Of Mist and Mirrors

More from Phase Publishing
by

Rebecca Connolly

Agents of the Convent
Fortune Favors the Sparrow
The Ears Have It

The Arrangements
An Arrangement of Sorts
Married to the Marquess
Secrets of a Spinster

The London League
The Lady and the Gent
A Rogue About Town
A Tip of the Cap

The Spinster Chronicles
The Merry Lives of Spinsters
The Spinster and I
Spinster and Spice

Of Mist and Mirrors

Agents of the Convent
Book Three

Rebecca Connolly

Phase Publishing, LLC
Seattle

Phase Publishing, LLC first paperback edition
February 2023

ISBN 978-1-952103-49-0
Library of Congress Control Number 2023901075
Cataloging-in-Publication Data on file.

Acknowledgements

To Princess Anne for being the hardest working Royal ever and one of the most impressive women in the entire world. You are an inspiration and an underrated example of dignity, grace, and class.

And to joggers for becoming my new favorite article of clothing. We're going to go a long way together.

Want to hear about future releases and upcoming events for Rebecca Connolly?

Sign up for the monthly Wit and Whimsy at:

www.rebeccaconnolly.com

A Proclamation

By Miss Leonora Masters
Headmistress of Miss Masters's Finishing School

Forasmuch as it has been thus Ordained by the powers that be that the Rearing of gently bred ladies requires some assistance, and in Keeping with traditions long established, It has been decreed that such rearing Needs proper establishment for training purposes, Given the span and scope of such development.

As it pleases the powers that be, Never forgetting the honor due to her subjects, Development and education of young ladies shall be Courteously and courageously given.

Owing to the need for such establishment, Unto the finishing of the female sex, Nobility shall be thus encouraged, Their patronage much desired, to Relinquish the education of such female persons as aforementioned Yet in their youthful and less informed state Into such qualified care.

Nevertheless, with charity and succor, females of a Lesser status shall be generously and Indubitably sponsored in their similar attendance herein For the purpose of gaining appropriate Education as befits needs and station.

Occupied thusly, this establishment shall henceforth Render such superior instruction and care, Defending the virtue and honor of her pupils, Engendering appropriate accomplishment upon all, Avowing to maintain the standards and Traditions of her forebears, and shall Henceforth fulfil all other obligations as so indicated.

Given under my Hand at Miss Masters's Finishing School in Kent, the 1st day of March, 1790, in the Thirtieth year of His Majesty's reign.

God save the King
Leonora Masters

Chapter One
London, 1826

The event was a crush if ever there was one. Every foot of the ballroom seemed to contain someone, if not two someones, and how there was still room for dancing was impossible to say. But music was filling what space was not filled by a person, ringing clearly throughout, and the cadence of dancers' steps was just as audible.

Minerva Dalton could not see any of the dancing, but there was no denying what she heard.

A crowded event would certainly make her assignment easier, as her motions and objectives would not be so easily observed, but it would also make things that much more difficult, given the sheer volume of guests. Had the Drummonds been unable to resist inviting all of London Society to their ball? Surely they were not on friendly terms with this many people, or even knew them beyond a passing acquaintance. Why would anybody choose to invite more people than a room had space for, particularly when their ballroom was the largest Minerva had ever seen?

Considering she had spent many, many hours in the ballroom of what had once been known as Beddingsford House, but was now the Miss Masters School for Fine Young Ladies, she thought she could safely make such a statement.

"I don't know that it is wise for Lady Beddingsford to frown so on her first appearance in Society," a familiar, warm voice murmured beside her, a gentle nudge tapping her elbow.

Minerva immediately forced a small, polite smile on her lips, praying it would look more serene than she felt. "Lady Beddingsford is unused to such events, Miss Bradford, and to this many people milling about. If one can mill about whilst colliding into another person."

Miss Bradford, headmistress of the Miss Masters school, otherwise known as Pippa, and professionally known to Minerva as Milliner, the chief female spy in all of England, grinned in amusement, looking years younger in her present finery. "I shall set my mind to finding the proper definition of milling once the evening has concluded."

"Please do, I am rather curious now."

The women shared a quick laugh before looking about them again. Minerva, for one, took the chance to study her friend and companion a little more. With all that Pippa had to do, both in her public life as the headmistress and in her private life as a spymistress, she was still taking the time to assist Minerva in her first event on this new assignment of hers. The fall term had started a few weeks ago, but the mission took priority over the students and coursework. It would not be possible to balance both coursework and the assignment, not when so much was required.

The new teacher, Lucy Allred, would be covering Minerva's courses until her return, and Pippa had assured Minerva that she would see Lucy was paid additionally for that.

The poor girl would need those funds.

Minerva calculated quickly in her mind, guessing that her friend and mentor was not yet five-and-thirty, and she so rarely bore the strain of her years as spymistress upon her countenance. She might not bear the first bloom one might expect of young misses in Society, but there was no denying that Pippa Bradford was still a lovely woman. It was so easy to forget when one was in the confines of the school and their rather simple attire there. But tonight, swathed in silk of azure blue, Pippa looked no more than five-and-twenty, and it would not surprise Minerva a jot if she were to be asked to dance several times.

But Pippa was only here in an advisory capacity, as herself, using the connection to the school and the Beddingsford family to introduce Minerva into Society.

As Lady Beddingsford, not as Minerva Dalton.

There was no Lady Beddingsford, in truth. Nor a Lord Beddingsford, for that matter. The title had fallen vacant and been returned to the king, though as far as the public knew, the last Lord Beddingsford had sold his estate, settled his affairs in England, and moved to the Continent or beyond, never to return. It was entirely possible that he had married there and had children.

That was the mystery they were playing on for Minerva's character in this assignment. Lady Beddingsford, wife to the heir of all things Beddingsford, returned to England for a time. Not to take up a place in the family estate, as it was now a school, but simply to return to Society. Or make an appearance, if she had never been.

The details of her story were entirely up to Minerva for construction, as the assignment would be a solitary one. No partners, no team, no co-conspirators. She always worked better alone in her operative assignments, and this would be no exception.

There was too much at stake to bring someone else in anyway.

But heaven help her, assignments taking place in a ballroom were her least favorite of all. This was not her first time doing so, but it was certainly going to be the most lasting and extensive. She was required to become part of London Society without being notable in it. Entertain several invitations, but not enter any scandal sheets. It required the sort of expertise that Minerva cultivated well—that of being everyone and no one at the same time, both visible and invisible, taking part and yet remaining aloof. Attracting attention and somehow remaining unremarkable.

Making an impression without anyone being quite able to place her.

There was only one other operative she knew of who could do the same thing, and the pair of them had, on rare occasions, discussed their skills. But the Gent was not here this evening, or if he was, he was nowhere to be seen. No matter, she could not remember his public name as it was.

Minerva inhaled, then exhaled in irritation when her inhale was constricted. "I don't know why Tilda felt the need to lace me so tightly. Just because I prefer the old style of stays does not mean I deserve punishment."

"I don't think she was offended in truth, no matter how she

played at it," Pippa assured her, though she did not look especially convinced. "Besides, you look absolutely exquisite."

That might have been true, but surely it was not too much trouble on one's fashion to breathe. But Tilda, the stage costumer who offered her services to many of the nation's operatives, had insisted on fitting Minerva out for her first foray as Lady Beddingsford.

She wore a crepe-lisse gown of Pomona green with low sleeves, the bodice wrapped in folds of white crepe-lisse, with a notched tucker bearing a corsage of white roses, the fabrics fitted so snugly to her stays, it was a wonder the lines of such were not visible beneath. Her arms were trapped in those sleeves, despite the fact that her shoulders were almost fully visible above them, encased in more notched ruches of the same white crepe-lisse and green satin rouleau. Thankfully, her elbows were free of fabric, but raising her arms would be a feat, indeed. More white roses and bows of the green ribbon decorated the skirts, the ends of the bows somehow connecting to wreathes of more green satin that swirled around the entire skirt. A thick row of puffed crepe-lisse and somehow more satin, this time wadded up, lay at the hem, the temptation to kick the thing almost impossible in Minerva's mind. Her waist was cinched somehow further by a wide satin sash of white, and all in all, she only felt more constricted in the aspect that was her hair.

Tilda had insisted on foisting a headdress on her, something in the same Pomona green as her gown but also bearing pearls. Her hair had been folded and shaped into actual bows, along with plaits, on either side of the headdress, and a comb fastening her hair with the tightest pulling Minerva had ever known in her entire life. If it was possible for one to have a headache at the crown of their head, she would have one shortly. She thought there were also white flowers and pearl pins in her hair somewhere, but as everything felt scratched and pulled, she could not be sure. Her necklace was gold and pearl, her earrings were gold and pearl, her long gloves were a perfectly pearl white, and she bore bracelets of gold on each wrist, which were starting to feel like manacles.

She did not feel exquisite, elegant, fine, or lovely. She felt trussed up, trapped, slightly itchy, and uncomfortable.

Was this what it was to be in Society? How in the world did any woman smile like this? They ought to have been marching on the villains who insisted this was the way of things and take over their own fashions. Something comfortable, perhaps, that could also be flattering. Surely that was not so difficult to accomplish.

"You hate this, don't you?" Pippa murmured.

Minerva cleared her throat, suddenly aware that the woman beside her was not only her friend and mentor, but her superior. "No, not at all. I am quite at my leisure," she told her, falling into the highly cultivated accent she had perfected over the last few weeks in preparation. She had injected a touch of a foreign tone to it, as someone who had lived away from England for some time might, and hoped that it would be believable to those who heard it. She had never had trouble with her accents before, so there was no reason to suspect this would be different.

Looking about her, Minerva smiled with the regal airs she had once seen the queen use for the public. "One must adjust to the dictates of fashion for appropriate events, yes?"

Pippa raised a brow, her smile slight. "I suppose…"

"Then I am quite well, indeed." She snapped open her fan and began to gently wave it, praying that somehow the breeze of it would infuse her lungs with more air than they could naturally exchange. "A pity they are not announcing guests this evening. If I am to expand my circle, it would help very much to be able to be selective rather than try for everyone when it may not be worth my time."

"A great pity, my lady," Pippa conceded without missing a beat. "But there are a great many people I can introduce you to myself, should you wish it."

It was not unusual for Minerva to play a part with other operatives she knew well, but it was rare, indeed, for Pippa to take part, given her public station as the headmistress of such a popular finishing school. But as this mission required a public persona, she was actually a rather useful connection for the person of Lady Beddingsford to have.

Which was undoubtedly one of the reasons they had chosen Beddingsford for the title in all of this. Not the sole reason, of course, but one of them.

"Voyez-vous quelqu'un que vous reconnaissez?" Pippa asked in a polite tone, her pronunciation as perfect as ever. *"Quelqu'un du passé, peut-être?"*

Minerva shook her head, biting back a sigh as she looked around the room, taking in each face and comparing it with the sketches she had studied in preparation. *"Non, pas un seul."*

Pippa nodded once. "Would you like to take a turn about the room, my lady? We could take stock of the guests and you could see if there are any introductions you would like me to make."

Nodding, Minerva gestured for Pippa to lead. "I would, Miss Bradford, thank you."

They made their way from their position to walk along the outskirts of the room, which proved to be some feat, given the sheer number of people about, but there was something about ladies in motion that prompted polite shifting of bodies to allow their passage. It proved to be an interesting exercise, as several people recognized Pippa and greeted her with smiles or brief comments, and yet attention was given to Minerva in equal measure, if not more. Pippa did not stop to talk with anyone, so introductions were not needed, but it was clear there was interest there.

Perfect.

It was entirely possible that their interest was purely curiosity and speculation, but that could be enough to garner the invitations she would need. They would begin to talk about the woman seen with Miss Bradford, the one arrayed in more finery than her, the one no one recognized or knew, and her name would find a way to reach all of them.

The next few days would be an intriguing set, indeed.

"Oh, Miss Bradford!"

Pippa paused a step as a voice called out rather loudly, almost warbling in its tone.

"Why do I know that voice?" Minerva muttered very softly.

Pippa patted her hand gently as the caller suddenly appeared through the crowd. "Ah, Mrs. Pearson, how delightful to see you!"

Minerva swallowed a groan and lifted her chin a little in preparation for introduction, though she already knew the woman perfectly well in her life as a teacher. Mrs. Pearson had four daughters, the youngest of whom was still at their school, and while Catherine Pearson held all the potential in the world for a promising future, her mother did not. She was a tyrannical woman when it came to her girls, repeatedly sending letters to ask that her daughters be excused from lessons in the more scholarly subjects so as to not grow too much like bluestockings. She wanted idiots for daughters. Not in so many words, but the result would be the same.

Luckily for their present aims, Mrs. Pearson also took no pains to know any of the teachers at the school, only Pippa. And if Pippa had not been in a position of authority, Mrs. Pearson would not have wanted to know her either.

"I am happy to see you in London, Miss Bradford," Mrs. Pearson told her with a broad smile that did not reach her eyes. "It is never too late for a husband, you know, and you are not so far beyond your youth as to make you unsightly."

Pippa did not so much as stiffen, well used to this sort of thing from her students and their parents by now. "Indeed, and thank you for the compliment. How did Catherine enjoy her summer holidays?"

Mrs. Pearson beamed in an almost eerie manner. "Oh, wonderful! She did not read any books at all, her dancing has vastly improved, her singing far better in pitch, and her embroidery more skillful than any of her sisters. Whatever changes you have implemented in your curriculum have been extremely beneficial for her."

"I am very glad to hear it," Pippa said warmly. "Mrs. Pearson, do you know Lady Beddingsford?"

Mrs. Pearson looked at Minerva with wide eyes, her complexion going a trifle pale in her awe. "Lady… Beddingsford?"

Minerva dipped her chin in a nod. *"Ravi de faire votre connaissance, madame.* Charmed, as you say."

The hasty curtsy Mrs. Pearson offered was almost laughable in its instability. *"Merci,* my lady," she replied in a dreadful accent. "Any relation to the Beddingsfords of Beddingsford House?"

"Indeed," Minerva answered, keeping her words clipped. "My husband's family. He was born abroad, you know, as was his father before him. I have only just come to London, and Miss Bradford is kind enough to help me to get comfortable here."

"Do you plan to stay, then?" Mrs. Pearson asked, her eyes suddenly growing bright, no doubt from the opportunity presenting itself. "Without your husband?"

Minerva looked away, pursing her lips. "I do not know, *madame*. We will see. And I pray you excuse me, I do not like to speak of my husband."

"O-of course, my lady," came the rushed reply. "No apology necessary, I did not mean to cause pain or offense."

"It is quite a delicate situation, Mrs. Pearson," Pippa offered soothingly. "Lady Beddingsford's plans are not yet settled, but perhaps once they are, she might call on you if need be?"

Minerva would have to step on Pippa's toes for that, but unfortunately, she wore satin slippers tonight, and nothing with a heel to make the excursion especially painful. As if she would ever want to call upon Mrs. Pearson or ever see her again in any fashion. And if Catherine were in the house, she might recognize Minerva, having just taken one of her courses at school.

Her disguise was excellent, there was no question, but her students surprised her with their attentiveness at times. Which was usually when she recommended them for the testing required to enter the secret operative training program also held at the school. It did not always work out that they did so, given the other requirements, but every now and again…

"I will inform Catherine that I saw you upon my return to the school, Mrs. Pearson," Pippa was saying, bringing Minerva back to the conversation she had been ignoring. "And, of course, let her teachers know of her improvements."

Pippa was quick to whisk Minerva away before Mrs. Pearson could respond further.

"Why would you tell that woman I would call upon her?" Minerva hissed.

"I said could, my lady," Pippa corrected in a low voice. "It would not surprise me a jot if that woman proved to be of interest."

Realization dawned and Minerva nodded slowly, smiling very slightly. "A little bias in that statement, Miss Bradford?"

"I haven't the faintest idea what you are talking about," Pippa quipped, sniffing very slightly.

Minerva choked a laugh, shaking her head in amusement. "Of course not."

They moved to another portion of the room, pausing in a slightly opened space to breathe a moment. Again, more people greeted Pippa or acknowledged her, and one or two took a closer look at Minerva.

"I wonder when the novelty will wear off," Minerva murmured, waving her fan gently again. "When the gawking will cease."

"Probably never," Pippa said bluntly, giving her a sidelong look. "But it should not stop you. Once you are more familiar with these circumstances and these people, you will adjust."

Minerva nodded once, her operative training and experience reminding her of that. "I always do. This is simply more exposure than I am used to."

Pippa hummed a very soft laugh. "And this isn't even all that public, my lady. All things considered, it is still fairly secluded, especially given what plans you have made."

"Thank heavens," Minerva said firmly, feeling an unsettling shudder run up her spine. There was nothing in her past that could have prepared her for this sort of assignment in all its particulars, despite all of the missions she had taken previously. Her skills as an operative were not in question, and her ability to adapt to any given situation in place. But finery was not part of her person or her nature in her childhood, adolescence, or adulthood. There had never been anything akin to high society for her.

She had been part of operations where she had needed to portray someone in high society, but it had been for one event only. Not an extended operation where she had to not only make connections, but maintain them for however long this assignment took. And it was entirely possible that it would take a very long time. So much so that they had made contingency plans for her position at the school, should the situation arise that she was unable to return due to her continuing assignment.

She could only pray that would not be the case. If she was trapped in this world for that long, she ought to be pulled from the position due to failure.

"Pardon me, my lady."

Minerva adopted her persona again and turned to the approaching woman, recalling her name with shocking ease. "Yes, Mrs. Mills?"

Mrs. Mills, whom she had met early in the evening, was absolutely bursting with excitement, which seemed in complete contrast to the woman she had met earlier. "My lady, I have the most remarkable news for you."

"Indeed, *madame?*" Minerva asked, wondering how anything could be remarkable news for a woman who had only just appeared in London Society. "Pray, do tell."

In another stark contrast to the woman she had met and the evening she had known thus far, the woman took Minerva's hands and squeezed them. "Your husband arrived almost an hour ago, my lady."

Minerva blinked, staring at this new acquaintance in shock. "I beg your pardon?"

Clearly thinking she was emotional in her disbelief rather than confused, Mrs. Mills only beamed. "Lady Beddingsford, your husband is here. Lord Beddingsford is just as fashionable as you, madam—a waistcoat of spun gold on him! He said nothing of your being here either, but I could not resist letting you know right away. Lord Beddingsford is here, my lady!"

The conversation around her softened dramatically, not to a full silence, but low enough that her reactions would be heard.

"Oh… oh my…" Minerva swallowed, unable to say anything else. "Thank you for telling me."

Mrs. Mills squeezed her hands again before she turned to gesture in the direction of the supposed husband.

Thinking quickly, Minerva put a hand to her face and turned to Pippa as though emotional, knowing her mentor would see her enraged and confused eyes. "You said there was no Lord Beddingsford!" she hissed.

Pippa put her hands on her arms to comfort her faux tears. "There isn't!" she insisted through a false smile. "Cap swore it was the perfect cover."

Minerva widened her eyes, grinding her teeth together.

What was this? Were they compromised so early in the mission?

Who else could possibly know about this title, let alone well enough to use it?

Could there possibly be a true Lord Beddingsford that none of them knew about?

For the first time she could ever recall, Pippa's eyes and expression held no answers, guidance, or instruction.

This was Minerva's assignment, and she needed to act. Somehow.

She took in a quick breath, then exhaled slowly before turning to look where Mrs. Mills had indicated.

A group of three or four men were staring back at them, one of them bearing the telltale gold-spun waistcoat and eyeing her with a mixture of confusion, horror, and even interest.

She could only hope her expression was less readable.

"Beddingsford, I presume?" she muttered to no one in particular.

Unfortunately, her words were heard.

"Oh, my lady," someone near her gushed, "has it been so long that you cannot remember your husband's face?"

This was becoming more and more a production, and the impending reunion of sorts was beginning to attract attention. Even a pathway between the supposed Beddingsfords had been created, despite the crush of the event.

There was a cruel irony in that.

"I just… I cannot believe he is here," Minerva managed with a measure of emotion for effect. She heard the gushing woman gasp, which seemed as much as she could hope for.

Now for the actual reunion, which could not be avoided any longer. Not if she wanted her cover to remain intact.

Sighing to herself, knowing several guests were now watching in anticipation, and could ruin the entire assignment if she didn't act quickly, she started forward. Swallowing her faux emotion, and a significant portion of her pride, she increased her pace until she was nearly flying at him.

"Oh, Beddingsford, I've missed you so!" she cried out, forcing a catch in her throat. She raised her trapped arms as high as they would go, seizing his gold waistcoat and wrenching him down to her, capturing his lips with hers in the most passionate, desperate, confounding kiss she could imagine.

Chapter Two

Well. This was unexpected.

Griffin Russell could not react for a moment as the exquisite woman in green thoroughly and expertly waltzed with his lips in the most sensual manner he had ever experienced in his entire life. He had been away from Society for some time, but was this how things proceeded now?

His surprise faded momentarily, and his training took over. He wrapped his arms around his supposed wife, hauling her close and quickly shifting control of the kiss to his favor. As much as was possible, anyway. It was not often he kissed someone he had not had a chance to study and analyze, let alone someone he had been surprised by, but this… This woman could very well be his dream come true.

She could also be a dozen other things much less promising, a few of them rather dangerous, especially given his current assignment.

But so help him, he was going to enjoy this moment as much as he could. While he was thinking twelve thousand other things, including possibilities for his next move.

The woman kissing him made a sound then, something he doubted she was aware of, and something he somehow heard in the back of his right leg. His hold on her tightened, and he ventured further with the kiss, curious as to her response.

She leaned into him, and suddenly his next move was entirely irrelevant. He might just stand here kissing her until the entire room cleared and the candles were doused for the night.

What he would do then, however…

Applause filled the ballroom, sighs and sniffles echoing all around them, and someone, most likely the host, instructed the musicians to play the next number.

Griff wasn't quite sure; everything sounded a little fuzzy.

The music seemed to jar the woman in his arms, and slowly, she disengaged from him, lowering her heels to the ground. When had she arched up on her toes? How had he missed that?

He stared down at her, her gaze locked somewhere around his cravat, and he could almost see stars dancing before her eyes, which ought to have delighted him were it not for the horde of agitated bees driven into a frenzy through his body. He doubted she was actually seeing him as she recovered, her panting matching the heaving sensation in his lungs, and she inhaled sharply as her hands slid from their hold on his neck—where they had landed when he'd taken over—and returned to his waistcoat, pressing there as though to steady her.

But who was going to steady him?

He watched her blink, then swallow, then look up at him, her eyes clear now.

He smiled slowly, amused and intrigued and, if he were perfectly honest, ridiculously attracted. She was stunning, especially bearing the look of the freshly kissed.

Tonight had become a great deal more entertaining, there was no doubt.

He drummed his fingers, which had come to rest just above the swell of her hips as the kiss had ended. "I say… good evening to you as well, wife," he said in a low, deeply amused tone. "I suppose it would not be too forward of me to claim this waltz after that. You always were a rather fetching dance partner."

Before she could say a single word, he swept her into the dance, his eyes fixed on her face the entire time. He watched as the dazed, almost confused light faded from her eyes as they danced, saw the exact moment clarity returned to her, and shortly thereafter, knew that he would die by her hand, if she could find a way to manage it.

Her clenching, painful hold on him during their waltz might have hinted at that as well.

There was almost certainly something odd afoot, and she was at the heart of it. No one should have been able to pluck up the Beddingsford title and use it for their own ends. He and Draper, his superior in covert operations and head of the Foreign Office, had looked into the matter extensively, and received reports from their assets on the Continent and beyond regarding the family.

Or lack thereof, as the case was.

But only they knew that, which was why they had picked up the title for Griff's present assignment. He might be the younger brother of one of the wealthiest men in England, but he had avoided taking any position in Society after earning his degree, which meant no one would recognize him here. Even his old friends from school would struggle to identify him, given the years and how changed his appearance was now. While every other gentleman in the room was perfectly clean shaven, Griff had kept three days' growth along his chin and jawline, just as though he had traveled from lands afar. His tanned complexion already added to a sort of exotic air, which would fascinate the members of Society he would be mingling with and lead to his being sought after by various individuals, further leading to the connections he needed to make for his assignment to work.

His first evening in this role, and someone else was bearing the title he was using and claiming herself to be married into the family he had taken such pains to adopt as his own for the time being. And then she had brought him into whatever world she had created for herself by searing him to within an inch of sanity. There was still a buzzing about his ears.

So now he was not only Lord Beddingsford, but he had a Lady Beddingsford, who, if the glare was to be believed, resented his interference and likely his taking control as well.

She would need to get used to that. He refused to have this mission upended by whatever dalliance she was planning.

And yet…

It was a surprisingly strong body he felt beneath his hand, her figure slender, but hardly petite or frail. The way she moved in the dance was graceful and lithe, barely needing his lead or, indeed, allowing it at all. The power he had felt in her grip when she had kissed him was unusual and remarkable for a woman of her stature.

Perhaps odd was not the correct word for him to use to describe this situation. Perhaps it was more nefarious than odd.

He continued to smile down at his supposed wife, who would soon be drawing comment from others about the lack of enjoyment she was taking from the waltz, as her expression was displaying all too clearly.

"You must have been surprised to see me here, my dear," Griff said with a wry smile. "It has been such a long time."

"It felt very long, indeed," she replied through gritted teeth. "One quite forgets the actual length of time because of it."

Griff laughed to himself. "Quite. I see you waltz even better than I recall. What a delight!"

She smiled very thinly, her eyes flashing, switching from blue to green to gray in the space of a blink. "You should see what else I do better than you recall, my dear."

He grinned at the veiled threat, finding himself more amused than anything else. "I am sure I will, darling. You always were a most surprising woman."

"You once found that my most attractive quality."

"Did I? How extraordinary. I thought it was your singing voice I adored most."

Her brows snapped down, and he bit back more laughter. Not musical, then. That was one thing he could say about her now.

"You jest, Beddingsford," she muttered, forcing a laugh that could have doubled as a guillotine. "My singing has not improved since we were last together."

Griff tutted softly. "A great pity. But I must say, your manner of greeting has greatly improved. A more enthusiastic welcome I have never received."

The heel of her foot landed squarely on his toe, turning rather forcibly once upon them. "Forgive my rashness. I know how you hate displays."

"Do I?" He pretended to think about that, then shook his head. "No, I don't think that is the problem. I believe I rather hated *your* displays. The usual version, mind. This one I quite liked." He moved his foot safely out of the way of her next attack on the next spin and smiled down at her invitingly. "If you would like, I'll go away for a few moments and then return so you may greet me again."

Her smile in response was perfectly feral. "Please do. I will surprise you in ways you cannot possibly imagine for the next greeting. You will be most impressed. A greeting you will not soon forget, my dear."

Oddly enough, he believed that one without a second thought.

Time to vacate this room, and he was taking her with him.

"Now, darling," Griff said in a low voice, keeping his smile as adoring as the public could wish, "I am going to take you into a grand series of spins that will take us to the edge of this group, and then we will further waltz out into that corridor in the northeast corner of this room. I have it on good authority that there is a small, rarely used study that way, and we will retire there to continue this conversation and…" He paused, letting his smile turn particularly wolfish. "Any other conversations that proceed from it."

Her mysterious, gemlike eyes narrowed, her lips somehow pursing while remaining flat. "Spin me away, Beddingsford. I have much to say to you in private."

Griff chuckled in a low, rumbling way. "You usually do, my lady. You usually do." He raised a brow at her. "Make it look good, or there will be more questions than answers for the gawkers."

She nodded once, her jaw seeming to tighten.

Had it ever been so delightful to provoke anyone?

He listened to the music for a moment, trying to anticipate the proper momentum there to propel the waltz as he needed. As though he had commanded it, a particularly grand swell began, and with a quick nod to his wife, started his series of what ought to appear as graceful turns to be much appreciated in a waltz. The image of perfection in his arms moved with just as much precision, her steps light, her control impeccable.

She was an operative of some kind, there was no question.

He liked her all the more for that. The most terrifying, and most surprising, operatives he had ever met were women, and he was certain this faux-wife of his would be as well.

Each hair on the back of his neck stood at attention as they reached the corridor, preparing for whatever danger awaited him. He had never yet had to fight a female operative, and it would challenge his honor to do so.

If he had to.

Various defensive moves played in his mind, offering themselves as options to the potential fight ahead of him. He could certainly defend himself against a female assailant without offending the tenets of being a gentleman. So long as he did not attack her, it ought to be fine.

Surely no one would disapprove of that.

He kept his wife's hand in his hold as he tugged her down the corridor. She did not fight that hold, did not resist the motion, did not give any indication that she was opposed to this impending interview.

That made him a trifle uneasy.

What sort of interrogation techniques could one impose on a woman?

They turned into the study, the room not lit but for the small fire in the grate. Griff released her hand and moved to the candles on the desk. "I suppose you will not kill me until the room is lit?"

"If you like."

Her tone held no concern in it, and the slightly foreign note disappeared from her voice entirely. The timbre and cadence were the same, the pronunciation slightly softer, which made it more difficult to place.

But he knew a practiced accent when he heard one, and she had perfected that. No one sounded that ambiguous as far as station and region, as though they were from everywhere and nowhere. Other than himself, of course. He had trained himself the same way, which allowed him to venture into darker and lower places both in England and outside of it without anyone suspecting his station of birth.

No one but his superiors knew he was the younger brother of the Duke of Kirklin.

No one else needed to know.

Griff lit the tall candles in the candelabras from the small fire, then began prodding the logs in the grate to build up the flames. One they were blazing and giving off a decent amount of light and heat, he nodded, rising from the floor and moving the candles back to best illuminate the room.

"I trust Mr. Drummond will not mind that I've made myself at home here," Griff said with a laugh. "He uses the study on the other side of the house for his own work."

"I know damn well where Mr. Drummond works in this house," his companion snapped coldly. "And what time he does so, what he takes for meals when he is in there, and what his wife is considering for the redecoration."

Griff nodded a slight bow of acknowledgment at that. "Vital information, I am sure. Mrs. Drummond must be so pleased to have additional input on her decorating thoughts."

Her eyes narrowed, and she folded her arms, standing perfectly balanced on her strong legs, the finery of her ensemble oddly not at all detracting from the dangerous air she presented. "Who are you?"

"Lord Beddingsford, madam," Griff replied, bowing in earnest as much as he could while leaning against the desk. "And you?"

She laughed darkly once. "There is no Lord Beddingsford."

"And yet…" He shrugged. "You expect me to believe you are Lady Beddingsford? I don't recall marrying you."

"Do stop talking."

"Do you have a better idea for how to pass the time in here?" He smiled crookedly, shrugging out of his elaborate jacket and laying it on the table.

Her eyes widened. "What are you doing?"

He gave her a look. "Don't get excited, darling. I'm making myself more comfortable. If you intend on killing me, I'd rather not be trussed like a peacock."

"At least you acknowledge it."

"If you think I dressed myself in this," he said with a snort, rolling his sleeves, "you need to relieve yourself of such delusions."

Her dark hum had an oddly ticklish effect on the base of his spine. "No, dressing yourself would be above your capacity and intellect. I had no doubt you had help."

Griff grinned at the snide barb. "And you expect me to believe you adorned yourself in that apparel? Without help?"

"If you knew anything about female attire and its processes, you would know better than to ask something so stupid and ignorant."

"I know plenty about female attire," he assured her, dipping his voice low and maintaining his smile. "And its processes. Especially its processes. Now, are you going to kill me or not?"

She said nothing, but her jaw shifted slightly from side to side. He could almost hear the grinding of her teeth and offered a moment of silence for what had surely once been a rather perfect impression of them.

Then, without warning, she wrenched her eyes from him and started to pace, muttering to herself.

His brows slowly rose, not that she would see it, and watched in amusement. Was she suffering from a mental affliction or was she simply pushed to the limits of her tolerance? He could see either option in the realm of possibilities for her, based on their engagement thus far, but one would make him sympathetic and the other delighted. He would hate to react incorrectly to whichever it was.

"Matarlo sería más fácil, por supuesto, pero ¿cómo explicarlo?" he heard her say, her accent perfection and her pacing rapid.

He cleared his throat. *"Solo diles que no se puede evitar,"* he suggested with a quick grin. *"Estoy seguro de que lo entenderán."*

She paused a step, glaring darkly at him. Was that for his answer or because he matched her language?

The pacing resumed then, and so did the rambling.

"La mia prima notte, e questo doveva succedere? La prima notte?"

Griff quirked a brow, noting the highbrow accent to her Italian. *"Preferisci la seconda notte? O il terzo?"*

Her eyes flicked to him with a murderous glint, which only made him grin.

"Jemand muss etwas erklären," she hissed, her tone turning almost cruel, *"und sie sollten es besser schnell erklären."*

"Entschuldige Liebling," Griff replied with as much sympathy as he could muster. *"Ich habe keine Antworten für sie."* He forced his expression to be appropriately dour.

It had no effect on her, except for the surprisingly animalistic screech that emitted from her clenched teeth.

Her pacing sped up, and she shook her head as she did so. *"Ego illum necabo. Sic me Deus adiuvet, ego illum occidam."*

He'd thought her surprises for him done with for one night, but nothing could have prepared him for Latin. *"Nunc hoc tibi, deliciae, lingua gravis est. Admiranda."*

She glanced at him with a wry smile that made him wary. *"Tha a h-uile dad mum dheidhinn iongantach, daor."*

He almost laughed at the shift to Scots Gaelic, finding this entire exchange worth the inconvenience now. *"Mar sin tha mi a 'faicinn. Seall barrachd dhomh."*

His agitated would-be wife looked up at the ceiling, her hands forming fists at her sides. *"Spasite menya ot etogo shuta, kto-nibud'. Lyuboy, ya vas umolyayu."*

Griff jerked to such an extent that he straightened from the desk. Russian? He could count on one hand the number of operatives he had encountered who could speak that, and she did so with ease. *"Krovavyy ad…"* he breathed, stunned by this woman he either needed to marry or terminate; preferably the former.

She exhaled loudly and stopped, turning to face him and glowering. *"As jy nie stilbly nie, man, ek sal jou self stilmaak."*

Now he gaped, and he did not care that she would see it. The woman spoke Afrikaans? That was utterly impossible to believe, and had he not heard it with his own ears, he would have scoffed at the thought of anyone speaking it. The British had only officially had the Cape Colony for twenty years, and operatives who had been sent there from any departments and returned to England for new assignments were few and far between.

Many of them actually wanted to stay there and start a new life, much to the disgruntlement of the locals. It was not a comfortable assignment, given the tension there, but apparently, it grew on a person. Griff had been there for six months a few years ago, and it was a stunning part of the world, but he was better suited for Europe than any distant lands.

This woman could speak that language?

She grunted once. "Have I stumped you there?"

Griff shook his head, still gaping. *"Ek het geen idee wat om te sê nie."*

Her brows snapped down as she scowled. *"Go n-ithe an tochas thú,"* she muttered.

There was nothing to do but bark a laugh at the Irish curse. *"Tá brón orm."*

A knock at the door kept them from exploring what other

languages she spoke, and Griff was instantly on alert, ready to defend himself and her, if it came down to it.

Unless she started attacking him as well.

The door opened, and they were joined by a woman of roughly the same stature, her hair bright and fair, her eyes an unclear shade, but her expression telling Griff she knew exactly what the situation was and the severity of it.

Was she the woman who had been standing by Lady Beddingsford earlier? He'd been so shocked by and fixed on her that he'd missed any and all companions she'd had.

"Right, glad to see you alive," the new arrival said, looking between the two uncertainly.

His wife gave her a doleful look. "You told me not to kill anyone."

Griff looked at the other woman in surprise, curious as to her reaction.

She smiled at her associate blandly. "Yes, but you don't always listen."

That was not surprising, and Griff barely bit back his laugh. Was this woman her partner? Her superior? Her mentor? The possibilities were endless, but at least this woman did not seem ready to kill Griff where he stood.

"Do you know anything yet?" his actress version of a wife demanded without manners. She gestured to Griff dismissively. "Like what this is?"

"Right here," he reminded her, leaning against the desk again and folding his arms. "Hearing every word."

He heard her growl. *"Tais-toi, espèce de bouffon exaspérant!"*

Now that was the most interesting language yet, even though it was only French. The most common language he heard besides English in his career. But it was rare he heard an impeccable accent.

She had one.

Was she a Frenchwoman who had been living in England? Was that where her allegiance lay? It would fall in line with his interests quite nicely, as well as the focus of his assignment. Surely that was too convenient, but he could only hope for so simple a connection so soon.

"I don't have any answers yet," the fair-haired woman said with a shake of her head. "I've sent a Hermes, so we should know something soon."

Griff glanced at her in some suspicion, keeping his expression blank. A Hermes was code within the British covert operatives for a rapid message up the ranks, and it was not a word to be used lightly, nor frequently.

Either he was working with in-house operatives, or the potential compromise in their ranks was far worse than anybody had ever led him to believe.

But he would give nothing away. If they were using the word to garner a reaction from him, he would disappoint them. He had not been in a deep cover assignment for the last two years on a whim, but because he had proven himself equal to such an intense level of scrutiny.

No pair of terrifying female operatives, no matter how capable, was going to change that for him.

Until Griff saw a familiar face, he would not say another word that could be used against him.

But how to pass the time, then?

The door opened again, this time without any knocking, and Griff straightened at once.

Georgie Canning, the current foreign secretary and the man Griff addressed as Draper, entered the room. He took one look around as he shut the door behind him, narrowing his dark eyes even as the light from the candles and fire glinted off his bald head.

"Hmm," he said softly, folding his arms and twisting his lips. He turned to face the fair-haired woman. "Well, Milliner, how do we resolve this?"

Milliner? Griff looked at her again, impressed in spite of himself. In the world of covert operations in Britain, the leadership, some of whom were in the highest circles of government, were known as the Shopkeepers, and Milliner was the head of the Agents of the Convent, an elite team of female spies whose missions spanned several countries. Griff had only ever worked with one of them in the past, and their interaction had been minimal.

They were beyond impressive in the ranks, their stories like something out of legend, and their training grounds doubled as a finishing school in Kent. His sister had just finished her schooling there, but he'd never heard if she'd suspected anything beyond what things appeared.

He looked at the woman posing as his wife with new appreciation, various pieces falling into place. She could not have been a more perfect fit for such a position, and looking at her now, she could not be over five-and-twenty in age, which meant her missions had to be particularly intense or she was particularly impressive in order to have mastered so many languages flawlessly. That was no bluestocking at work, but a concentrated effort of someone with a purpose in mind.

He would give anything to see her fight. To watch her interrogate. To see more of her skills, if not learn her entire mission history. He had enough connections who owed him favors to have a chance at reading the files himself, but there was something better about hearing from the operative herself.

"We needed the Beddingsford title," Milliner told Draper, her tone completely devoid of accusation. "Cap assured us it was open."

"It is," Draper assured her, "which is why we decided to use it for Mist here." He flicked his fingers towards Griff, and Milliner followed the gesture.

Griff nodded at her in respect, and she returned it, smiling tightly. "Your reputation precedes you."

"As does yours, ma'am," he replied with all due deference.

"Didn't you check with Cap on the title?" Milliner demanded of Draper, again without malice in her tone.

Draper shook his head. "Weaver. Clearly the two of them need to communicate better."

Griff smirked to himself, wishing yet again he could sit in on a meeting of Shopkeepers. What a row that must be.

"Mist?" his spiteful wife repeated with a laugh. "Quite a feminine name for an operative, isn't it?"

Used to such a jab, Griff only glanced at her. "And you are?"

"Mirrors," Milliner chimed in before another snide reply could meet the air.

Intriguing name, all things considered. He'd have to think back to know if he'd heard it before.

"We cannot undo what has been done," Draper said with a clearing of his throat, no doubt anxious to get back to his evening. "Mist cannot be pulled from his assignment. We have too much in place."

Milliner pursed her lips. "Mirrors cannot be pulled from hers. We have too much at stake."

Draper considered that, cocking his head. *"Bonsoir?"* he asked, which confused Griff.

She nodded once. *"Rhif un?"* she inquired in return.

Griff looked at Mirrors. "Any ideas?"

"Not a one," she replied, watching the exchange with interest. "Nor was I aware she spoke Welsh."

He grunted, returning his attention to their superiors.

"Could they parallel?" Draper went on, a more speculative look crossing his features.

Milliner tapped her chin in thought. "Possibly. She is my best."

"And he mine."

There was silence for a moment, and then they turned to their operatives in eerie unison. "Right, then," Milliner announced, as though a part of the conversation had occurred without the operatives knowing. "You will be Lord and Lady Beddingsford, and your missions will continue."

"And," Draper added, "you will help each other. Consider yourselves partners."

Chapter Three

$\mathcal{M}$inerva blinked at the balding man as though he had sprouted three heads and a tail. He might be a Shopkeeper, if his association with Pippa and his code name were any indication, but that did not mean the man was fully in possession of his sanity and intelligence.

"I beg your bleeding pardon?" she squawked, propping her hands on her hips.

"Mirrors," Pippa, now fully acting as Milliner, her superior, and not Pippa, her friend, warned in a surprisingly stern tone.

Minerva ignored her superior completely. "You expect me to truly pretend I am married to him? To focus on his mission as well as my own? Do you have a death wish for him? Because I will kill him before this is over."

"Aw, is our marriage already so ruined?" Mist asked from his perch on the desk. "I thought we were getting along rather well."

Biting the inside of her lip was the only way she could keep herself from lashing out with true venom and appropriate obscenities. "Stop. Talking," she ground out.

His chuckling was almost worse than his speaking, and she put a hand to her brow. "Please, Milliner. Draper. Don't make me do this."

"We don't have a choice," Draper pointed out, doing her the courtesy of not appearing even remotely patronizing. "Give us a moment to work through a few details." He turned to Milliner and gestured for her to follow him, moving to the fireplace, keeping their voices low.

Minerva shook her head as she stared after them. The maddening mongrel she'd had to march across a ballroom to kiss in order to save her own cover was now going to be part of her cover? She moved her hand to her mouth, trying somehow to press her further refusals into silence.

"If I don't have the chance to say so later," Mist mused in a voice ringing with amusement, "might I tell you, wife, that your gown is quite fetching? Suits you marvelously; it's no wonder all eyes are on you tonight."

She shook her head, the sound of him grating on her ears. Her hand fell to her throat now, and she turned to look at him. "Don't."

His dark brows rose. "Don't? Don't what?"

"Don't," she said simply. "Don't talk to me, don't tease me, don't pretend to flatter me, don't do anything except sit there and breathe."

"But we're to be partners, my dear," he replied, ignoring her demands with the same ease with which he crossed one ankle over the other. "We should get comfortable."

"I'd be more comfortable on a bed of nails," she snapped, folding her arms now, the tight pressure of them adding a strange comfort to this scenario. "Or perhaps being turned on a spit over a roaring fire. Let me make one thing perfectly clear: No matter what our superiors decide, however this must play out to make my cover believable, I will not fail in my mission. I have worked too hard and for too long, and your arrogance and idiocy are not going to get in my way. Now why are you smiling like that?"

He uncrossed his ankles, grinning as though she had confessed undying love or praised him as being molded by the hand of God. "Well, first of all, it's a relief that the woman who is apparently my wife is not the enemy. That would have been awkward." He winked at her, leaning forward a touch.

Minerva would have spat in his face had he been close enough.

"And secondly…" He shook his head, chuckling as he sighed. "I just can't stop thinking about that extraordinary kiss. I'm very much looking forward to the next one."

Her stomach clenched in distress and bile rose in her throat. "There will not be a next one. I would rather cut off my own toes."

For a man known as Mist, his smile turned rather stormy. "Better find yourself a sharp dagger, darling. You are the one who decided we are exuberantly married."

"Yes. And we could just as easily be passionately volatile, and I could throw something at your head," she suggested, the image bringing her a great amount of satisfaction.

He snorted softly. "You would miss, like you always do."

"I never miss," Minerva replied, emphasizing each word clearly for him. "Which you would know, were your memory intact after all the times I have thrown something at your head. If I had ever missed, perhaps it would not be so bad." She shrugged as nonchalantly as she could, hoping he would give her a reason to prove it.

The irritating bull only grinned again. "Marvelous spirit you have there, Lady Beddingsford. All the better in close quarters."

Minerva snarled, lowering her jaw to stare more murderously. "Are you certain you need him alive, Draper?" she demanded, raising her voice.

"Mist," Draper called without looking up. "Muzzle it."

Now it was Minerva who laughed, loving that particular image as much as she did the idea of her throwing something at his head.

Despite the brusque order, Mist still grinned at her shamelessly—silently, but the grin did not fade a jot.

It would have been so much better if his smile looked like a dog baring its teeth at an intruder, but unfortunately, the man was a handsome one, and his grin only enhanced those looks. Were he not the most annoying termite to ever don a cravat, she might have enjoyed looking at him. As it was, she could only resent every attractive feature wasted on him.

How could he not be as upset as she was about this? If he was the best operative the Foreign Office had, he should find the addition of another operative to his mission just as much of an inconvenience as she did. Yet he was grinning like a fool, teasing her, taking nothing seriously, and acting as though nothing could disrupt his irreverent mood.

Was he so skilled an operative that he could adapt that quickly to such a drastic change? Or was he simply so naïve that he hadn't thought far enough ahead to see the ramifications of this?

Was he an idiot or a genius? That was the question.

And apparently, she was going to find that out for herself sooner rather than later.

What fun.

She glanced over at him in irritation, and thankfully, his attention had shifted down towards the floor, though his smile remained in place. He appeared more bemused than irreverent now, and she much preferred it this way. She could make a quick study without him accusing her of taking an interest or any other ridiculous idea of his own self-indulgence.

There was something about his sleeves being rolled to his elbows that made him more approachable and less impossible, that humanized the image of finery he had presented in the ballroom, that drew the eyes in a way that even Minerva could not resist. The man bore a natural insolence that was damnably attractive, there was no mistaking that, and when stripped of the accoutrements that one generally saw among gentlemen…

Well, he could have had any woman with a pair of eyes and a pulse.

Until he opened his mouth. The sensual image of him was shattered with a single complete sentence. Even an incomplete sentence. Anything longer than three words strung together.

Not even the dark hair, dark eyes, shadow of scruff, and perfectly chiseled jaw could make up for that. Nor the broad shoulders, long legs, and rather intriguing impression of muscles in the presently exposed forearms.

All right, now she was staring, and there was nothing about a character study in that.

Just observation.

Her eyes flicked to his face, and his eyes were on her, smiling in an entirely new way that immediately lit her throat on fire.

He raised a brow, nodding at her. "My lady."

Minerva looked away quickly, her face flaming.

There was something about him that made her want to look at him, but it was not something as simple as attraction, though he certainly had an appealing visage. It was more… puzzling. Not quite familiar, but he did not seem particularly a stranger either.

She had never worked with him before that she was aware of,

but there had been several interactions with assets and operatives in passing, and disguises were a natural and expected aspect of life. She could not be certain of anyone's appearance at any time, which made trust rather difficult without proof.

Which meant she did not trust at all.

But there was something…

"Mist," Draper announced then, turning to face them with Milliner. "You will give up your apartments first thing in the morning."

"Fine," Mist replied with a nod, his attention on Draper now. "Where am I going?"

"Upper Grosvenor Street," Milliner answered, her smile tight. "We have a residence just off the square. Fully secured, fully staffed. Mirrors, you will prepare the staff for Lord Beddingsford's arrival."

Minerva blinked at her superior, arguably the most powerful woman in England, and bit down hard on her tongue to keep from arguing. "So, it's settled, then?" she managed when the urge to screech subsided enough to be contained.

Draper looked at her, his expression remaining unmoved. "Can you think of another way, Mirrors, for both missions to move forward and your covers to remain intact? It is not ideal, but what's done is done. We will debrief you both on the details of each assignment tomorrow when Mist is settled in, and then it will be up to the two of you to accomplish both. How you do so is your own business. Can you avoid killing each other for the duration?"

"Certainly, I think so," Mist answered before Minerva could do so. "We are both professionals, after all."

Oh, he had to bring that up, did he? Emphasize that they ought to be adaptable and accommodating, given their previous experience? Make her seem less professional by voicing so many complaints?

She was not about to take that.

Minerva only nodded, folding her arms more tightly. "Less paperwork when nobody dies," she mumbled.

"Very true, my dear," Mist replied, though the statement had not been directed towards him in any way.

"I have nothing against paperwork, Fog Brain, and I will spend the next year filling mountains of it out with a smile if I wind up killing you," Minerva snapped, raising her voice and flicking her eyes towards him without actually seeing him.

She could hear him snicker, and oddly enough, she wanted to smile at it.

But she was still too irritated to give in to that impulse born of superiority and a well-fired barb. There would be time for reveling in such things later. If she was going to be trapped in a house with him for the duration of their missions, she would undoubtedly have plenty of time to insult him creditably, as well as smile about it.

Minerva pressed her tongue to the front of her teeth and looked at Milliner, knowing she would be able to interpret the expression perfectly.

Sure enough, Milliner gave her a sympathetic smile. "We have every confidence that you will be able to accomplish both missions working together, and that nothing will hinder your work by this change of plans."

"Really?" Minerva asked, intending for the response to be sarcastic, but it came out sounding more curious than anything else. She cleared her throat. "Nothing?"

Milliner's brows rose. "Apart from yourselves, yes."

The message was clear enough: It was done.

The decision had been made and that was all there was to it. There was no point in arguing about it anymore. The mission parameters had now changed, and resisting would not get her anywhere.

She was going to be the wife of this imbecile in the eyes of Society and the world until they finished their missions, and because of that, she would have to live with him as well. Would have to confide in him. Would have to trust him. Would have to work with him. Would have to…

Oh heavens, what if she had to kiss him again? Why had she been so stupid as to choose that as her reaction to seeing the elusive Lord Beddingsford so unexpectedly? He was right. Now that was going to be their reputation, and she would have to be rather familiar with him to keep that impression going. Unless she wished to start rumors of a rift between them, some disagreement of sorts, but that would have to be explained somehow, and the Beddingsfords were not going to parade their personal details for the world.

Not if she had anything to say about it.

Minerva swallowed her further resistance to the plan and nodded once, glancing at Mist quickly. "Will there be a chance for Mist and me to do some training together? If we're to be working together, and mostly alone, we need to trust each other completely, and that sort of connection takes time we do not have. The least we could do is practice."

Mist sobered at once, nodding as well. "I actually agree with that. I haven't had a partner in some time, and it would not serve anyone for me to put Mirrors in danger by my lack of recent experience. Twice the mission is twice the danger for us, so let's not present more weakness than we have to."

It was the most intelligent thing she had heard him say yet, and there was a great relief in that. She had begun to wonder if he could take anything seriously, and if the operatives in the Foreign Office were some of the lowest qualified in the entire British operative ranks.

This, at least, proved that not to be entirely true.

"Excellent thought," Milliner praised, bringing Minerva's attention back to her. "We will want someplace safe from suspicion." She looked at Draper, her brows knitting. "What if the Beddingsfords take a trip into Kent to view the historic family estate?"

"It would have to be more than a day trip," Draper pointed out even as he was nodding. "These two might make it to Kent and back without fuss, but the Beddingsfords would most certainly not do so. We will need at least five days, if not more. Can we spare that?"

Silence rose in the room as they all thought about it, tried to consider possibilities and solutions that would allow both her and Mist to perform to the best of their abilities in their missions, now that they would be working together.

Minerva bit her lip gently as she thought, then looked at the two Shopkeepers in the room. "I received an invitation for a house party, also in Kent. It came just this morning, and I have yet to give my answer. It could be the perfect timing for Lord Beddingsford and myself to leave London to spend some time together, now that we have been reunited. No one would expect us to attend the party after tonight's surprise, would they?"

Mist grunted once and she looked over at him. He was smiling a bit ruefully, shaking his head. "Not after that scene, no. I expect they'll have a very clear idea of why the Beddingsfords want to spend time away, and they'll be talking about it for quite some time."

"Yes, rather," Minerva said quickly, her cheeks flushing as she returned her attention to the others. "My point is that a great many others will be away from London during the house party, so we could be as well. I can confirm the dates when I return to the house."

"Perfect," Milliner replied with an approving nod. "And it would be only fitting for the Beddingsfords to dine with the Kirklins while visiting the family estate, so we can arrange that. Might even be good for the assignments to do so, all things considered."

"Undoubtedly," Draper agreed, though something about it made him smile, which Minerva had yet to see him do. His gaze darted to Mist a moment, but he said nothing and looked at Milliner again. "Whatever you think is best, Milliner, will do well. I trust you have retained Fists up there?"

Milliner laughed once and nodded. "We could never get rid of him. Of course he's there."

Draper dipped his chin. "Good. He'll be familiar with Mist's training, then." He exhaled and pulled out a pocket watch, frowning at it before snapping it shut. "I think the Beddingsfords would do well to return to the ballroom, or else someone is likely to come looking for them." He looked at Minerva and Mist in turn. "Stay as long as you like but leave together. Even if you aren't staying in the same place tonight, you must give the impression. We'll pay a call tomorrow and give you all of the information for each assignment that we can."

Minerva nodded, though she wasn't entirely certain Draper was speaking to her. Still, no matter how anyone looked at it, any of the Shopkeepers outranked her, and she would take orders from them as such.

She and Mist were a team now, which meant she was temporarily part of the Foreign Office as well as acting in her usual position in the Agents of the Convent. His mission was now her mission, and hers his.

One could only hope they would coincide without too much

inconvenience.

Minerva cleared her throat and turned to face Mist, ready to tell him to rearrange his attire for their return. But he was already rolling his sleeves back down, one already fixed with a cuff link. How he had managed to do so without help was unclear, but she could see the secure and glinting link in place for herself.

Her momentary glimmer of regret at his forearms being hidden once more faded into her more structured, mission-oriented mind. His smug smirk was gone for the moment, and a serious, focused expression remained.

That was even more attractive than anything she had seen yet. Unnerving.

He glanced up at her as he finished rolling the sleeve down. "Care to fix my link, my lady?"

She moved to him, holding her palm out for the cuff link. She glanced at it, smirking slightly at the elaborate gold-and-ruby B on the face. "Tasteful, my dear. Really." She shook her head and went to work on the sleeve.

"I bought them just for you, darling," he replied with a soft snort. "Do you think the Beddingsfords are the sort to stay into the wee hours of the morning at an event like this? Or are they the sort to make their mark and retire early?"

Minerva shook her head, exhaling roughly. "I haven't the faintest idea. Whatever plan I had for the evening is now moot, isn't it?" She finished fastening the link and tugged on his sleeve to check the closure.

He shrugged a little. "Not necessarily, but I see your point." He nodded and slipped into his jacket. "I was only making an impression this evening myself, so I am at my leisure."

"Oh, you made an impression?" Minerva quipped, not bothering to soften the edge to her voice. "I hadn't noticed."

Mist chuckled easily, his fingers now working expertly at the linen of his cravat. "Well, I thought I had, but I dare say I was outshone by my wife yet again. Certainly, no one will forget how she flew at me in a passion. Though I may say, I did respond rather well, all things considered. One must be a match for one's spouse, don't you agree?"

Minerva ignored that, wishing she could go back and change her reaction to one of cool indifference rather than abject adoration. It would have made things far simpler and possibly have rid her of this mess, though her rational mind told her that was likely not true. Milliner would not have risked her in such a way, and they would have needed to discover the connection between the operatives using the title as it was.

So she might still have wound up in this situation with the maddening man, only without the precedent of physical affection.

Far more preferable, given the insufferable airs of her supposed husband.

"The spectacle has already been created," Minerva said shortly, straightening his cravat while he saw to the buttons. "Questions will circulate, and we need not answer them. We may do the same amount of work by sharing two more dances. Not consecutively, given we need to establish connections outside of ourselves for any of this to work."

"Excellent thought, all things considered. With this interlude here, perhaps we should part ways in the ballroom for the space of two dances?" He reached up and adjusted her headdress, finding a pin with shocking ease to affix it all more securely. "I will do you the courtesy of looking in your direction with frequency, so as not to raise additional questions about loyalty and the like. Perhaps you might spare me a glance or two?"

Minerva nodded, ignoring how the feeling of his fingers in her hair sent a shiver down her spine and made her fingers quite warm. "Certainly. After the third dance, I believe we will have proven our point well enough and we may depart. Agreed?"

"Agreed." He stepped back, looking her over quickly and giving a nod. "Perfection, my dear. It would do my reputation well to kiss you soundly to turn your lips a brighter shade, but I will refrain." He spread his arms out a little, raising a brow. "Do I meet with your approval?"

Cheeks warmed from his rather blasé suggestion, Minerva offered a clipped nod. "Well enough. Shall we?"

His grin told her he saw through her brusqueness, which might have been the most unsettling realization of all. He gestured towards the door through which they had entered, and which, apparently, their superiors had already exited without her notice. "After you, my lady."

Minerva dipped her chin in a hint of a nod, lacing her fingers together, and moved with every ounce of practiced grace she possessed out of the room. She was only too acutely aware of the presence of the man behind her, whom she now had to encourage openly for the public and endure professionally in private.

For all the missions she had undertaken in her career, this one now bore the most anticipation of them all. Nothing was as certain as it had seemed only a few hours ago, and every imagined strategy was now gone. She was walking into an unknown, despite weeks of preparation, and even knowing she now had another skilled operative alongside her brought little comfort. In fact, it only made everything worse.

Infinitely worse.

Chapter Four

London in the morning was an interesting atmosphere, there was no doubt about that. Men walking this way and that, carriages moving with a strange hush that did not exist in the afternoons, riders on horseback dressed in all manner of states, honest working folk about their usual business. Far more people than Griffin had anticipated seeing, and far many more knowing him than he had been introduced to the night before. Was London always so bustling, regardless of the hour?

Griffin had little experience with it, given his recent assignments on the Continent and his secret rustication at Worsley Park, his estate in Suffolk. His brother thought he was never there, and likely still believed him to be somewhere in Italy, as his last letter to him had indicated. His official position at the Foreign Office had him stationed as an attaché of sorts to any number of ambassadors, which kept him out of England for all intents and purposes. He had certainly operated in such a position a time or two, but not nearly as often or for as long a time as his siblings thought. He was in England a surprising amount of the time, just not in a position to enlighten them as to that. And Worsley Park, for all it belonged to the family, had become a cache for his work.

Suffolk was a bit far from his superiors for their liking, but it was the best he could do under the circumstances. His brother, the duke, had insisted on keeping both of the estates in Wiltshire, which made no sense at all, but Hawk was a stickler for tradition, and both estates had remained in the holdings of the Duke of Kirklin for generations. Never mind that he also had the traditional seat of Kirkleigh in Kent, which would have been a perfect alternative for Griffin, if he'd had to remain in the family holdings.

Better still would have been for Hawk to sell off Millmond or Elmsley Abbey and take Worsley back, giving Griff the money and the freedom to build his own estate where he pleased.

But while his brother knew nothing of Griffin's true work and life, none of that could take place.

So Worsley Park it would be when he was out of London, and whatever lodgings had been arranged for him while he was in it.

For the present, he was relocating to the house on Upper Grosvenor Street where his wife was waiting.

His wife…

He still had to laugh at the idea. There was no question she despised him, and he was honest enough to admit that he had given her ample cause. He hadn't meant to be incorrigible; he simply had retreated into his natural irreverence to cover his own distrust and forced adjustment. In some circles, ladies found such behavior charming.

Mirrors had not.

Which, he could also admit, was utterly fascinating.

She was a stunning woman, and clearly suffered no fools, which landed her squarely in his preferred category. He had never found the naïve, ignorant, vain girls of Society to be in any way attractive, despite what beauty their appearance displayed. Perhaps it was due to having an active and engaged mother who was well-read and outspoken, perhaps it was his fondness for his impudent and independent sister, or perhaps it had always been something his tastes had tended towards. Whatever it was, a woman who challenged him in some regard was instantly worth his attention.

And his wife certainly challenged him.

He had heard of operatives being legally married for their missions before, and fleetingly wondered if the same legalities would be extended here. It would not necessarily help matters between them, as they were both established operatives with ties to the highest authorities in the land, and Society already thought them married in every respect. Neither of them was utilizing their true identities, so there was no risk to their futures, unless they were to become hopelessly compromised. And if their story of being married abroad was true, no curious minds could seek out their marriage license.

So they were free to be as unencumbered as they had been before.

Apart from now having to cohabitate and present a united front, of course.

Which was why he was now walking from Bloomsbury to Upper Grosvenor Street, complete with the most elegant walking stick Tilda could find and taking great care to be seen proceeding to join his wife in the home she was renting.

What a great joke, he had said to inquiring minds the night before, to surprise his wife in London after many months apart.

Yes, of course they would be moving in together for the foreseeable future, he had declared. Hadn't they already spent too much time apart?

He could not possibly accept invitations yet, he had sadly related, as his first devotion must be to his wife and making up for time lost. But naturally, once all was satisfied there, invitations would be welcome.

It was an exhausting act, even for him, but the rumor mill would be spinning on his work, and likely hers as well, though he had yet to overhear any of her statements on the subject for the gossips. No one would doubt Lord Beddingsford's marital satisfaction, nor his eagerness to indulge himself in time with his wife. He half expected someone to approach him this very morning and inquire as to his not already being at the house in Upper Grosvenor, after the display between himself and his wife the night before.

He had an answer ready for that as well.

What sort of gentleman would he be if he did not let his wife have some true rest after such exertions? And he could not have left the Drummond home with the proper clothing for this morning as well as the ensemble he had worn there, so he simply had to return to his Bloomsbury lodgings to change before his things were moved.

But despite the looks of several gentlemen he passed on his way, and some intrepid ladies up and about too early, no one approached him with so direct a question. Other questions, certainly, but not that one. Truth be told, he would not have been surprised if he saw the

Drummonds themselves ambling about, attempting to appear to meet him by chance despite carefully orchestrated efforts.

Perhaps there would be a suspicious gathering of individuals situated outside the doors of the house on Upper Grosvenor, each engaged in pointless conversation for show, hoping to catch a glimpse of the captivating couple away from the ballroom.

On the one hand, this could be the most fun he'd had inhabiting a role for a mission. On the other...

Well, he had a task to accomplish, and indulging in gossip to deflect the kind of attention that could upset matters would grow tiresome rather quickly.

Particularly if his partner in all this despised every aspect.

He could only hope that the few hours of sleep she had received had softened her demeanor towards him, though he highly doubted he would be so fortunate. After all, he was not so changed with the same, so why should he expect such a thing from her?

He turned onto Upper Grosvenor Street then, plastering a ridiculous smile on his face for the benefit of any gawkers presently anticipating him. There were some, though hardly as many as he had imagined. He could only be grateful for that.

Their primary objective was to accomplish their missions, and the scrutiny of others would make the task more difficult. He was, of course, accustomed to acting in a course hidden beneath appearances much observed, but this was something new. London rarely deviated from topics of fascination without something new to divert them, and he had difficulty imagining something more fascinating than a separated couple no one had heard about, reuniting with a passionate embrace in front of dozens of Society's finest.

Gads, this was a mess. He could not blame Mirrors for acting as she had, adapting to an unforeseen complication with an admirable rapidity that had compromised nothing and no one. But it would complicate matters infinitely.

Why had the Shopkeepers not discussed their business with more clarity? Why were there not measures in place to keep open titles from being used between offices? This could all have been avoided and both missions could have proceeded as planned unencumbered.

But the situation was what it was, and it could not be changed now.

Griff's approach was now being noticed by those lingering about, and he did them all the courtesy of tipping his hat at them. "Good morning, all. Has my beloved incomparable made her appearance yet?"

He was going to get a thrashing worth remembering if Mirrors caught wind he'd called her that, which, oddly enough, made the thing worth it.

"No, my lord," an intrepid onlooker replied, doing him the credit of not pretending their presence there was an accident. "There seems to be a great deal of bustle about the place, but Lady Beddingsford hasn't been seen."

Griffin grinned at the stranger, his eyes scanning through those gathered, not a familiar face among them. "That would be for me, I'm afraid. My little joke in surprising my wife, you know. Now that I've revealed my presence in London, I really must take up residence with her. I could not even trust the staff with my surprise, given their fervent loyalty to my lady, so I caught them all unawares. Hardly fair, but there it is." He chuckled with a sheepish air, which seemed to prompt laughter from the others.

Word in London must spread faster than he'd thought, if the previous evening at a ball could create attention for himself and Mirrors that morning. That would have an interesting impact on their missions, whatever hers happened to be. But if their higher-ups were to be believed, they would both find out all they needed to about both missions shortly. And then they could figure out how to accomplish those missions together.

And what their next move would be.

Or first move.

Last night did not count. It had only been the introduction to the missions, and then the rapid adjustments to the slight oversight of the title. And now the missions were being adjusted, so there would need to be another introduction to them. Together this time. As partners.

He hadn't had a partner in years.

And he had never been distracted by a partner.

Not that he was distracted by Mirrors. Such a thing required repeated opportunities to attempt to focus and work beside her so that he might actually feel distraction, should it arise. His focus on her the night before had been for show, to further the proof of their identities, and to remove the possibility of more astute questions from the public. And as he was quite skilled in his tasks as an operative, it had been his responsibility to convince the world of his fervor for the woman who was his wife, particularly on their first exposure as a couple. And he had done so, as was his task.

Surely he could not be blamed for that. Surely even Mirrors would wish for him to convince the world. After all, she had been the one who…

Well, what else was he supposed to do when she had kissed him utterly senseless without warning? A man could only be expected to endure so much.

This could all be construed as her fault, if he wished to pursue such a line of argument.

But he would settle for receiving one of the better bedrooms in the house they would share. As the master of the house, that could not be too much to ask.

Griff looked around at the strangers who apparently waited for him to do something extraordinary or entertaining, and only gave them a foppish sort of smile. "Well, if you do not mind budging up slightly, I think I must venture within to indulge my wife." He gestured slightly with his walking stick, smirking to himself when the gawkers parted like a sea before a certain ancient prophet.

He strode through them without hesitation, tapping his hat with the handle of his stick. "Much obliged. Do disperse now. We are not in the habit of displaying ourselves for the world. I am sure we will see you all by and by." He grinned, quirking his brows in whatever suggestion they might read in it, then proceeded to the door, rapping upon it three times.

It opened to reveal a face Griff knew well, the man having played his valet, his driver, and even his master on various assignments in his past. But having no idea of the man's present name, he could not very well address him.

Lord Beddingsford could afford a minute of idiocy, at any rate.

"Good morning, my man," he greeted for the benefit of those listening in. "I'll recollect your name one of these days, but it has been a terribly long night."

A twinkle in the eye was all the good butler gave away. "Carne, sir. Pleasure to see you again." He stepped back, nodding a perfectly clipped dip of the chin.

Griffin swept inside with as much grandeur as he thought Beddingsford might employ. "Of course it is," he replied, lowering his voice and turning with a far more natural grin as the door was closed.

Only then did the butler turn back, chuckling freely and shaking his head. "Always knew how to make an entrance, Mist."

"You taught me how, Pick," Griff returned with a laugh. "Can I help it if I learn well?"

They came to each other, hands outstretched, and shook hard, gripping each other's arm tightly. "Where the devil have you been?" Pick demanded, thumping him on the back after releasing his arm. "I lost track of you after Austria."

Griff exhaled a sputtering breath, thinking back. "Oh, let me think. After Austria, there was Athens, followed quickly by Santorini—narrowly escaped that one by the time the mainland Revolution broke out. Hunkered down in Catania for a few weeks, then took up a position in Naples for several months… Then there was Zürich, Graz, a quick stint in Belfast, a whole year in Glasgow…"

"Deuce, man," Pick exclaimed, shaking his head again, this time in disbelief. "It's a wonder you haven't gone mad yet with all of that."

"Oh, it's not so bad," Griff protested without fuss. "I had a lovely nap between each assignment, and I don't need much else." He smiled and patted the older man on the shoulder. "Quite a mess we find ourselves in, this. Seen my counterpart this morning?"

Pick snorted once. "Of course I have. She sleeps as little as you do. Up before most of the maids, that one."

Griff hissed softly, grimacing. "Has she been cursing my name?"

"No, actually," the older man said, surprising him. "But she doesn't rant or confide, so I wouldn't have heard."

"Lovely," Griff grumbled. "Suppose I'd better go and see her before Draper and Milliner arrive."

"Undoubtedly," Pick agreed, gesturing down the hall. "I'd wager she's pacing that drawing room there. Seems to think on her feet."

Griff gave him a rueful smile. "Perfect. So do I." He nodded at his comrade and moved towards the room, the fingers on his right hand absently rubbing together as he did so.

He had not slept well the night before, thinking of all the things he would now have to consider and rearrange. The beauty of this particular assignment was that it was adaptable. He had no idea what he would be getting into, and bringing Mirrors into the mix did not change that. He had a few individuals he needed to strike up an association with, none of whom had names as yet, but he had very clear illustrations of their features, and a fair idea of allies, which seemed as good a place as any to start.

Surely the disappearance of one scrawny would-be operative could not be so difficult to uncover, and yet, the entire London League had failed to do so. Given the incredible skill set of every man in those ranks, Griff could not help but take the whole thing that much more seriously.

So they had turned to the Foreign Office, where that would-be operative had come from, to begin their own investigation into the matter.

Or they would have, had his files been where they ought to have been.

Which created the bigger problem.

No files meant no name, no history, no contacts of note, and absolutely nothing to go on except what the League could give them.

And no one within the Foreign Office to trust, given the files had not walked away of their own accord. Someone had removed them—either the operative himself or someone who knew more than they should about the whole matter. Until they discovered the operative himself, or his fate, or some traitor in their midst, Griff would have no allies but those Draper had given him.

It would have been daunting had he not been accustomed to working alone.

Although now, he would have a wife, wouldn't he?

Heaven help them both.

He reached the drawing room and peered in. Sure enough,

Mirrors was pacing, this time rather simply arrayed in a grayish-green calico, nicely fitted without being perfectly tailored. Her body was not any less impressive for its being dressed in less finery, and her strides against the floor were powerful, lithe, and entirely unladylike in their pace. Nothing sedate about this woman, despite the grace and airs she had mastered the night before.

This was who she was, unobserved and stripped of disguise.

He liked her more now than he had five minutes ago, and she hadn't said anything yet.

"Morning, darling," he greeted with a pointed yawn as he entered, feeling a slight pang of regret at having to break her ardent concentration.

Her eyes flicked up to him as she turned, the long plait of her hair whipping around to drape on the opposite shoulder. "Mist," she replied, continuing to pace without the barest hint of interruption to her actions. "Sleep well?"

Griff scoffed and dropped himself into a chair. "No, as it happens. You?"

She shook her head just a little. "Not particularly. Quite a lot of tossing and turning."

"I have that effect on women, I do apologize," Griff offered with a playful grin.

Her expression became the most sardonic thing he had ever seen in his entire life. "Does that sort of thing ever work as flattery? Or is it your intention to put off every woman you encounter?"

Griff threw his head back on a laugh. "Ouch, my lady. That cuts me to the quick."

Mirrors sighed with raw impatience, now stopping her pacing and turning to face him. "Would you do me a very great favor and not do that sort of thing with me? I am not some conquest for you to strive for. We are to be partners now, and if I am to trust you, I would much prefer not being uncomfortable in your presence."

Normally, such a statement would have earned another wry remark from him, but he found the frankness refreshing and the lack of dramatics sobering.

And she had an excellent point.

"Of course," he found himself saying. He nodded quickly, then pushed to his feet. "Of course, you have my word." He held his hand out, rather like he had done with Pick a few moments before.

She took it with only minimal hesitation, her grip firm. "Thank you."

"I realize our situation is rather different from other partnerships we may have had. Likely a good deal more intimate, so to speak," he told her, not relinquishing her hand quite yet. "So here, in our base of sorts, feel free to call me Griff, if you like."

She seemed to take that with the same good graces with which he had offered it and nodded. "Minerva."

He shook her hand once more, then released it. "Pleasure. Where are you from?"

"Norfolk," she replied without much interest. "Near Downham."

"Really?" He cocked his head, sliding his hands into his pockets. "I was raised in Wiltshire but spent a deal of time near Martham. Do you know it?"

She shook her head at once. "Only by name. I rarely went to the coastal towns, though I've been to Norwich a time or two."

Why he had felt the need to test her, he couldn't have said, but something about this spirited woman being from the exact county of England where his estate sat seemed unlikely. Still, almost nobody had been to Martham that claimed to be from Norfolk, but at least she'd gotten the location correct.

"Were you a governess there?" he asked, forcing his tone to be light. "If you're one of Milliner's operatives, chances are you have worked at the Convent."

"Still do," Minerva replied, resuming her pacing once more. "I teach comportment, elocution, logic, and philosophy."

Griff raised a brow, rearing back a little in surprise. "Blimey. And for the less public students?"

She glanced over at him, her mouth curving in a raw way he found intriguing. "Comportment and elocution. Adaptation, stagecraft, acting, accomplishment, and the like."

Ah, now that made far more sense, and he grinned without reserve. "So you are quite literally the perfect person for an assignment requiring infiltration into Society?"

Minerva only shrugged. "I have some skills, and I was available when needed."

"I suspect you were," he murmured, more for himself than for her ears. "And I suspect someone was readily available to cover your teaching assignments, which must be rather convenient."

"Quite." She turned in her pacing and stopped, giving him a quick look. "Apologies, have you eaten? I am sure something could be brought up for you."

Her sudden recollection of household duties made him smile without any hint of jesting. "I have, actually. Don't worry, I'll make myself quite at home here. Were we not anticipating our superiors any moment, I'd probably be examining each of the bedchambers and testing out which bed suits me best."

"I've already put you in the master's rooms," Minerva said dismissively with a quick flick of her wrist. "Seemed most appropriate. And you can always change out the beds."

Griff watched her for a moment in amusement, her long strides kicking at the skirts of her dress. His humor had completely missed its mark in his delivery, and that was a rarity. Minerva was quick enough to have caught it, and certainly witty enough herself to grasp his meaning, if not volley banter back. But in this moment, she had either not heard his tone of playfulness, or she had not found the idea of his examining rooms and beds like a child in any way amusing.

If not both.

"Nervous, Minerva?" he asked innocently.

"No," she insisted on a sharp turn in her pacing. "I simply want to know what is going to happen and what the new expectations of us are."

Griffin watched as she continued to move, finding the motion oddly soothing. "Do you always pace when you are anxious?"

"Changing the word does not change the truth," Minerva snapped, rather like she had done the night before. "I am not nervous, anxious, excitable, or whatever word you choose to use that means I am overwrought. I am only thinking and trying to plan."

She could call it whatever she liked, but there was a desperate edge to the thing that spoke of anticipation, if not uneasiness. Perhaps she was thinking and plotting, but that was not all there was.

"Would it help if I promise not to get in your way?" Griffin offered. "Whatever your assignment is?"

Minerva scoffed loudly, rather like Griffin had heard his sister do dozens of times over the years. "No, it would not help. You see, I would not let you get in my way. Should it come down to it, I would charge you down on my own two feet, trod upon your incapacitated form, and march on my merry way. Understood?"

Griffin whistled low and held his hands up in surrender. "Yes, my lady. Quite clearly."

"Good." She nodded once, then her eyes moved to something behind him. "Yes?"

A soft throat clearing answered her. "Your guest has arrived, my lady," Pick's voice chimed in.

Minerva's brow creased. "Guest? Singular?"

Griff turned to face Pick as well, now curious himself. "Are we missing something?" he asked his comrade-turned-butler.

Pick smiled a little. "She said, and I quote, 'Go open the kitchen door after announcing me.' I thought I might do as she said, given everything."

Griff looked over at Minerva, whose face now held something of bewilderment in it. "I won't pretend I know what she refers to, but yes, I suppose you'd better," he said.

Pick's footsteps faded into the corridor, and another set approached.

"Good morning, Beddingsfords," Milliner greeted as she entered the room, dressed in a fine morning gown he hadn't anticipated from the headmistress. "I hope you don't mind this slightly dramatic and cloaked approach we've taken this morning. Draper and I could not think of a single reason why he and I would be paying social calls together this early in the morning, so he has kindly offered to come in disguise as the grocer man through the kitchens. Kindly do not mock his ensemble, whatever it is, for he is quite proud of it."

Griff turned away from her a moment, more to stifle a laugh, and glanced at his wife, who now looked utterly exasperated as she met his gaze.

"This is never going to work," she hissed to him.

He could only shrug before returning to the seat he had vacated earlier. It might be a disaster, but there was no help for it. Once Draper arrived, their assignments would be given, and the true work would begin.

Chapter Five

"*R*ight, we've notified all departments of the situation, and all are on the alert to help the pair of you in any way, should they meet you socially."

Minerva blinked at Draper's succinct beginning to their meeting. "Help? Help with what?"

Draper looked at her, his simple grocer's ensemble doing nothing to lessen his aristocratic appearance from the shoulders up. "Whatever you might need. Connections, a cover story, information… We will not be tripped up again, and neither of your missions can be sacrificed at this point."

Minerva glanced at Pippa for any insight, but she was in full Milliner form, and revealed nothing. It was maddening when she did this, but she supposed in this particular situation, her friend had to be her superior first.

They'd only been at this meeting a few minutes, and already, Minerva was desperate for it to be over. She had never had much patience for lengthy discussion, nor for taking ages to reach the crux of any conversation. She wanted to know what she needed to know and get on with things. Perhaps it came from not being gently born and bred, despite what she portrayed for the world, and not being trained up to endure dithering on. She could pass it off well enough when she was in character, when she was meeting with students or parents, or the like, but when she was herself…

"And our missions are…?" Mist prodded, as though his mind was in line with her own. His posture was one of casual inelegance in the chair, though he hadn't removed his jacket or rolled his sleeves again, thank heavens. But neither would anyone looking at him guess him to be the resplendent Lord Beddingsford from the night before, though his morning ensemble did hold a touch of refinement above the common attire.

Unlike Minerva's at the present.

Mist—Griff, she corrected herself—had to face those people who had been wandering about outside of the house all morning, so perhaps he had only dressed that way for their benefit. There was no telling how he would dress here in the privacy of their home.

The house, that was.

They did not have a home. They were not married. This was an assignment, nothing more.

An assignment which she did not yet completely understand, as there was now a second part to it.

If they would ever get to the discussion of it.

"Mist," Draper began, nodding towards his operative, "will be looking into the disappearance of the clerk who used to work for the London League. He was one of ours before he started there, and his disappearance has become a great cause for concern. There is a great potential for danger and compromising of identities both in the London League and the Foreign Office, and what with the compromise that has already occurred with the League, you can imagine we wish for progress quickly."

Minerva found herself gaping a little bit, having heard about this missing clerk, of course, through the network of conversation that was the operatives of England. It was all the League could talk of, now that Trace had been restored and everybody accustomed to his reappearance. The opportunity to examine the clerk's disappearance and present whereabouts was something any operative who loved their work would wish to take on.

"Jealous?" Griff asked with a laugh, no doubt catching her expression.

"Very," she admitted without hesitation, giving him a look. "I've heard there is nothing to go on. Is that true?"

Griff shrugged, looking rather pleased with himself. "His file is sparse, if that is what you mean. I have his last used identity, and his birth name, but without anything to corroborate…"

Pippa cleared her throat pointedly then. "It is best for us all if Draper and I are not here long. Perhaps the two of you could discuss the details later?"

Griff raised his fingers in a sort of apology and gestured for them to go on, but he cast a quick look at Minerva, winking a little.

She felt a quick burst of something within her chest at that. Anticipation to hear what he knew, what he had uncovered, what his plan was. An eagerness to imagine how she would undertake the same mission, what avenues she would explore, anything that would stir her more creative strategies. An excitement to engage in a pair of assignments with an operative who felt just as much pride, challenge, and satisfaction in their world as she did.

This could all work out brilliantly after all.

"Mirrors," Pippa began, drawing Minerva's attention to her, "will be hunting Faction operatives. More particularly, tracking those who might have been smuggled into England before the coastal houses they'd been using were shut down. We've had word from operatives in France that certain figures are missing from Society there, and we are keen to use the likenesses captured by Sketch and Sphinx on their mission last year to find them here. And with their discovery, the same for any others they might have converted here to their cause. Given the murder of Mr. Hubert, time is of the essence."

Minerva heard an almost pained exhale from the man near her and flashed him a quick grin. "Now who is jealous?"

Griff scowled at her, though it was quickly replaced by a rueful smile. "I'd have drugged any operative on either side of the Channel to get this one."

She gave him a flat look. "If I wake up feeling in any way suspicious and find you away from the house in pursuit of this assignment, I will end you in ways you cannot possibly imagine."

That seemed to intrigue him, and he quirked a brow, turning towards her. "This is not my first foray into danger, madam. My imagination can extend quite far."

"Not far enough for what I am capable of, darling," Minerva insisted, shaking her head slowly. "Not far enough."

"Don't tease me with that kind of promise," Griff growled at her, his smile turning particularly devilish.

"You're a right pair, the two of you," Pippa said from her chair, her eyes fixed on Minerva with a mixture of amusement and severity. "We speak of compromise of identities and the murder of an asset, and you both are envious of each other's tasks. Ought we to be concerned about your humanity?"

Minerva gave Milliner a surprised look. "No, of course not."

"No, ma'am," Griff said with equal solemnity, turning back to them. "It is simply rare to find an operative with similar tastes in missions and the capacity to satisfy the requirements. You might call it a mutual respect between colleagues, though we know little of each other's missions. Which brings me to a question." He looked between the two superiors. "Have we your permission to tell each other about previous missions? As it relates, of course. Calling upon past experiences to assist our current work and the like."

The two Shopkeepers looked at each other, then back at their operatives. "Permission granted, of course," Draper told them. "Now, a few additional details. Mirrors, when is that house party you spoke of last evening?"

Minerva relayed the information quickly, sensing the man wanted to be gone rather soon. The house party was in a week, would last a fortnight, and would likely be spoken about for a great deal longer than that among the social elite. All the more unfortunate that she and Griff would have to miss it, but needs must.

And there was no question that they must.

Both of them going into an unknown, now doing so together, and without any sense of what the other was capable of, was unthinkable. More than that, it would put both of them in danger. And the whole point of a partnership, aside from completing their tasks, was to keep each other from danger.

A fortnight of playing pretend, and likely not much operating in their assignments, and then they could get to work. And Minerva was desperate for work.

Suddenly, Draper and Milliner were rising, and Minerva blinked, uncertain how they got to that point but adapting well enough to bid them farewell. Griff showed them out of the room, and Minerva was quick to sit back down, her mind racing ahead with her speculation.

Her notes and details regarding the mission were safely stowed in her rooms, and secretly done even then. Though the house was entirely run by operatives, she had long ago learned not to fully trust a single person. It was easier, safer, and altogether less complicated that way. She had no choice but to trust Griff with the details, but his neck was on the line as much as hers. And with the sensitive details of their particular missions, the Shopkeepers would have been even more selective as to those they assigned to such tasks.

If she was going to trust anyone, Griff would be a decent enough choice.

"I can see the steam of your thoughts whirling from your ears," commented the wry voice of her returning husband, who closed the drawing room door behind him with a firm click. "What's got you spinning?"

Minerva looked up at him quickly, ignoring the humor. "Why are you parading about Society if your information on the clerk is so sparse? Was he assigned a Society position before?"

Griff's brows rose. "Right into the fire, then? Do you ever relax, Minerva?"

"Yes," she replied simply. "Every night when I go to sleep. Which, as I understand, is what that is for. Would you like a game of billiards before we get to work? A stroll in the park? Perhaps you would prefer to go to the house party instead of the Convent?"

He folded his arms, exhaling heavily. "Fine, you've made your point. Are you always this driven?"

"Are you always this annoyed by the prospect of work?"

He gave her a dark look and moved to sit on the sofa opposite, slouching at once. "The clerk, whose given name is Charles Martin, had a simple role in a mission before his transfer to the London League six years ago. He was part of a team that moved about in Society to glean information after the Cato Street Conspiracy. The Home Office had its own ideas of infiltration, but Draper was anxious to quell any outside influences."

Minerva found herself nodding at that. "Understandable. The Scottish Insurrection followed, and the opinions against England…"

"It was an interesting time for us, that is certain," Griff concurred. "I've contacted those who worked on the team with him, and not one of them could give me insight as to his character and person. So I decided it would be best to do my own infiltration of Society and bandy his used name about a little."

"Which was?"

"Thomas Abbott." He sighed and rubbed at his brow. "Do you have any idea how difficult it is to track a man named Charles Martin who was born in London in eighteen hundred? We cannot afford to bring many in for assistance, given the risks, so I was left to do most of the early paperwork myself. I have never actually wished for my eyes to bleed until I did that."

Minerva hissed in sympathy, feeling that pain all too well. "Why is his file sparse? Surely he went through the same proper training as everyone else."

"He was recruited from Eton, siphoned out by our plants there based on his particular skills and intellect. Training happened after he completed his education, of course, and then he spent some time at Oxford, funded privately, as per usual." Griff smiled flatly, not elaborating when Minerva nodded in understanding.

It was the same with the Convent. When a young lady at the Miss Masters School proved herself worthy of interest by those working for the covert ranks, opportunities were made available to her that might not have been otherwise. It was one of the reasons why they had started the companion project, the Rothchild Academy, for the poor girls who would never have been provided any education at all, and could not afford finishing school of their own accord. Some of those who'd had the roughest start in life could prove the most useful of all, once given the chance.

Minerva could testify to that personally, though she'd never had to.

Not many knew of the true purpose of the Rothchild Academy, and it was better that way. A charitable act it was, but not necessarily a selfless one.

"So why was he given to the London League as a clerk, if he had done his duty as an operative?" Minerva asked, frowning as she considered the picture of the man as a whole. "Would that not be seen as a step down?"

Griff shrugged his shoulders, making a face. "Not necessarily. He was brought on to help and was tasked initially with aiding Eagle with structuring and organizing their tasks and assignments. As they became more active and employed, they required some assistance. And he was a mastermind at reworking the manner in which they operated. Eagle offered him assignments, but he preferred to stay as he was."

That was odd, and the more she thought on it, the more Minerva straightened. "He did not want to be an operative in the League?"

"Not in the traditional sense. But not all do, you know. Look at Sphinx."

That was a point, and she could not deny it. Sphinx was a gifted codebreaker and decipherer, and his recent on-site assignment in Paris had been one of his only missions outside of office space. Yet she would never have considered him in a lower position than anyone else because of it. Simply different. Different skills, different tasks, different needs, but vital to their work all the same.

Minerva shook her head slowly. "If he was that involved in their details, why has the League not been shut down with his disappearance?"

Griff gave her a humorless smile. "You presume the League gives everyone equal access to all things. There is apparently enough not shared to render disbanding unnecessary. Although I do believe that all of the families have been moved into protection."

"That is something, at least," Minerva murmured. "I cannot imagine how they feel about this."

"I wouldn't know, I'm not personally acquainted with any of them." Griff somehow shrugged without actually shrugging, unfolding his arms and lacing his fingers across his midsection. "At any rate, I'll also need to do some slumming for my assignment, if that makes you feel any better."

Minerva sniffed some version of a laugh. "I prefer slumming most of the time. There is nothing more unnerving than being constantly on display."

He gave her a slight smile. "True, but I do love a good display from time to time. Now, what about your own mission? Had you given it much thought beyond your entrance into Society?"

"Oh yes," Minerva assured him, now offering her own smile as a thrill of pride rushed through her. "I have planned everything out."

"Of course you have."

"Which now must be rearranged, due to the unforeseen complication."

"Sorry."

She ignored him. "But it was rather neatly constructed, so I trust I shall be able to do the same soon enough with the adjustments."

Griff raised a brow slowly. "Minerva, you do realize that missions do not follow a set plan, no matter how well constructed, do you not?"

She rolled her eyes, tempted to match his posture by slouching inelegantly in her position, but avoided it. "Of course I know that, I am no amateur. I carefully construct a plan and then adapt to my changing situations and new information as need be. It is orderly, not ironclad."

"If you say so." He waved a dismissive hand, seeming to shudder. "At any rate, what was your plan?"

"Ingratiate myself with the social climbers, of course." She batted her lashes mockingly before snorting at the idiocy of her actions. "Given the penchant for the Faction members to seek out funding and influence, it seemed the best option. I've also studied the drawings Sketch had done from Paris and would take stock of anyone in my company or at an event and see who I find. Well, that is the obvious avenue, at any rate."

Griff grunted once. "And the less obvious?"

Minerva leaned forward, resting her elbows on her knees. "It is entirely possible that the missing Parisian society members do not need the British society members for their present aims, which would mean they are looking for their own sympathizers or operatives already here. Those that are in lower orders, of course. So I've tapped into Gent's network of gossips and tails, with his permission, and the occasional slumming would take place based on their information."

If her plan impressed Griff, he gave no indication. He simply nodded, his brow creasing just enough to indicate thought.

When he continued to say nothing, Minerva gave him a pointed look. "What have I said that confuses you?"

"Nothing," he said absently. "I follow perfectly."

"Marvelous," she quipped in a dry tone. "Then kindly enlighten me as to why your mental efforts are requiring such concentration. Or is that how you normally look when you think?"

His dark eyes flicked to hers, his lips quirking. "Sharp tongue, wife. Excellent shot." He sat up with a groan and rubbed his hands together slowly. "I was only thinking of the sort of coordination we will need to have in our social schedules to allow us to accomplish both of our tasks. Not that we always need to be in the same place at the same time—that would be even more suspicious than anything else. We've already established that the Beddingsfords don't mind attention. In fact, they attract it."

"Unfortunately," Minerva grumbled as she considered more occasions of needing to feel like a pin cushion and a porcelain doll at the same time.

A fleeting smile crossed Griff's face, but it vanished with her glare. "Given that both of us worked to be rather flamboyant in our attire, we should probably coordinate ensembles for the larger events. I don't know about you, but I did not have my valet prepare a full wardrobe for Lord Beddingsford."

Minerva made a face. "No, I have a few gowns prepared for smaller things, but it was always the plan to have other elaborate gowns created once I had made my mark."

"And what a mark you made. I can still feel your lips if I think hard enough."

"Griff…"

"Sorry, sorry." He exhaled heavily, smiling at her in a rather lazy manner. "You cannot blame me for teasing you about that, you know. It was the most unexpected thing that has ever happened to me, mission related or not, and that is saying a great deal."

Minerva's cheeks flamed at once. "I did not mean to… I just could not think what else to do under the circumstances."

He waved that off. "Oh, from an operative standpoint, it was an utterly genius move, there is no question there."

The utter certainty in his voice did more to cool her embarrassment than anything else. Respect from a colleague was always to be appreciated, far more than any flattery or compliment from anyone else. But as the circumstances were what they were, Minerva had to smile just a little.

"Unfortunately, though, you did set a precedent."

Her smile vanished. "I what?"

Griff shrugged. "We are a spectacle, and utterly exuberant people. So, as I highly doubt you wish to kiss me regularly and with great fervor, we are going to have to appear as though we would do such things, if we were able."

Minerva's throat tightened, but somehow she managed to swallow. "As long as I don't actually have to kiss you, I can pretend almost anything."

"Well…"

She pressed her tongue against her teeth as her defenses rose like an eager drawbridge. "Well what?" she eventually forced between clenched teeth.

He held up his hands as though she were a wild horse he needed to tame. "I mean this with all due respect and in utter seriousness."

"I doubt that."

"If," he continued, giving her a warning look, "the situation arises in the course of our mission where I must return the gesture, I only want the assurance that you won't stab me in the kidneys. I am not saying I plan on such a course of action, but as you said, the circumstances were unexpected. Given that, and the precedent you set and I heartily embraced, would I have your permission to kiss you without prior discussion?"

She stared at him with all the darkness she could ever imagine, only for that darkness to slowly ebb when he did not so much as crack a smile at her. Not with his lips, not with his eyes, not with his frame.

She swore very softly in Greek. "You're entirely serious about this," she breathed.

He gave her a firm nod. "Look, I may be a cad in character, but I take the treatment of a lady seriously. You are my partner, and a respected colleague, but our situation requires a level of familiarity that isn't exactly standard practice, let alone something comfortable. I've never been married, I don't know how a happily married couple behaves, and I don't want to make you more uncomfortable than my natural provocation attempts do. I'll not have it said later that I forced you to do anything, or forced myself on you, or behaved ungentlemanly… And I don't want you to feel as though I am taking advantage of our situation to be less of a professional. Or a gentleman."

Minerva blinked at this man, feeling that this might be the most unexpected moment of her life, mission related or otherwise.

This man—this strong, clever, experienced, incredibly attractive man—was asking for her consent to do to her what she had done to him if their mission, or lives, depended on it. To act in their roles as a couple might, were they truly who they pretended to be. To ensure she knew of his respect, regardless of what situation they found themselves in.

She sank back against the cushions of the couch, staring at him in bewilderment. "You're serious."

"Yes," he said slowly, giving her a wary look. "I've said that."

"No, it's just…" She laughed once. "You're a confusing individual."

"I've heard that one before."

She smirked and heaved a sigh. "Very well, I consent. You get one return sign of affection without my demanding an explanation, as it is only fair. Anything else will require a full debrief when we are safe to do so. Agreed?"

His grin was potent and playful, and it curled something in her stomach. "Agreed. More than I expected, but I am glad for the clarification. And I don't mind admitting, I think I'll enjoy every opportunity, required explanation or not."

Minerva's amusement faded but could not completely abate. She rolled her eyes. "Oh, good heavens."

"That is a compliment. You are an excellent kisser, Minerva."

"I don't care, and it doesn't matter."

"I beg to differ, it very much does. Ask any red-blooded man, and he'll tell you."

"Shut up or be shut up."

Chapter Six

"This will be worth it, this will be worth it, this will be worth it…"

"Are you all right, Griff?"

"This will be worth it, this will be worth it…"

"Griff."

"Shh, Minerva, I am trying to calm my anxieties."

"Oh, for the love of… We are seeing a costumer, Griffin, not an executioner."

Griff cracked an eye open to look down at his partner in crime, walking purposefully beside him. "Have you ever met Tilda?"

She snorted and brushed at one of her gloves. "Yes, of course I have."

He nodded once. "To any man alive, she is as terrifying as an executioner and twice as cunning. I had to apologize to my throat and neck this morning in preparation."

Minerva gave him a startled look. "For what?"

"The amount of starch that will soon be strangling them both. It is no laughing matter. You would not believe how difficult it is to eat in such a contraption." He shuddered, wishing he was exaggerating.

All right, he was exaggerating a little, but it was not far off. Tilda, whose surname was as unknown as her background, was the ultimate costumer for the operatives in England, and her skills were legendary. She owed someone in the higher ranks a favor somewhere, either for a crime or a rescue, but her loyalty had never once been called into question. She was the most well-protected asset outside of official ranks that Griff knew of, though he doubted anyone else in the ranks knew just how protected.

And she had free rein of everything within her scope.

Tilda also worked in the theaters of London, with her actresses ranging from actual stage players to those who had more interpretive definitions of the thing. Griff had asked around, and no one was entirely certain if she preferred her work with the actresses to that with the operatives, but the woman never seemed overburdened or fatigued by her tasks.

Griff, for one, suspected the woman actually was an operative, but his superiors had never confirmed nor denied that notion.

He blinked as they entered Covent Garden, suddenly not entirely certain where the entrance to Tilda's workshop was or why he was allowing himself to be subjected to the torture. He had a valet. An imaginative one, perfectly trained by the Foreign Office for any and all tasks. It would be simple enough to allow him to take over his full costuming and would surely be a delight for the man. Not to mention how much more comfortable Griff would be that way.

This was wholly unnecessary. He would go back home and write to Draper of his decision. He would leave Minerva to the trussing, as it was far more important for a woman to be splendidly arrayed than a man. He did not have to be involved at all.

He would not be.

"Don't even think about it."

Again, Griff blinked, this time looking down at his companion with a quick jerk of his head while he tried to adjust to his course of action being scratched out without him expressing it.

He cleared his throat. "Do what?"

Minerva's look was derisive and all too knowing. "Run away," she said simply.

There was no need to hide his shock. "How the devil did you know?"

"You think you are the only one dreading this?" She snorted softly, fussing with her gloves as though the fabric of them irritated her palms. "We are about to let Tilda do whatever she likes to the both of us. She has never had completely free rein before, if what I've heard is true. I would rather face a battalion of snipers blindfolded."

"A battalion of snipers?" Griff repeated, barking a laugh. "Where would you encounter such a thing? And why?"

Minerva was unruffled by his mockery. "Blindfolded," she repeated. "Standing in the middle of a square with a battalion of snipers all around me, high and low, and no notion of where the shots will come from."

He'd have laughed again, but he suddenly pictured the image she described, and the humor was harder to come by. Not that he pictured her in the center of the square, but himself. Blindfolded. Knowing shots could begin at any time and from any quarter.

He'd been in a number of dangerous situations before, but that one, farfetched as it might be, could become his nightmare.

And Minerva would rather face that?

Over corsets and frills?

"I think it will be fine," Griff announced with a slight clearing of his throat, lifting his chin. "Perfectly fine. I think we are worrying for nothing."

"Like hell you do," Minerva laughed, slapping his arm as they strolled towards the theater. "You simply hate snipers."

Griff heaved a massive, if dramatic, sigh. "I do hate snipers. Dirty cheaters, the lot of them. Hiding behind this and that, firing a gun at a stationary object. Where is the challenge?"

Minerva snorted softly as she jammed a finger beneath the ribbons of her bonnet at her chin. "Remind me to introduce you to some acquaintances of mine so you might express those opinions to them."

"At any particular distance, or point-blank range?" he queried, eyeing passersby and plucking Minerva's hand to loop it in his arm.

She stepped closer to him smoothly, her fingers drumming on his arm now. "Either," came her reply. "I have found them to be quite skilled at both."

He smirked in amusement at her words. "You're not the only one who knows such individuals, you know. I've met several myself."

"And you came through without holes in your person? Interesting."

They said nothing further as they neared the small alley beside one of the theaters, moving forward without hesitation and without fanfare. It wasn't unusual for alleys to be used to get from one point to the other, but they did not exactly want to create attention by doing so. As they had avoided any kind of finery in their apparel, no one should mark their particular shortcut.

The Beddingsfords were not on parade today.

Tomorrow, however…

"Here," Minerva hissed, flicking her fingers towards the second door on their right.

Griff looked down at her in surprise. "You sure? Not the first?"

She nodded once. "Trust me."

Trust her? They'd known each other for a handful of days, started off by kissing each other into oblivion in front of Society, and only managed to not kill each other because their superiors intervened and insisted they work together. They were being forced to trust each other.

But did they?

He nudged his head towards the door, looking down the alley protectively as Minerva moved across him, opening it with a near-silent creak. She slipped in, and he followed, surprised by the weight of the door as he pulled it shut.

They were immediately encased in darkness.

"Now what?" he whispered loudly.

"Shut up, I am letting my eyes adjust," Minerva replied in the same tone.

He grinned in the darkness, finding great enjoyment in poking her with the proverbial stick. She didn't blush and didn't flinch, which was entertaining, and she tossed barbs right back at him, which was refreshing. In a way, it was like bantering with his younger sister Adrianna, only far more enjoyable.

Because he was not related to Minerva.

And she was still a mystery.

And he really could not forget kissing her. In fact, he replayed that moment far more often in his mind than he would ever have admitted, even under torture.

He could not be blamed for that. He was a man, after all. And really, it had been a magnificent kiss.

Clearing his throat yet again, he found his loose cravat suddenly seemed terribly constrictive. He hooked a finger on the belt of

Minerva's dress as she started forward.

"What the ever-loving…?" she growled, looking over her shoulder.

At least, he thought she looked over her shoulder.

"I cannot see yet," he whispered, shrugging even though she wouldn't quite make it out. "I'm afraid of being left alone in this place." He indicated she continue on, adding insult to injury by twirling his finger in a gesture that she ought to turn around. "Lead on, please."

He would swear he could see her roll her eyes, and she strode forward, not resisting the slight tug of his finger hanging on to her. She muttered something under her breath that he didn't fully catch, mostly because it was in rapid and rambling Russian, but it was very foul, indeed.

He bit back a laugh. Whoever Minerva really was, she was no fine lady.

Or if she was, she hid her true nature supremely well.

He wasn't sure which version he preferred.

She led him down the dark corridor, startling him by turning left at one point when he fully expected to turn right. But he was keeping close, so his hold on her belt had no effect on her progress, which was a small mercy. If he had done anything to set her off balance, he was certain she would whirl and land a sound jab on his jaw, if not his eye.

He could see almost perfectly now, but he saw no reason to remove his finger from its place. After all, if Minerva was confident in her direction, he would be following anyway. This way, he could almost guarantee she wouldn't abandon him.

Almost.

"We must be nearly to the Thames by now," Griff mused in a half-whisper when they continued to walk.

Minerva only exhaled in exasperation and turned to the nearest door. "Here," she ordered.

"Really?" he asked when she turned to face him. "Or are you just depositing me here and continuing on alone?"

The dim light of the corridor did nothing to minimize the potency of the derision in her look.

She only pointed a finger towards the room, and he released his finger from her belt, holding up his hands in surrender and doing as she indicated.

This room, unlike the corridors, had candles and lanterns aplenty, enough that Griff had to squint as he entered. Once his eyes adjusted, he nearly turned around to flee.

Only Minerva standing directly behind him kept him from doing so.

Rolls of bright fabrics were to one side of the room, next to a mountainous stack of even more fabrics, each of which were interwoven with something metallic that made them glisten in the light. Bolts and bolts of something that looked suspiciously like satin were behind the rest, and the outlines of at least a dozen evening jackets hung on mannequins against the wall. Ribbons, lace, and pristine white linen sat in baskets on a table, as well as bowls of buttons that shone like freshly minted coins.

It was something out of his nightmares, and he hadn't known it could exist in reality.

He blinked, noting that Minerva still was not beside him.

A faint tightening at his back told him that fingers were gripping at the tails of his coat. He glanced over his shoulder, seeing only a bonnet that faced directly between his shoulder blades.

"What are you doing back there?" he asked, his voice only slightly less strangled than he felt.

"Hiding," she bit out in a surprisingly weak tone. "How bad is it?"

He somehow managed a smile. "How do you know it's bad?"

Her fingers tightened their hold on his fabric. "You inhaled like you were drowning. I couldn't move when I heard that, so please, tell me… are we going to die?"

"I am, that is for certain." He looked back around, trying to see the horrors from a lady's perspective.

When he noted the differences, he wanted to gather Minerva into his arms and hold her like a child.

"There are five female mannequins in the front," he told her slowly, trying to force calmness and compassion into his tone. "Each of them is draped in lace, and three of them are practically filigree.

Silk underneath, I think. And if those bolts of fabric are any indication, there will be at least a dozen more gowns to come."

Minerva whimpered and leaned her head against his back.

He tsked sympathetically. "Three more female mannequins behind the table have the start of riding habits. They aren't so bad; they look more like military uniforms."

"I can handle that," Minerva replied in a muffled voice that vibrated against his spine in an almost ticklish way.

"Ooh, that's a lot of gloves," he blurted before he could stop himself, the rows and rows of them on the second table startling him. "Long gloves, short gloves, white gloves, champagne gloves, opera gloves, riding gloves, lace gloves, button gloves…"

Her grip on his jacket began to pull at his shoulders. "Stop saying gloves," she choked out, "I beg you."

Griff bit his lip hard, knowing there would be gloves for him as well, but hardly to the same degree. Yet hilarity was welling within him as much as the fear.

Hilarious terror. What a concept.

Then he saw something that made him hiss. "Do you want to know about what seems to be undergarments?"

"No, I do not," she ground out. "Anything resembling hair accessories?"

Griff scanned the surroundings, then nodded. "Affirmative. Combs, ribbons, flowers, pearls… is that a butterfly? Oh gads, Min, that's a set of jeweled butterflies. I count at least seven, and I think you're meant to wear them all at once."

"And look like a hydrangea bush? I think not." She yanked on his jacket tails, pulling him backwards. "Let's go, we'll find another way."

He was hard on her heels when another figure entered the room, blocking their exit.

She was tall, regal, beautiful, and smiling at them.

A dark, knowing, almost predatory smile.

"Good morning, my lovelies," she all but purred, her barely gray locks pulled back into an elegant mass of curls at the back of her head, her lips painted a deep red, her eyes sparkling with an impish light Griff mistrusted.

"Tilda," Minerva greeted in the smallest voice known to humankind.

The dancing eyes flicked to her, a neat hand with long, slender fingers reaching out to tip her chin up into the light. "Mirrors. I've said it before, but you are a beautifully blank canvas, my dear girl. I can do anything with you. Such a treat."

It was much to Minerva's credit that she did not yank her face away from the piercing eyes of the woman.

But then those eyes were on Griff, and he barely managed a swallow.

"Ah," Tilda exhaled slowly, the sound almost hoarse. "Lovely to see you again, Mist. Very nice. Clean lines and angles, elegant throat, fascinating scruff… You play both scenes, don't you, darling? High and low, you flit among it all."

Griff frowned a little. "Are you a poet?"

Tilda smiled broadly, showing the very first signs of lines at the corners of her lips. "Only in my mind, darling." She eyed the two of them, the smile remaining. "I've been told I must dress the pair of you for the excesses of the world. Are you siblings or married?"

"We are—" Minerva began.

"It's not—" Griff said at the same time.

Tilda laughed and wagged ring-laden fingers in their direction. "Assignment, darlings. Assignment. No need to look embarrassed or scared."

"I am feeling a great deal of both at the present," Minerva muttered as she tugged at her bonnet ribbons.

Griff swallowed hard. "We are assigned to be married. Lord and Lady Beddingsford, at your service, I suppose."

The beaming grin such a response provoked on Tilda's face was unnerving. "I don't often get what I wish for, but here it is in the flesh. I can see I must refresh my memory on the subject of prayer, for this definitely warrants words of gratitude and thanksgiving."

"We have very different understandings of gratitude and thanksgiving," Griff said without reservation.

"And prayer," Minerva added.

Tilda lowered her chin just enough to give them each a more direct look. "You have your callings, and I have mine. And unless you would like to fail in yours, you will indulge me as I do mine."

Had she pulled a knife on them and sprung four bodyguards, she could not have said anything more intimidating.

"Yes, ma'am," they said together, their voices blending in the most morose tone uttered by a person over the age of twelve.

If she found their reactions amusing, she gave no indication. She simply tilted her head back towards the room and folded her arms.

Griff took Minerva by the arms and backed up with her, turning themselves until they practically backed into the wall to allow Tilda to pass, followed by three rather plain-faced, unadorned women of indeterminate ages.

Assistants? Actresses? Operatives in training? It was entirely unclear who they were, or what they were about.

Tildas in training, perhaps.

That was almost more terrifying than the room they were in.

Tilda turned and looked them both over again, blinking twice. "Well, don't just stand there. Take off what you can and come here so we can begin measurements."

Griff didn't release Minerva. "Take off...?" he repeated slowly.

"Oh, you're a pair of children, the both of you," Tilda snapped. "Take off the headwear, cloaks, and coats. Weskit and cravat, too. Any layers that can go without disrupting modesty. Honestly, I'm not about to strip you down to unmentionables or stark naked in front of each other. Stop internally screaming and come here!"

The bark of her voice had the desired effect, and Griff inadvertently pushed Minerva away from him, which earned him the sort of glare that could have been accompanied by daggers.

He only shrugged and began unbuttoning his coat, tossing his hat into a corner. She flung off her bonnet with much the same energy and went to work on her spencer. He turned away with a faint swallow, his ears turning a little warm. It wasn't personal; there was just something about a woman fumbling with buttons at her chest that was inherently awkward.

"Thank God, I can take my cravat off," Griff announced to no one in particular, forcing levity into his tone. "It must be my least favorite article of clothing."

"Then you will not be pleased with what I will be teaching your valet, *cherie*," Tilda replied without any sympathy.

There was no helping the groan that Griff released, and he did his best to ignore Minerva's snickering. After all, he might be strangled, but she would be suffocated and unable to bend over. He might be encased in starch, but she would be wearing yards of fabric and hardly able to move. His hair might require cutting and cleaning, but hers…

Well, Marie-Antoinette would have surely been jealous.

May she rest in peace.

Griff heaved a sigh, free of his outerwear, cravat, and weskit, and turned, walking over to Tilda. "Well?"

Her painted lips quirked, and she gestured for him to stand on a stool nearby. "Up you get. We've several measurements to take." She made a face as he did so. "Did you have to wear trousers, love?"

"Should I not have worn trousers?" he asked with a curious tilt to his head. "It's the middle of the day and we're not in character. It's a perfectly reasonable article of clothing."

"For the anonymous, unimportant fellow without the benefit of a tailor or fashion artist, perhaps," she replied as she lowered herself to his ankles and gathered the fabric in one hand. "For you, darling, not at all." She pulled the gathered fabric tightly until there was nothing left to the imagination of his lower leg, then wrapped it around him and pinned it securely. "You will be in breeches and stockings. No arguments."

Griff squawked in outrage, glaring at the top of her head.

Tilda peered up with a raised brow. "That constitutes an argument. Silence."

He clamped his teeth together, grinding them hard and throwing a look to Minerva.

She was on her own stool now, her slender figure on display as one of the assistants took her measurements. Her gown was not only simple, but it hung rather limply on her. Fashions had begun to widen at the skirts for women, but it was clear Minerva had not taken up such a trend. The critical eye might have declared her ten years out of fashion, if not more, but the insult would have missed its mark.

And besides, the simplicity suited her. Furthermore, it would suit her assignments as Mirrors. Any woman in the world could look so unremarkable and never be noticed by anyone. Why in the world would they have chosen her to so splendidly stand out, then?

He watched as Minerva frowned at the assistant, who was now measuring further down her rather slender waist.

"Why so low?" Minerva asked her. "I am not arguing, for the record, only inquiring."

The clarification made Griff smile.

"Fashions are leaning towards a longer torso," the assistant replied, wrapping the measuring tape about her. "We'll be fashioning you new stays."

"I have stays," Minerva insisted as her nose wrinkled up. "No one will see them, so…"

"Your structure has to be pristine," Tilda overrode without looking. "It must be impeccable, and some of your gowns will be so perfectly fitted that the slightest flaw in your undergarments will be noticeable. Now, would you like to draw this out by questioning us, or would you rather we get the mortification over quickly and send you on your way?"

Minerva bit down on her lip and met Griff's eyes, not quite looking murderous, but certainly unpleased.

He had no comfort to give her, and as Tilda was now pulling the fabric of his thighs as tightly as his calves, he had no amusement to spare for the moment.

They were trapped, and that was that.

Chapter Seven

$\mathcal{L}$ife with Griff in the same house was unpredictable, and that was a rather simple way of saying so.

One morning, he would take breakfast in the morning room, another the dining room, and another in his own rooms. He would ride in Hyde Park, walk in St. James's Park, take the dogs to Regent's Park. And if she understood correctly, he had actually gone for a swim in the Serpentine. Whether he had done these things as himself or as Lord Beddingsford was unclear, and she did not dare ask. After all, they were partners, not spouses, and she would not be his keeper.

He was certainly not hers, for which she was eminently grateful. She did not want to explain her slipping out into the London night to spar with Ears and her husband, or her headlong rides at dawn in Richmond. Riding out to Richmond as a lady was shocking enough, though she did so before any gently bred woman would have risen from bed, but to then race at breakneck paces…

Lady Beddingsford would never have recovered from the scandal of the thing. But such a scandal would never materialize, thanks to Minerva's biggest asset. She had never been more grateful for her nondescript looks in her life than now.

They'd enjoyed a humorous dinner with Lord and Lady Rothchild, both of whom knew precisely who they were in reality and what their work would entail. Lord Rothchild was one of the Shopkeepers with Draper and Milliner, and his wife knew enough to not ask questions, but both of them were also squarely in the upper crust of Society. A private dinner with such esteemed individuals would do wonders for the reputation of the Beddingsfords, but it was also the most relaxed Griff or Minerva would be for the duration of their assignments.

Tonight, they had a ball to attend, and then they would leave for the Kent countryside in the morning. It would be a relief to focus on training with Griff and not have to play a part for a time. Though she was accustomed to acting when on assignment, some roles came more naturally than others.

Being at the height of Society in both fortune and fashion was as unnatural a role as Minerva had ever been forced to play.

She winced now as her maid fastened her stays, though they were her own stays and her usual settings. It was not the fact that she was wearing stays, as she was quite accustomed to that, but the fact that after this last item of her own natural garments was placed upon her, the ridiculous ones would begin. And then there was the fiery pain along her scalp. Her hair was tightly bound with pins and plaits, some of which would be released after her gown had been donned and arranged, as a few of the pins were there to help create curls, apparently. But it did not change the fact that her head ached before she had even left her own rooms.

One could only hope that Anna would not also douse her in ridiculous quantities of perfume. There was only so much torture a head could take in such a short space of time.

"Minerva?" called the too-loud voice of her husband from the corridor.

"Do not come in here!" she bellowed back, clutching at the front of her perfectly modest stays.

She could almost hear his snort of derision. "Wasn't planning on it, thank you. What color are you wearing?"

Minerva looked at the closed door in almost disgusted confusion. "What?"

Now she did hear a sound from him, a heaving sigh. "Tobin wants to know the color so we can match."

"We don't have our costumes from Tilda yet, how can we possibly match?" Minerva snapped. She raised her arms to allow Anna to slip the dress over her head and glanced down at it as her arms slid into the puffed sleeves. "It's peach. And lace. And ribbed at the hems and… good heavens, Anna, are those clusters of ribbons meant to resemble actual peaches?"

She heard Griff laugh behind the door and glared at it again. "Shut up, husband. Have fun with your cravats."

As she hoped, his laughter stopped, and she heard his footsteps fade down the corridor.

"Do you… wish to change gowns, Minerva?" Anna asked hesitantly from behind her.

Minerva shook her head even as she frowned. "No. I suppose I would dislike any gown that makes me feel pushed and prodded and cinched."

"Are the stays too tight?" Anna fumbled at the back of them quickly. "I can adjust them."

"No, they are fine," Minerva assured her. "This is the only article of clothing of my own. Thank heavens we don't have Tilda's creations yet. I would not put it past her to stuff me into some new creation from France or some such place that would render me truly breathless instead of merely uncomfortable."

Anna hummed a soft laugh. "Oh, she would, aye. My days with her were quite entertaining, indeed."

Minerva grinned at her maid through the mirror. "I can only imagine. I thank you for not using her excesses on me for your own amusement."

Anna returned the smile. "You know I won't have a choice when it all comes in. She has eyes everywhere, and she'll know if we don't play by her rules."

"Yes, I suspect she would." Minerva craned her neck from side to side as Anna began to do up the buttons. "I suppose there are worse colors than peach for my complexion."

"With your complexion and features, any color would suit. And this one is very pretty. The bodice, in particular, with the lace patterns…"

Minerva tuned out whatever praise or descriptions Anna was about to wax effusive on, neither appreciating nor caring for such things. The dress was her tool to blend into her surroundings, nothing more. She would be uncomfortable the whole night, and she allowed a small smile that her partner would be suffering alongside her. Not to the same extent as she, naturally, but at least he would not be comfortable.

And if she happened to spread the word that Lord Beddingsford adored dancing and preferred to never take a rest…

Griff, in his character of Lord Beddingsford, would never be anything less than perfectly polite, and while ladies did not ask to dance, an influx of available young women clearly angling for a dance would certainly garner invitations for themselves.

But she mustn't make it impossible for him to do his duty as far as their missions were concerned.

As it happened, they had yet to discuss what they would even do tonight other than socialize and make general ninnies of themselves. Establishing the Beddingsfords was still the most important thing they could do.

Then they could see who, or what, came out of the woodwork.

Anna seemed to take ages to get Minerva fully situated for the evening, and by the time Minerva could look at the entire picture of herself, she had to admit one thing.

She looked ridiculous.

"What, in the name of all that is holy, has happened to my hair?" Minerva demanded, afraid to touch the lace, ribbon, and pearl-strewn monstrosity presently sitting atop her head.

The scratchy pins preparing her curls had been released, but the remnants were not much of an improvement, scratching aside. There were so many curls alongside her face that the width of her head seemed to barely fit within the looking glass. Perfect curls they might have been, but the mass of them was intimidating.

What a monstrosity.

"I've copied it exactly from the most recent issue of Ackermann's," Anna insisted in her Irish brogue as she somehow found another place to jam a pearl-crusted pin. "It is the height of fashion."

"It is the height of the Great Pyramids, Anna!" Minerva swallowed hard, despite the clenching sensation of her throat. "And as wide as an ocean! What have you… Has the entire world lost their minds?"

If Anna had truly been only a maid in the house, she might have cowered or simpered to please her mistress. But as Anna was actually an operative herself, albeit one on a different scale, with separate tasks to assist Minerva, and now Griff, she did not have to take orders or cater to Minerva's whims. Really, she did not even have to listen to her complain if she did not want to.

Her task was to make Minerva's task easier. Which she was doing.

More than Minerva liked.

"Probably," Anna said without any concern. "There, all done. Let me get your gloves." She turned to the small table at the toilette and picked up long, pristine white gloves.

Minerva groaned. "Oh, please, no. Please let me wear the short ones."

Anna tsked softly. "Sorry, not an option. You have short sleeves, so you must have the long gloves."

That was the most ridiculous thing Minerva had heard yet. She plucked at the ridiculous puff to her sleeves, which, admittedly, barely covered the whole of her shoulders. "These? They're voluminous. Needlessly. They use the same amount of fabric that could have covered shoulder to elbow, but instead, it just billows out with more starched stiffness than a cravat Griff could gripe about."

"It's not starched," Anna replied simply. "It's crepe."

"Oh, that makes me feel so much better." Minerva rolled her eyes and huffed as she shoved her hand into her stupidly long gloves. "Crepe. Lovely."

"Structurally, yes, it is," Anna quipped, as if it was a marvelous thing. "So many uses, but everyone always thinks of crepe as a mourning material only."

It was all Minerva could do not to roll her eyes again.

At long last, she was freed from her rooms and started down the corridor, shaking her head and noting that not a single thing on, about, or hanging from her head moved with the motion. There was something deeply uncomfortable about that, but her training would not let her march moodily down the stairs or slump in defeat or do anything except glide and keep her chin elevated and her head steady. Perfect composure and comportment, or nothing at all.

Fully arrayed as she was, she had no other option.

Griff was pacing at the base of the stairs, clearly waiting for her without standing in anticipation, and the fact that he was distracted enough to not have heard her yet gave her opportunity to observe him.

Not for long—he would notice soon enough—but she was a spy, so a moment was all she needed.

He was a stunning specimen of a man, his dark dress coat contrasting brilliantly with his near-white breeches, and his perfectly coordinated peach waistcoat peeking through the top and bottom of the coat. His cravat was radiant and billowing with the same skill and extravagance that Minerva's hair had been arranged, though he had escaped with only two pins rather than several. His scruff had been trimmed, but not shaved, and that made him more appealing, rather than less, even in his resplendent attire. His dark hair was perfectly combed back, possibly also trimmed, and none of his tan had faded with a week in England.

Were he not a married man in the eyes of Society, he would have been a very, very popular man, indeed. As it was, he would still be flocked, but for entirely different reasons.

Was it strange to be grateful he was her husband, given all that?

Pretend husband, naturally.

Not that it had any impact on the pounding of her heart that he was her pretend husband. No, that thundering within her chest that was wrapping itself in fire could only see a handsome man that was living in her house and would be shortly taking her hand.

Swallowing became a slight challenge as she managed the next few stairs, and Griff chose that moment to notice her.

His smile was slow, which somehow made it better, and something in his throat visibly ticked. "Well, well… Lady Beddingsford. Loveliness has never known a more perfect illustration."

Minerva smiled at that, though a burst of nerves lashed at her stomach. Griff was the sort to say all manner of things and had engaged in flippant flattery from the first moment they had met. It was something she had asked him not to do, and he had complied, but it was entirely possible that he was doing so now. Which would mean he did not necessarily feel as he spoke, which would have been easy enough to brush aside had she not wished for a sincere compliment from him at that moment.

Any sincere compliment.

"Truly?" she heard herself ask in a small but dubious voice.

When had she become this insecure woman trussed up in finery? Never before had she needed the approval or assurance of another human being in order to find confidence in herself, and she hated that she needed it now.

But need it she did.

Griff extended a hand to her, his eyes never wavering from her face. "Honestly. Which is a right sight better than truly."

"Is it?" Minerva asked, ignoring the faintest skip in her heart as she placed her hand in his.

His thumb brushed over her knuckles, his smile turning almost fond. "Of course. Honesty is preferred to truth, which is subjective to the teller. Honesty can always be trusted. Honesty is not flattery but observation, and honesty is irrefutable."

Minerva gave the man a wry look as he led her to the door, where their cloaks waited. "You're making that up to make me feel better."

"About honesty?" He shook his head firmly and took his hat while the footman fastened his cloak around his neck. "I am not. My parents drilled the importance of honesty into me and had me recite all sorts of things as punishment. I could write you a soliloquy on the subject."

"Oh, please do not," Minerva begged. She smiled her thanks to the maid, tugging her cloak into a more comfortable position. "You've already a way of filling the air with nonsense. I could not bear to hear any more of whatever it is you call sense."

"I beg your pardon," Griff protested, offering his arm and leading her out into the night towards their coach. "I paid you an honest compliment and defended the virtue, and you're inferring that my sense is in question?"

Minerva grinned at him. "Of course not. I am only inferring that what you think is sense is in question." She quirked her brows and entered the carriage, situating herself on the far side.

Griff glared into the darkened coach, though there was still a playful edge to his smile. "My lady, you are in for a very long night if you continue to plague me."

"Am I?" Minerva queried primly. "But you plague me incessantly, my lord, and surely a small bit of revenge is called for in such a case."

"I didn't say it wasn't. I only thought it fair to warn you." He climbed into the coach and sat opposite her while the footman folded up the stairs, closed the door, and stepped back.

The coach pulled away, and Minerva felt her playful air fade as she considered the night ahead of them. It was not going to be a difficult night, simply an opportunity for the Beddingsfords to continue spreading their particular appeal to all in Society. Those connections were the ones that would hopefully lead to her French connections making themselves known, and Griff could try to make progress on his mission. Whatever contacts he imagined he would need there.

They really had not sat down to plan their missions out together, other than that first day after they became aware of the assignments. Perhaps that was something they could do as part of their training at the Convent. It could only help each other's missions to involve the other, given their previous experiences, and fresh eyes could bring much needed insight.

Glancing across the carriage now, Minerva could only hope that Griff was capable of much needed insight.

He caught her looking and smiled easily, their earlier teasing apparently forgotten by him as well. "Nervous?"

Minerva shook her head, then shrugged as she made a face. "Not particularly. Uncomfortable, certainly, but as we're really only playing parts tonight and not looking for specifics, my nerves are at a minimum."

"You do act exceptionally well," he praised as he turned his attention to his gloves. "In another life, you might have made a very fine actress on the stage. In the most respectable sense, of course."

"I've acted most of my life," Minerva replied carefully, flashes of her past springing to mind, both good and bad. "It is why I am still alive."

Griff paused in his glove adjustment, his eyes returning to her with a serious air. "On missions, or…?"

She only shrugged. "Both. Neither. Survival is not easy for

everyone, but we manage, do we not?"

A furrow appeared in his brow, but he nodded all the same. "I suppose we do. And there is always the state of existence without really living, which is just as much of a tragedy. I've seen that too many times to wish it upon anyone."

"That sounds confining," Minerva murmured.

"It's bloody suffocating, is what it is." Griff sniffed dismissively and tugged at his gloves once more. "How many dances would you like this evening, Lady Beddingsford?"

The shift in discussion did not go unnoticed by Minerva, and she found that interesting. He would ask about her slip into the personal realm, but his own slip would be bypassed and swept under the proverbial rug?

Interesting.

But they hardly knew each other, so she could hardly blame him there. They were partners in this mission, however long it went on, and they would undoubtedly come to know more about each other than they might ever wish to, but there was no need to rush themselves into such familiarity. It would not serve them to force such things.

It would do nothing to build their trust if it was forced.

"Twice," Minerva said on a sigh. "If we need to meet people, I should be available to do so."

"Is that regret I hear in your voice?" Griff inquired, crossing one leg over the other and raising a teasing brow. "I know there are not many men as skilled at dancing as myself, but you mustn't let that prevent you."

Minerva gave him a scolding look, shaking her head. "I suppose you may continue to say things like that tonight, as we have a reputation to uphold. I will do you the courtesy of seeking you out regularly and smiling, or some such."

Griff grinned. "Some such is my very favorite. Please do that as often as you like."

Minerva ignored that. "We have the excuse of leaving for Kent in the morning, so we do not have to stay late, if it suits us to leave."

"Excellent, these things can go on, rather." He glanced out of the window and made a soft grunt of acknowledgement. "Well, they certainly spared no expense on candles. Every room is lit. Who are these people again?"

"I haven't the faintest idea," Minerva admitted without shame. "Milliner secured our invitation for us."

"So it's an entire night of improvisation from start to finish," Griff said, rubbing his hands together. "My favorite."

Minerva cocked her head at the curious man across from her. "What about all of this is not your favorite, Griff?"

His grin was completely and utterly boyish. "The cravats. If we were doing all of this on the Continent, I wouldn't have to wear cravats, and it would be perfect."

"That is not true."

"It is, in the right circles."

"Liar."

"Spy."

There was nothing to do but roll her eyes and look out of the window as the carriage pulled to a stop. "Well, thankfully we'll soon be training in Kent, and you won't need to wear a cravat for a fortnight."

Griff laughed once. "Don't remind me. I'll make the evening a short one in a shocking display of enthusiasm."

Minerva glanced at him as she scooted to the edge of her seat. "Don't involve me in that enthusiasm."

His mouth curved. "It could only be you, my lady."

That made her throat dry, and she was grateful the liveried footman opened the carriage door at that moment, offering her a hand. She took it and got out quickly, adjusting the seemingly voluminous mass of her skirts while she waited for Griff.

"How is my hair?" she asked him absently when he stood beside her. "Besides ridiculous, I mean."

Griff looked it over quickly, nodding once. "Ridiculous, but pretty and intact."

"Thank you." She looked up at the windows and every set of lit candles in every window. "The Beddingsfords have arrived. Care to shout it to the world?"

Griff looped her hand through his arm and walked them both to the door. "Trust me, darling. Once we enter, they will know without either of us saying a word."

Minerva hummed an almost laugh that did not quite reach the definition. "And it will get worse once Tilda's creations arrive. Aren't we the most fortunate?"

His groan was answer enough, and her mouth curved into a smile at the prospect of his misery. Perhaps she would mention his affinity for dance to someone prone to gossip. Just to test her theory.

They were met by the host and hostess, who were effusive in their greetings and barely took a breath throughout, and were eventually released to the ballroom, where dancing was already in progress.

"One pass of the room for good measure?" Griff murmured through a smug smile for the onlookers.

Minerva dipped her chin in what she hoped was an appealing nod. "Oh, why not?"

She heard him chuckle, which made her smile grow, and suddenly the whole thing felt like more of a game than she had previously given it credit for. A promenade in the park might be the thing to do for young ladies, but it could not possibly match a promenade in a ballroom when in cahoots with one's promenading partner.

It was a strangely beautiful thing.

"Lord Beddingsford! Lady Beddingsford!" cried out a feminine voice.

"So it begins," Griff hissed, pausing their walk to turn them in anticipation.

"I know that voice," Minerva replied as she held his arm more tightly. "Ah, Miss Bradford! I was wondering when we'd see you this evening."

Pippa curtsied in greeting, folding her hands elegantly before her as she smiled at them both. "My, you are both looking as glamorous as when I saw you last! You will certainly be the envy of all, and the tailors and modistes will have you to thank for their improvement of business."

Minerva tried to blush, if such a thing could be forced. It was not like Pippa to call out in public, especially on an assignment, so Minerva's mind already spun on possibilities for her reasoning. "You are too kind, Miss Bradford. Truly."

"You are looking rather lovely yourself, madam," Griff complimented with a slight bow. "Blue is perfectly fetching for a complexion such as yours."

Pippa smiled at him with warmth. "Thank you, my lord. You are too kind."

"Rarely true, Miss Bradford," he quipped at once. "I am always just kind enough."

"One of his better qualities, to be sure," Minerva grunted.

Pippa's lips quirked. "Did I hear the two of you will not be attending the house party at the country seat of Viscount Partlowe?"

Considering the woman knew full well they would not attend, Minerva found it hard to contain confusion from her polite smile. "Yes, unfortunately. His lordship and I are bound for some time in the country. In Kent. We would dearly love to visit your school, if we may. His lordship has heard so much about his ancestral home, and it would warm our hearts to see the place where his family had been so happy."

"I shall certainly see that done," Pippa assured her. "But the school is not so far away from DeRaven Park. Surely, the pair of you might make some appearances? A few days here and there while you are in the same county?"

Minerva's eyes widened and she leaned into Griff a little. "Well…"

He put his hand over hers. "Do you think it would be worth the sacrifice, Miss Bradford? I am… new to this. Unused to the people and the way of things. Is it your opinion that we should make the effort while we are enjoying our private time together?"

Pippa nodded very firmly. "It is, sir. I think the opportunity should not be missed. Moreover, I do not think the viscount or his lady would take issue with partial attendance. Do say you will go. It will do you both good."

There was no mistaking the message. They would be attending the house party while completing their training at the Convent. They would be splitting their time playing their parts while learning to work with and trust each other.

"Then it would appear we shall," Minerva managed to say

through newly numbed lips. "I will have my maids adjust the items in my trunks accordingly first thing in the morning."

Pippa nodded again, her smile maintained, her eyes showing understanding. "Excellent."

Griff suddenly steered Minerva towards the dancing. "Do excuse us, Miss Bradford. I cannot resist this song or the chance to dance with my wife." He moved them away, hissing under his breath. "Damn."

"I should have said it first," Minerva whispered. "Among other things."

"Indeed," he grunted. "Three dances tonight, darling. I think we need it."

Chapter Eight

*M*inerva snored.

Not loudly, not excessively, and not constantly, but she did.

There was something oddly adorable about that.

They'd been on the road to Kent for several hours now, and both of them had slept, but Griff had been woken by the unexpected sound of his companion's symphonic breathing. Why such an unremarkable sound should have woken him, he couldn't say. He had spent several excursions dozing while traveling post over the years without such sounds troubling him, some of which had been much louder and much more inebriated, but something about Minerva's snoring broke his own slumber.

He'd watched and listened for a while, unable to believe that his partner, lovely and dangerous as she was, would do something so mundane as snore in any way, shape, or form. But after several minutes wherein Minerva did not wake, stir, or give any indication that she was acting, there was absolutely no doubting it, and now he could only smile.

The stubborn woman who so hated high fashion and was immune to his flattery snored when she slept. How utterly perfect was that?

She was a fascinating creature, this pretend wife of his. She danced as perfectly as any young miss trying to snag a husband, she was cleverer than most of the operatives he had worked with in his career, and she was unencumbered by the airs or status that were so ingrained in people of station, yet mingled among them without difficulty. He had yet to engage in training with her, so her physical abilities as an operative were still to be tested, but as yet, he was impressed with her. Then again, he had never met one of Milliner's agents who was anything less than remarkable, though he'd never worked with them closely.

He was looking forward to spending more time with her without the parade of their characters getting in the way, which meant that the revelation the night before that they would need to also attend the house party was more than a little inconvenient. They'd had no explanation at the ball, but it was hardly the setting for such things. Milliner would be hosting them at the school starting from tomorrow, but tonight, they would be staying with the Duke and Duchess of Kirklin.

At no point had Griff explained to Minerva that the Duke of Kirklin was his brother.

He was rather looking forward to the revelation.

The only question was how much his brother knew about the situation. He had married last year, much to the surprise of everyone who had ever known him, but Griff had been on the Continent on assignment with the Austrian royal court, and there had been a bit of confusion about the identity of the woman who was now his brother's wife.

She had been a teacher at the Miss Masters school, according to their sister Adrianna, which meant that Minerva would know her. But was the Duchess of Kirklin also one of the Agents of the Convent? That was less clear. Not all teachers at the school were, and it was not his way to ask Minerva to disclose the identities of those who were. It was also likely against the principles and limited code among operatives to do so. Besides, he did not know the teachers at the school. He did not pay that much attention to his sister's letters.

Minerva might be walking into this particular situation knowing more than he did, but she would not know everything. For now, that was enough.

And at least he knew that she snored. She might not even know that herself.

What a delicious little secret he had.

Griff smirked as he watched Minerva sleep now, the swaying of the carriage on the roads doing nothing at all to disturb her. She'd curled up into a ball on her seat rather than simply leaning against the wall, and while she had attempted to keep her skirts appropriately draped, she hadn't quite managed, giving him a decent glance at the entirety of her right lower leg, safely encased in white stocking. It was trim and feminine, but also shockingly muscular for a woman, and he'd be lying if he claimed not to be imagining sliding the opaque material down her calf.

He was also well aware that there would be no way that would happen, without her being on the short side of death, that did not end with him getting stabbed, strangled, or shot, if not all three. And even if she were at that point of death, he might still end up dead himself.

No woman was worth that risk.

Unfortunately.

His attention moved to her face, tracing each feature with the quick attentiveness he had honed throughout years of training. He'd spent days with Minerva, danced with her several times, but somehow, he'd never managed a complete picture of her in his mind. Her face changed shape ever so slightly, the dusting of freckles was greater or less, her brow was higher or lower, her lips…

Well, her lips were always the same, and it was better not to look at them for long. He knew what those lips felt like, and the memory was a scalding one.

He swallowed and forced his attention elsewhere. What color were her eyes, anyway? Brown? Green? Some combination? Were they a dark blue? Suddenly, he couldn't recall their shade in the slightest, and his memory was impeccable.

What was this skill she had to become no one in his memory? To change form and figure, shade and coloring, even to someone who was coming to know her. It was as though he knew nothing, when, in fact, the opposite was true. How could he forget such details?

Suddenly, she was a much more dangerous and skilled operative than he'd realized, and a crucial asset.

His focus on her intensified, though no specific feature captured his attention.

Who was Minerva Dalton, really? How had she come into the ranks of operatives? What was she doing teaching at the school when she could have done anything? What was her story? There was something more to her than the scant basics she had shared, that much was clear, but he also sensed that she would not share such personal details readily. Perhaps not even under torture or death.

There were walls and layers to the woman, of that he had no doubt. But just how many? And how impenetrable were they?

And how badly did he want to break them down?

The carriage hit a divot in the road, jolting Griff's attention away from the fascination that was his wife and breaking his concentration entirely.

Unfortunately, it also broke the adorable melody of Minerva's snoring, and she was soon righting herself upon her seat and rubbing her eyes.

Somehow, that was even more adorable.

What the devil was wrong with him?

"How much further?" she asked sleepily, blinking hard. She inhaled a soft sniff, looking out of the window, her brow furrowing in concentration. "Oh, nearly there, then."

Griff laughed very softly. "You know the roads to Kirkleigh?"

She nodded. "I've been there once. The duchess and I were both teachers at the school, and she invited some of us to the house after her marriage to the duke." She swallowed and looked at him, her posture and expression growing less fatigued. "Have you been to Kirkleigh?"

A better man would have explained to Minerva at that moment just who he was and how many times he had been to Kirkleigh, but there were still marks on her face from her sleep, and he was too bemused by them to be fully honest.

"Once or twice over the years, I believe," he replied with a faint shrug.

Minerva was too clever. She raised a brow. "You believe?"

Griff held up his hands helplessly. "I've been everywhere in Europe and England for missions in fine courts and houses. Despite my best efforts, they all blur together, and I cannot be counted on to remember this duke or that earl, sometimes even that prince. It is all devoted to what is necessary for my mission at the time and nothing more."

To his surprise, Minerva nodded at that. "That I can understand. I have not a perfect memory, unlike some of our colleagues, though it might be skilled enough on any particular mission. I have not moved in such exalted circles as you, perhaps, but…"

"No, you were in rather sunken ones, were you not?" He grinned at the mental images that brought up. "What were you? A thief? Washer woman? Seamstress? Oh, please tell me you were a fishwife."

Minerva's lips quirked in a peculiar almost smile, her eyes taking on a new light that intrigued him. "I've been nearly everything at least once. Whatever you can imagine in the slums of London, I'd wager I have been close to it."

Griff tossed his head back on a hearty laugh but found the laughter fading more quickly than he'd anticipated as he thought up some of London's seedier aspects. Surely, she was not suggesting she had been attached to a brothel in some way. Those were rampant in London if one knew where to look, and he could not think that Milliner would send her agents into such an establishment willingly. They certainly had the resources to pay existing ladies of such places to act in their interests, and he could not imagine a single scenario where an operative herself would need to infiltrate such.

But Minerva, for one, had her own mind, and he would not put it past her to act in a dramatic fashion if it would see her mission accomplished more effectively. Not all aspects of missions were dictated by their superiors, after all.

Good heavens, had Minerva really taken such risks with herself?

He stared at her, helpless against the concern and agitation such an idea roused, though she was not presently watching him and would not see. He could not bring the topic up to her. Not now, not just before their arrival at Kirkleigh.

But if she ever hinted at such a thing again, he would have no choice but to inquire.

For his own peace of mind, at least.

There would be nothing he could do about it, should she answer in the affirmative. Nothing he would do about it. Nothing could change, and their situation would be exactly as it was before. It would serve nothing for him to know.

Except that he would know.

And somehow that made him feel better.

Or would, anyway.

The carriage hit another rut as they turned onto the drive for Kirkleigh, and Griff heard Minerva scoff softly. "You would think," she said with a wry smile, "that the duke would ensure his roads are better cared for."

"What, a duke should never encounter ruts in the road?" Griff asked, folding his arms. "I shall be sure to inform His Grace of the fact."

"You will not," Minerva protested on a laugh. "You would not be that impudent with our host."

"I might." He shrugged, making a nonchalant face. "You never know."

Her expression took on a rather warning look. "Griff…"

He rolled his eyes. "I will be perfectly well behaved. The most inoffensive version of myself."

"If only I knew what that meant," his partner muttered. "Most inoffensive does not necessarily mean entirely inoffensive."

"I'm not about to get us thrown out of Kirkleigh," he insisted, feeling oddly stung. "It is not impossible for me to actually behave."

Minerva seemed to consider that. "No, I grant you that, given you've had several successful missions. It is not impossible at all. Only unlikely." She gave him a politely sweet smile and batted her lashes.

Oh, it was going to be sweet justice, indeed, when it was revealed that he was related to the duke, and that this was one of their ancestral homes. But he was not going to tell her so yet.

Just a few minutes more.

Minerva scooted to the very edge of her seat as she took in the approaching house. "My goodness, it's even grander than I remember. Her Grace must have had the ivy trimmed, as I do not believe His Grace cared. It is such a striking place, especially given the coastline. Do you recollect it now?"

Griffin made a show of moving to her side of the coach to get a better look at the place. Truth be told, he hadn't been to Kirkleigh in several years, as it had not been one of his brother's favorite estates until his marriage. He hadn't even been sure he would recollect much of it when they arrived, but as it happened, he remembered it perfectly. The gables, the tall windows, the shade of stone in this light, the trajectory of the vines of ivy creeping up… it was an almost nostalgic experience to see it again, flashes of childhood now appearing in his mind as though called upon willingly.

It made him smile almost without meaning to.

"Yes," he murmured, the game of teasing her all but done. "Yes, I think I do."

His voice must have given something away, for Minerva gave him a suspicious look. "Suddenly? Just like that?"

Griff's smile turned impish, if he did say so himself. "Well… I may be closely acquainted with the Duke of Kirklin."

Her eyes widened. "You may be? Just how closely acquainted are we possibly talking about?"

The iciness of her tone was perfection, and he would have grinned had he not recalled that she could kill him quite professionally. As it was, his smile became a shadow of a grimace. "I could be related to him."

Minerva frowned, her eyes growing hooded. "How related?"

Griff made a face and moved to the relative safety of his side of the carriage. "My name is Griffin Robert Stanwick Russell. Lord Griffin, technically. I am the duke's brother."

The silence was as deafening as it was frigid.

There was nothing to do but wait for his partner to fully react, and for his fate to be revealed.

"Well," Minerva began primly, "that should make the introductions rather simple when we arrive."

Griff blinked. "Indeed…" He watched her cautiously, waiting for the rest of her tirade to commence.

But she said nothing else and resumed looking out of the window as they pulled up to the house.

He raised a surprised brow. "That's it? That's all the reply you're going to make?"

Minerva returned his look with surprise of her own. "Would you like more?"

"I expected more," he told her bluntly. "That is not the sort of secret people usually enjoy discovering."

"Why should you have told me about your identity before this?"

Minerva asked with a slight tilt to her head. "It would have served nothing, and our identities are generally the most protected aspects of ourselves. Your proximity to the duke changes nothing."

Well, well, this was a pleasant surprise, indeed. No railing against him, no offended airs, no fury at his keeping something from her that she might have wished to know.

It did take some of the fun out of things, but as he was not feeling the sting of a slap across the face, he would take it.

A pair of footmen sprang forth from the house and presented themselves to the coach, one opening the door and standing at attention.

Minerva proceeded out of the carriage without assistance, brushing at her travel attire while Griff stepped out as well. They shared a look and each nodded before starting forward, Griff offering her his arm more for the sake of the servants than to put on any kind of show for his brother.

Servants did talk an excessive amount.

Minerva cleared her throat as they approached. "You did tell them we were coming, didn't you?"

Griff nodded, biting his cheek to keep from laughing. "A note was sent, yes."

"And what did the note say?" she pressed in a tight voice.

"That Lord and Lady Beddingsford were coming. They know what that means."

Minerva's hold on his arm tightened perceptibly. "And do they know that you are Lord Beddingsford?"

Griff allowed himself to smile down at her. Just then, the door to Kirkleigh opened and Stafford gaped openly. "Good heavens. Master Griffin? What in the world are you doing here?"

Minerva's sigh was heavy with irritated resignation. "You idiot…"

Griff, on the other hand, was delighted by the utter bewilderment on the stately butler's expression. "Stafford, my good man! My, you are looking well. The coastal air does you good."

"Th-thank you, sir," Stafford managed, still blinking as though Griff were a hallucination. "Is… is His Grace expecting you?"

"Yes and no," Griff quipped easily, which earned him a sharp jab in the side from his pretend wife. "Keep my secret a trifle longer. Just announce us as Lord and Lady Beddingsford, for as such we are."

Stafford blinked again, then looked at Minerva for a moment before returning his attention to Griff. "You've married, sir?"

"Not as such, and yet…" He shrugged, loving the evasiveness of this game. "Come on, man, let us in and do your duty. Hawk will never believe it."

"Of that we are both certain, sir." Stafford looked at Minerva again, clearly understanding her expression well. "I expect I am to sympathize with you, my lady."

Minerva nodded once. "Yes, I expect you are, thank you."

He stepped back and let them into the house, quickly instructing the footmen and the coachman before closing the door and turning to face them.

Poor Stafford. He really did not deserve the frazzled expression Griff had put upon his features, but there really wasn't anything for it. The situation was so delightfully perverse, crossing his worlds without the embarrassment or dramatics he would have expected on the occasion of the revelation of his true career to his brother.

Of course, he had yet to technically do that…

Technically.

"Is His Grace about?" Minerva asked Stafford as she stripped her gloves from her fingers. "Or Her Grace, perhaps?"

Stafford nodded. "Both are, my lady."

"You don't have to call me…" Minerva paused, trailing off and looking confused. "Actually, I suppose I must be Lady Beddingsford here as well, mustn't I? Otherwise, it will get far more confusing."

"Undoubtedly," Griff offered with a grin, knowing it would not be helpful to do so.

The butler gave Minerva a pleading look. "Please don't confuse me further, my lady. I have quite enough to be getting on with now that Master Griffin is in the house."

"I beg your pardon," Griff protested.

Stafford ignored him and kept his attention on Minerva.

She nodded with all the sageness a woman in her assumed position might hope to have. "I quite understand. Truly."

Griff looked between the two of them in disgruntlement, though most of it was pretended. "I am right here, you know."

The looks he received in return assured him more than any words might have that they were well aware of his presence and proximity.

Respect was distinctly lacking in this great hall. One could only hope it was not also lacking in Kirkleigh as a whole.

"Stafford? Did I hear our guests arrive?" a feminine voice called from somewhere nearby.

Griff had only met his sister-in-law once, but it was clear hers was the voice that spoke, as it was certainly not that of his sister Adrianna.

Small mercies.

He had no idea how he would explain any of this to his sister.

Clara, Duchess of Kirklin, appeared from somewhere deeper in the house and paused a step when she saw them. "Minerva?" She tilted her head, her brow furrowing. "Griffin? What in the world are you two doing here? And together, at that."

Stafford heaved a sigh. "Your Grace, may I present Lord and Lady Beddingsford? I shall see to having the Cedar Room prepared for his lordship. Would you… recommend any particular room for her ladyship?"

Well, that was a delicate way of putting it.

"The Willow Room will suffice," Clara murmured, her eyes flicking between both of them with the same calculating expression he had noticed upon his first meeting of her. It would not surprise him in the least if she had been an operative for Milliner, and, if she was, he wanted to know every detail of any assignments she'd had.

And putting Minerva in the Willow Room… She could have had the Aspen Suite or the Birch Room, the Oak or the Ash, Beech, Yew, or Elm… But the Willow Room had been a favorite of their mother's when they would visit their uncle, the duke. The Willow Room was delicate and bright and feminine, refined without being ornate, and its murals of the willow itself reminded the inhabitant of its flexibility and intricacy.

Griffin could have described the entire room in exact detail and walked it blindfolded for the number of times he had gone to jump on his mother's bed or take in the view from her windows.

And that was where Minerva would be resting her head while they were here?

He'd better not dwell on that too much.

"Hawk!" Clara suddenly bellowed in a surprisingly booming voice that was entirely unfit for any duchess in the world. "You'd better get down here! Now!"

Chapter Nine

Flat on one's back was a terrible and discouraging situation to be in.

Particularly when the person who had put you there was laughing in victory.

The fact that it had been the fourth time in this fighting session that Griffin had landed Minerva in such a position was utterly maddening.

Even if he was a powerful and quick man.

She had taken down larger men before, but she had yet to render him even remotely injured.

Minerva ground her teeth and closed her eyes as she lay on the mat, her hands forming fists at her sides.

"Doth the lady require a respite?" Griff chuckled from his corner of the mat, sounding only mildly out of breath.

Drawing in a slow breath, Minerva uttered the foulest Russian curse she knew, taking no pleasure in hearing the choked sound of surprise her partner and foe made.

Heavy footfalls shook the mat beneath Minerva, and she felt more than saw the figure looming over her.

"Had enough, Mirrors?" the gruff voice of Fists asked without much concern.

Minerva shook her head firmly without raising her head. "No. I am mentally berating myself and will only be a moment."

"Do you want to know why you failed?"

"Not yet, but I trust you will tell me shortly."

The gravelly grunt told her she was correct and, reluctantly,

Minerva rolled to her side and sat up. She adjusted the sash about her tunic, cinching it with jerky motions as she muttered wordlessly under her breath. It was maddening to continually lose to a man whose motions you were actively studying, to feel as though you had learned nothing despite your best efforts, which were usually more than enough. Even in the simple setting of training, nearly identically garbed in trousers and tunics, barefoot, without weapons, he was beating her.

Literally.

She exhaled slowly and closed her eyes, replaying the most recent disaster of their training session back through her mind to find her error. He had feinted left after a series of jabs and spins she had blocked, and she had recognized the feint, as he was fond of using it, but somehow in anticipating it, he had thrown her off balance and left her open for a knee swipe that not only sent her to her back but had wrenched her leg behind her in the tumble.

She opened her eyes with a heavy sigh, shaking her head, and looked up at Fists glumly. "I overcorrected."

Fists pretended to consider that. "Well, yes, but that was not the problem."

"It wasn't?"

He shook his dark, graying head, folding his arms. "You over-anticipated. You were growing confident as you blocked, and in your confidence, you thought you could continue to do so. And your greatest issue?"

"Let me know when you'd like me to chime in here, Fists," Griff broke in, grinning crookedly.

Thankfully, Fists ignored him. "You aren't fighting. You are defending. Reacting to what he is doing rather than engaging. Of course he is beating you—you aren't doing anything, Mirrors."

Griff was snickering in the background, and Minerva wished with all her might she could send beams of fire directly into the pit of his stomach and let his internal chaos commence.

"So should we reverse the situation, then?" she asked Fists, cocking her head. "Have him react to me so I change my tendencies?"

Fists shrugged at that. "We could for a round or two, if it will help you find your footing. Or we can train with mannequins for a time.”

“Oh, let’s keep with the live targets however we can,” Griff insisted, once again interjecting himself into a conversation in which he need not participate. “One does so rarely encounter an immovable foe in the real world.”

Minerva pressed her tongue to the front of her teeth, her brow snapping down as she continued to stare at Fists alone. The man had encountered his share of arrogant operatives before and knew full well how to upend them, and if the quirk of his tight mouth was anything to go by, he was about to give her a trick to do just that.

The anticipation of such a beautiful moment was enough to get Minerva up from the mat without any hesitation or reluctance.

“Right, then,” she chirped, turning to face her partner, who came to the mat as well. “Ready to be reactive?”

“I am always reactive,” Griff insisted. “It is my best quality.”

“That is not saying very much.” Minerva wiped at her palms and flexed her fingers by her sides in anticipation.

Fists stepped closer to her, his mouth near her ear. “He lacks your speed and agility. Disorient him. Then drive into the solar plexus; he has been protecting that. Once you do, a simple toss will land him.”

Minerva managed not to smile, knowing Griff would see it. “You observe the most incredible things, Fists.”

“So could you, if you knew what to watch for.” He patted her shoulder and stepped back, whistling once to indicate they start.

Griff circled slowly and Minerva did the same, trying to notice more about him and the way he moved, not to anticipate his actions, but to prepare hers.

It was an interesting experiment in her approach to fighting. In her previous experiences with physical altercations, she had usually had the element of surprise, or their weaknesses had been obvious to anyone with clear vision. It had been years since she had been matched with someone even moderately capable physically, let alone fully trained as she was.

Griff moved like a cat, despite his size. Lithe and fluid, even the slightest motion intentional and powerful. But there was also a pattern to his movements, and the more she watched, the more evident it became. Had she failed to notice this when he had been the attacker? Or had his motions truly changed enough that she would not have seen any such pattern then?

Seeing the pattern now, however, made her smile just a little.

She noticed the widening of his eyes, though his smirk did not move a jot, and she knew her long pause before beginning her attack was throwing him a little, if not irking him. But he was not making a joke about it, which was oddly flattering. Did he trust that she would have some skill, some tactic that he would need to watch for, despite her outright failures in their training thus far?

She was a skilled fighter. She was. She only needed the opportunity to prove it.

With a readying sway from left to right, Minerva suddenly lunged and whirled, kicking at Griff's left hand while slashing her right hand at his newly exposed neck. He countered by ducking away from a subsequent blow and grabbing her left hand, twisting her arm behind her back. Minerva kicked backwards into his knee, launching her right elbow back as well and landing a blow in the center of his gut. He grunted at the quick succession and loosened his hold on her arm, making it easy to wrench away and repeatedly drive hits into any vulnerable position she could find, practically dancing out of his way when he would attempt to counter.

Fists was right—using her natural speed and agility, she was rather at an advantage. Griff was quick in his own way, far better than an average assailant, but now that she had seen his methods and his tendencies, she could adapt and improve her own style. He would have more power than she would, but power was not everything.

This time.

Her overthinking had proved a momentary distraction as Griff landed a blow into her ribs, sending her off balance, but she recovered with a quick roll that allowed her a solid kick into the side of his right leg, leading it to buckle nicely. Springing back to her feet, she circled him and struck sharply at his exposed lower back. He swung for her, but she ducked and jabbed up at his nose, a resounding crack emanating from it with his accompanying grunt of pain. Using the opening, she whirled and punched with all her might at his solar plexus, just as Fists had suggested.

Griff wheezed and hunched, blood beginning to trickle from his nose as he angrily started towards her.

Heart pounding at the opening, Minerva turned again and grabbed his arm, whirling hard and bending low to send him over her back, using his own momentum and instability to drive him hard into the ground.

Flat on his back.

There was silence for a moment, Minerva staring down at her breathless and bleeding partner, her own chest heaving with exertion, pride and energy pounding through her veins. She couldn't even look at Fists for his reaction, waiting first to see what Griff would do.

To her utter surprise, he began to laugh. Deeply and with a telling catch to his breath that made her outright grin.

"Bravo, Min," Griff coughed through a laugh, spreading his arms out wide on the mat in a sign of utter submission. "I am beaten."

"For now," she protested with her own laugh. "And that was your trick at the end."

"I know," he praised. "You did a damn fine job of executing it."

She faux curtsied in her fighting ensemble. "Thank you."

Slow clapping came from another corner of the mat, and Minerva glanced over to see Fists applauding her, though his expression showed little pride or satisfaction. "Good. Much better. Do it again."

"Give a man a breath, Fists," Griff groaned, still laughing. "The woman has dreadfully pointed elbows." He fussed at the neck of his tunic and dropped his head back to the mat with a groan. "Hell and damnation, I haven't been thrown in ages. I'm out of practice."

Minerva started to smile at the admission, then she caught sight of something around his neck through his now-loosened tunic opening.

A thin strap of leather, worn and dark, hanging down to nearly the top of his breastbone even in his supine position. A necklace of sorts, which she had never noticed before. Why would she? Every other time she had seen him, he'd had a suffocating cravat on, hadn't he? But he was not a sentimental man, by everything she had noticed, so what he could he possibly wear around his neck?

He shifted on the mat, rolling to his side, and the necklace fully fell from the tunic, hanging from his neck like a talisman and swinging loosely in its freedom.

Minerva followed the leather strap down, her heart oddly skittering in a manner she dared not interpret when she caught sight of the charm sitting at the end of it.

A faded gold button swung almost tremulously from the leather, dark in spots and almost misshapen with age. Even from her vantage point, she could tell that the carvings on the surface were nearly smooth at this point.

But she knew that button. She knew every detail, every scratch, every faint etching, and she knew the tiny initials that had been laboriously scratched into the underside. She knew that leather strap it hung upon, and she knew where it had come from.

She had cut that strap herself. Had threaded the button upon it. Had worn the charm herself as a talisman against danger and loneliness. Had clung to it during hundreds of dark nights while crying for her losses.

It was her button, her leather, her talisman.

She had not seen it in almost fourteen years.

Not since the night she had happened upon a scene on the London docks where a young man had been shot by whatever contact he'd come to meet and had been left for dead.

She had been a street urchin then, one of dozens running around various parts of London with the sort of willful independence that only luck could provide. She had been running errands and procuring information for the man they called Gent at that time, a newcomer to London who took an interest in the children wandering the streets. Her friend and sometimes fellow errand girl Jack had been with her, and once the danger of getting shot themselves had passed, the two of them had worked quickly to move the young man from the docks to a safer location.

Minerva had gone by Hatch in those days, a token of her birth name, Minnie Hatcher, and no one had known anything of her story. She had preferred it that way, not wanting to claim sympathy or pity from anyone, and she had done her best to prove her toughness and resourcefulness on the streets. But no girl of thirteen wanted to be taken advantage of, so she and Jack had taken to dressing as the lads did, which proved useful in many respects.

She and Jack had decided that Jack should go for help while Minerva would tend the man and do her best to keep him alive. So, bearing the now nearly unconscious and incoherent man on her young back, Minerva had carried him to one of the nearby warehouses, picked the lock, and hauled the man onto a low pile of crates. His chest and arm were bleeding profusely from the shots, and though the chest wound was likely what rendered him unconscious, the shot to the arm was deep and streaming blood in a more concerning way.

Even now, all these years later, she could remember how her mind had raced, and she had stripped off her shirt to staunch the bleeding to his chest. Her chest binding and too-large stays gave her a modicum of modesty, not that anyone else would see her, and she had found a loose brick to lay upon the padded chest wound in an attempt to keep pressure there while she focused on the arm.

This man, whoever he was, did not deserve to lose his arm, and she had done enough observing of Suds, the unofficial doctor of the streets, to have a general knowledge of what to do. She had taken off her necklace, the only emblem of her father, and tied the leather strap tightly above the arm wound as a tourniquet. Then she had gone to work, pulling the needle and thread from her small kit of tools and beginning to stitch the now slowly bleeding flesh. Her patient, not so insensible as to be unaware of new pains, winced and groaned against her attentions, but thankfully, was too weak to move against it.

Pounding footsteps echoed outside, and between the groans of her patient and her own pounding heart, she had been positive they would be discovered and both killed. She had covered the man's mouth with her hand and whispered a frantic plea into his ear, not knowing if he would even hear her. But he had quieted, and the sounds faded into the distance. She had just finished stitching his arm when the door to the warehouse burst open, and she had whirled, drawing a dagger from her boot to defend her now deathly still patient.

But Gent had been the man she had seen, with two other men as well as Jack standing behind him, and he had sworn when he'd caught sight of the patient.

"Nice work, Hatch," Gent had praised with a pat on her head as they'd moved to the man and carefully lifted him up, carrying him out of the building and into a wagon.

The others had driven him away, but Gent had given Minerva a thoughtful look. "Come see me this week in White Lyon, any day around eleven. We need to talk."

She had agreed, and later on that week found herself invited into the ranks of operatives in London. Being a child, she hadn't been thrown into work straight off, but she had been adopted into the Rothchild Academy and found herself taken out of the streets for good. Educated beyond her wildest dreams, along with other girls from poor situations, and secretly trained in the skills of operatives at the same time, which only a few of the other girls were doing.

Jack had not been invited to come, and Minerva had not seen her since. Nor had she ever learned the fate of the man she had worked so hard to save.

Until now.

Minerva swallowed hard, her eyes moving quickly to Griff's still-grinning face. It had been thirteen years, but she could see it. She had spent enough time that night looking into the man's face as she worked, preparing to take whatever extraordinary measures might be required to save him. But time had also done enough to make her doubt, just a little. No one else had a reason to have her father's button, but if it had proven lucky for the man she had saved, it was entirely possible it could have been passed on when he had no need of it. Or if he had died on some future mission, perhaps a partner would have taken it up.

But in her heart, she knew.

Griff was that man.

The only other proof she would need to make her wholly convinced was to see the scar on his arm. Likely an ugly scar, due to her hurried, inexperienced, and poor stitching.

She was not about to ask him to lift his sleeve so she might examine his arm, and she was also not about to reveal her secret to him. Not with so much at stake for their missions and the depths to which her identity had been altered for her future.

But heaven help her, she was unsettled. Shaken to her core.

Unable to fight him anymore.

Today at least.

She hastily cleared her throat. "I'd like to savor my victory a little longer," she announced as she turned from the mat, hoping she would sound more cavalier than she felt. "Let's throw knives."

Without waiting for anyone else, she moved to the lanes designated for archery or the throwing of sharp implements, and picked up a pair of small, newly sharpened daggers. She ran her thumb along the blade of one, feeling the new tension in her throat and neck with the revelation of her connection to Griff. The feeling of cold, sharp steel against her skin reminded her of those hungry, feral days on the streets of London.

Her father had died, her mother had been dead for years, and there was no relation to take her in. Rather than submit to an orphanage or poor house, she had taken herself into the streets and learned how to survive on her own. She had made friends with the unfriendly and unsavory, had seen goodness in the darkest places, had found prosperity in scarcity, all without thinking of the future before her or any possibilities for her life.

And look what she had become through that.

Look what improvement fate had handed her, and what she had done with the opportunity.

She did not want to remember those years with such clarity, rarely allowed herself to think back at all, and being forced back into that place and those feelings…

Taking both daggers by the hilt, she hurled one after the other towards the stuffed mannequin at the end of the lane, releasing a sharp cry that surprised even her. Pain such as she had rarely known surged into a fire within her chest, and her eyes burned at it.

She inhaled a shaky breath through her nose, blinking to clear her vision as she tried to examine her work.

A low whistle behind her told her more than her eyes managed to.

"Damn," Griff murmured as he came to her side. "Dead on. That's oddly terrifying. Were you imagining me?"

Minerva swallowed, keeping her eyes on the daggers that were almost perfectly side by side over the heart of the figure. "No," she replied in a low voice, straining for calm while painfully aware of the man beside her. "No, I was not. Your turn."

Chapter Ten

The house party had an exceptionally ridiculous number of guests, most of whom were idiots, Griff was certain, and now he was among them.

The guests, rather, not the idiots.

Although he rather felt like an idiot at this point.

The items of clothing they had been forced into obtaining from Tilda had arrived, and tonight, he was wearing chartreuse.

Chartreuse.

Had a more disagreeable color ever been created in fabric?

The only consolation was that Minerva matched him, though the color looked far more attractive on her. Which, he supposed, was the point.

He wasn't certain what to expect from his partner this evening. Ever since their training session the day before, she had grown oddly reserved. Not quite distracted, but certainly not the fiery woman he had begun to grow accustomed to sparring with. If something was bothering her, she was not sharing what it was, and he could not blame her. They were not exactly close, despite their partnership, and a day or two of fight training would not change that. Which was why they had wanted two weeks of full training before they engaged in further missions, but there was no arguing with their superiors.

What exactly their assignment for the house party was, he could not say with certainty. They would be here for three days, then back to the Convent for further training, before returning for another batch of days. He had received some insight from Draper as to some potential contacts, but if any of them had distinct ties to the missing clerk from the London League, Griff was not aware of them. And Minerva had been tight-lipped about her own plans for contacts relating to the Faction members in England, so he had no insight into her thoughts.

They had only been blatantly directed to come, and they would have to go on instinct here.

If he knew what Minerva's instincts were, he might feel more comfortable about the whole thing.

As it was…

"And it was at precisely that moment that the nephew of my hostess appeared, bearing the full regalia of a member of the King's Guard, the red clashing dreadfully with his ginger hair and freckles, and his utter gangly appearance was preposterous in the uniform."

"Is that so?" Griff mused thoughtlessly, only half listening to the equally overdressed man currently engaging him in pointless conversation. Honestly, would it have been such a great sacrifice to dance with his wife all night instead of endure this?

"What was the chap's name? Drat, it will come to me in a minute." The man heaved an apologetic sigh Griff did not care about. "He's a cousin of our host, as it happens. Was headed to work for the Foreign Office when his commission was up. I certainly hope they made better use of him than the army, if his bearing was any indication. Martin, I believe. The surname, I mean. Couldn't tell you his given name, but it was dreadfully boring."

Griff's ears began to burn, and he quickly looked at his droning companion with new interest. "Indeed? A cousin to the viscount?"

If the man noticed the sudden interest of his companion, he gave no indication. "Indeed, sir. A first cousin. Close in childhood, if the stories are correct. And the viscount, being the head of the family, is very invested in the details of his relations. Devoted family man, he is. Why else would he and his wife be so very committed to raising their brood and expanding it so? Five daughters in seven years of marriage—it is unthinkable."

Griff began to tune out once more, not finding any need to discuss the proclivity of the viscount and his wife to produce children. If the ginger-haired, lanky cousin of the viscount was who Griff thought he could be, the invitation to the house party could be far more beneficial than he'd previously thought. Was it possible that Martin would keep in touch with the head of his family, despite his mysterious life? Would the viscount have more information than the government with regards to his whereabouts?

If foul play was afoot, would a ransom have been requested of the viscount for his cousin?

Griff needed to get into Partlowe's study, and he needed to do it sooner rather than later. He needed to spend ages of time in there, and he needed to do so now.

They'd been at DeRaven for a full day now, and the only thing Griff had managed to collect up to this point was a bevy of annoyances now claiming acquaintance, though Partlowe himself was a good enough chap. A trifle preoccupied with his own wife for Griff's taste, but satisfaction in marriage mustn't be criticized, given it was such a rarity in Society. If Minerva had found success in her day of social engagement, she had not shared the information with him. Separate bedrooms were an even greater annoyance than he'd previously thought, though the politeness of the thing must be forgiven.

Unfortunately.

Next time—if there was a next time—Griff would scandalize the world by insisting he and his wife share a bedroom. Nothing less would be tolerated.

Though what they would actually manage in arrangements for sleeping was another matter altogether.

He scanned the room, looking for his wife now, and cursed the varying shades of yellow and green that floated about the place. Was it really so popular a fashion these days? And how could the annoying shade he and Minerva had donned blend in so perfectly with the rest of the array?

Would it be too much to shout for Lady Beddingsford among the horde? Or would that push his cover too far and irk his wife into a display of rage unworthy of them both?

"There you are, darling! I have been looking everywhere for you."

Relief had never tasted so sweet.

Griff fixed his most charming grin upon his lips and turned to his left to see the resplendent, if chartreuse, figure of his wife approaching. Her voluminous skirts swished and crinkled as she neared him, and the towering mass of her coiled plaits was somehow still perfectly in place atop her head.

Majestic creature. Chartreuse, but majestic.

He really did need to find something else to fixate on.

"My beloved," he purred, taking her hand and kissing it in a not-quite-perfunctory way. "The pleasure of seeing you surpasses all else this evening has afforded."

He could almost see her gagging behind the adoring façade. "A dance, my lord? Or would dancing with your wife prove too much ecstasy for one evening?"

Griff choked on a stifled laugh. "I must bear it if I can." He pressed the hand he held, and she moved it in the direction of the dance, letting him lead her to the floor.

"If you kiss my slippers tonight, I will drive my knee into your face," Minerva hissed between beautifully smiling teeth.

"I actually despise feet," Griff assured her with a faint squeeze to her hand. "Disgusting things. Even yours, no offense."

"None taken; I am quite relieved." She kicked her skirts slightly as they took up position. "Though I am not certain I possess feet any longer beneath these mountains of fabric. It is as though I have been carefully placed through the top of a bird cage and must move with it."

Griff raised a brow as he moved into place beside her. "That is your concern with our apparel? The breadth of it? Have you been looking at us? The shade is something out of a handkerchief when one has a particularly putrid cold!"

Minerva snorted not quite delicately, which was no surprise.

"Yes, that," he reiterated. "Scads of it. That is what we are."

"Shut up," she managed, the edge of laughter eminent. "We'll never have to wear them again, all right?"

"Thank heavens for the stupid offenses of fashion," Griff allowed with a nod of satisfaction, if not consolation. "One must never wear the same thing twice."

The dance commenced then, so their private conversation was cut off by the motions, though Griff did a fair enough job of praising his wife's grace and beauty for the company's ears. And Minerva accepted such flattery with becoming blushes and fond smiles, which likely meant he would not get pummeled later.

They came together for a long stretch of turning with each other, and Griff leaned close, smiling. "I need to get into Partlowe's study. Soon."

Minerva nodded once, artistically arching into him while pretending to look away. "And I need to find the room for Mr. Galveston. He looks familiar, and his voice sounds practiced."

The fact that Minerva also had action to take was a relief to him, and he felt nearly as much pride in her efforts as he did in his own analysis of snippets of droning conversation. Perhaps the evening would prove useful after all.

But there was one problem, as he saw it.

Chartreuse. Shimmering, elaborate, extensive chartreuse.

He frowned down at his ensemble as they moved away from each other, knowing there would be no time to actually retire to their rooms and change. He could make do with his breeches and linen shirt, as there was nothing remarkable about fawn and lawn on a person.

Minerva, however…

He ran through the layout of the house in his mind, moving in patterns of the dance without thought or emotion, though he was fairly certain he kept some semblance of politeness on his features. Some habits did not change, after all.

He and Minerva circled again. "The butler's pantry," they said together.

Griff grinned in both surprise and delight. "Clever girl, you thought my thoughts."

Minerva raised a patronizing brow. "Might I remind you of my skillset and our same knowledge base? Surely it is not that remarkable."

"Oh, but it could be. Try it again." He curved his mouth to one side, pretending he could send his thoughts to her in some wordless exchange of ideas.

His wife rolled her eyes in response.

"There it is again!" He laughed and moved around the woman

beside him before returning to Minerva. "We are brilliant."

"You are an idiot," Minerva corrected. "Your wife will want to take the air when the dance is over, and you will oblige her. The terrace has a door connecting to the servants' halls, and it will be unlocked for the evening. Understood?"

Griff looked appropriately obedient. "Yes, ma'am. If I behave, may I have dessert?"

Minerva heaved an irritated sigh, but he caught the quirk of her pert lips. She found him more amusing than she wanted to admit, and he would get her to develop a ready sense of his humor yet. If not her own.

A few more passes of the patterns, and the dance was complete. Griff brought his wife's hand to his lips again, then looped it through his arm as he led her grandly to the terrace, the crisp evening air bringing a renewed vigor and energy to his legs and lungs. A faint hint of jasmine wafted towards them from the gardens, and for a moment, Griff wished he could walk his wife through them and delve deeper into the scent.

He blinked to remind himself that Minerva was not, in fact, his wife, and that wandering through jasmine-infused gardens with her was not going to get him anywhere he wished to be.

Wait, wished to be?

What the devil…

He cleared his throat, which had nothing to do with the trouble of jasmine or wishing, and surreptitiously glanced about them for any onlookers.

There were none.

"Go," he hissed to Minerva, who moved quickly, tugging her skirts up enough to keep them from dragging on the stone of the terrace.

As she had predicted, the door was unlocked, and they were able to slip into the servants' corridors without observation. Griff noted the trouble Minerva seemed to be having with her mass of skirts in her haste, and he seized hold on some and hefted them above the floor, pressing gently against her back with his free hand.

She glanced over her shoulder and nodded once wordlessly, slipping down another corridor that would lead towards the butler's pantry and out of the main thoroughfare.

They reached the room in question, but a quick check of the handle told them what Griff had feared.

The door was locked.

He hissed a favorite Spanish curse, dropping Minerva's skirts.

"Oh, stop being dramatic," she scolded, turning towards the door more fully. "Here, hold this." She held out a length of the front of her gown and a wad of petticoats, drawing the length up her leg.

He took them automatically, his eyes darting from the fabric to her leg repeatedly. "Hold… What the hell are you doing?" he demanded, his voice rising in pitch as the top of her knee was revealed.

Minerva ignored him and fumbled for something at her thigh, producing a rolled leather pouch of sorts and opening it. "You can drop them now," she told him without concern as she unfurled the leather.

He did, but with a swallow that did absolutely nothing for the tension in his throat at present.

Focus, man. Mission. Locked door. Paperwork.

Odd how none of those words distracted from the image of the most fetching length of leg he had ever seen in his known life.

He looked heavenward as he tried for sanity, paying no attention to whatever his wife and partner was doing with the door before her.

Until the lock clicked.

Then his eyes went there in shock.

Minerva grasped the handle and turned it, opening the door with a soundless ease.

Griff gaped, then grinned, almost all thoughts of leg forgotten. "That was under thirty seconds. What skills you possess, my dear. You'd have made a very good thief in another life."

She raised a brow, her mouth curving in an almost smug smirk that was rather becoming. "I *was* a very good thief in another life. Some things not even time can erase."

With that stunning pronouncement, she moved into the room and immediately began stepping out of excess petticoats, nearly startling him again.

Right. Chartreuse.

He removed his coat and tugged at the ruffles of his cravat with a mental apology to his blessed valet. His weskit was an annoying hue of gold that supposedly complemented chartreuse, if such a ludicrous thing could truly be accomplished, so that was also discarded and tossed alongside his other articles of clothing. A quick flick of the button at his throat and he was perfectly at his leisure, aside from the stupidity that was male footwear for a ball. Nothing to be done about that unless he wished to travel with a separate pair at all times.

He was prepared for Beddingsford to be a peacock, but even that was too far.

Setting his hands at his hips, Griff looked over at Minerva with smugness.

Which was quickly replaced by something distinctly more aghast.

Masses of petticoats were on the floor, as were her gloves, but her gown…

She'd managed the lowest button, but that was no hardship. There were at least a dozen buttons on the monstrosity, and her flailing arms were entirely incapable of reaching them. He knew full well her strength and flexibility, but the cut of the garment, and no doubt her stays beneath, kept her from being able to use her arms as fully as she might have done otherwise.

They did not have time for this.

"Here," he grunted, coming over and undoing the top button.

She jerked as though he had scalded her and whirled. "What are you doing?" she demanded in a harsh whisper.

He gestured at her gown. "Helping you get it off. That is what you were aiming for, yes?"

"Of course. I cannot possibly go rifling about in this." She slapped the fabric in frustration, and it swished loudly in response, illustrating the point.

Griff nodded dramatically. "Yes, and you cannot get it off yourself. Ergo, I have decided to help you so we can actually do something useful this evening."

She glared at him darkly. "I don't want you to see me."

He exhaled with the same sort of impatience he usually employed with his sister. "Did you bring something else to wear, Minerva? A new outfit, perhaps?"

Her jaw worked from side to side as she ground her teeth. "No," she mumbled.

"Then I am going to see you in your unmentionables while we do this," he explained as though to a child, "and I will see you while I help you out of your gown. There is no choice."

She held her gown tightly across her chest, though it was in no danger of slipping with the number of buttons still left. Her eyes held a cold fury, an indignity, perhaps, but he sensed it was all a defense against something else.

Vulnerability.

He'd love to dwell on his prickly partner's vulnerabilities when he had the leisure to do so, and he'd never dream of ignoring them in ordinary circumstances, but at this moment, they were operatives, not people. Certainly not a gentleman and lady.

"You know," Griff said with a brisk exhale, folding his arms, "despite what you may think, I am capable of seeing a woman in stays without turning into a feral hyena lacking in morals."

Her brow creased and some of her stiffness softened. "I know, but…"

"We don't have time, Minerva," he interrupted, cutting her off with a quick slash of his hand. "So you need to decide now if it's more your pride or your modesty at stake, and whether you can trust me with both."

Her lower lip puckered, no doubt due to her biting the inside, and then she huffed and turned her back to him. "Fine. Hurry."

He stepped to her without comment and his fingers flew down the length of her spine from one button to the next. The gown soon gaped, and the ribbons of her stays were exposed.

The sheer volume of their crisscrossing pattern was enough to make him blink. "Hell and the devil," he said as she shrugged out of the gown. "They've imprisoned you in layers. I don't know that my dagger could cut through those ribbons, there's so many of them."

Minerva snorted softly, tucking a rogue curl of hair behind her ear as she stepped fully free of the skirts, her long white chemise seeming to flow from the stays themselves rather than being bunched by them. "Let us hope I will not be required to engage in acrobatics tonight. These new stays are longer than I am used to, so I can only bend enough to sit, if one can call such posturing sitting."

"The decorum teacher complaining about posture?" Griff tsked playfully, kicking aside the pile of skirts as they moved for the opposite door of the pantry. "What will your students say?"

"I will apply for a new subject to teach directly," she quipped, adjusting a strap of her stays more securely on her shoulder. She turned, one hand covering her exposed skin above the stays and chemise. "Do you promise you can handle this? I will not be gawked at."

Griff rolled his eyes and gestured for her to lead the way. "Yes, I can handle it. And I've no time for gawking anyway, Mirrors. Let's go."

Apparently consoled at last, Minerva nodded and turned, hurrying out of the room, Griff hard on her heels.

He'd never followed a woman in her unmentionables throughout a house before, and he could not say that he'd even considered such a thing as possible in his baser imaginations. He had every confidence that Minerva was more dangerous now than she had been ten minutes ago, given the removal of certain restrictions, so he would be a fool to let his guard down and find any sort of enjoyment in the matter. But it did give him pause.

They would be fortunate, indeed, to not be spotted during this outing of theirs. They could have waited until night, he supposed, but it was far easier to investigate when people were awake and distracted than when they were asleep and unpredictable. It was entirely possible they might have to sneak out for further investigation then as it was, but for now, they needed something to go on.

The more they knew, the more they could do, and he'd be damned if he'd spend his time at this house party being merely decorative when there were possibilities to explore.

He suspected Minerva was feeling much the same way.

She led him silently to the housekeeper's parlor, the sounds of servants' activity all too plain beyond the doors. "Look for her ledger," Minerva whispered as she moved around the cleared desk and began to pull open drawers. "She'll have every guest and their preferences recorded."

Griff nodded and scanned the shelves behind the desk for

anything that might prove useful. Row after row of ledgers sat there, carefully notated by year, but nothing indicating the present one. The housekeeper at DeRaven was evidently meticulous, which ought not to be a surprise, given the precision of all details associated with the house party. There were at least fifteen years of records here, and he made a mental note to examine the housekeeper's parlor at any house he was investigating in the future. He knew not all of them would be like this one, but he'd take less and be satisfied with the source.

"Here," Minerva hissed.

He turned and came beside her, his eyes darting across the open pages. "Where?"

"Completely opposite of us, of course," she replied, tapping his name. "We'll have to go now."

Griff nodded. "He needs an extra blanket? Poor chilled frog. What does it say about us?"

"No," Minerva told him as she snapped the ledger shut and replaced it in the bottom drawer. "You can snoop for gossip on your own time. The longer we are gone, the more likely we are to be missed."

"I am quite certain they will draw convincing conclusions for themselves," Griff assured her with a laugh, once again following her. "After all, we are the effusive Beddingsfords. All they need do is go in the butler's pantry…"

"Shut. Up," Minerva ground out, each word carefully enunciated.

There was the teacher once more.

He grinned at her back, resolving to be more teasing in their next sparring session. Her ire could make for a most intriguing fight.

It was much to Minerva's credit that she had studied the servants' passageways as much as the rest of the house and could lead them both up the nearest stairwell, creaky and tight though it was. He had spent years sneaking around buildings of all sorts, but even he was a little disoriented when they walked out into the corridors of guest rooms.

Some operative he was.

Minerva looked one way, then the other, then nodded and gripped his arm. "This way. Come on."

Chapter Eleven

$\mathcal{I}$t was not the first time Minerva had been forced to work in less-than-ideal attire, but it was the first time she had had a partner of the opposite sex working closely with her while wearing the less-than-ideal attire.

She'd never been more aware of the revealing nature of stays in her entire life.

But she had to focus now. Had to be at the top of her game. There was no time to distract herself from her work or her skills. Time was their enemy, and there would be no recovering from being discovered, especially dressed as they were.

No matter how attractive Griff looked thus.

Minerva cleared her throat as softly as possible against the cruel tightening of it. She would not think about his attractiveness at the moment, or at any moment. It was not helpful, especially given what she knew about him now.

Where was the necklace at present? She could see clearly it was not about his neck, and his sleeves were rolled as they hurried down the rows of rooms, so it was not on his wrist. Had he left it in his room? Was it even at the house party?

Why did she care? She had thought about the trinket for years, knew how she had lost it, but oddly, had recovered just fine from the loss of it. Her memories of her father had not dimmed with its absence, nor had her affection for him as the years had passed. But she needed to know why Griff had worn it during their fight. Did he know who she was? Or was it simply something he had kept?

If the latter, why had he kept it?

If the former… why had he not said anything?

She bit the inside of her lip as they neared the room she needed. Probably for the same reason she had not said anything to him about it.

Secrets were safety. And privacy was paramount.

It was all about protection, even from him. From anyone. Everyone.

The bedchamber in question was before them, the door closed, as she expected it would be. She was fairly confident Mr. Galveston was still in the ballroom, but she was not going to take any chances. She placed her ear at the door, and after a few moments of only hearing her own heartbeat, she took the handle and pressed her way in, Griff immediately behind her.

He had been far too jovial for her liking as they had begun their investigation that evening, but she also knew she was on edge due to her present appearance. Still, if she would have to explain everything she was looking for and wanted him to do, she would go insane far more rapidly than she was already destined to.

Thankfully, he did not stand about helplessly, but immediately went to work carefully inspecting every item and detail on the far side of the room, including tapping panels of the wall. They had no reason to suspect the Partlowes as being involved in anything, but they also knew better than to write anyone off.

Minerva went to the bureau in the room first, inspecting each and every clothing item carefully, particularly the buttons. The reports had stated that particular buttons were used to indicate operatives, but the lack of such buttons would not clear Galveston. Compromise of information could occur at any given time, and their investigation must consider that.

No such buttons were found, and though she felt a stab of disappointment, she moved on to the trunks in the corner of the room. She ran her hands along the outside, finding no telltale notches or grooves, then lifted the lid, eying its dimensions and appearance thoroughly.

Cocking her head, Minerva tilted the lid back and ran her fingers along the velvety lining of it. Whatever the exact fabric was, it was rather fine for a trunk of such wearing. One might have the insides reupholstered, she supposed, if that was the term for it. But something was certainly suspect about this lid and its lining.

She ran her fingers along the surface in the center, noting how the fabric shifted in shade ever so slightly with the change in direction of the fibers, just as velvet had the tendency to do. She blinked as she did the motion once more, then looked at the edge of the lining with far more interest.

Repeated contact with a fabric such as this would lead to wearing of sorts, a more permanent alteration to the pattern of fibers, possibly even to distort the appearance entirely. And who would think to change the direction of the fibers of the lining of their trunk lid to avoid detection of a secret on closer inspection?

Determined to examine her own trunks when she returned to her rooms, Minerva caught her breath as she saw exactly what she had been seeking: a distortion.

She hooked her fingers into the rim of the lining and gently pulled, finding the panel of fabric giving way with far too much ease to be a mistake. Tilting the lid back fully so as not to have any contents spill out, Minerva rose and came to the side, adjusting the panel to see within.

She discovered documents, some looking to be maps, others letters, and another…

"Griff…" Minerva whispered, her fingers almost seeming to tremble as she reached inside for the proof that confirmed her suspicions.

He was at her side in a moment, crouching beside her. "What is it?"

She pulled the page out and showed him, a thrill of pride racing through her veins when she heard his own breath catch.

A page of music ought not to give anyone so much reaction, but when it was the music for *"Suspendez à ces murs,"* one felt the intense desire to either bellow in victory or heartily embrace the nearest human.

Neither of which Minerva would do at this moment.

"Gotcha, you bastard," Griff breathed, a slow grin crossing his lips.

They shared an elated look, the air between them suddenly heavy and warm and brilliant.

For some godforsaken reason, Minerva glanced at Griff's crooked grin, the heat of her delight seeming to concentrate in the center of her chest and, oddly enough, on her now buzzing lips.

Griff was a spy, which meant his senses and skills of observation were as attuned as hers. Which meant he noticed. More than that, he did the same to her, sending sparks flying throughout her being.

Heavens…

Or was the feeling hellish?

How could it be both?

"We… don't have time to look through all of these now," Minerva whispered through her still-buzzing lips, dragging her eyes down to Griff's exposed throat. "Not if…"

"Not if we want to go to the study as well," he finished, his nod painfully slow. "Right. Think we can come up with a reason to come back in here another time?"

Now she nodded, feeling rather stupid as she did so. "Undoubtedly." She could think of several reasons to come back in here, but none of them had anything to do with the paper in her hand.

Why was her head swimming? She needed to focus, needed to think of the next step, the next course of action, needed…

Griff swallowed, which was suddenly the most fascinating thing she had ever seen, and then he took her hand and brought it to his lips, which was a far more exhilarating experience than it had been before, now that her gloves were gone.

"Well done," he praised roughly, squeezing her hand. "I think we'd better go."

Minerva blinked. Then blinked again.

Right. They should.

Her hand buzzed with the same strange sensations her lips had managed, and she found herself slipping the music back into the hidden panel of the trunk before she recognized the action. She replaced the lining, made sure it did not appear disturbed, and closed the trunk entirely. Griff moved to set other things to rights, and the separation from him was like a blessed breath of crisp air for her body and lungs.

With it came the clarity she sought, and she moved to the door, doing her best to ignore Griff in any way, shape, or form.

He joined her and nodded once, indicating she lead the way.

Must he be accommodating at a time like this?

The corridor was as silent as when they had arrived, and Minerva was more than tempted to race back to her bedchamber and find something resembling a fichu to cover herself while she and Griff were at work. She wasn't necessarily scandalous, given the lack of particular endowments she possessed, and the neckline of gowns at present, but it still felt rather exposing, and she was not comfortable with it. And it was more exposing than she had been yet with him, or with anyone with whom she shared a working relationship.

How in the world could he respect her as a colleague when she looked like this?

Then again, she had been gawking at him as well.

Perhaps there was little room for self-pity here.

Silently, they found the servants' stairs again and descended as quietly as possible. The ball would be continuing for several more hours, so none of the servants ought to be preparing rooms as yet. If Minerva had learned anything about the running of a great house in the country during her life, it was that the servants would catch glimpses of the finery and entertainment whenever they could. As such, she was convinced that the maids and valets were ensconced in some room with a hidden view of the ballroom, no doubt critiquing the ensembles and the guests against whatever rubric they found necessary.

Back on the main floor, Minerva was desperate to return to the butler's pantry, but knew full well they needed to venture to Lord Partlowe's study first. It was not a difficult trip to make, which was why they had chosen the butler's pantry for their hiding place, but she was beginning to feel the length of time they had been absent and did not like the idea of speculation among the guests, who had surely noticed they were not in the ballroom, nor on the terrace. She'd have begged to investigate the study at another time if she were not already committed to doing so now.

She paused to let Griff go ahead of her this time, hoping to hide herself behind him as they moved into the corridor that led to the study. They could no longer hear the sounds of the ballroom, which was to be expected, but the silence of their surroundings made every motion of theirs louder in Minerva's ears. It was as though she had never been a spy in her entire life before this moment, and every tiny creak of floorboards or ripple of fabric made her wince. There wasn't even particular danger, only embarrassment, but the stakes felt the same.

If only she could do this on her own. Without a partner, without distraction, without hindrance, without having to consider any other subject but her own aims. It would all have been so much easier, not to mention quicker. She could have handled both missions alone, she was sure of it.

But having Griff with her…

It was far and away the more complicated way to manage things.

She hated when she could not work alone, which was why she rarely agreed to such things. She wouldn't have agreed to this, had she been given a choice.

Griff stopped suddenly, and she slammed into his back, gripping his waist for balance to keep herself from falling. She knew better than to ask questions and only waited in silence as one of his arms stretched behind him to either steady her or protect her.

Footsteps echoed in her ears, their location unclear, though they seemed to be at a distance. Minerva held her breath once more, willing the person away so they could continue and get this over with.

As though conceding to her wishes, the footsteps faded, and Griff's hand, which had landed on her arm when he'd shot it out, patted her twice.

They moved again and found the study in short order, only three doors down from where they'd been forced to pause. Thankfully, this room was unlocked, no doubt due to the unlikely incidence of anyone wandering there during the ball.

Minerva closed the study door silently behind them while Griff began rifling through the large mahogany desk in the room.

"What do we need?" she hissed, curious as to what had piqued his interest in Partlowe's study.

"Family names," he replied without looking up. "Anything documenting extended relations. Trust me, something will be here."

Trust him? She was barely keeping her head above water, and he wanted her trust?

But there wasn't another option, was there?

She began scanning the rows of books on the shelves, looking for any sort of family Bible or history among them. Some of the older, more established families in the peerage had such tomes in their libraries, and she had not studied Lord Partlowe's line well enough to know if his would be among them.

Her fingers ran across the peeling spine of a large book, and she looked more carefully at it, her eyes not quite adjusted to the dim light of the room as yet. But she pulled it down and felt a jolt of excitement as she opened the cover to see that it was, indeed, an old family Bible. She moved to the window, where moonlight offered only a trifle more illumination than the dying fire.

Neat and tidy writing listed family births going back a hundred years, including branches off of the original family line.

She scanned the lines for the present generation and placed a finger on the family she had looked for. Glancing over at Griff, who was eyeing pages from an account book from one of the drawers, she made a faint but sharp hissing sound. He looked, then came to her side as she indicated.

She tapped the family name. "Martin," she whispered.

He nodded and ran his finger down the page. "Charles Alexander William Martin," he breathed. "Seventeen ninety-seven. Older than I thought."

"Surely not," Minerva retorted. "His service record…"

"Shows nothing," Griff overrode, his whisper firm without being harsh. "I only discovered tonight that he was in uniform, and that should have been in his file in London. There must be discharge papers somewhere, but it would be at least ten years ago."

Minerva frowned as she closed the Bible once more. "Hardly much of a military career."

Griff only shrugged. "Perhaps he was wounded and on pension. Now that I have a name and birth year, perhaps I can discover that. I need discharge records to prove it."

"Why would Lord Partlowe have his cousin's discharge records?" Minerva asked as Griff moved back to the desk.

"Why would he have the certificate of banns for his second

cousin's wedding last year?" Griff returned, plucking up a slip of paper and waving it at her. "The man is a document hoarder, no doubt trained into such by his predecessors. But it will not all be in here."

He closed the account book and exhaled roughly. "I was hoping for the same success as yourself in here, but I need hours of time and a more specific aim." He shook his head and replaced the book in the drawer. "Let's go, or we'll be missed."

Minerva nodded, returning to the shelves and setting the family Bible back in its place. Griff waited for her at the door, giving her a querying look, which she nodded again at. They slipped back into the corridor and moved as swiftly and silently as possible back towards the butler's pantry.

How much time had passed, Minerva could not guess, especially since she had somehow lost the ability to comprehend anything for a stretch of time in Galveston's rooms. It could have been an hour, it could have been twenty minutes, it could have been half the night, though she highly doubted it was that long. But they had to make an appearance at the ball before too long, or rumors would abound.

Well, more rumors than likely already did about the Beddingsfords, anyway.

Her breathing was shallow as they moved, anticipating their imminent discovery at any moment, but no impending footsteps interrupted them, and the faint sounds of the ball were once again heard as they neared the butler's pantry. She exhaled fully as they entered the room, Griff shutting the door behind them with the faintest click.

Minerva immediately stepped into her petticoats, yanking them back up into place and tying the ribbons tightly. She didn't dare look over at Griff for his process; there was no telling what his expression would be or if she would feel anything from it.

She'd like to think she would feel nothing, but she had already felt too much this evening, and more was entirely possible in this state.

Curse feminine appreciation of a well-formed figure.

She suddenly heard a sharp hiss and whirled, seeing Griff standing perfectly still in his fastened weskit and loose cravat, eyes wide.

"What?" she mouthed.

"Gown," he whispered harshly. "Now, Min. Now!"

She nearly dove for the gown and scrambled to foist the skirts over her head. Shimmying them down, she shoved her arms into the tiny, tight sleeves, praying she wouldn't rip anything.

Then she heard it: keys jingling outside the door.

Minerva cursed sharply in Gaelic, hefting the bodice into place and adjusting her arms fully within the sleeves.

Griff was instantly at her back, working at the buttons, but she could feel him fumbling in his haste.

They weren't going to make it.

The lock clicked and they both froze, looking at the door. A stately man in slicked back hair and a simple but formal ensemble entered, his eyebrows slowly rising as he caught sight of the two individuals within his workspace.

Minerva could only swallow, suddenly feeling a chill in the air right where her stays were exposed and above.

"A thousand apologies, my good man," Griff said after a moment of strained and burdensome silence. "But you see… my wife presented such a fetching picture this evening, and I was mad for a, erm… private audience. You understand."

"Indeed," came the low rumble, no hint of amusement in the tone.

Griff laughed uncomfortably. "The door was unlocked, and I have no notion of how, precisely, we came to be here. We are almost rearranged and presentable, as you see. Would you be so good as to keep this from your master for the evening? I will, of course, address the impropriety in the morning, with my deepest apologies. But the evening is going on so well, and I would hate to disrupt his hosting duties for something so unfortunate as my poor choices. And I would spare my wife her blushes, as you can imagine."

The butler's eyes flicked to Minerva, who did not need to feign her blushing, and he finally seemed to develop a shade of emotion, though it was certainly more pity than sympathy. "Of course, my lord… Beddingsford, is it?"

"'Tis indeed, my man." Griff puffed with the sort of delight one might use for being recognized at White's rather than indecently dressed in a butler's pantry. "You are a good sport. And truly, my mortification knows no bounds. Will you forgive the unwelcome intrusion?"

"Certainly, sir," he replied, not sounding as though he would. "And I shall take more care with locking the door in future."

Griff gave him a sage nod, pulling Minerva gently, but decidedly, closer to him. "So I should hope. Deuced tricky things, locks. We had trouble with so many of them in our house in Calcutta, did we not, my dear?"

"So much trouble," Minerva mumbled through blazing cheeks, wishing she could find the strength to smile for all their sakes. "So distressing."

The butler blinked, suddenly seeming a touch uncomfortable. "Well, things are different in Calcutta, I daresay. In… several regards. But you need have no distress for my part, Lady Beddingsford. I shall remove myself, and you may both… finish your restorations and return to the ballroom. At your leisure."

"It shall be very swift," Griff assured him, placing both hands on Minerva's barely exposed shoulders. "Truly, we are almost to rights now."

The butler nodded once and backed out of the room without any further conversation, shutting the door with a decisive click.

Griff exhaled sharply and leaned his head against Minerva's towering plaits, his fingers seeming to tremble against her skin.

Minerva was not much better; she leaned into him just as much and tried to find a steady breath amidst the torrent of rushing air from her lungs.

They stood like that for a moment, not so much taking comfort from each other as using each other to remain upright, realizing what could have happened, what they had risked, what might have been ruined…

Only when she felt Griff working at her buttons again did Minerva allow herself to open her eyes and find her defenses once more.

"Sorry," he murmured, his fingers brushing against the exposed skin of her back just above her stays.

"It's fine," she waved off, wishing she had a looking glass to examine her hair after all of that.

She heard Griff laugh once. "No, that was a hazard of tiny buttons. I was apologizing for the excuse I gave the butler."

Minerva glanced towards the door, which was still closed, and kept her voice low, just as Griff had done to spare them from eavesdroppers. "There was no other logical explanation. I suppose I should be grateful you didn't have me shoved up against the wall."

"I thought about it…"

She bit her lip on a restrained laugh, reaching behind her to whack him lightly. "Cad."

"Prude." He finished her buttons and patted the now-closed gown. "There. Perfect."

Minerva stepped away and reached for her dropped gloves before turning to face him, watching with interest as he haphazardly tied his own cravat. "Is anyone going to notice that your cravat isn't as florid as before?"

He shrugged. "It's possible, but I can blame it on the lack of proper starch or losing my cravat pin. I am not overly concerned about it."

"So I see." Minerva flexed her fingers, now encased in the satin of her long gloves, and exhaled slowly. "We'll need to address what happened tonight."

He raised a brow. "How do you mean?"

She gave him a look, hoping he was not thinking of the same thing she was not thinking about. "We were almost caught. Easily. We won't be so fortunate another time."

"I know." He sighed roughly and picked up his chartreuse jacket and shrugged into it, fastening the buttons and shaking his head. "We need to practice more. I haven't been taking it as seriously as I should have."

"Nor have I," Minerva admitted. "But I think you'll agree, that was too close."

He gave her a quick nod. "I do. And we will fix it. But not tonight. Come on, back out to the terrace and into the dance with us. I've got a very important conversation with Lord Partlowe in the morning, and I don't envy the butler trying to keep a straight face when he sees us again."

Chapter Twelve

"Thank you for agreeing to see me this early, my lord."

Lord Partlowe gestured for Griff to take a seat in his study, which looked oddly different by morning light. "It is nothing. I am an early riser regardless of the events of the night before. I trust you found breakfast to your liking?"

Griff nodded as eagerly as he dared, though he could not, in all honesty, say that he had enjoyed the food provided to them.

The Partlowes were in desperate need of a better cook.

But that was beside the point.

"What can I do for you, Beddingsford?" Partlowe asked, spreading his hands out as he sat behind the desk Griff had been snooping around the night before.

Griff smiled uneasily for the act, though he truly wished to be rather smug about his evening. "I am afraid that your butler—what is his name?"

"Griffin," came the easy reply.

Of course it was.

Griff ignored the impulse to laugh. "I am afraid that Mr. Griffin witnessed a bit of an awkward situation last evening. My wife and I… Well, we have been separated for some time due to business and family affairs and the like, and I surprised her by appearing in London. No doubt you heard about that."

Partlowe chuckled. "I certainly did, and with that welcome you received, I can only imagine how agreeably your time has been spent since."

"Just so," Griff replied with a genuine laugh, more due to his imagination of Minerva's expression on hearing such a statement. "And last night, during your excellent ball, we moved out to the terrace. I am afraid that the… the fragrance of jasmine takes us right back to our life together in the Indies, and we… Well, to be frank, we were in need of some secured privacy, and neither of us wished to make the journey to the bedchambers for the liaison. We found the butler's pantry available and made use of it. Your butler walked in on us as we were righting ourselves. There was no indelicate exposure, but we were not fully restored to proper appearances, you see. I am afraid we rather shocked him, and I did not wish for you to hear of the issue from him."

To his credit, Partlowe looked rather bemused instead of offended, and seemed to be holding back laughter.

That was a good sign.

"Poor Griffin," he finally replied, a hand going to the corner of his mouth as he shook his head. "Thank you for telling me, but it was not necessary. There is no scandal here. It is not as though you were discovered by all of the guests in the orangery, although, even then, you are married to each other, so…" He shrugged, sitting back.

"You are a man of remarkable understanding and tolerance," Griff praised, allowing himself to further relax into his own chair in evident relief.

Partlowe seemed to brush that off, making a slight face. "I try. Affection in marriage is rare enough; expression of it ought not to be hindered. I'll speak to Griffin and let him know we have talked, make certain he is not so affronted that he cannot look you in the eye, or some such." He paused, grinning at Griff as though they were old friends. "Perhaps, upon your next return to the house party in a few days, we might have you and your wife share a bedchamber to make things simpler for everyone. And more convenient."

Griff laughed heartily, nodding in agreement. "I suppose you might wish to do that, no question. Truly, it is not our habit to take such liberties in a house that is not our own, so I hope you do not think—"

"Oh, come now, what man has not wished to escape a ball for more pleasant diversions at one time or another?" Partlowe overrode, leaning forward to rest his forearms on his desk. "And should the impulse overtake you once more, find a better place than the butler's pantry, man."

This was starting to get uncomfortable, even for Griff.

And yet, when opportunity knocked…

Praying Minerva would forgive him for the impression he was about to set forth, he offered his host a sly grin. "Such as?"

"My archives room." Partlowe rose and gestured for Griff to follow him. "Trust me, no one goes in there. I mean, I do, but not during events. My wife doesn't use it, and I have never seen the need to lock it. I think you will find it conveniently located, as well."

If Griff had debriefed Partlowe as to his mission and his needs, he could not have been more accommodating than he was at this moment. Not only was he going to show him the exact room that Griff would want to visit most, but he was giving him express permission to spend personal time in it.

With Minerva, engaging in certain activities, but it was access, nevertheless.

He did not need to know what Griff, and Minerva, by extension, would truly use the room for.

Partlowe led him down the hall to a door just off of the direct thoroughfare, one that might have been ignored as a person rounded the corner on his or her way elsewhere. Partlowe pushed the unimpressive door open and stepped in, spreading his arms wide. "Welcome to my cave of history, Beddingsford."

Griff allowed himself a low whistle of appreciation. The room was spectacular, as far as rooms went. What must have once been the library of the house was now wholly devoted to preserving the history and artifacts of the Partlowe family. Shelves towered high above, ledgers of varying states of distress neatly lined among them, as well as some boxes that must have contained letters or jewelry, or some other sentimental items. There were trunks in some places, and an overwhelming scent of moth with a hint of lavender. He could also detect the smell of paper, which was no surprise, given the sheer volume of it in the space. Tall windows were covered with green velvet curtains, though they were not fully closed at the moment, and a simple desk sat far to one side, nothing upon it, while a plush armchair sat next to a ladder that leaned against the shelves.

It was a library in appearance and setup, despite the fact that it was all archives of the Partlowe family.

He was suddenly dying to ask if Partlowe regularly read his grandfather's journals.

Griff turned to Partlowe, who was looking at him in expectation. "This is not what I was expecting," he admitted with a laugh. "But my family is a series of one child per generation for ages, which is why we no longer have a family home in England. I would not know where to begin with this."

Partlowe shrugged and looked around them. "It became part of my training from my father so I could continue the work when I inherited, so I know nothing else. I've actually culled some of the contact with extended lines because it was getting ridiculous. But I do know the next five potential heirs, should we fail to produce one, and every detail of their personal and professional lives."

"I am sure solicitors would be glad for that," Griff murmured, eyeing the shelves again. "And you say this is culled?"

"Well, not this so much as what I regularly take in from the current generations," Partlowe admitted. "First and second cousins only, unless they have a claim to the viscountcy."

Griff glanced at him. "And how many cousins fall into the category of first and second?"

"Eighty-four."

There was no helping the coughing fit that suddenly overtook Griff then, and he gaped at Partlowe through the gaps in each cough. "Are you bloody serious?" he asked, completely forgetting to put on a finer tone to his voice.

Partlowe grinned. "Entirely. You see now why I've done some pruning of the family tree."

"I'd have gone further than you did, and I won't deny that." Griff took in a full, clear breath at last and tried to find some way to bring up the mystery cousin in easy conversation. "Ah, I see a military scabbard up there. History of military service in the tree?"

"Rich one, in fact," Partlowe replied, looking up at the scabbard with a fond smile. "Several generations of uncles and cousins and the like. A few served with Wellington, several more in the American War of Revolution. Some in the Navy as well. There are a few boxes of medals in here, honors from various monarchs. My father's sister has a son who was injured in service some years back. You should see the reports of valor in his discharge papers. I was quite envious."

Griff's ears perked up at the mention of a cousin, especially a close one, having such a sterling military career, though the man did have an inordinate amount of first cousins. But an injury would explain the early discharge from the army, given the man's age and history with the Foreign Office. And yet…

Had anyone ever made note of the clerk's having a limp or disability? What sort of hindrance would keep him from continuing in the army and still allow him to be recruited for their work?

Recruited during school, yet given a commission in the army?

There were so many disconnecting points with this story, Griff wasn't certain what to believe anymore.

And he wasn't entirely certain that this missing clerk was, in fact, missing at all.

No one's backstory was this complicated as well as true.

No one's.

"Were you, indeed?" Griff murmured, setting his hands at his hips as though impressed. "I was always fascinated with the soldiers and naval officers coming in and out of the Indies when I was a boy. I am afraid that fascination has never fully left me."

Partlowe chuckled and moved towards the shelves. "Were you a lad always playing with toy soldiers and acting out battles?"

"Of course I was," Griff returned with his own laugh. "I'd have joined up myself, if my father had permitted. But alas, only son, and all that."

A sympathetic tsking sound came from his host, who now looked up at a particular shelf with a thoughtful expression. "Well, I don't have the time to show you all that I have on the subject, but feel free to wander in here when you wish to avoid company or events, even if your wife is occupied. This shelf here is usually where I keep all military records and medals from the family. Far more interesting than the land records over there."

Griff faked a shudder and made a face. "Only if I need sleep."

"That is usually when I pull them out as well." Partlowe grinned and gestured for them to leave. "As I said, make use of this room as you like. Plenty of privacy. And Griffin won't wander in randomly."

Well…

Griff had to bite his tongue to keep from quipping at the joke only he would appreciate. "Thank you, my lord. You've been very generous with your time, particularly given how our conversation started."

"Think nothing of it," Partlowe said easily. "My wife has planned all manner of things for this party, so I wouldn't blame you for disappearing a time or two."

There was an invitation, if Griff had ever heard one. And he had never been one to turn down an invitation.

They walked back through the quiet morning corridors of DeRaven, though there were certainly sounds of other guests stirring within the place. He had no doubt Minerva would be rousing shortly, and they would need to talk about the night before, and how they intended to proceed from this point. The ball had gone late the night before, and he hadn't wanted to extend the embarrassment of their near miss into a lack of sleep as well.

He was far less patient on minimal sleep, and there was no telling how Minerva would be, considering her standard impatience.

But perhaps that was just his effect on her.

Griff parted from his host with a congenial nod and opted to pay a visit to his wife in her chambers before she made her way down to the other guests. They were due to depart today and return to the Convent to resume their training and strategize on how they might better work together as a team rather than two spies forced to blend their missions, but this conversation could not wait.

He smiled at every guest he passed, more men than women heading down to breakfast, and there were several servants bearing trays to guest rooms, which allowed him the chance to smile at them as well. One should never underestimate a servant's ability to be of use to an operative, and he had yet to take the time to sniff one such out here. Perhaps Minerva had been paying more attention.

Smiling at the woman leaving the room beside Minerva's, Griff gently knocked on the door.

"Come," said the voice within, fully awake and almost bright.

But it was Minerva, so it could not actually be bright.

Unless she was inebriated, but he suspected she was a violent drunk and not a pleasant one.

He would pay a great deal of money to find out.

"Come," she called again, a little louder than before, bringing his attention back to the present.

He grinned and pushed open the door, bearing a sheepish expression on the chance that his wife was more indecent than the night before. Which, he thought, was the perfect level of indecency, but that was beside the point.

Minerva was smiling in her bed, looking quite the lady of leisure, splayed out as she was with a breakfast tray in her lap. She raised her brows at seeing him enter. "My lord, what a pleasant surprise for my morning."

"I hoped it might bring a smile and not a frown," Griff teased with a fond bow towards her. He closed the door tightly behind him, nodding and letting his smile ease as he moved to the bed. "May I sit?"

Minerva sat up further and nodded, gesturing to an open spot.

Griff lowered himself, then brought his feet up to sit cross-legged, as he had so often done on his mother's bed as a boy. "Partlowe accepted my apologies."

Minerva took a bite of toast and exhaled. "I suppose that is a good sign. And he took it well?"

"Very," Griff said with a light laugh. "He has offered us the use of his archive room for any such future endeavors, as we would be far less likely to be interrupted there."

Groaning, Minerva covered her face. "I am not going to be able to look him in the eye. We must leave as soon as possible."

"I have no doubt we will," Griff tried to console through more laughter. "But there's a curious thing about the archive room."

"That does not seem likely," Minerva muttered as she returned to her breakfast, cutting into her eggs.

"It is a family archive room," Griff went on, as though she hadn't expressed her doubts. "A very large and involved family. Cousins and all."

The cutting into breakfast ceased and Minerva's blue-green eyes locked with his. "Interesting cousins?"

Griff nodded very firmly, smiling further. "Very. And as I am such an avid studier of all things British military, his lordship has given me permission to examine anything on that particular shelf and its contents at my leisure."

Now Minerva smiled, a slow and rather maddening smile, he would freely admit. "You do love military records."

"Indeed, I do." He grinned widely and slapped the bedcovers in enthusiasm. "We have an in, Minerva! I know we're leaving today, but upon our return, I'll know exactly where to go and have the freedom to do so whenever I like! And you can, too, since we've now earned ourselves a reputation."

Swallowing with some difficulty, her smile wavering, Minerva placed the back of one hand to her reddening cheek. "I suppose I shall have to endure that for this mission, shan't I?"

Griff nodded again, this time slowly and sympathetically. "Afraid so. And when we return to DeRaven for our next stretch, Lord Partlowe is going to give us a shared bedchamber."

Minerva's hand dropped. "He's what?"

"He thinks he is being indulgent and giving us what we want," Griff explained with a wince and a shrug.

Minerva was shaking her head before he finished. "The Beddingsfords do not share rooms."

He snorted once. "The Beddingsfords certainly do. Or would you wish to disappoint everyone who saw us in that ballroom? And the dear butler last night, not to mention Partlowe himself."

She gaped wordlessly for a moment, her mouth trying to form some semblance of conversation and failing madly. "Surely no one expects our reconciliation to go on this long," she eventually managed.

"Well..." He trailed off, giving her a look.

Minerva blanched. "You're joking."

Griff sighed heavily. "I'll say it again: you started it."

She groaned again, putting her face in her hands "I should have slapped you in that ballroom."

"I probably would have grabbed you and kissed you soundly," Griff admitted without any semblance of shame.

Minerva peeked out from between her fingers. "You would not."

He shrugged, allowing himself a cheeky grin. "You were not in my head when you came marching towards me. Nine out of ten scenarios I thought up had me kissing you right there and then."

Her hands dropped, her eyes going wide. "And the one that didn't?"

Griff hesitated before admitting, "I carried you out of the ballroom over my shoulder. And then I kissed you."

Minerva stared at him, slowly shaking her head, her cheeks beginning to turn pink. "Unbelievable."

"Not really," Griff told her with a slight wrinkle to his nose. "You're a stunning woman, particularly in high dudgeon."

It wasn't like him to admit such a thing so openly and without shame, but really, what was the point in pretending that he hadn't been immediately attracted to her? That he wasn't still attracted to her, in all honesty. It didn't prevent him from working with her, nor respecting her skills as an operative. It didn't cloud his judgment nor his abilities. It had nothing to do with anything, except that it existed.

And sometimes, it really existed.

"And so you would've kissed me regardless?" Minerva asked, amazingly without any hint of shyness and not that much outrage. It seemed more unbelievable to her, which was unbelievable to him. Who wouldn't want to kiss Minerva? He'd kiss her right now, if she wouldn't injure him severely.

Was it worth that risk?

There was something rather delicious about the rumpled look she presently bore and the remnants of curls from her hair the night before. The breakfast tray in her lap might be an obstacle, but he could knock that aside. Surely that would not be too difficult a mess for the servants to contend with.

But he didn't dare kiss her on the bed. He knew how she could kiss, and one must not tempt fate and decency above what one's limits were.

Not if one wished to live.

"What if I were an assassin?" she asked when he didn't add anything.

Griff shook himself and tried to appear nonchalant amid his present thoughts. "Then at least I would have died after an extraordinary kiss, which is really all any man wants."

Minerva's cheeks were now an astonishing shade of near-scarlet, and she swallowed with some difficulty, her eyes dropping to the bedcovers. "I don't know what I'm supposed to say to that," she admitted in the smallest voice humanly possible.

"I'm not sure you're supposed to say anything," Griff assured her with a gentle pat to her foot. "As much of a compliment as it is, it is also a simple statement. You don't need to be uncomfortable with me, Minerva. I hope you know that."

She nodded, something seeming to shut behind her eyes as they met his. "I do. But you need to understand that attention is not something I will ever be comfortable with. I am used to avoiding such and hiding from anything associated with it. Even before I was an operative, attention was my enemy."

"What were you before an operative?" Griff asked, cocking his head as he looked at the presently vulnerable woman before him.

"Governess," she murmured, shifting beneath the tray of food in her lap, suddenly seeming to recollect that she had breakfast before her. She began to eat again, but slowly. "Only thing available to me, all things considered. And nobody wants a governess who attracts attention, trust me."

That was undoubtedly true, but Griff wasn't certain about something in her story, simple though it was. Lacking in details though it was. Something did not sound right, but he could not put his finger on what.

He knew nothing of Minerva's life or childhood, other than her being a teacher at the Convent. It was clear enough that she had no interest in sharing such personal details, and he could understand that. He was the brother of a duke, so his life was hardly relatable to the average Englishman, let alone an Englishwoman. But he had been an operative for long enough to experience life in nearly all stations and situations, which kept him from being too high in the instep. He had seen and learned enough not to judge anyone based on where they were born, what circumstances they had been born in, and what they had done with their life of their own volition.

Minerva could have told him anything, and he would have nodded and asked her to tell him whatever she wished about the thing.

But what she had said was not the truth. Or at least, not the whole truth.

Did that matter?

Not particularly, he supposed, but it did sting a little.

He hoped they could grow familiar enough with each other, trust each other enough, to share the deeper truths of their lives and themselves. Such comfort and trust took time, and they would have opportunities with training and work to improve relations between them.

But trusting someone with one's life was different than trusting one's secrets.

The former was easy. The latter…

Well, it was rare.

Very rare.

Griff offered his wife-partner a crooked smile and patted her foot again. "Eat up and get packed. Something tells me we've got a great deal to do today, and we have to get to the Convent before we can do any of it."

"Don't tell me what to do," Minerva ordered around a bite of toast, kicking his hand away from her foot.

Why that was encouraging, Griff could not say.

But encouraging it was.

Chapter Thirteen

"So you just stood there? With the butler gaping like a fish?"

"Not quite like a fish, Hawk, but basically, yes."

Laughter coursed its way around the table, and even Minerva, cheeks heating under the memory, had to laugh with the rest.

Days away from the occasion helped.

She sipped her Madeira, hardly tasting it, and resumed her meal, relieved to be dressed more like herself and less like Lady Beddingsford. It was lovely to not feel on display, even if she was at the dining table of the Duke and Duchess of Kirklin. They had been invited to supper upon their return to the school, and Pippa had come with them, which was a lovely addition to the table.

As the duchess was an operative herself, though presently enjoying a reprieve due to the forthcoming birth of her child, they could discuss case details without shame and elaborate on the life they enjoyed as operatives.

The duke had taken some time to fully comprehend his brother's true occupation when they had first arrived the week before, but he seemed to be completely supportive now.

Indeed, he was presently leaning on one elbow in his chair, grinning at his younger brother in the most casual, carefree manner Minerva had ever seen from him.

It made the brothers look even more related than a cursory observation could provide.

Minerva mentally shook her head. She had known His Grace for over a year now, as Clara had been a fellow teacher at the Convent before becoming an operative and, by extension, the duchess. She had refused to sever ties with her fellow teachers and friends despite her change in station, and so Minerva had seen them on several occasions, both at the school and outside of it.

Never once had she seen the duke so at ease.

Miraculous what being in one's home among his comfortable circle could do for a person.

But then, was not it so for Mr. Darcy in the novel by Miss Austen?

"You seem very pensive," Clara murmured, leaning close to Minerva, keeping her voice down to avoid attracting the attention of the others.

Minerva smiled at her, chewing a bite of potato more carefully. "I am afraid I was. I should add more to the conversation."

Clara waved that off, her deep golden hair catching candlelight in an elegant way that reminded the viewer of its true hue rather than the darker one evening light bestowed upon it. "Nonsense, this is no formal dinner. It's practically a family dinner, really. Griffin and his brother need to get reacquainted, now that secrets are gone, and Hawk is vastly interested in the missions his brother was engaged in while abroad. Believe me, the only formal undertaking we will continue this evening is for the ladies to retire while the men talk, simply to give them the chance while you are both here."

That was an image that made Minerva smile, and she glanced at Griff, who was talking to his brother with great animation at the moment. "I think Griff needs it. Conversation with his brother, I mean. I couldn't say why; he has never talked to me about it. Even so."

"You are partners, you are bound to notice things." Clara smiled with genuine warmth and a mischievous twinkle in her eye. "Now what were you so pensive about?"

Minerva felt her cheeks grow a trifle heated. "I was comparing your husband to Mr. Darcy."

Clara's brows rose and she glanced down the table at the man in question. Her expression softened and her mouth curved in a sweet smile that spoke of fondness, if not outright adoration. "I can see that. He is a marvelous man."

"I am sure he is," Minerva mumbled awkwardly, reaching for her glass again. "But I was particularly considering how Mr. Darcy was relaxed and easy when at Pemberley."

Clara blinked and looked back at Minerva in surprise before laughing. "Yes, that makes far more sense coming from you. Oh, heavens… As though you would see my husband as Mr. Darcy in any other light!"

Minerva had to snicker at that, bringing her serviette to her mouth to smother the sound.

Griff gave her a curious look, smiling a little but doing nothing to interrupt her conversation or stop his own.

She averted her eyes quickly, or she was destined to laugh further still, and far less delicately.

Clara put a hand to her chest as her laughter faded. "Oh goodness, Minerva. Yes, I must say that Hawk is far more comfortable here than you might see him anywhere else. And with his siblings, you will find he is either relaxed and at ease, or he is even more stiff and strict than one might find him. Province of the eldest brother, I suppose." She indicated the happily chatting brothers at the other end of the table. "I have never seen those two like this. I never dreamed I would be able to."

Minerva eyed the brothers cautiously, not wanting Griff to make her laugh or blush somehow. Thankfully, he was fully invested in the conversation with his brother and Pippa and did not notice her looking.

He did seem easier than she had seen him since they'd started working together. Less of the forced charm she had seen in public, less of the teasing man she had known in private, less of the focused operative she had worked beside.

This was simply Griff the man. And there was something inconceivably attractive about Griff the man that had nothing to do with a visible throat or fighting skills or a crooked smile. This was a whole, real, all-encompassing human whose outer appearance had a rather heart-stopping nature, but whose entity, stripped of the characters he inhabited, was soul-stirring.

And her soul was stirred.

Which, ironically, had the unfortunate effect of making her heart feel like it was stopping. Starting, too, just a few seconds late. Starting and stopping. Stopping and starting.

All because of Griff.

That wasn't good.

And yet…

"You're smiling," Clara said.

Minerva immediately looked down at the table, letting herself smile at the linen. "I thought of something amusing."

"I am sure you did," Clara murmured with the same awkward tone Minerva had employed earlier. Thankfully, she appeared to move on. "Griff is a very amusing fellow. And now that I know the truth, I cannot fathom how I never considered him as an operative. It should have been obvious."

"He is very good at being one," Minerva said with as much consolation as she could muster. "And to be fair, you are still new at this. How could you possibly expect to identify your new brother-in-law as an expert operative?"

Clara made a face of consideration and resumed her meal. "I suppose that is true. It does not stop me from feeling rather stupid, though."

Minerva turned towards her more fully and covered her hand. "Griff would not want you to feel that way. You know as well as I do that we do everything in our power to keep our status a secret, especially from those we are close to. You and His Grace were more protected not knowing, and now, while you may feel comfortable and relieved with knowing, you are at an increased risk."

"I know." Clara offered a small sigh and turned her hand to squeeze Minerva's. "I have no regrets about that, nor about my own choices. And I think Hawk is rather proud to have his brother be an operative for the Crown. I cannot tell you how many times he has bemoaned the waste of his brother being some pseudo-ambassador to the social circles of Europe. Now…"

Again, Minerva glanced at the brothers.

It was all too clear that their relationship was warm and engaging, and the revelation of Griff's status as an operative had done that. Had shifted his brother's view of him and gained him the respect that he deserved for the work he had done and the service he had given to his king and country.

There was something to be said for having no more secrets, she supposed. She wouldn't know the same herself. Her life, her background, was nothing but secrets.

And always would be.

Loud laughter erupted from the brothers, and they were nearly inconsolable in their mirth for a few moments.

Clara looked at Pippa curiously. "What in the world is that about?"

Pippa, grinning in a way she rarely did, could only shrug. "I haven't the faintest idea. Some private joke I do not understand but clearly is rather hilarious."

"Evidently." She flicked her attention between her husband and his brother, and Minerva could see every shift of emotion across the woman's face as she observed them. There was amusement, love, delight, relief, and something softer, sweeter, more touching that Minerva wasn't sure had a definition.

"Clara?" she pressed when she noticed a sheen of tears in her eyes.

Clara shook her head slightly, swallowing. "I have never seen my husband like this. Not to this extent. I am not certain he has ever been like this with his brother. Ever."

"No?" Minerva asked in a low tone, suddenly finding her own heart beginning to warm at hearing the continued laughter of the brothers, despite having no personal investment in the thing.

What did she care if Griff and his brother had a closer, more personal relationship? What was it to her if the brothers were laughing in a way that they had apparently never done? Why should it affect her in any way to be witness to this new stage in their brotherhood?

None of that mattered to her except as to how it would impact her partner's ability to do his job and keep her safe while doing so.

If her heart would stop skipping at every snicker she heard Griff utter, she would succeed in convincing herself of any of that.

"I love this," she heard Clara whisper in a choked voice.

Minerva watched Pippa give Clara an encouraging smile, some new understanding passing between the women.

Logically, Minerva could understand why a woman who loved her husband as Clara did would wish for this sort of comfort and happiness among his family. Who wouldn't wish for such a thing? But why should Pippa seem to truly feel it in a similar way? Not to the extent of tears, granted, but she was not unmoved, and it was more than Minerva was feeling.

How strange. Pippa had no husband, no children, and never mentioned family of any kind, apart from her niece that she was guardian for at the school.

How could she possibly comprehend more fully what Clara was feeling than Minerva?

Perhaps Minerva was emotionally inept…

That would not be surprising.

Years of no personal connections, only professional ones, would do that to a person.

A strange yearning started somewhere in the pit of Minerva's stomach. Slowly taking in all of the other individuals present, she could see the importance of connection in each countenance. Even Pippa bore a satisfaction to her expression that Minerva had never known, was certain she had never displayed. Three members of a family, along with another person who had experienced the depth of such precious connections, all enjoying this glimpse of a particular heaven that was entirely elusive to Minerva.

She had never felt so lonely in a room of people in her life, and she was not unfamiliar with the sensation.

But this was different, poignant and painful. She would have given anything to be part of a family in some way. Something that lasted longer than the length of a mission. Something that she could truly feel rather than pretend to feel. Something she could hold close to her heart in the middle of the night instead of recalling chilled nights alone on the London streets with an empty stomach and aching limbs.

She'd known warmth and affection in childhood, adored her father to distraction, and clung to the faint memories of her mother. But it had been so long since any of those things had been enough to give her pleasure rather than pain. Those things had not served any purpose while she had been learning how to be tough and scrappy, so they had been placed in a steel box in her mind, only to be brought out for reconsideration in moments of true privacy and security.

Distance and lies had been her life and continued to be from day to day. The only person who knew the full extent of her truth was Pippa. Others had glimpses, bits and pieces, but no one could place Minerva in any particular setting for any length of time.

It was a solitary existence, but she knew of no other way to live.

No one to mourn her should disaster strike on a mission, no one to welcome her home after successful assignments. No one to object to her actions, no one to celebrate victories. No one to advise her on details of life, no one to hold her when it all became too much.

Griff was a fortunate man, indeed. A loving family who would move heaven and earth for him, who would complain at an imposed distance and beg for more of his attention. An occupation that allowed him to serve his country, risk his life, give him purpose, drive him to succeed in several avenues, and show him the world. A life that extended beyond his present tasks and assignments.

Something permanent.

Something his own.

An unsettling sensation of hollowness curled within her stomach and began to expand up through her chest. With that, her eyes began to burn, stinging with the desire for tears.

But she would not let them form. And she certainly would not let them fall if she failed in stopping their formation. She would flee from the room before she would let that happen.

A curious scene would be better than a vulnerable sight.

"Ladies, shall we leave the gentlemen to their port?" Clara announced, rising from her chair.

Minerva swallowed hastily, pushing her chair back.

"Minerva drinks port," Griff pointed out with a grin. "She could stay."

That made her pulse skip. Did he want her to stay? Or was he simply teasing her?

Clara speared her brother-in-law with a look. "All three of us drink port, Griff. We simply prefer our own commentary while we do so."

His Grace snorted a laugh and covered his mouth, casting a bold wink at his wife while Griff chortled. They both rose as the women left the dining room, looking almost like twins in their shared mirth.

Minerva couldn't bear to look at them and hurried to follow Clara out of the room, Pippa coming up behind her. She needed to be away from the splendid happiness of her partner and his family for a time, or she would begin to wish herself actually his wife instead of pretending to be so. And Griff deserved to have someone desire him as a husband for his own sake and not out of envy.

What Minerva wanted was a family.

No, not a family, necessarily.

She wanted to belong.

And that was something she could never admit. Not to anyone. Her work as an operative gave her some sense of belonging and allowed her to devote her life to a cause greater than herself, but when all was said and done, this occupation was all she had.

Sometimes, it was enough.

Other times…

"You're very quiet," Pippa murmured as they entered the drawing room Clara led them to.

Minerva offered her friend and mentor a slight smile. "Am I? I do not mean to be."

Which was true—she did not mean to be blatantly silent. She simply had a great deal on her mind and not a great deal to say aloud.

Pippa's dark eyes surveyed her carefully. "I read your report on the DeRaven incident. It was handled very well."

That made the smile tight. "Thank you, but it should not have happened. Griff and I have addressed the issue, and the last two days of training have helped us a great deal."

"Indeed?" Clara inquired, hearing the conversation now. "Do tell."

Minerva hesitated, looking at Pippa, as Milliner, for confirmation, but also hoping she would suggest that the topic was not necessary.

"Oh, come now," Clara interjected before Milliner could do anything at all. "I have been away from the field for weeks now and never had a partner. Surely this is important for me to know."

It was a reasonable argument, but it did not help Minerva feel more inclined to speak.

Only when Milliner cleared her throat did Minerva sigh.

"The fighting style one employs with a partner is very different to what one employs alone," Minerva explained, hedging around the implication of working in close quarters with Griff. "Even when one is facing a single attacker. We had been practicing against each other's fighting styles to grow accustomed to them, but then Fists brought in additional attackers for us to fight at the same time. At times, we only fought side by side, and at other times, we fought together. They are not the same thing, you see."

Clara was nodding as Minerva explained, and asked no questions, which was a relief, as she did not wish to explain anything in great detail. The fighting practices had been the most comfortable she had felt throughout the training, as her growing confusion and emotions were able to be worked out through aggression and physical activity. The only moments she felt even remotely out of sorts when fighting was when she caught sight of the button somewhere on Griff's person.

She was going to have to ask about it at some point. Innocently, of course, just as a partner would when something peculiar was noticed. Thus far, she had seen it around his neck, on his wrist, and around his ankle, on the occasion they had been focusing on body work on mats and had not been wearing footwear. Any partner would have noticed its appearance by now, and she had not asked about it.

She couldn't bear to bring it up. It was perhaps her greatest secret, and if he suspected… if he knew…

"Is Fists pleased with your progress there?" Clara asked, handing over a small glass of what Minerva suspected was a watered-down port.

She wished very much for a full-strength dose.

She nodded as she sat back more comfortably in her chair. "He is, finally. And Thistle came by to give her opinion on our partner fighting. Her mastery of footwork is truly remarkable."

Milliner nodded at this. "She is the best partner operative we've ever had, which makes her refusal to reenter the field disheartening. But I won't argue it, as she continues to train our girls."

Minerva nodded somberly, feeling the brief pang of sadness for her friend and colleague, and for the loss the Shopkeepers must have felt in having her removed from the active ranks. But Thistle had lost her entire team on her last mission, and the damage of such a loss had been great, indeed. Minerva suspected that Thistle had actually been in a relationship with her partner, Dart, but nothing had ever been confirmed.

If she had been, his death would have been even more compounded for her.

Thistle had been unable and unwilling to take on any assignments since that loss, and it was going on three years now.

An image of Griff lying on the ground in a pool of deep red, the same color spreading from his chest, sprang to mind, and the agony with which Minerva's stomach clenched was acute.

She sipped her port in an attempt to settle herself, and hopefully, remove such pain—and imagery.

"What of the other training?" Clara pressed, sitting forward in her seat. "Surely you have done more than fight training."

"We have," Minerva affirmed as she swallowed the weak burn of port. "Abby has been very thorough in setting up various parts of the school for simulations, and we've only died five times."

"Excellent," Milliner praised, looking rather impressed, while Clara looked positively horrified.

Minerva took a moment to chuckle at the extremes between the two.

Clara looked at their superior in shock. "Excellent, you say? How?"

"The average operative dies a dozen times for every three different scenarios," Milliner explained with an almost pitying smile. "When death is an imminent risk, at any rate."

"I never died," Clara reminded them both, still looking bewildered.

"No, because death was not an estimated outcome for your assignment," Milliner went on. "Discovery was your greatest risk, and you were discovered a great many times before you improved."

Understanding dawned, and Clara began to nod. "That is true. So, as my assignment was so specific, we did not complete the death outcomes training?"

"Correct."

"But should I take on new assignments in the future where a

death outcome is a risk…"

Milliner was nodding before she finished. "We would put you through death-outcome training scenarios. But the average operative who receives a more well-rounded training at the beginning goes through them naturally."

"Don't let your husband hear you discussing possible death-outcome assignments," Minerva urged in a teasing whisper, grinning at her friend. "He might take great offense."

Clara's eyes widened and she looked at the door to the dining room quickly. "Shh!"

Minerva shrugged and sipped her port again.

"May I ask what all was practiced in scenarios?" Clara inquired innocently, though she still looked uncomfortable at the prospect of her husband appearing while death was discussed. "Aside from the possible death and capture aspects. Those seem rather obvious."

It was difficult to avoid wincing at the exclusion of the two things that Minerva would have been more comfortable discussing with their practices, but there was nothing to be done about that. Clara was quite right to consider such options as obvious, though Minerva could have discussed the various ways and means in excellent detail.

"Detection avoidance," Minerva began with a soft sigh, "intelligence discovery and replacement, memorization, infiltration, costume changes, escape adaptations…"

"Costume changes?" Clara interrupted sharply, eyes going wide. "Are you serious?"

Milliner interjected before Minerva need do so. "Given the high visibility of Lord and Lady Beddingsford, they will be forced to investigate during societal events, such as what took place at DeRaven. We must take great care to enable them to fill both roles as much as possible."

Clara settled as she nodded in comprehension, but there was a noted tension in her features that Minerva did not miss.

"We have decided that I must wear breeches beneath my gowns," Minerva told Clara with a quick and hopefully reassuring smile. "And a short chemise to act as a shirt or tunic. In some cases, Tilda believes a jacket could be hidden in layers of petticoats, fastened to my waist. And some of my gowns will have hidden hooks in the front so the buttons and lacings need not be disturbed when on a mission. Unfortunately, no matter how I argued, we cannot do anything about my stays." She made a face at this, recollecting the heated argument with Tilda all too well.

"You brought Tilda up from London?" Clara shook her head in amusement. "She must have been delighted to revisit her designs."

Minerva snorted once. "Considering more than half of our costumes are still in her clutches, she had no issues with the adjustments. And someone gave her permission to keep a few items as they had been." Her eyes flicked to Milliner with this accusation.

Her superior was completely unruffled. "You will not always be sneaking around during events. And I did allow her to create street wear for you. And gave permission for a hidden-weapons fitting."

"That is only a small consolation," Minerva grumbled.

"What's a small consolation?" Griff boomed as he and his brother entered the drawing room.

Minerva raised a brow as she looked over her shoulder at him. "My aim being better than yours," she lied without reservation.

His Grace barked a laugh. "No surprise there. Griff's aim was the worst in the family growing up. Even Adrianna can best him."

"Lies!" Griff protested as only a younger brother could. "Shameless, bald-faced lies!"

Chapter Fourteen

Kirkleigh at night was a curiously peaceful, comforting thing, even for someone as unfamiliar with it as Griff.

It was one of the family houses, so of course he knew it as well as any of the other estates he visited infrequently, but it had nothing on Millmond or Elmsley Abbey, where he and his siblings had spent most of their time together. Kirkleigh had recently become Hawk's favorite, so he was there more often than not, but Griff had his own house in Worsley now, so he was rarely lingering at one of the Kirklin estates. His brother had often complained about that, never understanding why Griff was at a distance when in England.

He understood now, and the relationship between the brothers had never been better.

And oddly enough, being at Kirkleigh with his brother was rather perfect.

The amount of time they had spent here as boys, no doubt driving their uncle, the previous duke, to distraction at their rambunctiousness… The coastline they had explored, the caves they had discovered, the adventures they'd imagined… All of these things, Griff had then been able to add to his life as an operative, while his brother had been left with only the memories as he'd taken up the responsibilities of the dukedom.

He would have to come back to Kirkleigh in between missions and spend time with his brother without the pressure of assignments and see if they could recover some of that impishness from their youth; for Hawk's sake, if nothing else. They'd been up for hours the first night Griff arrived here last week, catching up now that there were no secrets regarding Griff's occupation and identity. It was astonishing how easy it was to confide in his brother, once he was free to do so, and how understanding his brother was about everything. He supposed he would need to privately thank Clara at some point for how her own work as an operative prepared that ground. Her exposure as a fraud had been a bitter sacrifice to his brother's heart, as he had considered Clara a traitor and a thief rather than an operative at first. But deciding she was worth it, he had pursued her, and therein discovered the truth.

Rumor had it that Hawk had even been involved in some of the interrogations that had taken place at Kirkleigh once their prey had been captured in the trap set up at her coastline, but Griff had not been able to verify that with any reports. And his brother had been so full of questions that first night that Griff had not been able to ask.

He supposed they could have had just such an evening of revelations and questions tonight, but they'd spent a long enough time in company with Milliner and Clara and Minerva that they'd all retired after it ended.

Griff didn't mind that so much. Tonight, he simply wished to wander the house and see the place as he once had. And he couldn't sleep, thinking of the next phase of their mission. Returning to DeRaven better prepared and with plans in place, making as much progress as possible before returning to London, pushing themselves to the closest possible risk of discovery for the sake of what they could find…

All so the return to London would be one of near-constant activity rather than bored societal interaction.

Although he could not completely avoid the societal interaction, more's the pity.

Griff wandered the silent corridors, passing each bedchamber and reminding himself what the interior looked like, as far as he could recall. It was an amusing quirk of the place to have the rooms named after various trees, but there was a definite allusion to the specific tree in the respective rooms, which was elegantly and subtly done. Griff's preferred room when in residence was the Cedar, but he always admired the others for their particular beauty and light as well.

He browsed the gallery, noting the addition of a few more

paintings, no doubt done by the skilled hand of his sister-in-law, though, he was surprised to find, there were no portraits of herself or Hawk among them. He'd have to recommend that to them, even if another artist was brought in to do so.

He did not think Clara would be satisfied with her own attempts at them, given her exactness with landscapes.

Proceeding down the stairs, Griff moved towards the back of the house, the faint sounds of the waves crashing against the shore seeming to draw him out to the terrace. He had donned a dressing gown before beginning his nightly stroll, though it appeared more like a banyan or a greatcoat as it billowed out behind him in the strong breeze from the ocean. The moon was full and bright, barely above the horizon at the moment, but granting him light enough to render any candles unnecessary, just as he had considered them to be inside the house.

He moved to the railing of the terrace, leaning upon it and gazing out at the unsettled sea. There was something impossibly calming and compelling about it, and he had always felt that, even as a young man. He'd often thought about joining the Navy but had never managed to convince his brother to help him obtain a commission. And then he had not needed to do so, once the Foreign Office had recruited him. Several assignments on the Continent and beyond had given him the adventure he had craved and the overseas ventures he had sought.

And yet there was still nothing like being on land and looking out at the sea. Kirkleigh was not his home, but there was something of home within it.

His estate in Suffolk was far enough inland to avoid even a hint of the coastline, but someday, if he had his way, he would sell the place and find another situated near the water.

But that was an almighty if.

"Oh… I did not think anyone else was out here."

Griff glanced to his right, smiling a little as he saw Minerva coming up the terrace stairs from the path. "I've only just arrived. Found myself wandering the place instead of resting peacefully. What are you doing out here?"

Minerva shrugged, coming over to him and tucking a loose strand of hair behind her ear. "Just wandering. Couldn't sleep, and I wanted to walk the coast."

"At this time of night?" He shook his head. "A trifle dangerous, even for a spy, unless you know the terrain. You must be careful."

She smiled a little, and something about that very slight curve pricked at something in the vicinity of his ribs. "I was." She pulled her long, loose plait of hair over her shoulder, absently playing with the ends. "I've little enough experience with the coast that it still feels new. I've been overseas, of course. But I don't know that I've ever just enjoyed the seaside."

"I was just thinking that myself," Griff admitted softly, subtly taking in the full image of his partner just like this. So relaxed, so easy, so delightfully natural with her hair plaited and a thick dressing gown cinched at her waist, so free of the adornments their mission required her to put upon her person. She was lovely in any state, he was coming to learn, but this was his preferred version of her, and he'd have admitted it to anyone.

"There is something magical about it, I think," Minerva said as she matched his pose against the railing. "Even in the moonlight."

"Especially in the moonlight, I'd say," Griff replied, looking up at the night sky before examining the rippling reflection of the moon on the water. "I've explored this coastline dozens of times, but never at night. Somehow, my mother and my uncle always knew when I tried and sent me straight back to bed."

Minerva laughed, the sound low and throaty, igniting four of his right ribs. "Of course they did. Are you tempted to go explore now?"

Griff nodded, fumbling for a laugh himself as he became achingly aware of the woman beside him. "Wildly," he managed.

"Why not go?" she pressed, nudging him.

The contact left him at ease to look at her and answer, in all truthfulness, "I find myself quite at my leisure here just now. Just like this."

Her eyes widened and she looked away, clearing her throat.

Good. He shouldn't be the only one mildly uncomfortable and yet perfectly comfortable.

What a conundrum.

A strong gust of wind rippled across them, and Griff's talisman slipped from the loose neck of his nightshirt, swinging madly against the fabric and clapping almost audibly against his chest. He took hold of it and straightened, tucking it back beneath the shirt before resuming his leaning posture.

"What is that?"

Griff turned slightly to give Minerva a careful look. "What's what?"

She slid her eyes to him, not fooled. "That thing you wear. I've seen it before. Around your neck, your wrist, your ankle… Do you always wear it?"

"Are you studying me, Minerva?" he asked in a suggestive voice, quirking his brows.

"Yes," she admitted bluntly, startling him.

He blinked, all teasing gone. "Really?"

Minerva nodded, the motion of her chin and neck suddenly the most fascinating thing he had ever seen. "I cannot help it. You are my partner, and I am trying to figure you out. Like a puzzle or a word game of sorts. Some assignment I've been given, upon which rests all future assignments. I refuse to believe we've been thrown together like this by sheer coincidence. We are both arguably the best in our fields independently, yet never part of the great duos or teams we know. Surely there is some meaning in that, and something we can learn from each other."

That was undoubtedly true, but it was something rather extraordinary to hear said aloud. And he would admit, there was an inkling of disappointment if her studying of him had been purely for their tasks. He wanted her to be fascinated by him, not as an operative, but as a man. He wanted to be interesting to her. Attractive to her. Compelling.

Worthy.

Something shivered in the center of his spine, and he struggled to swallow, though he had no idea how the two things could possibly be connected.

"And we are playing spouses," Minerva went on, giving him a more direct look that made it impossible to look away. "I need to study you, to know you, to be comfortable with you, not only work beside you."

"Aren't you comfortable with me?" Griff heard himself ask with real concern. "I know I say ridiculous things, but—"

"You do," Minerva overrode with a quick laugh. "But yes, I am comfortable with you. Why do you think I'm here instead of racing inside? I am technically indecent, after all."

Did she really have to say indecent? It would only highlight what he was trying to ignore, and quite frankly…

"I think you are perfectly decent," Griff said without thinking. "I… honestly, I prefer you this way."

To his utmost relief, Minerva smiled widely, her eyes crinkling at the corners. "And I prefer you this way. So it only follows that we are forced to dress in costume constantly, yes?"

Heavens, it would be miraculous if he avoided devouring her with reckless kisses before they returned to the safety of their individual rooms.

"Yes," he all but coughed. "The costumes are our fate."

And so was burning. Dreadful, agonizing, brimstone and hellfire burning.

Ages of it.

"So," Minerva chirped with another nudge that did not make Griff feel any better, "that talisman, or whatever it is. Will you tell me?"

If it would settle the madness at war within him, he'd recite his entire life story for her.

"It's from my very first mission as an operative," he began, his voice rather gruff and low, even for speaking softly in the night. "I was working down in the dockyards, looking for some connections Trace had passed over to us. Confident, or perhaps only arrogant, in my own information and sources, I went to meet a new contact at the docks in the middle of the night, despite the warning to always have backup with these sorts."

He slowly shook his head, the memories flooding back to him as though it had only been the day before. It was the most idiotic thing he had ever done in his entire life, and sometimes, he still had nightmares about the experience.

But that bit he would keep to himself.

He cleared his throat, finding brief consolation in another breeze off the sea that tousled his hair. "Something went wrong. My intelligence was flawed or something, I am still not certain what, and I was shot, once in the arm, once in the chest. I hit the ground rather suddenly, which should not happen, as I am certain you know. Two shots ought to allow us to get a block away at least or find some cover. But my attacker had remarkable aim, and I was shot through a lung and had a bullet tear apart a major vessel in my arm."

Minerva was silent through his telling, but he felt her edge closer to him. There was something comforting in that, and he was no longer overwhelmed by thoughts of her. On the contrary, he was back in the London dockyards, lying there on the ground, yet somehow watching himself lie there as well, and feeling the coldness spread into his limbs.

"Someone found me," Griff said, his voice sounding rather distant to his own ears. "A girl. Somehow, she carried me to a warehouse or something—the memories are hazy. But she tended my wounds. Bound my arm in a tourniquet with this strap." He pulled out the talisman, showing her the leather, his fingers running over the surface of the faded gold button at the end of it. "I was carted off to Suds sometime after. According to him, it saved my arm. She stitched up the wound crudely, but enough to keep the blood loss at a minimum. The bullet from my chest was found on the streets after, so they figured I'd heal well there. Suds had to fish for the one in my arm, though. Kept the strap in place until he was certain it was out, and the stitches would hold. I could still have lost my arm in the aftermath, but I was fortunate."

"May I?" Minerva murmured, reaching for the button.

Griff nodded, leaning in so she could see it.

Her fingers dusted over the surface, looking it over. "A button," she whispered. "I wonder what it meant."

"Who knows?" Griff exhaled shortly, his breath catching short tendrils of hair at her brow and causing them to dance. "I tried to find her afterwards to thank her and to return this. Hatch, she was called. But there was no hint of her on any of the streets, and no one would say a word. So I kept it. A talisman against such stupidity and recklessness. I've never been as close to death since, even when I was in prison in Portugal. It's habit to wear it now. And there is an uneasy feeling about me whenever it's gone."

Minerva released the button and looked up at him, her eyes dark and luminous in the night. "Thank heavens it worked," she said, her voice barely audible above the distant waves. "That she was there."

Griff nodded very slowly, his eyes searching hers, his fingers reaching up to touch her cheek as a tendril of hair escaped from her plait. He tucked it behind her ear, his thumb tracing her jaw gently. "I have thanked God a thousand times for both," he murmured, the friction of his thumb against her skin impossible to resist. "And the button reminds me daily that I owe my life entirely to the deeds of another. And not to waste a single moment."

"No," came the breathless response from the most perfectly parted lips known to man.

Such a moment ought never to be wasted.

Griff applied the slightest amount of pressure to Minerva's jaw, tilting her face up as he leaned in. There was no time to pause, to reflect, to think. There was only what was about to be and how badly he ached for it.

He touched his lips to hers once, shivered at the contact, then pressed against their fullness further, finding no hint of resistance from Minerva. On the contrary, she returned the pressure, her lips parting enough to catch his upper lip between them in the most delicious action he'd ever experienced. There was a slow give and take to the kiss, a perfect, leisurely waltz that had a rawness to its edges and something unrefined in its beauty. It reached for his soul and clutched it tightly in its grasp, wringing everything that made him who he was until he couldn't breathe for wanting more of her. More of this.

More of them.

Griff captured the fullness of Minerva's bottom lip, tugging ever so slightly and smiling against the faint moan he heard from her at it. He kept his hand carefully against her face, his thumb continuing to brush her jaw in encouragement. There was no madness to this kiss, no frenzy like what they had shared in the ballroom when they'd first met, but that had been the Beddingsfords putting on a show.

This was Minerva and Griff, and there was no one to see them.

There was no forcing anything here, no desperation, no pretense.

Nothing had ever felt so real.

Nothing.

Minerva sighed against him, and Griff let the kiss fade on his part, more than willing to continue if she wished, but satisfied if she chose to end it. Her lips fell from his, and her nose brushed against his chin as she leaned against him.

Griff wrapped his arms around her, touching his mouth to her brow, more to keep her from slumping against his chest than anything else. But also, being positioned this way helped him to feel more stable in spite of trembling knees and completely numb toes. His arms could feel her there, and his breath brushed against her hair, reminding him that he was alive, breathing, and well, and that she was not pummeling him to death in outrage.

She was actually holding on to him as well. Loosely. Limply. But holding all the same.

Inhale. Exhale. Inhale. Exhale.

"Do I need to apologize?" Griff asked against the sweet texture of her skin, the focused breathing doing nothing to help steady his lungs.

He felt Minerva exhale, the sensation of her breath at his throat making his fingers splay against her back. "No...?" she replied, belatedly turning the word into a question.

Griff chuckled and kissed her brow. "Fair enough. Are you going to hit me?"

"No," she said again, this time with more firmness. "No, that… I didn't mind." She swallowed and pulled back, meeting his eyes. "At all."

The change in her demeanor made him smile, and he stroked her cheek again. "Good. I didn't mind it either."

Now she smiled, which was a brilliant sight to behold under the circumstances. "I didn't think so." She tilted her head to one side and tugged on the edges of his dressing gown a little. "Better than the ballroom kiss?"

The sole of his right foot caught fire and he leaned in, brushing his nose against hers. "Oh yes," he purred, brushing the rim of her ear now with his thumb. "Far more preferable. Though I'd never argue against a repeat of that one either."

"Of course not." She flicked her hand against his chest sharply, still smiling.

"Ow," he scolded, though there was only pleasure and delight. "You said you weren't going to hit me."

Minerva narrowed her eyes at him. "I changed my mind. I do have that prerogative."

"So long as you don't change your mind about kissing me, I've no objection," Griff assured her with a cheeky grin.

"I don't think that's likely," she muttered without spite, averting her eyes and fidgeting with her hair.

Sensing he was rapidly going to lose this ethereal creature to her more rational counterpart, he took her face in both hands. "Minerva."

Her eyes returned to his face, and he could see hesitation, if not fear, reflected back at him.

He let himself smile in spite of the sharp edge to his own feelings at the moment. "It's fine," he said softly. "You, me, the kiss, standing out here like this… it's all fine. Don't overthink it. No recriminations. It happened, and I'm glad that it happened. Do you know why?"

"Because you've been obsessed with kissing me since I started it that first night?" she suggested glumly.

Griff glanced up at the stars as he laughed once. "Sure, there is that, but no, that is not the primary reason." He looked back at her, his smile not nearly as forced. "Because there was no pretending there. I don't want to pretend with you. Not anymore. Not about anything."

Her eyes seemed to brighten at that, even in the darkness of the night around them. "I don't want to pretend with you either."

"Good," he said simply. He leaned in and gave her a quick, perfunctory kiss, pulling back as soon as it was done to keep things simple.

Even if his lips did buzz and tingle with the desire for more.

Minerva gave him a scolding look, which made him grin. "What?"

"You will not keep doing that, do you hear?" She jabbed a finger into his stomach, making him jump. "Just because I may occasionally be amenable does not give you free rein for such things."

Griff held up his hands in surrender. "Yes, ma'am. Understood. I only thought I would seal the agreement between us. No more pretending."

"A handshake would do just as well," she said primly, holding her hand out in a businesslike fashion.

He took it, shaking firmly. "But not nearly so enjoyable." He brought her hand to his lips, chuckling against the skin as she shivered, despite the disapproving look.

"You are incorrigible," Minerva groaned, trying to tug her hand away.

"You already knew that," he replied as he looped her hand through his arm politely. "Surely you are not surprised." He started towards the house with her, and she came quite willingly.

"I am not, you are quite right." She craned her neck from side to side, a resounding crack coming from one part. "Don't tell Clara I did that. It is so unbecoming for a lady."

Griff snorted once. "But rather refreshing for anyone else. Nicely done. How long has that been brewing there?"

"Since you tossed me in the twist on Thursday. Excellent move."

"Thank you, I was inspired by your interpretation of Ivy's trademark spin."

"Ah, you liked that, did you?"

"Liked it? I dreamed about it for days afterwards!"

"Too far, Griff. Too far."

"What? What's wrong with that?"

Chapter Fifteen

"*I* feel like a bleeding ice queen in this rig."

"Thank heavens you are not a bleeding ice queen, or I would have to answer a great many questions."

Minerva ground her teeth at Griff's unconcerned quip. "Your lack of sympathy is noted."

"And your common tongue is noted. I like it."

She'd have at him, but he was carefully far enough away that she could not easily reach in the tight, restraining cap of her sleeves. It was astonishing how even her narrow shoulders could feel too wide in a gown, but here it was, presented for the entire world. Thankfully, the neckline was such that she did not feel unnecessarily exposed, though it would not take much adjustment to make her feel such.

A triumph for fashions everywhere—one wrong step away from ruinous display.

"Stop scowling, darling, you'll make the people worry." He led her towards the stairs, his chin elevated to the proper height for the Beddingsfords, his ensemble far more sensible than hers, as only the waistcoat matched her gown, and such an article was barely visible for the dark evening jacket and breeches.

Fortunate man. He would have full freedom of movement this evening while she had to be fully prepped beneath her gown for their future endeavors.

She was already perspiring in her extra layers, and the dancing had not even begun.

"Can I have a moment?" Minerva whispered as her breath suddenly caught painfully in her lungs.

Griff looked at her sharply, steering her towards the wall. "What is it? Are you all right?"

Minerva exhaled slowly, flicking open the fan hanging from her wrist and waving it before her face. "I am carrying nearly a full stone in layers and starch, I am convinced of it. Everything feels impossibly heavy, including these paste jewels around my throat. I cannot bend at the waist, I cannot move my arms, and I have an itch in the center of my back."

Griff tsked sympathetically and glanced around. "I cannot do anything about the itch at the moment, but we could remove some of the underlayers without offending anyone. Tilda isn't here, she'd never know."

"She would," Minerva corrected, sagging against the wall and leaning her head back against it. "She has spies everywhere. Possibly every house in Britain. And each layer contains something we might need."

"Are you serious?" He looked down at her skirts intently as though he could see beneath the fabric. "Have they turned you into a pack mule?"

The image made Minerva chuckle in spite of herself. "Hee-haw," she recited obediently.

Griff met her eyes, grinning. "I love your laughter, you know. You should laugh more."

"If I had a reason, perhaps I would." She sighed and made a sputtering sound. "Anna is going to speak with the housekeeper about guests and such, see if we can get additional information about my mark and who he has been spending time with."

"And Tobin is going to sidle up to the mark's valet, so we'll see what he comes up with," Griff recited, though they had gone over the plan for the evening at least three times since their arrival that morning.

There was no time for rest and respite, not when there were only three days left to the event. Whatever they uncovered tonight, Tobin could race up to the Convent for them to give a report or turn items in, or they could simply formulate a plan for London. Having information to act upon was the goal for that, and being able to place shadows on an individual was ideal. They already had enough information on Galveston to do that much, but Minerva wanted more.

She wanted enough to string the traitor up.

She exhaled slowly, wishing her stays and bodice allowed for the sensation to offer actual relaxation. But all it did was remind her that she was due to make a splash shortly, and she needed to use being the center of attention to her advantage however possible.

And then she needed to become invisible, which was something she was rather good at, but to do both in the same event was a challenge.

"Min?"

She opened her eyes and stared at her husband-partner. "Yes?"

Griff gave her a searching look, though there was minimal concern there. That was oddly comforting. "Ready?"

Minerva nodded, grateful he did not ask if she needed to go back or if she wanted him to do the work tonight or any such thing. He was not questioning her abilities or her willingness to do her job. He respected her enough to know better.

It was entirely possible that she had never been fonder of him than at this moment.

She pushed off of the wall and looped her arm through his, the ice blue of her glove matching her gown in an eerily perfect fashion. Tilda made no mistakes when it came to her ensembles, and yet Minerva had no name to give when asked about her gown. Tilda was no modiste, though she could certainly spend her retirement as one, if she wished. For this assignment, should she be asked, Minerva was only to say that her gown came from France and to see what shook out from such a statement.

No one had asked about the chartreuse gown, oddly enough, but tonight, she had a feeling.

Griff kept her close as they moved down to the ballroom, their steps in perfect sync with one another as though they had practiced such a promenade. Their return to DeRaven was praised by many, even those to whom they had only briefly been introduced. Truly, it was an example of Society's idiotic craving for high connections if she had ever seen one.

The dance was already underway, and she and Griff had made

an agreement about never dancing the first with each other if it could be helped. He bowed over her hand, kissing her glove in a polite, perfunctory manner before winking and striding away to get his name on other dance cards or spread his influence in some other way.

Strange how watching him leave gave her a sort of bereft feeling, despite knowing they would be circling one another all night.

Partnership was a strange thing.

Taking a survey of the ballroom as a whole, Minerva began to move at a leisurely pace, fixing her expression into something rather indulgent and open, smiling at each person whose eyes met hers. She had already noted where Mr. Galveston was in the room, but without reason to greet him, she dared not approach directly.

How, then, to proceed?

Her smile deepened as she caught sight of Lady Partlowe moving in the direction of the man and his group, and Minerva moved quickly to intercept her.

"Lady Partlowe!" she called when close enough.

The fair-haired hostess paused in her progress and beamed at Minerva as she approached. "Lady Beddingsford! I had heard you were back. What a delight to have you and your husband here again for our last few days!"

Minerva inclined her head in demure appreciation. "The delight, my dear Lady Partlowe, is in your permitting us to come and go as we please. You are very good to indulge our whims. The disruption to your arrangements cannot be easy to navigate, and for that I must apologize."

"Not at all!" Lady Partlowe gushed, patting Minerva's arm gently. "It is only natural that your husband should wish to see his family's former estate and acquaint himself with the heritage in the county. I am only glad you have made time for our little party in your endeavors."

"How could we not when there is so much pleasure to be had here?" Minerva smiled and covered the hand on her arm. "But you were on your way somewhere. Do not let me impede you further."

"Oh, you may come with me, if you wish," Lady Partlowe insisted with a tilt of her head in the direction she had been moving. "I am only going to greet some guests. Let me acquaint you with them. You will find them truly entertaining, I think."

"Marvelous!" Minerva cried with only partially feigned enthusiasm. "I do adore entertainment."

She could swear she heard Griff snort in amusement at that, but he was across the room engaging in his own diversions at the moment. She'd have to recount all of this for him later. He did love a retelling of humorous words and deeds.

She had little enough of those anecdotes to share from her own adventures.

Lady Partlowe moved easily towards the group, instantly causing a widening of the circle to accommodate her. "Good evening, all," she greeted. "Are you all acquainted with Lady Beddingsford here?"

Minerva stepped forward beside her at the invitation, smiling around the group without lingering upon any one person in particular.

"Lady Beddingsford," the gentlemen greeted almost as one with identical bows. The few ladies in the group curtsied, each of them eyeing her gown with varying degrees of admiration.

"Lady Beddingsford has spent much of her life in the West Indies," Lady Partlowe explained to the rest before giving Minerva a smile. "No doubt you heard of her husband's surprising her in London a fortnight ago."

"Ah, yes," the gentleman next to Mr. Galveston broke in with a wry chuckle, his words perfectly crisp and English. "Quite a display, as I understand it."

Rude little twit.

Minerva ducked her chin, forcing a blush. "Yes, my parents would be quite horrified that I forgot my strict British upbringing in favor of something so very Continental in behavior. They would never have taken me on such trips in Europe and in the Indies had they known I would be so impacted by looser cultures."

"Oh, I would not remonstrate yourself too harshly, Lady Beddingsford," another man interjected. "We like someone to ruffle stiff British feathers now and again. And one does enjoy the occasional devoted couple, do we not?"

Rumbles of agreement rounded the group, but not all expressions bore the same.

"Vous êtes bien trop gentil, monsieur," Minerva murmured with a shy

smile.

His expression did not alter, and he toasted her with the drink in hand.

A few exchanged glances among the ladies told Minerva that some were not quite as fluent in French as might be considered accomplished, but each of the gentlemen were unmoved.

"Your gown is exquisite, my lady," the woman on Galveston's other side praised. "I am quite envious. Wherever did you find such a creation?"

Minerva fussed with her skirts as though self-conscious. *"C'était une boutique chère à Paris. Je n'aurais pas dû me donner tant de mal."*

The woman shook her head at once. *"Au contraire, cela valait bien les fonds."*

A perfectly smooth transition into French without any apology or effort. What a marvelous revelation that was.

"Non," Minerva contradicted sadly, heaving a sigh, *"j'ai peur que ce soit trop. Je ne me fond pas parmi les autres dames anglaises."*

The bait was out there now, hanging before all of them like a carrot before a cart horse. Would any of them comment on not fitting in with the English ladies? Was the hint enough to garner certain conversations she would welcome with open and waiting arms?

"So elegant to speak French so well," one of the other ladies whispered loudly across from her. "She must be the toast of Society there, too."

"Êtes-vous récemment allée à Paris, madame?" the rude gentleman from before asked, his voice a trifle tight.

Minerva shook her head. "Not in an age," she said with a groan of longing. "I simply send my orders to my modiste, and she sends me her gowns wherever I am. But I do so long to return to Paris and to stay a length of time. Perhaps when my husband and I have satisfied our curiosity for the English heritage we share and the lovely society we have found." She offered what she hoped was a flattering smile for the group as a whole and was gratified when it was returned by nearly all.

"Would you favor me with this dance, Lady Beddingsford?" Mr. Galveston suddenly asked, his English passably pristine, but not perfect enough to be natural.

Feigning surprise, Minerva took the proffered hand with a nod. *"Enchanté, monsieur."*

He led her to the floor without another word, and Minerva wondered that he had been so quiet in the group yet should be the one inviting her to dance. The rude one would have been a more obvious choice, but he had made no move to do any such thing.

She'd make a note to inquire about him when she had the chance. Galveston was almost certainly not alone in this, and any of his associates were suspect enough.

"Vous préférez converser en français plutôt qu'en anglais?" Galveston asked as the dance began, taking the few skipping steps towards her.

Minerva circled with him. "Not necessarily," she admitted in a low voice. "It is only the habit I fall into when ill at ease. French is comfortable in a group, as not all will understand me. Less of a risk to bungle things up."

He raised a brow. "I would have thought English your first language."

"It is," she replied as he backed away. "But we spoke several languages at home, depending on where my father would be assigned next. And I found a natural affinity for French, and the English in the Indies is not nearly so refined. I fear I might embarrass myself in higher circles by a poor word choice."

"Yes, the English can be particularly brutal with ridiculous things," he admitted with surprising rancor for someone pretending to be English. *"Je préfère les manières des Français moi-même."*

Minerva gave him a sympathetic smile as she passed him on her way to the man beside him. *"Je comprends."*

He returned her words with a clipped nod, watching her more carefully than the woman currently proceeding in the dance towards him.

Giving her attention to her new temporary partner, Minerva turned with him, laughing politely at his blatant flattery. She glanced beyond him to see Griff watching, toasting her briefly and casting a quick wink of encouragement.

Or perhaps that, too, was flattery.

Either way, it warmed something in her fingertips.

She did not feel like an ice queen now.

She returned to Galveston, her smile remaining in place for him. *"Vivreriez-vous en France si vous le pouviez?"* she ventured to ask as they promenaded in line with the other couples.

"Oui," he replied without any hesitation. *"Je ne serais pas du tout en Angleterre si je n'avais pas à y être."*

Minerva averted her eyes to smile at Griff, more to cover her surprise than anything else, and to avoid giving Galveston any reason to suspect her of something. To announce that he preferred France to England, to wish to live there and imply he was forced to be here…

She had not expected such blatant remarks from him, considering what she knew. Someone who was deeply undercover would not dare be so careless with their opinions, particularly with a stranger. But perhaps he was testing her out for recruitment, or he was new to the field. Perhaps it was the rude gentleman who was the superior, and it was Galveston who did the filtering.

Either way, she was getting into something rather entangled, she could sense it.

"Have I offended you?" Galveston asked in clear English, forcing a laugh into his tone. "I am told not to say shocking things, but I never listen."

Retreating, was he? Well, two could play at that game.

She met his eyes squarely as they returned to their positions in line across from each other. *"Non, monsieur. Mon mari et moi ressentons la même chose que vous."*

She caught the widening of his eyes, the tightening of his jaw, and something almost smug in his expression, clearly taking him slightly by surprise with her agreement to his sentiment. And to throw Griff into the mix as someone of similar views could hardly be taken for granted. A somewhat exotic couple with staunchly British roots who embraced the decidedly less British views of the world would be an important recruitment indeed.

And by the way Galveston was glancing over his shoulder towards Griff, he was certainly interested in making that connection.

Check.

"Perhaps I might convince you and your husband to sit among my friends during supper?" Mr. Galveston asked when they drew close again for the dance. "They are quite amiable, and their discussion will likely be of interest to such widely traveled people as yourselves."

Minerva acknowledged the offer with a nod. "Thank you, Mr. Galveston. I may answer for my husband; he is still rather keen on pleasing me, though I know he will find himself taking great enjoyment in such conversation."

"Excellent," came the simple and very British-sounding reply as he swept her back into a promenading pattern with the rest.

Minerva allowed herself a soft exhale as they moved. The only question now would be if she and Griff escaped for their exploration of the archive room before supper or after. Splitting the evening between both missions was not ideal for either of them, but there were little other options, considering the guests in question and their own host. They must accomplish as much as possible in both assignments before they were left to other fields where information would be more difficult to come by and the avenues for their quarry increased in complication and variety. The containment of a house party was too convenient to pass up.

The remaining conversation of the dance with Galveston was innocent enough, though he did slip into French a time or two. Never with the same sentiment as before or with any particular topic, but it was an interesting habit he was displaying. Whether it was for her benefit or his own cover, she could not say. After all, she had been using French to bait whoever might take it, and it could be that he was doing the same. She was open for a double crossing now, which meant she would need to be even more careful.

If the conversation at supper leaned in a suspicious direction, they would know more. If they were directly approached to do more than dine with the group, they would know more. If they never spoke a word to any of them after supper…

Well, then things would get interesting. The Beddingsfords might not be intriguing enough for them, but they were certainly not going to be ignored.

Though how she would regain lost ground in such a situation was beyond her, apart from belting out *"Suspendez à ces murs"* at the top of her lungs in the center of a ballroom.

She had no great singing voice, but if she pretended at enough wine, perhaps that might be forgiven.

Griff would likely never recover from such a sight, should she stoop to such.

She danced and chatted with several others once Galveston deposited her at the end of their set. She uncovered the identity of the rude gentleman, as well as the French-speaking woman near them, and could honestly say, at this point, she was simply biding her time. She had not seen Griff in some time, no matter how she looked out for him, and she was beginning to wonder if he had gone to the archive room without her.

She would deliver an almighty jab to his gut at the end of the night if he had, though she would not blame him for taking advantage of an opening.

Resent him, certainly, but not blame him.

And if she was trapped speaking with this insufferable woman whose name she had already forgotten for much longer, she was going to create a scene for her own sake that had nothing to do with Lady Beddingsford in the least.

But needs must.

She moved her fan a trifle more quickly, deepening her breathing and making it a trifle more audible. She slid her free hand to her abdomen and widened her eyes, praying the woman would notice the change sooner rather than later. Forced swooning was never altogether pleasant, and she knew that from experience.

It was not the wooziness so much as the landing that was distasteful.

"My lady?" the older woman asked in some alarm. "Are you quite well?"

"I fear…" Minerva faux wheezed, her fan trembling in her hand. "I may need some air…"

"Oh dear," the woman chirped loudly, her hands flapping in her distress. "Lord Beddingsford must be around here somewhere, surely. Can anyone see Lord Beddingsford?"

A few moments later, with the sound of jostling to accompany it, strong arms came to Minerva's elbows. "Darling, not again. I've warned you against excessive dancing when those gems are about your throat. Come now, you'll be right as rain with a walk."

Minerva followed the pressure at her elbows, letting her eyes flutter in a swooning manner, though she was not even remotely light in the head. Griff steered her perfectly through the crowds, half carrying her at times, and assuring everyone that this was common for his wife, and he would remain with her until she could resume dancing.

The rush of cool night air as they reached the terrace was a welcome sensation, even without being desperate for its healing properties. She let Griff settle her on a bench to one side and sighed heavily when he sank beside her, blocking any view of her from those inside.

"Did you have to go completely dead weight?" he asked her with a soft laugh. "It was like maneuvering a statue with a fountain pool attached."

She whacked his knee with her fan in retaliation. "I cannot help the weight of this rig," she protested in a low tone. "And you could easily have picked me up rather than steering me."

"In that gown? I don't think so." He shook his head firmly. "I was not about to risk exposing certain parts of you. Treacherous thing, that neckline."

Minerva gave him a sour look. "Do you have any idea how secure and immovable everything is in the structure of these fashions? Good heavens, Griff, it's like wearing armor."

He folded his arms, his smile going shamelessly crooked. "I'll test the armor theory, if you like. For the sake of being thorough."

"Must you always play the rake?" She kicked her skirts moodily. "Are they ignoring us yet?"

Griff glanced over his shoulder. "Not quite. I said we would walk, so let's go down the stairs. That door will be closer for us anyway."

Minerva nodded and offered a hand for him to pull her up. He did, moving his hand just above her elbow to the exposed skin and letting his fingers rub there gently.

"Just for security," he murmured as he slid behind her, taking loose hold on her skirts for the stairs. "You are supposed to be weak, after all."

If he didn't stop doing that, she was going to be weak, and then where would they be?

Once completely out of view of those in the ballroom, they moved quickly, Minerva hiking her own skirts above her ankles and rushing through the corridors towards the archive room. Griff had told her where it was, but he had been the only one to see it, so he led the way. As promised, the way to the room was completely empty, the servants being occupied with the ball and all other guests remaining in the ballroom or in its vicinity.

They entered the darkened room, and Griff moved to the windows while Minerva shut the door behind them. Griff focused on opening the drapes as wide as possible for maximum light without the need for a candle while Minerva went to work on her gown. The hooks at the front of the bodice were easy enough to undo, and stepping out of the petticoats was a chore, but she managed it, delighted by the freedom of her short chemise and white breeches. She dug into the petticoats for the layers of additional resources, tossing the jacket around her shoulders and unravelling one of the three satchels for whatever documents they found.

Satisfied with her progress, Minerva turned towards the shelves, only to find Griff staring at her in outright bewilderment. "What?" she demanded in a whisper.

He shook his head. "That was the most ridiculous thing I have ever seen."

"You're welcome," she spat. She gestured impatiently to the shelves before them. "Shall we?"

Griff huffed and waved her over. "Come on. Let me show you where to look."

Chapter Sixteen

"This is unbelievable. I mean truly, why would anyone keep these things?"

Griff snorted at Minerva's near-disgusted tone as they rifled through the papers they had pilfered from Lord Partlowe's archive room. "For people like us to find?"

Minerva gave him a despairing look before continuing to sort whatever she was looking through. "I mean it. Surely preserving family history did not mean saving the laundry bills from a military assignment in Bruges."

"If the lad was anything like me," Griff said on a would-be patient exhale, "he saved everything and sent it to Partlowe out of spite, under the guise of being thorough."

"That may be the least surprising thing you have ever said since I've known you," came the immediate and unemotional reply. "Remind me to send Kirklin a bottle of expensive wine as condolences for being responsible for you."

Griff sneered at her, though she was not looking and therefore would not see it.

He was not overly concerned about that. She would know, and that was enough.

They had spent less than half an hour in the archive room, grabbing anything they thought might be related to their search. Minerva's petticoat satchels had proven invaluable as a means of transportation for what had been located, and Griff had admitted his error in judgment upon such a realization. She had related what she had discovered in her evening thus far, and with minimal fuss, they had righted their ensembles and returned to the ball.

There had been much relief at finding Lady Beddingsford so well after such a scare, and several guests had been particularly attentive the rest of the evening.

The desire of so many to pathetically ingratiate themselves to those they felt to be of influence was truly astounding.

Supper had gone well enough, though the conversation that had been promised to be of interest had proven to be only that of hot air by those who were bored of England. That was not to say that there were not individuals of interest, but if Galveston had hoped he would persuade the Beddingsfords to join some cause of the Faction, or anything else, through that experience alone, he was sadly mistaken. But Griff had paid particular attention to those Minerva had noted early, gained their names, and hopefully said enough to pique their interest.

He had not quite managed a dance with the woman, a Miss Pryce, but only because she had been dancing every single dance already. There would be more opportunities to improve their acquaintance in the next few days before the party broke up, especially if she considered herself accomplished in lawn games or archery, but he would not know that until the morning.

They had stumbled upon something with that group, of that he was certain. As was Minerva, though she was not saying nearly as much on the subject as she was about the paperwork they were examining at the present.

How was her mind spinning on the topics of concern for them? Was she even now filtering through the information she had memorized to see what was relevant and what was not? Could she separate his mission from hers while she worked, or were they combining into some greater conspiracy in her more wayward thoughts, as his thoughts were? Was she concerned for the rest of the party, or was she more concerned about London?

Damn it, he wanted to interrogate her as though she were a suspect of some sort, but without the vicious edge one might use under those circumstances. He wanted her to explain how she thought, where she saw things of suspicion and note, how she saw the mission playing out if she had her way. He wanted to know the truth of how she came to her position with the Convent and what her life had been before that. He wanted to know about every one of her previous missions and how close she had come to discovery or death in any of them.

Even the word death made his throat tighten, and he had to look at the flames in the grate to find any sort of focus.

He wanted to unearth everything that made Minerva who she was and have every one of her secrets laid bare. He wanted…

He wanted to tell her everything about himself and his life, his missions, his fears, his thoughts.

He had never wanted to be known by another living soul, but suddenly he wanted that with Minerva.

He desperately needed to get to London, or he was going to be truly believing in this farce of a marriage, and nobody needed that.

"You're distracted," Minerva murmured, her eyes never leaving the papers in her hands. "What's wrong?"

Griff put his pages down and pinched the bridge of his nose. "I couldn't say, honestly. My thoughts are all in a jumble."

That was true, after all.

He was reflecting on the day, he was thinking about London, he was thinking about her…

"What would help?"

He glanced over at Minerva, her features softly illuminated by the fire, her dark hair back in that long plait over a shoulder that he so enjoyed, the furrows in her brow made deeper by the shadows and yet doing nothing to lessen her loveliness.

Why wasn't he an ordinary man who could afford to spend time dwelling on such a woman and such a simple thing as finding himself attracted to her?

"Griff."

"What?" he asked, shaking himself from the thoughts of her.

Her eyes flicked up to his. "What would help?"

He exhaled heavily. "Spot of brandy, change of subject, engaging in pure conjecture…"

Minerva sputtered softly in derision. "I am not finding you brandy at this hour, but I'd be happy to engage in pure conjecture, if it'll stop the words from blurring before my eyes." She set her papers down and adjusted her position so that her knees were bunched up beneath her chin, her nightgown and wrap somehow not the least disturbed by the change.

More's the pity.

"Do you think Martin is really missing?" Minerva asked in a very low voice, as though she was concerned about being overheard.

Griff leaned back on his hands, looking at her intently. "What makes you think he isn't?"

She shrugged. "Missing people have a trail, don't they? They aren't meant to disappear completely, in record and in life. It all seems rather intentional."

"It does, doesn't it?" He'd be lying if he said he hadn't thought the same, but there was nothing to go on with the thought. Someone with an excellent record in the operative ranks and within the Foreign Office was a great loss, and their disappearance an investigation of the highest priority. Usually such an investigation resulted in discovering the person dead or imprisoned, as in the case of Trace, though he had been presumed dead due to the circumstances surrounding his disappearance.

There had been nothing of the sort with Martin.

He had simply vanished.

"We need proof one way or the other," Griff finally said, arching his bare feet towards the fire for warmth. "The Shopkeepers won't want to believe desertion."

Minerva nodded once. "He should be easier to find. Even if he deserted. What did the investigation of his lodgings show?"

"Nothing," Griff told her. "I mean literally nothing. It was a neat and tidy room without any personal touches at all. The clothing left behind was unremarkable in every way and there was nothing to say that that man specifically had been living there. His workspace was immaculate, reports he had been working on left behind as neatly as though he would pick them up the next day. No current missions of the League had been compromised, no intelligence missing."

"Current," Minerva interrupted softly. "What about previous missions?"

Griff gave her a crooked smile, laughing softly to himself. "I asked the same question."

"And?"

He shook his head. "The only thing that could even possibly have been missing, according to them, was a few of the old Hawks Company missions."

Minerva's brow cleared in surprise. "The Hawks? But that's practically ancient now. What use could any of those be to them?"

"Those are the missions that Trace himself admitted to confessing details about when he was imprisoned by the pirates," Griff told her, his fingers drumming against the floor as though in delight, though what he was sharing was certainly not for entertainment.

"That still does not explain what use they would be. Surely they were already proven outdated and complete after he confessed details." Minerva's eyes narrowed and her chin rested on her knees. "Why would they want old missions everybody knows about?"

"They who?" Griff pressed before sighing and craning his neck. "Is it the Faction? Is it some revolutionary group raging against Parliament? Is it some aspiring author who wishes to write an adventure novel based on true events? Until I can prove anything, I have nothing."

Minerva rubbed her eyes, groaning in frustration. "I don't even know who Martin is, but I want to murder him, if someone else hasn't already."

"After I am through questioning him, you may do so with my compliments." Griff smiled at her and raised a brow. "Your turn. Do you think Galveston is in charge?"

She shook her head. "No, I don't. He's an idiot."

Griff barked a laugh and lay back on the floor completely, his hands resting on his chest. "That's quite a statement coming from the woman who married Lord Beddingsford."

"I'm serious!" Minerva protested, looking over at him with a smile. "He has all the subtlety of a bull. It feels planted, which is why I am looking at Chorlton and Miss Pryce. Less clumsy and more intense. I think Galveston might be their more recently arrived French associate, while they are British recruits."

"Makes sense to me." He focused his attention on the ceiling above them as his mind spun on that for a moment. "Galveston would be more likely as one of the faces Sketch can't name, if he is French. We'll have to visit her when we return to London. You couldn't do a quick sketch of him, could you?"

Minerva scoffed rather loudly and chucked a rumpled page at him. "I am capable of sketching, yes, but it would not help identify him from any other man in the world."

"Not very good, then. How disappointing."

That earned him a swift heel to the hip, which made him laugh and attempt to slap it in retaliation, but she'd already resumed her position, her feet safely tucked beneath her nightgown.

"Think they're meeting while they're here?" Griff asked, sobering. "I mean officially. Plotting."

"Potentially," Minerva conceded, though her nose creased in indecision as she admitted it. "Or recruiting. But why would they do so here?"

Griff pushed up to his elbows. "What do you mean? Recruit? Why not? There's such a selection of people."

Minerva shook her head, her mouth twisting. "Any of it here. It is not as though they could possibly recruit the Partlowes. They're as British as the Thames, and there doesn't seem to be anyone specifically powerful in Parliament or Society here. Some respectable fixtures, certainly, but no leaders. Why is this house party worth three of them?"

That got Griff thinking, and he slowly pushed up fully to a seated position, staring into the fire in consideration.

Why would they be at such an event? Griff and Minerva were only here because of them, if he understood the change in their itinerary well enough, unless someone had uncovered the relationship between Partlowe and Martin, which was possible. Even so, Partlowe had told Griff that he had been the only last-moment addition to the group. Everyone else had sent their acceptance days before the event.

What was it about this place?

His eyes widened as a connection was made. "Minerva…"

"What?" she asked sharply, his tone no doubt startling her.

He turned to face her, a strange energy pounding through his limbs. "What if they are looking for the same thing we are? What if there is a connection between Martin and the Faction, and they are looking for the same proof?"

She immediately scrambled from her curled position to sitting on her heels, her jaw tight. "To obtain it for themselves? Or to destroy it?"

"Either," Griff barked, running a hand through his hair. "What if we are all looking for the same thing here?"

Minerva shook her head, gaping at the thought. "We have to check, Griff." She scooted closer and put a hand on his arm, gripping hard. "We have to know. If they are looking for him as well, or information about him, the investigation becomes that much more dangerous and important."

"I know." He swore under his breath and squeezed his eyes shut, thinking quickly. "Do we have anything passing for servants' attire with us?"

"I can make anything work," Minerva assured him, squeezing his arm before rising and moving to the trunk. "It's the middle of the night, the servants won't be in uniform. All we need are simple things, like a cap for me. I've got a bit of prosthetic material somewhere; I think we can give you a false nose and use some ash for scruff. The Partlowe servants don't wear wigs, so you're safe from that."

Griff was nodding as he pushed to his feet, loosely tucking his nightshirt into the back of his trousers. "Unless you think I ought to wear a wig."

Minerva paused, eyeing him quickly. "You know, it would not hurt. But let me just try…" She came over and reached up, threading her fingers through his hair and tugging this way and that, brushing and spreading his thick locks about in a manner that was destined to make him purr shortly.

"There," she said just as he was debating kissing her. "You look quite common."

Well, there went that sensation.

"Thank you?" He snorted and shoved the rolled sleeves of his nightshirt down to his wrists before moving to the fire and dipping his fingers in some of the ash at the edge. He rubbed it along his jaw and under his nose, then in front of his ears to give him the look of additional hair there.

"Nose," Minerva said, placing the cool material into his palm.

Griff turned to the looking glass and put it on, adjusting his features in a few different expressions to test its fit. "Good enough. You?"

"Ready."

He turned to look and smiled a little.

He could see that it was her, but she looked so perfectly common herself, by virtue of her own appearance and the haggard expression she wore, that no one would mistake her for Lady Beddingsford.

"Aye, so y'are," he offered in a harsh brogue. "Shall we?"

"Yessir, I heard a noise," she informed him in the most perfectly common northern accent he'd ever heard.

Griff cleared his throat. "Bes' check tha oot, then." He opened the door and glanced out, examining the corridors for any actual servants or other guests that might be up and about.

Thankfully, there were none, and he waved Minerva out. On a whim, he took her hand in his as they moved towards the nearest servants' stairs, and she did not pull away or stiffen at the contact.

There was something to be said for that.

But he had to focus on the mission now, especially with this sudden change and potential threat. His pulse seemed to accompany every step he took with a pounding in his ears and feet, each breath seeming to burn in his chest.

This was the sort of energy he was used to on his missions, this heightened alertness and rapid observation of every detail about him. This was where his training and experience came back to him with pure instinct, reminding him of innate risks without giving him doubts or questions. He was acutely aware of the sounds they made in their movement, that of the branches of trees tapping against the windows nearby, the very texture of the wooden steps beneath his feet. The smallest details could prove important; even those that seemed innocuous.

Though no one had ever asked him about the texture he walked upon.

He could not be selective in what he noted, not in this state. He simply existed in it.

The entire house was almost silent as they came out onto the proper level, their steps even more cautious and swift. They would come to the corridor of the archive room at the next corner, and there was no telling what they would find.

Griff brought Minerva's hand to his lips and kissed the back quickly before letting their hands fall away from one another.

Their characters needed to come to life now, regardless of what they found ahead of them.

"I can hear something, William," Minerva announced in a loud whisper, her northern accent ringing out. "The master won't be pleased with disruptions."

"The master won't be pleased with false alarms either," Griff replied in his brogue, matching her tone. It would be audible enough for those wishing to be quiet and on the alert for sound but would not disturb the rest of the house or anyone else in the vicinity.

It was a smart move on Minerva's part to start speaking before they got there. If there was no one in the area, it would do no harm. If there was anyone trying to avoid detection…

"It's coming from this direction," Minerva said in the same tone, pointing towards the archive room.

"If ye say so," Griff replied, giving her a questioning look.

He wasn't hearing anything yet, but if she was…

She gave him a brief nod as they rounded the corner, the door to the archive room slightly ajar almost directly ahead of them.

There was no light from within, but it was open.

That was enough.

Then he caught a faint rustling sound, and felt a smile cross his face. There was someone in there, which meant the potential for a fight was rising. He hadn't engaged in a real fight in ages; it would be a thrill to take on the intruder himself. And if Minerva was feeling herself inclined to the same, they could do a great deal of damage.

"Perhaps it was nothing after all," Minerva suddenly said in her loud whisper, startling Griff.

He paused his step, staring at her wildly and mouthing, "What?"

She lowered her hands in a calming gesture and mouthed back, "Trust me."

He'd never wanted to do anything less in his life.

She knew as much, and her look became scolding. "I am sorry to have disturbed you, William. I'll just see to the windows; one of them has likely been left open. Good night."

Griff gritted his teeth, heat rising from his chest and directly into his face. "Good night," he managed, not having to feign any sort of impatience.

Minerva waved him further against the far wall, but encouraged him to keep walking, as she was. Doing so kept him in shadow while she would be more visible for whomever was within the room. They couldn't leave without being seen now, and they would know that. But what good would only believing there was one servant approaching do? It was only going to risk Minerva more, and that was something Griff was not at all comfortable with, even if she could manage the most threatening situations alone.

She adamantly refused to look at him again as they walked, and he noted that she was no longer making an effort to muffle her steps. She wasn't exactly stomping or making her presence known, but simply ambling down the corridor as she might have done on any given Thursday for tea.

What exactly she had planned, Griff could not have said, but he did not like it, and he continued to muffle his tread on the off chance that was what she wanted.

They reached the door to the room, Griff losing his ability to see within by being in the shadows, but Minerva had full access, and started inside, only to stop at once.

Griff heard a pistol cock and instantly went numb.

"What are you doing down here at this hour?" a male voice hissed.

"I h-heard a noise and thought…" Minerva stammered, though she gave no other sign she was distressed.

Griff moved ever so slightly to try and see into the room and could only glimpse the tip of the gun at Minerva's brow.

Her left hand twitched behind her back and his eyes darted to it.

One, she signaled. Then she held her hand out in a halting motion.

Stop? Wait? Whatever that was for, Griff wasn't about to let his partner get shot in the head. His stomach clenched at the thought and suddenly he couldn't swallow.

"Who are you?" the voice in the room demanded.

"Myra," Minerva recited. "I'm L-Lady Partlowe's maid."

The voice seemed to laugh. "You aren't going to tell anyone about this, are you, Myra?"

"No, sir," she said at once. "Are you stealing from my master?"

"That is my business, not yours. Do you know any of the guests at the party?"

Minerva whimpered, and Griff wanted to die at hearing it. "No. I've been upstairs tending to my mistress and her gowns. I don't know anyone, sir!"

"Shut up!"

"Please don't kill me!" she begged, throwing a catch into her voice that nearly took Griff out at the knees.

He needed to get in there, drive her aside, and tackle whatever blackguard had a gun to her head. He needed to throttle the man, needed to...

Again, Minerva held out a hand, reading his mind without even looking at him. She had some sort of plan in place, and he trusted her enough not to disrupt, but the rising bile he was tasting and the rampant unsteadiness of his pulse were also reminding him that he could not take much more of seeing her in danger.

Griff was going to kill her himself shortly, of that he was quite certain.

After he kissed the ever-loving life out of her.

"I don't want to," the voice hissed. "I don't want to leave a mess that would have to be explained, nor do I want any sort of disruption to the party. So you are simply going to clean up the mess I've made, and forget any of this happened, aren't you, Myra?"

Minerva nodded emphatically. "Yes, sir."

"Good. Take two steps forward so I can get by."

She did so, and Griff flattened himself into the shadows. He wasn't going to take out the man as he walked by. That would be too disruptive to whatever the aims were. He only needed to see who it was and let him believe he was getting away without identification.

That had been Minerva's plan, or at least part of it. He could see the wisdom in it, but he still wanted to throttle her.

The pistol's cocking mechanism was released. "Good girl, Myra. See that you do. I will know if you don't." He moved behind her and exited the room, marching by Griff's hiding place without a second glance.

Griff, however, had quite a good look at him.

Chorlton.

Several rather dark German curses sprang to Griff's mind while he waited for enough time to pass so he could join Minerva in the room. When there were no more footsteps and the house was silent again but for Minerva's cleaning up the mess, he moved within.

He waited against the wall a long moment, watching her move from mess to mess, tidying as though it truly were her task, the linen cap on her head looking as unruffled as anything in the world. One would never know that the woman had just borne a pistol to her head.

Why wasn't she shaking? Why wasn't she afraid? Damn it, why was he afraid? The danger was over, and nothing had taken place. He had seen far worse things happen to colleagues and associates, far worse threats, and not been so upended by it. He had lost people he had known for years in the course of missions and assignments, and never had he known such all-consuming terror and sickness by such things. By even the prospect of them.

Minerva looked at him then, knowing exactly where he was, and cocked a brow. "Are you going to help?" she whispered.

Griff swallowed and pushed off the wall, heading directly for her rather than to any of the messes. Her eyes widened as he approached, and he saw her defenses rise as though by drawbridge.

He didn't care. He wrapped his arms around her and hauled her into his chest, gripping her hair beneath the stupid linen cap and holding her as tightly as he dared. She stiffened in his hold, then slowly wrapped her arms around his waist.

"Griff?" she asked softly, seeming truly curious over his reaction.

"Bloody hell, Minerva," he breathed in a rough, raw voice, one hand moving to her face and tilting it back just enough for him to kiss her hard. Then again softly. Then he simply rested his lips against hers. "Bloody hell."

Her arms tightened around him. "It's all right," she whispered, her hands moving in soothing motions on his back. "I'm fine. It's fine."

"No, it is bloody not," Griff insisted, pressing his lips to her brow and forcing himself to breathe slowly in his fight for calm. "I'd kill you myself if I weren't so relieved at the moment. And if I could feel my legs."

"I didn't mean to…" Minerva cleared her throat and tilted her face up, resting her chin against his chest. "I'm an operative, Griff. I know what I am doing."

"I know that," he whispered. He put a hand alongside her cheek and smoothed a tendril of hair back with his thumb. "That is the only reason I didn't barrel in here and kill him. But it didn't stop me from being so bloody terrified, I thought I was going to be sick." He swallowed hard, the memory tightening his throat. "Did you know that was going to happen?"

Minerva smiled a little, her hands still moving in slow lines along his back. "I had an inkling. I knew at once that one intruder against two servants wouldn't be ideal for him, and he might choose the window for his escape, and we would never know for certain who it was. But one female servant? He could threaten her, and you could identify him secretly. Did you?"

Griff nodded, his eyes tracing every single aspect of her face for sheer memorization. "Chorlton."

"I knew it," she hissed in victory. She buried her face against his chest with a heavy exhale that he felt through to his spine. "He was masking his voice, too, so I could not be sure. Tomorrow, you'll have to be beside me when we see him again so he suspects nothing. We'll greet him warmly and invite him to partner with us for bowls or something."

"Minerva," Griff broke in, his voice dipping low.

She looked up at him again. "What?"

He smiled very tightly. "Could you kindly refrain from discussing what we must do tomorrow to cover for this at the moment? I'm still fighting the impulse to go upstairs and toss the man from a very high window, so the idea of being his chum in the morning is more than I can tolerate."

Minerva looked a trifle surprised. "All right… Shall we tidy up, then?"

Griff shook his head. "Not yet. I need to hold my wife a little longer and absorb her calming influence."

She snorted and laid her cheek against his chest. "Partner," she corrected.

"Whatever," he replied, curling his arms more securely around her. "Whoever she is, I feel better with her in my arms. Give me a minute. Perhaps ten."

"I'll give you five," she murmured, snuggling against him.

"I'll take it."

Chapter Seventeen

$\mathcal{G}$riffin was being unreasonable, and it seemed he did not care. No matter what Minerva said or did, no matter how she protested, he was almost literally at her side every waking moment. He hadn't left her for a moment during the remainder of the house party, playing to the rumor that Lord Beddingsford was ridiculously attached to his wife, and he had not slept a wink on the trip back to London, despite the fact that there was no one else with them.

At this rate, she would have to retire from being an operative because she came attached to her very own nanny.

It was utterly maddening.

And, she would admit, a trifle adorable.

But only a trifle.

He refused to admit that it was because of what had happened with Chorlton, but it was the only explanation for his sudden attention. The house party had finished off without a hitch and there had been no sign of recognition from him where Minerva was concerned. Anna had related no strange messages or gossip from the servants downstairs, and Tobin had no insight from the man's valet. But Griff had refused to breathe easily, and had resolutely kept watch at Minerva's side, engaging in the same silliness others had witnessed Beddingsford take up throughout his time in London.

In a way, it was a clever protection for themselves, but surely even the devoted and excitable Lady Beddingsford would have found this tiresome by now.

London was more dangerous than any house party in Kent, Minerva was certain of it, but London was where they were both destined to be more comfortable. Surely he could not continue to keep watch over her at every moment here.

"Ah, there you are," the man in question suddenly called as Minerva yawned upon reaching the ground floor.

She was not quite sure where his voice was coming from, but replied, "Here I am."

Griff appeared from the nearest drawing room, smiling easily. "Sleep well?"

Minerva gave him a puzzled look. "What are you up to?"

"Why should I be up to something?" Griff asked, folding his arms and giving her what he likely thought was a dubious look.

It fell far short of the mark.

Minerva matched his pose. "Because it's you, and I know you. Explain, please."

He flashed a crooked grin, but at Minerva's stern look, he settled into something slightly more sheepish. "All right, fine. I've asked Sketch and Sphinx call upon us to discuss what we've found and their insights for us moving forward."

"All right…" Minerva said slowly, not entirely grasping why that should be such a fuss and render him suspiciously pleasant.

She ran through the words in her mind again, combined it with his behavior, and slowly let her expression morph into one of disbelief. "You've asked them now, haven't you?"

"Technically, I asked them last night," Griff admitted with a shrug. "That way they could be here early this morning."

"Rather than us venturing to their house in the very dangerous and secluded part of London known as Mayfair," Minerva drawled sarcastically, her folded arms tightening against her body. "Such trouble there, one might be approached by a gentleman or a lady, of all things. Hardly worth the risk, you are quite right."

"Minerva—"

"No, no," she overrode with more spite than she probably ought to have expressed. "I don't know what I would do without you thinking for me and keeping me so protected that I needn't ever leave the house again. What a gallant knight to exert yourself so for a weak and simple damsel like myself. Will you bring my marks to the house as well, so I might investigate them here? Or are you intending to take that over as well? You clearly know best, so I'll defer any decisions to you. Let me just send a note to Milliner so she might add you to the roster of Convent agents. Draper won't mind you being part of two departments, will he?"

Griff had slid his hands to his hips and remained silent throughout her rant, his expression shifting to a resigned impatience as she spoke. When she did not continue, he asked, "Are you finished?"

Minerva sniffed once. "That all depends."

"On what?"

"If you are also finished." She tilted her head in a distinctly impertinent manner, daring him to answer.

She saw the flash of anger cross his features and felt her hackles rise, complete with gooseflesh raising on the back of her neck.

But then his shoulders moved on a hefty exhale, a muscle in his jaw ticked, and he nodded once. "Fine. I don't like it, but fine."

"You don't have to like it," Minerva pointed out, letting the ire of her argument fade. "You only have to remember that I am an operative, as well trained as you are, and I don't need saving or protecting."

"To a point," Griff corrected, holding up a finger. "You are still my partner, and partners protect each other."

Minerva allowed that. She craned her head from side to side. "Yes, but we are not nannies or captors. Protect, not restrict."

He did not care for that, she could see clearly enough. But she refused to allow him to keep her from doing her job, which was one of risk and danger. It always had been. Just because he had witnessed the risk and danger she was willing to put herself in and had felt the fear of it did not mean he could act in a manner that would soothe that fear while constricting her freedom.

She dared not reflect on the reasoning for his fear, nor the depth of it. Doing so wouldn't help either of them. It was simply part of the process in working with a partner, which they both needed to completely adjust to.

Griff's eyes were fixed on her face, darting from feature to feature with the same intensity, his thoughts less obvious than they had been previously.

Minerva couldn't say anything, did not say anything. She was not going to pretend to understand what he experienced while watching her helplessly that night. She had made the decisions then, and he'd respected her enough to abide by them, but she'd known full well he had not liked that either. It was what she'd had to do for the mission, and it had worked out perfectly, but no partner enjoyed being forced to witness without acting.

What he was doing in response, however, was a complete overreaction, and it was keeping both of them from fulfilling their assignments.

He needed to understand and accept that. Just as Minerva needed to understand and accept his need to avoid returning to a similar situation as the one she had placed him in.

She would do her best, if he would give her the freedom to do so.

"So long as you never have a gun pointed at your head in my presence again," Griff finally said in a clipped tone, "or if you do, that I may intervene, then I concede."

Minerva tsked slightly. "I cannot promise that, given our occupation. But I do promise to try."

Griff pressed his tongue to the front of his teeth, inhaling slowly and exhaling the same. "Accepted. Now, can we go speak with Sketch and Sphinx? Or would you rather they continue to hear every word to our argument?"

"I am quite certain they are perfectly familiar with the arguments of partners being forced to portray a married couple and the particular struggles of such an arrangement," Minerva grumbled as she started past him for the drawing room from which he had originally come.

"Yes, I am sure we will all have marvelous stories to share when all of this is over," Griff quipped dryly as he followed her.

Of that, Minerva had no doubt. She had sat with Hal, code named Sketch, upon her return from Paris, and she had been shocked to hear that the operatives, who could not have been more different, had chosen to remain married in actuality. Somehow, amid the stresses and strife of the mission, they had found love and affection beyond the partnership.

Minerva knew full well how unusual that was, especially for a woman like Hal, who had been perfectly content in her life as a spinster, working as an asset for all of the operative departments. And for Sphinx, arguably the most reserved man Minerva had ever met, to find the fiery and independent Hal his perfect match…

It was a story that no one would believe, if they had not actually seen the pair of them together and heard the story from their own mouths. But the stories of the mission itself, apart from the apparent romance, had not been in Hal's descriptions at that time out of necessity and security.

Now Minerva would be able to hear just about anything she wanted from the pair of them.

And as they were now sitting in Minerva and Griff's house, not their own, it would be up to them to decide when they'd had enough and take their leave. She could question them to her heart's desire, and their tolerance would be the only ending factor.

It was rare that she got to question a fellow operative about a mission, but she had always wanted to do so.

Come to think of it, she and Griff had not yet sat down and discussed one another's previous missions. They had permission to do so, although she thought there was a caveat of relatability to present assignments. But if she knew Griff, and she was fairly certain she did, he would go far beyond the relatability factor and start sharing details of whatever mission he wished to.

And that was a conversation she wanted to have. Someday.

She entered the drawing room and grinned at the two operatives within, curtsying a little in greeting. "Are we formally greeting the Pratts as the Beddingsfords? Or are we being more casual than that?"

To her surprise, it was Sphinx who chortled. "The formality is for the public, Mirrors. We greeted poor Pick like he was a grand vizier or something, just to keep up appearances. I'd much rather keep this as relaxed as possible."

Hal smiled and linked her fingers through her husband's. "How many times have you heard him say that?"

"Never," Griff answered firmly. "Not even once."

Sphinx only shrugged, not even remotely embarrassed. "Despite evidence to the contrary, men can change. Apparently."

"Thank heavens," Hal added, fluttering her lashes in a would-be-sweet manner.

"That's enough out of you," Sphinx scolded. He smiled at her with a peculiar look that made something in Minerva's stomach tighten and her cheeks heat, and she caught the change in grip of their hands, some brief increase in pressure there.

Hal winked at him, and Minerva looked away, feeling she was intruding on some private, adoring moment between this couple.

Griff was looking at her, his smile tight but understanding.

Was he also looking away from them? Was he noting the same thing she was?

It was a strange moment of unity between them in the presence of their friends and colleagues. Something rather bolstering and, she would admit, a little wistful.

Odd, that.

"So," Hal said in a louder, clearer voice, shifting on the sofa. "What can we help you with?"

Minerva almost sighed with the blessed relief of moving on. "Are you both aware of our missions?"

Sphinx nodded, flicking his fingers in Griff's direction. "Mist gave us a quick overview before you came down. You are looking for some of the Faction sympathizers or associates based on the information we uncovered in Paris, if not some of the actual people we encountered. Mist is looking for the missing London League clerk."

It did not seem fair that her mission took longer to explain than Griff's, but she supposed that wasn't something that could be helped.

Minerva nodded quickly. "Yes. During the house party we attended, we found a copy of the song hidden in the lid of a guest's trunk, along with other materials that were less easily understood. We did not worry so much about those documents as we did about identifying his associates. His alias is Mr. Galveston, and the more we got to know him, the more certain we became that he is French and that he is not the main player of his group."

"Can you describe him to me?" Hal asked, taking up a piece of paper and a pencil and then settling her silver spectacles upon her nose. "Let us see if we know him already."

Minerva suspected this would be coming and had begun cataloguing the features of the man in her mind. She ran through each of them, hoping the descriptions she gave would be enough for Hal to draw the man accurately. She was insanely talented when it came to artwork, and sketching suspects in various missions or assignments was the task she engaged in more often than not. If anyone could accomplish such a thing in England, it was Hal.

"Well, well," Hal murmured as she finished, looking at the sketch as a whole. "I do believe we have now seen Monsieur Degarmo on British soil."

Sphinx looked at the drawing, then nodded as well. "So it would seem." He returned his attention to Minerva. "Who else was acting with him?"

"No one else who struck me as French," Minerva told them both, smiling in gratitude at the maid who entered with a tea tray. "But there were two British associates who seemed to work closely with him, and quite possibly were his superiors in the matter. A Mr. Chorlton and a Miss Pryce."

Hal took up another sheet of paper and nodded at her, so Minerva began with her descriptions of both, first Mr. Chorlton, then Miss Pryce. The drawings could be copied and then circulated among operatives in varying assignments at all levels of Society. They knew more than anyone that an agent or spy could be in finery one day and sweeping chimneys the next without batting an eyelash. It would be important to give their likenesses to the other operatives in the field as quickly as possible, if for no other reason than to put them on alert.

One could only hope that their likenesses were recognized by someone from previous assignments and missions so as to flesh out their roles and dangers.

"I've never seen either," Hal said as she finished, looking between the two with a furrowed brow. "But that only means that I have never actually laid eyes on them or that I have never drawn them. And I can assure you that not all operatives have me draw their marks."

No, that was true enough and Minerva knew it, but enough did that it was unlikely Chorlton and Pryce were known in the ranks.

Which was both a positive and a negative. Positive because it meant Minerva had uncovered valuable new information that could help untold numbers of operatives and citizens. Negative in that it meant there was no additional information to be handed over on them, and no insights that Minerva and Griff could use further in their work.

Mixed emotions were to be the order of the day, it seemed.

"I'll get their information circulated through the ranks," Sphinx told them. "How certain are you of their names?"

Minerva had to shrug. "As certain as I can be with introductions at a house party. They could be aliases, as is the name by which they know me."

Sphinx nodded at that. "True enough. It's as good as we are likely to get. I'll send word if there is anything you need to know. If nothing else, we can establish a watch on them."

"That would help a great deal," Minerva said, glancing at Griff, who was nodding in agreement. "We'll likely see them again in upcoming social settings, and they did seem to like us."

Griff shrugged. "I was more concerned that Chorlton would recognize Mirrors from the archive room incident than in ingratiating myself to him."

Hal's eyes narrowed. "Tell me about that."

"What?" Griff asked. "His recognizing her?"

"No," came the brisk reply. "The archive room."

Griff leaned back and turned his attention to Minerva, the tension in his face evident. "Why don't you tell our friends, dear?"

He was never going to fully forgive her for that, she suddenly realized. He was never going to let go of the memory of his fear, nor feel anything other than disgruntlement from the event. It was the most intense reaction she'd ever had from mission-related actions, including ones where she had been reprimanded by superiors, and she was not entirely certain how to cope.

Her throat suddenly dry, Minerva nodded and focused on their guests, quickly relating what had happened with full and honest truth. If there was any doubt it was the truth, one only had to observe Griff's shift in posture and how tightly his arms were folded against his chest. Smoke would have come from his ears if there had been enough friction among his thoughts.

And if Minerva needed to feel any worse, she caught a faint hiss from Sphinx when she said she had signaled for Griff to stay back even with a pistol to her head.

Thankfully, Hal had no reaction to the sequence of events.

"And that is really it," Minerva finished lamely. "He didn't seem to recognize me later or throughout the party, which is what I assumed would happen. No one ever does." She shrugged a shoulder and looked down at the tips of her fingers, trying not to look too embarrassed or ashamed.

"I have heard Gent say the very same thing more times than I can count," Hal said with a laugh, lightening the mood notably. "You are blessed with remarkably fluid features, my dear, there is no question about that."

Sphinx cleared his throat. "But not, I think, particularly comfortable for those of us without fluid features that confuse a mind. No one likes a partner to take solo risks."

Hal put a hand on his knee, her face tightening slightly. "Sometimes they are necessary. Working as a team is difficult, we all know this."

Nods bobbed around the group, and only then did Griff seem to relax.

But only marginally.

"So we know that Chorlton is not to be trusted and is dangerous," Sphinx summarized with a brisk clearing of his throat. "Do you know what he might have been looking for in the archive room?"

Griff sat forward at this and bent over the side of his chair to retrieve something. "As it happens, we have a fair idea, based on what sort of a mess he made, but we cannot be certain he did not search for other things as well. Or even take them." He set the pages of information they found on the table between them, just beside the tea tray. "This is the information we gathered on our own visit to the archive room, all relating to the missing clerk from the London League, Charles Martin."

Hal looked at all of the papers with wide eyes. "All of this on a man that the best operatives in England could not get a whiff of? Are you sure?"

"As sure as I can be." Griff started to spread the papers out, looking them over himself. "The Partlowe family has a long and healthy tradition of keeping any and all family documents. Cousins send such things to Lord Partlowe so he can keep them with the rest of it. I had a quick look, and there are documents and relics from the seventeenth century in there. If I had more time, I could likely find things even older."

Sphinx whistled low and began to look through the pages. "What a daunting task to inherit with the title. How much useless information is in there?"

"How much useless information is in here, I wonder?" Minerva mused with a quick gesture to the pages. "It is more than we have had yet to consider with this man, I grant you that, but what use is any of it really?"

"Well, this document is a forgery, for one thing."

The room went utterly silent as all eyes turned to Hal, holding one of the records in hand.

She said nothing else immediately and only continued to look it over, her eyes darting to various points on the page behind her spectacles.

Griff looked at Sphinx and then Minerva, but she refused to take her eyes from her colleague and friend.

"A forgery?" Minerva repeated.

"Mm-hmm." Hal nodded firmly, a slight smile at her lips. "A good one, I'll grant them that. But I can see it."

"How?" Griff demanded, his tone a trifle hard. "I've been staring at those pages for days and found nothing suspicious."

Sphinx made a calming gesture with his hand. "This isn't a slight on you, Mist. She has an exacting memory for things she has seen, and we've begun to use that skill of hers as often as we use her drawing. She knows what she is looking at."

Griff held up his hands in surrender. "I am not saying she doesn't. I simply want to understand how I missed it."

Minerva heard the stung note in his voice and knew that his pride had been tweaked by having such a thing pointed out within moments of viewing the paper, whatever it was. Griff was a dedicated operative and took great pride in being so. He spared no efforts to accomplish his assigned tasks and went to extraordinary lengths to ensure success. The very notion that he missed something that could move his mission along would truly bother him, and he would likely spend hours reviewing every detail after this so he would never make the same mistake again.

But there was no mistake made here, only a different skillset.

One that Griff would now attempt to attain for himself, if possible.

"I've seen dozens of military records," Hal informed them as she finally raised her eyes to them all. "All sorts of forms. This one, the discharge report? The formatting is wrong, and the order of personal details is incorrect. There should not be any mention of the pension in the discharge report, as the pension information is handled by a different department entirely and has its own reports. So we must assume that the accounts of his accomplishments and battles are incorrect."

"He got his assignment in the Foreign Office based on that," Griff murmured, eyes wide. "He had been supported through schooling by the Foreign Office to become an operative, but they wanted him to pursue military action beforehand. You are telling me that this is not his report?"

Hal shook her head. "It is not. I can say with absolute certainty that whatever Mr. Martin did in the military, this is not it."

Griff sat back in shock, then rifled through the papers on the table. "Then what about his enlistment report?" He found the paper and handed it to Hal, his eyes intent.

Minerva would have taken his hand to attempt to calm or support him, but their chairs were separated, and they were not actually a married couple, unlike the Pratts.

So all she could do was wait in silence and occasionally look at her partner.

Hal slowly shook her head. "This is legitimate. We can certainly say that Mr. Martin did enlist in the military and was first sent to join the regiment at Maidstone. But we can safely say that these are not his discharge papers."

Griff looked between the two documents, then at Minerva. "What the devil is going on here?"

Chapter Eighteen

"Griff! They're here!"

A sigh of relief had never felt so sweet, and Griff pushed himself out of the chair behind his desk, where he had been analyzing every document on Charles Martin he had in his possession. He could recite any detail about the man's life and roles that anyone could ask for.

The problem was that he had no idea what was truth and what was fiction.

Which meant, in all actuality, that he knew nothing.

Absolutely nothing.

He hated knowing nothing. It was worse than the beginning of any mission, where he always knew enough to have a direction of aims, at least. But when all of his groundwork and research prior to this mission beginning turned out to be untrustworthy, he felt like a schoolboy taking an exam for which he had not studied, and worse yet, had not even heard of the subject material.

With insight from Sphinx and Sketch, and a healthy dose of input from Minerva, he had proceeded with requesting all records related to Martin from the headquarters of his former regiment in Maidstone. If there were any. And he had gone a step further and requested every school note and report from Eton and Oxford that they had, whereas before the mission, he had only asked for confirmation of his attendance.

But if the calls of his wife were any indication, there were, indeed, records to be had, and now they had them.

He could not wait to see what these uncovered.

He hurried to the parlor where they had met Sphinx and Sketch the other day, which had no front-facing windows, and found Minerva already spreading the papers on the floor. He joined her, taking up her arrangement of Eton and Oxford to one side and military on the other.

"I'll take schooling," Minerva said, shoving the military ones towards him. "You take the regiment."

He nodded, his eyes scanning each paper quickly. There were not likely to be any forgeries in the documents presented directly from the regiment, but they would have Sketch look at any promising ones before they acted upon them. It was the only way to proceed now, given the history of it all.

The room was quiet between them for a while, only the sounds of rustling pages and faint breathing audible. Every now and then, one of them would inhale with a bit more force, but there was never any expression of the details they were looking at, just a strange rise and fall of energy without a single word or look being exchanged between them.

There was something rather uniting in the near-silent experience, oddly enough.

Griff put down an after-action report and pinched the bridge of his nose, exhaling slowly. "Anything on your end?"

"Not unless you wish to know his measurements for the Eton uniform or his marks in his Oxford exams," came Minerva's dry response. She shook her head and met his eyes. "I see the trend in his studies that attracted the Shopkeepers, which makes me wonder who their asset in the education ranks is, but beyond that, he is the most unremarkable student. No demerits at all. Never became head boy, but he was made a prefect." She shrugged, looking somewhat lost.

"Well, I never made head boy either, so…" Griff grinned at her, hoping to lighten the mood.

She raised a brow. "Tell me something surprising." She looked at the papers again, twisting her lips. "What about your documents?"

He shook his head, sobering. "After-action reports from drills and a few skirmishes, but so far, nothing of note." He cocked his head looking over the next report. "This is mildly interesting. He was injured in a skirmish in September of nineteen. He joined the Foreign Office in eighteen twenty, but there was no mention of a fault to his gait or his bearing."

"Perhaps it was not significant, then?" Minerva asked, leaning back on her hands and crossing her ankles. "Most likely they have to report any injury to save from lawsuits or some such."

"Perhaps," Griff murmured as he continued to read the lines. "But this seems to be a marked injury. A surgeon was called for." He looked behind the pages for any continuation of the report or documentation of surgical care. The next sheet had him nodding with satisfaction. "Yes, surgery was performed, and he was transferred to Aylesford for recovery."

Minerva's right foot danced up and down as it was propped over her left, and he glanced at the distraction, then at her face. Her brow was creased in thought, her mouth still twisting to one side. "Aylesford? That's not exactly known for its recuperative settlements, is it? Surely the doctors would have kept him in Maidstone for recovery, so his commanding officers might be better informed of his progress."

Griff considered that, returning his attention to the pages. "Yes, you're quite right. Why Aylesford? It is four miles away, but there does not seem to be anything significant about it. Strangely, it seems that he disappeared some days later. Simply vanished from his cot."

"What?" Minerva sat up sharply, her eyes going wide. "Disappeared? How did they lose a patient?"

"I don't know," Griff replied somewhat distractedly, continuing to read through the files. "Apparently, a search was performed, and it was deemed that he had deserted."

Minerva snatched the papers from him, looking over them herself. "The Charles Martin I've been reading about would not have deserted. Particularly if he was injured as badly as they said. Did he ever return to his regiment?"

Griff rifled through the remaining pages, his eyes darting across words for the particular ones he sought. "No, not that I can tell. And yet, in here, it says that they received notation of his discharge with the proper paperwork in London."

"And they accepted that?" Minerva cried. "How could he be discharged from his regiment if his regiment did not sign the paperwork? And after being labeled a deserter?"

"Seems the authority was incontrovertible." Griff sputtered and pushed to his feet. "I'm going to get the other papers and see what they say. At the moment, I'm not certain of anything."

"Nor I," Minerva admitted, leaning over to look through the military papers.

It was only a few minutes before he returned, and Minerva was exactly as he had left her, rather reminding him of a small girl engrossed in a book on the floor of a large library, oblivious to the rest of the world and perfectly content as she was and where she was.

Except he knew full well that she was not particularly content at the moment, nor was he. They were in the middle of a greater mystery than they'd thought, and the knots of it all were proving far more entangled than was comfortable.

"Discharge papers," Griff announced as he reentered, holding the pages aloft briefly. "Which we now know to be a forgery. His reason for discharge is injury, though it does say wholly recovered. And the signature of the authority figure is illegible, naturally."

"How could they not question an illegible signature?" Minerva demanded. "That would be…" She trailed off and looked at Griff closely. "Could it pass as being Palmerston?"

Griff studied it, then nodded. "I suppose so. Anyone who knows his signature, however, would know—"

"You're anticipating that the Maidstone Regiment heard from the minister of war often enough to know his signature?" Minerva interrupted dubiously.

He looked at the paper again, then smiled at his partner with genuine amusement. "True enough. They would likely hear from the general in chief command, and this signature is certainly nothing close to that of the Duke of York."

Minerva nodded, looking down at the papers again and biting her lip. "What do we do with all of this information? How does it help us? Forged documents of discharge, his reputation was in question before that due to suspected desertion, which was out of character, being sent away from the regiment to heal from his injury—against wisdom…"

An idea prickled in Griff's mind, and he narrowed his eyes. "What were the measurements of our chap at Eton? His last ones, when he would be nearly grown."

"Erm…" She shuffled through papers and picked up a thin piece resembling a tailor's report one might find in any shop in London. "The exact numbers?"

Griff shook his head. "Unless you can translate those into an estimation of his height and stature. I'm having a thought. Just let me know what your impressions are."

He watched as her mind worked, her eyes moving from number to number, her lips moving soundlessly as she appeared to calculate. "Stocky sort. Decent size, and he would have filled out the uniform nicely. Average height."

It was a strange experience to have a realization steal his breath from his lungs, rather as though the organs themselves had been removed from his chest and only a quivering emptiness remained. And yet, there was, with the emptiness, a shrieking new awareness of his limbs in illuminating aspects. All from seemingly insignificant information suddenly becoming connected into a larger puzzle and bringing the answers alive.

"Martin has always been described as gangly," Griff said, his voice almost a whisper. "From the moment he was discharged and returned to his family and his work with the Foreign Office. He was gangly and ill-suited to the uniform, according to an eyewitness. And my interviews with the members of the League confirm his appearance as being so."

"That's not possible," Minerva replied, her eyes round. "Not with these measurements. In order for this man to turn gangly, he would need to be starved for months. And then he would need to gain height beyond what is reasonable."

Griff thumbed through his papers and snatched an innocuous proof of uniform fitting from the mass, thrusting it at Minerva. "Here. Are these numbers possible when compared with those numbers?"

She took the paper and compared the two, shaking her head almost at once. "No. Not unless he had experienced a significant period of dramatically ill health, which would have raised questions at his discharge. Given the length of time between his disappearance and his discharge, that could not be possible." She lowered the papers, her eyes taking on a faraway look. "It's not possible. It is not possible."

"My thoughts exactly," Griff said, choosing not to tease her about the repeated phrase. "It isn't. So our Charles Martin, the one we seek, is no Charles Martin at all. The real Charles Martin is probably dead, killed for his identity, buried in unconsecrated ground somewhere between Aylesford and London years ago. Our clerk must have looked enough like Charles Martin to pass for him, even within family, and his cousin would, no doubt, ignore the dramatic changes and blame it on his poor memory of distant relations."

"They were not close, then?" Minerva asked, looking up at him. "I've no cousins at all; I do not know how any of those connections might work."

"The same as any other relations, I imagine," Griff replied with a shrug. "Some families are close on such a level, others are not. I could not pick my cousins out of a formed line if I tried, and others are closer to their cousins than to their siblings. Partlowe's family is so extensive, I doubt he knows one from the other, aside from their paperwork."

Minerva grinned at him, a brilliant smile that illuminated her features with its own source of light. Something stirring and captivating that made him want to do nothing more than gaze upon her in complete adoration. Like an artist with the vision of his muse.

When her face fell, so did his heart.

"What?" he asked in a strangely weak, almost desperate voice. "What is it?"

Minerva wet her lips, a fascinating sight if he ever saw one. "If the real Charles Martin is dead, and the Charles Martin you've been investigating is not him… Griff, that means that we know nothing about him. We know he is a fraud. We know he was likely not abducted but left for his own nefarious reasons. But we know nothing about him."

The thought had occurred to Griff when he'd suspected a difference in measurements, but the reality of the speculation hadn't truly sunk in. With Minerva's explanation, his momentary euphoria faded into the disheartening realization that his investigation would now have to begin anew and in a completely different direction.

He knew nothing about the man that he had spent months studying. He had no information to go off of for the future, and nothing to offer the superiors or other departments.

Other than that they had all been fooled and betrayed by the man who had joined their ranks.

He would get to deliver that crushing blow to the British operative teams.

No proof of what exactly he had done, or how betrayed or compromised anyone was, but the proof that he was a traitor would be enough to send alerts throughout the kingdom.

"Blimey," Griff muttered, rubbing a hand against his unshaven jaw. "That complicates everything, doesn't it? Where do we begin to look if we have no idea where we ought to look?"

Minerva scoffed softly and craned her neck, eliciting a resounding series of pops. "The neighborhood of the League offices? Surely a gangly, ginger-haired fellow would attract attention if he went anywhere at all, no matter how he tried to hide it."

Griff moved to a nearby chair and leaned his arms atop it, looking at Minerva in thought. "It's been so long since he's been there, do you really think they'll remember anything of note?"

"You'd be surprised what the lower orders can remember when they wish to," she said, almost to herself.

That was worth a brow lift, but Minerva was not looking at him, so the invitation to continue such thoughts went entirely unnoticed. Whether that had been an intentional choice of hers or a simple trick of fate in the moment, he could not say.

But he had a sneaking suspicion that his partner knew more about the topic than she would ever admit to him. The only way to test that theory would be to do just as she suggested and explore the streets of London.

"Very well, when should we go?" he asked in a carefully innocent voice. "Tonight?"

Minerva winced. "Unfortunately, tonight won't work. We're promised to the dinner party at the Gateses', and Mrs. Gates is of the annoyingly observant persuasion. She would most certainly know if we disappeared for a length of time and would despise our departing early."

Griff groaned with genuine displeasure, wishing for the thousandth time that their assignment did not involve the higher ranks of Society. It was always far more convenient to be an operative in a world and at a level where politeness was not so restricted to certain behaviors, where expectations were lower, and where judgment was minimal at most. And then there was the fact that he, Griffin Russell, hated dinner parties given by people he only knew by polite association.

It truly was unbearable, even for the manners he had been raised with and the good nature he had cultivated. Was it really so necessary to participate in superficial engagements just to maintain a certain standing with the gossips? What had the gossips ever done for him? What had being brother of the Duke of Kirklin ever done to improve his personal associations?

He knew full well that he had been born into a certain standing and fortune, and that such fortunate placement had given him far more freedom and opportunity than he would have received had he been born anywhere else. He was not so naïve as to believe that he would have ended up where he was if he had been born on the other side of the blanket in Whitechapel or some such, but he did believe that his nature and his skills would have been innate regardless. He was a man of fortune and status, but he was also a man who was not defined by those things. Who did not wish to be defined by such things.

If someone liked him, he wanted it to be for who he was, not for the connections he could provide them.

Granted, this particular dinner party was inviting Lord Beddingsford, who was a bit of a featherbrain and obsessed with his fetching wife, but exotic enough to be a curiosity for the public. And no one questioned the Beddingsford bloodline, despite its being out of England for generations. Somehow, the name still held sway, and he would bank on that for all it was worth until the mission was complete.

Which had been the point all along.

Still, Griffin Russell hated dinner parties.

Lord Beddingsford, however, undoubtedly loved them.

More's the pity.

Griff let his head hang with the weight of his reluctance, dreading the social engagement without reserve, and he knew Minerva would feel the same way. Neither of them appreciated the high society life they were forced to live in at the moment, which made them perfectly suited, in some respects, but neither of them had the luxury of begging off. Not when there were more connections to make, more loose threads to tease out, more opportunities to find holes in the stories they had heard from others.

But if memory served, more than half of one's social engagements in these circles were entirely pointless and fulfilled nothing at all within a person's life. And when one had a secret mission to accomplish, such evenings were even more tedious to bear.

"Will there be anyone worth speaking to at this dinner?" Griff asked morosely, grimacing in anticipation.

"How the devil should I know?" Minerva replied with a delightfully sharp note that made him chuckle. "I am not Mrs. Gates, and the invitation did not list other invitees."

Griff glanced up at her with a crooked smile. "Not looking forward to the fun either, Lady Beddingsford?"

She gave him the most derisive look he had ever seen, which was saying a great deal, considering the ability of his younger sister to portray such emotions. "If you think I would rather sit around a dinner table with a bunch of fine ladies who have nothing worthwhile to say among them and focus entirely on the manner in which I hold my chin in relation to my spoon, you are sadly mistaken, sir. It is an entirely useless pursuit more often than not, and the terrifying ensembles we must be forced into to attend such farces are not worth the endeavor to don them. Does that answer your ridiculous question?"

Clamping down on his lips did little to keep Griff from laughing, and he could only shake his head. "I would dearly love to know how you truly feel, Minerva. Don't hide your real feelings. Let them out, give them wings. Share your truth with the world."

Minerva rolled her eyes and got to her feet. "I rarely leave anyone unsure of how I feel."

"Why do I doubt that?" Griff mused aloud, straightening

slightly.

"What is that supposed to mean?" she demanded, propping her hands on her trim hips.

Griff noticed, and did not mind her noticing that he noticed, before shrugging his shoulders. "You have the most carefully cultivated mask I have ever seen in my work. Even when you are not in character, you have that barrier up between you and the world. You are so skilled at your inhabiting of characters, their mannerisms, their opinions, their very being, that you do the same with yourself. Even the you that I know is a version of yourself rather than the truth of yourself."

Minerva tilted her head ever so slightly, not seeming exactly displeased with the accusation, but not at ease with the thing either. "And you expect me to believe that you have entirely opened yourself to me?"

"I am not a complicated man," Griff answered as he let his amusement fade just enough to appear more genuine. "You've met my brother, you undoubtedly know my sister from the school, and you've seen my nature. Ask me anything, and I'll tell you."

Her brow creased faintly. "Anything at all? You mean that?"

He nodded, not intending to engage in this sort of exchange, but willing to continue if it would allow Minerva to open herself a bit more to him. "Anything at all."

Her throat moved on a swallow, and he wondered just what was working behind her eyes, what her thoughts were processing. He would love to know how that quick mind of hers worked and in what directions it would tend.

"Where is your talisman at this moment?"

The question caught him by surprise. Of all the things she could have asked, that was what she wanted to know?

He blinked and rolled his sleeve back, showing her the leather strap and button wrapped about his wrist. "Here. Tonight, I'll wear it around my neck, and tomorrow, when we go out in London, I'll wear it around my ankle beneath my boot."

She nodded at the explanation. Her lips twitched, and she sniffed once. "What does the world think Lord Griffin Russell is doing with his life?"

Griff grunted softly. "That he is a social ambassador with more charm than his brother, but far less respectability."

"What was your first impression of me?"

The question came so hard on the heels of his previous answer that it startled him, and when he replayed it in his mind, his knees almost buckled. From a question about his talisman to his first impressions of her in scarcely a breath. What sort of a test was she putting him through?

But if he wanted to strip away the layers hiding her true self, he needed to be willing to do the same with himself for her.

Honesty or nothing.

God help him.

"I thought you were the most magnificent creature to ever march in my direction," he admitted, his voice dipping low with an almost guttural edge that he had no strength to hide. "I wasn't sure if you were mad, or an ally, or a threat, and I was not certain I cared. And when you kissed me, I was a hairsbreadth away from giving up on the entire mission and throwing myself headlong into you. Then I heard your mastery of so many languages, your fierce temper against my antics, and got a sense of just how dangerous you could be. I was absolutely certain that you were the most perfect woman God had ever placed upon this Earth and felt particularly blessed to have crossed your path in such a grand collision of a course."

The room was silent as he finished, his words almost tumbling from his mouth once he had started his confession. His eyes had remained fixed on her, and the beautiful, maddening mask she wore had not moved for the longest time. But as he had continued, her expression had begun to soften, and her eyes had turned curiously bright.

Gads, she was even more beautiful like this than she was at any other time.

He felt something in the center of his chest tug, seeking to draw him to her, and he wondered if she felt the same thing. If the pull between them was as strong for her as it was for him, and if either of them would act upon it this time.

He fought against it on his side. He'd just admitted the strongest emotions he dared to her, and the onus was now entirely on her part.

Minerva's eyes dropped to the chair before him for a moment. "Why don't you say things like that more often? It's… rather stirring."

He laughed softly, a breathless feeling inflating his chest. "When we have so much work to do, you think I have the mental capacity to compose my thoughts and feelings into something anyone wants to hear?"

"I think you have more mental capacity than you give yourself credit for," Minerva murmured, her fingers rubbing together as she brought her eyes back to his. "And I think your thoughts and feelings deserve the words you clearly have for them."

"That may be the nicest thing you have ever said to me," Griff pointed out, smiling in spite of the oddly emotional response he was feeling at her words.

"It may be the truest thing I have ever said to you as well." She managed a smile in return, her fingers still moving in that almost fluttery manner.

If she said or did nothing else in response to what he said, he'd read between the lines. She was not unmoved, and perhaps her own thoughts and feelings were less able to be put to words as his had been. He was almost certain he had done a complete botch job of expressing himself, and yet she had appreciated it.

What would he feel when she finally found her own words for this madness?

Griff remained in his place behind the chair but gave her the softest smile he could manage under the circumstances. "So the real Minerva likes words, does she?"

The perfection that was her lips spread further, a genuine thing of beauty breaking like the dawn. "She does. And the young Minerva would have laughed to know that."

"Would she?"

Minerva nodded, her expression not turning guarded for a change. "She was a poor, uneducated thing. Words were foreign objects for other people. A means of communication and nothing more."

Griff's heart thudded at the sound of truth, and he shifted his weight ever so slightly. "What a revelation was in store for you."

She laughed very softly, her smile spreading in a nearly wistful manner as nostalgia washed over her in an almost visible wave. "Yes. Why else do you think I began absorbing so many languages?"

He'd never thought of that. He had learned languages as part of his regular education, and then for his wish to become an operative in various far corners of the world. It had come entirely because of ambition, nothing more. Minerva had developed the same skills out of pure, unvarnished curiosity and a love of words, language, and communication. The deprivation in her childhood had spurned a craving for words that had lasted well into her adult years, and probably still existed within her.

He had never felt more like a heel for something he had worked so arduously for.

Such wholesome, personal motives on her part. He had not been prepared for that, and he suddenly felt rather inclined to take her in his arms and hold her simply for the pleasure it would give him and the desire to cling to something good.

As though she could sense the warmth of his thoughts, Minerva ducked her chin slightly. "I'll send these papers to Sketch for her confirmation of their legitimacy. We'll need that seal of approval before we send information to the Shopkeepers."

"Right," Griff said in a low voice, finding further words impossible at the moment.

She nodded once and picked up the pages in question before moving from the room, her step faltering ever so slightly as she passed him.

It was as good as a connection between them.

Almost.

Griff exhaled slowly when he was alone and shook his head to himself.

Minerva was going to be the death of him.

Unless she was the life of him.

Which could very well be his death.

Chapter Nineteen

$\mathcal{L}$ondon at night was beautiful.

Not many people in this part of London would have thought so, but Minerva always had.

Even when she was an urchin forced to live on the streets, when nothing had been beautiful and everything was a struggle, the nights were actually beautiful. The noise and bustle of the day went quiet, the chaos calmed, and everything around her settled, which allowed for the beauty of the city and the skies and the unique aspects of London that everyone missed to show themselves for those keen enough to notice.

She could breathe it in deeply and sigh with the glories of it all. Not quite nostalgic, given she did not miss the streets in the least, but there was an odd sort of comfort and familiarity to it that she had never lost.

The only thing she needed to guard against tonight was giving Griff any indication that she had been the girl who had saved him that night on the docks.

He had said nothing about it, and she had been kicking herself ever since she had asked him about the talisman the day before. Why did it matter where he wore it at any given time? Why did she want to cry every time she glimpsed it? Why did she feel a need to hide from their connection in the face of her growing feelings for him?

Well, that latter question was an easier one to answer. Hiding was what Minerva did. It was what she had always done. Strong feelings and connections had never ended well for her, as evidenced by the death of her parents, and the lack of any familial support when her father died. No friends had stayed by her side on the streets. She had never trusted anyone completely, not even her fellow agents.

She did trust Milliner, she had to admit. She knew the whole of Minerva's story, apart from that night on the docks. Although Minerva supposed it was in her private files, so perhaps Milliner did know that much. She had never asked, and she had never been asked. And that was how she liked it.

The less anyone knew, the better.

Except…

She glanced to her right to the figure of the tall man walking almost entirely in step with her, looking perfect in the common clothes of the streets and entirely at his ease. Granted, most of the male operatives were able to flit between the stations with ease and agility, so it should not be a surprise that Griff was excelling without even trying.

But did he have to excel so attractively?

It was nearly as bad as the night before at the dinner party, which had proven to not contain any useful guests for their pursuits but had provided ample time for the two of them to exchange longsuffering looks and secret smiles.

Which had not been useful in her attempts to keep emotional distance between her and Griff and had only caused her stomach to do a dozen or so turns within the space of each hour. And her fingers to tingle, her lips to buzz, her ears to catch fire, and her toes to lose all feeling entirely.

She was barely able to put together coherent sentences for him, though she had no trouble with anyone else in attendance. Playing a part was easier than playing herself, and he was the only one in the audience for those particular performances. The only one who made anything uncomfortable. The only one to whom she was at risk of losing herself entirely.

And hearing his statement when asked what he first thought of her…

Had she any feeling in her legs, she might have run to him and confessed things that she could not face in a looking glass.

Blessedly, she had not felt her legs, and thus had avoided such words from which there would have been no return. And she had managed to avoid him all day, which had allowed her to settle and regain sanity as well as clarity.

Tonight was entirely about their mission, and in spite of his expertise in the field, he could not know the streets of this part of London as well as she did.

No one could.

"I have no problem at all in letting you lead," Griff announced, wisely keeping his voice down and his accent common. "After all, once I led us to the location of the League, which I am all but certain you did not know, I had no set agenda for the evening. But now I think I must ask… where exactly are we going?"

Minerva huffed, not having to feign her irritation, which was always an advantage. "We are going to visit a woman I knew in my youth. She lives in this part of London now and is blessed with the sort of open countenance that allows gossips and neighbors to confide in her unreservedly."

"Ah," Griff said, slipping his hands into the pockets of his trousers with the sort of nonchalance that belonged in their surroundings. "Excellent, I do love a well-placed asset."

"She's not an asset," Minerva said sharply, biting the inside of her cheek at the defensiveness in her voice. She inhaled slowly, then released it in a short burst. "Look, we were poor girls together, all right? We looked out for each other. She was not as fortunate as I was and had a very difficult life. Several children by different men, and barely has the means to keep them fed, let alone housed and healthy. She was forced into working in a brothel before anyone ought to even think such things, and…"

Minerva paused, swallowing hard as she considered the sort of life Cathy had been living since Minerva had left the streets and gone on to improve her own. It had only been a stroke of luck that had put her in Griff's path and allowed her to help him. Cathy would have been too young to do as fine a job and tend his wounds, but she would have risked her life to help him all the same.

Yet Minerva was here, wealthier than she'd ever dreamed she could be and moving in the high circles of Society with ease, educated and secure in her future. And Cathy was living exactly the sort of life that they had been destined for. That they all had been destined for.

"I'm sorry," Griff murmured in a low, barely audible tone.

Minerva cleared her throat, tossing her head as though it would mean something, though her hair was carefully pinned and tucked into a cap, and she was dressed as a newsboy. "Whenever I am in this part of London, I pay her a visit. And she does not know this, but I send money through a trusted third party so that she need not return to the brothel. It is not enough to offend her pride, but it should keep the children fed well enough."

"You've a kind heart, Minerva," Griff said, nudging her arm with his elbow. "I know full well you don't make a fortune."

She shrugged and averted her gaze, knowing she was nothing of the sort. She felt guilty for abandoning so many other children and finding success and happiness in a life free of starvation, thievery, and whoredom, and that was all she could say for herself. She paid money to Cathy because her children deserved better than what they'd had. Because Cathy deserved to have some dignity in her motherhood. Because if her work as an operative did not benefit people of all stations, what was the bloody point of it at all?

"Minerva?"

She shook her head quickly. "I have never used Miss Clark as an asset or informant. I have never had to. I have no guarantee that she will be of any help, but I do know the sort of information I hear from her when I pay my visits, and it could prove useful if it relates to our person."

"I look forward to making her acquaintance," Griff replied without irony or airs. "How many of her children live with her?"

"All of them," Minerva said as they walked, turning a corner and taking in the faintest aroma of the laundress's soap, something she used to find rather comforting as a child. "I believe the oldest is twelve now."

Griff cleared his throat. "How many children has she borne, Minerva?"

"Nine," she admitted, praying that Griff would keep an open mind as he met Cathy and her children. She was the sweetest woman, and her children were remarkably well-behaved and resourceful for the lives they led.

He whistled low, shaking his head slowly. "I cannot even imagine such a trial. And to be able to keep all of them with her and not send any away for young apprenticeships or the poor house? Remarkable."

"Ten, actually," Minerva corrected quickly, wincing. "If you count the one she lost three years ago. It all but broke her heart, least of all because she was a little relieved. Her sobs of agony were as much sobs of guilt for that."

"She cannot be faulted for mixed feelings," Griff protested. "With her lot in life, anyone would feel the same. And surely, she did not truly wish the child would not have been born."

Minerva smiled sadly at him. "That is what I told her, but she would not hear it. I cannot confirm it, but I believe the following child might have been conceived in recompense rather than by accident."

She caught sight of the door to her friend's apartments and turned to Griff quickly. "Please don't be appalled by the living conditions. It could be better if she managed her finances well, but she has not the benefit of such education or resources, and she is doing the best she can, all things considered."

Griff reached out and took her hand, smoothing her clenched fingers into an open palm. "Easy, Min. I am not going to judge your friend for anything. I do not know her life, nor her struggles. I am not unfeeling, and I am well aware of the good fortune of my own birth. I have been in true hovels, and I have been in poor family homes, and I can tell the difference."

Minerva nodded shakily, watching his thumb rub along the lines of her palm and each finger, something perfectly comforting in the motion, and oddly enough, not at all unsettling. She felt the edge of her nerves begin to wane with each stroke and let herself sink into the consolation of his being with her. Visiting Cathy was as much a joy as it was a reminder, and there were mixed emotions for Minerva each and every time.

Griff might not be able to understand that, as she had not told him the true details of her life, but he seemed to understand enough, if his attentions to her trembling hand were any indication.

She ought to give him more credit for his intuition than she did.

"Breathe in," he suggested, though she took it as more a command.

She inhaled deeply, then exhaled slowly.

"Better?"

She nodded and swallowed. "You can let go now."

Griff cocked his head and drew a faint circle in her palm with his thumb. "Pity. I was enjoying that." But release her hand he did, and they continued to walk, his fingers brushing against hers with almost every step.

The occasional connection was as jarring as it was amusing, and it was with that conundrum in her mind that Minerva knocked on the door. She had sent a note ahead of time for Cathy, as she always did, and she only prayed that their visit would not disrupt the sleep of her younger children. Cathy seemed to rarely sleep herself, based on the times at which Minerva had visited over the years, but she also supposed that the middle of the night was the only time her friend enjoyed any quiet or privacy.

Perhaps the sacrifice was worth such a reprieve.

The door opened, and a haggard but smiling Cathy greeted them, the rounding of her belly telling Minerva all she needed to know about how the family was faring.

"Min," she said with more warmth than her appearance seemed capable of. "It is good to see you again." She turned to Griff and her smile turned more polite. "Evening, sir. Do come in."

"You may call me Griffin, Miss Clark, and it is a pleasure to meet you." Thankfully, Griff had used his more common accent, no matter how politely he had borne his greeting.

Cathy's cheeks flushed just the right amount of pink, and she stepped back to let them both in, gesturing down the narrow, poky corridor. "Up the stairs, if you please, sir. First door on the left."

Minerva smiled at Cathy as she passed. "How are you?" she whispered, taking her friend's hand.

"Tired," came the heavy response. "And distracted. But that can wait." She cast her eyes after Griff and returned them to Minerva. "You did not tell me he was a looker, Minnie."

Minerva cleared her throat. "He's also bloody irritating, and I'll thank you to remember that first of all."

Cathy closed the door, snickering. "Oh, believe me, I know what irritating can do."

Face flaming, Minerva all but marched after Griff up the stairs and through the first door on the left without saying another word to her friend.

The sitting room had been partially turned into the laundry room as well as the dining room, ramshackle chairs and benches now pushed together in a cluster in the corner and draped with drying linens belonging to very small individuals. Six pairs of shoes sat before the meager fire beside a tattered wicker basket containing more clothing, though whether those items were needing to be washed, already washed, or needing to be darned was unclear. The few windows in the room were filthy, streaked with attempts to clean or clear it, though nothing had been an improvement.

There was an armchair, patched in places, and a rocking chair, likely the best-quality item in the whole place, and a faded sofa with one leg propped on a block of wood to keep it even. The walls held no artwork, only peeling and stained wallpaper, and there were three candles alight, all in mismatched holders. Two children sat near the fire, one darning a stocking and another whittling some yet to be discerned figure.

Minerva recognized the children at once, the twelve-year-old girl looking more like her mother than ever before, and the boy, who must be almost eleven now, holding almost none of the innocence of youth in his features now.

"Laura," Cathy called softly as they entered, closing the door to the stairs, "Michael, do you remember my friend Minnie?"

Laura looked up from her work and nodded, smiling prettily. Michael glanced over but did not acknowledge Minerva at all.

"And this is her friend, Griffin," Cathy continued, gesturing to Griff.

Again, only Laura made any sort of greeting.

In polite society, both would have risen and greeted them with respect, regardless of recognizing them. But here, there was no politeness, only genuine responses.

There was something perfectly refreshing in that.

"I am sorry that I do not have refreshments, sir," Cathy murmured as they sat in various places. "I would have made more of an effort to be welcoming, were it not…"

"We require nothing," Griff overrode in the gentlest voice Minerva had ever heard him use on another human. "Truly, I am only grateful to be in a warm home such as this."

Minerva could have kissed him for that, and more for its bringing about Cathy's sweet smile when she was so clearly uncomfortable in her own home.

"Something tells me this is not a mere social call," Cathy said, sitting back in her chair and resting her hands on her rounded stomach absently. "What brings you to my very humble abode?"

Griff looked at Minerva and gestured for her to take the lead in this, for which she was grateful. It was his mission, but Cathy was her friend, and this was her home. And she was no operative. She had no stake in their world, and Griff, she knew, was not going to pretend that he could treat this visit the same way he might have done under other circumstances.

"Do you still hear everything from this neighborhood?" Minerva asked without preamble or preface. "The gossip that nobody needs and the comings and goings of all sorts?"

Cathy snorted softly. "Unfortunately, yes. I cannot take the washing to the line in the old mews without hearing at least four things each way, none of which improve my day or my mind."

Minerva nodded once, glanced at her partner for his confirmation, then lowered her voice. "We are looking for a gangly man in his early to mid-thirties, ginger hair, unremarkable in fortune. He would have been in the Forts Alley region, perhaps Bricks, too. He wouldn't have been seen lately, but he would have been a regular for several years. Worked with the likes of Gent and Rogue."

"Ah, now you are getting interesting," Cathy replied with a quick grin, sitting up a trifle in her chair. "There is nothing the neighborhood loves to speak about more than Gent and Rogue."

"Do they really?" Griff asked, leaning back and linking his hands around one knee. "You must know all sorts of stories."

Cathy nodded almost smugly. "Far more stories than anyone would guess, I can assure you."

Minerva caught her friend's eye and shook her head ever so slightly, warning her away from saying much about their mutual past with Gent and his colleagues.

She did not need to have that particular discussion tonight, of all times.

Cathy caught the look without expression and returned her gaze to Griff. "We are very proud of our own personal detectives and protection here. And feel rather protective of them ourselves. So yes, I have heard of your ginger-haired friend, and the noted disappearance of him of late. No one knew his name, of course, only that he worked with Gent and Rogue. When we stopped seeing him, everyone was concerned. We saw Gent's children rushing here and there with their errands, but there seemed to be a new edge to whatever they were doing."

"I don't doubt that," Griff murmured, shaking his head.

Cathy acknowledged Griff's comment with a nod. "Sally Titchum, who runs the boarding house at the end of the row, swears she saw him a month or two ago out by Mr. Blaine's residence. You know Mr. Blaine, the moneylender? Brutal man."

It was all Minerva could do to keep from stiffening at the mention of him.

She knew all about Mr. Blaine. All of the London operatives did. It had been the most complicated and quickly arranged operation anyone had recalled in years, and though Minerva had been at the Convent in Kent for it, she had read every single report on the event prior to beginning this assignment. And her friend and fellow teacher, Ears, had been the one to uncover the truth of Mr. Blaine's associates and aims.

But as the general population would not know of that, Minerva would keep silent on the subject.

For now.

"I've heard the name here and there," she hedged carefully. "Does Sally have an honest eye?"

Cathy nodded without hesitation. "I've never known her to be wrong. She was positive it was him, though she said his hair was not so ginger as she recalled."

"Would she know him well by sight?" Griff asked with a furrowed brow. "If his hair was different…"

"I asked the same thing," Cathy said, laughing a touch. "I says, 'How could you know him without the mop of ginger hair?' And the look she gave me!" She shook her head. "As it happens, the man lodged at Sally's for a time and left without paying the remainder of his balance. She told me she never forgot anyone who owed her money."

Griff chuckled at the statement. "Then I utterly believe her. And will do my best to avoid being in her debt."

"Wise choice." Cathy looked at Minerva then, an air of expectation in her countenance. "Will that help? I could ask some questions about him, see if anyone else knows more—"

"No," Minerva interjected quickly, smiling for her friend. "We don't wish to attract attention to our hunt for him. But thank you for your offer. And yes, I do believe that will help us a great deal."

Cathy smiled in return and seemed relieved by the answer.

Poor woman, she must have thought she had nothing to offer Minerva upon her visit. Little did she know that her friendship, her companionship, her genuine goodness in spite of the circumstances in which they had both been raised, were all enough for Minerva.

And at the moment, she only wanted to speak with her friend and forget anything at all related to her mission.

She looked at Griff, biting her lip in hesitation, hoping he would understand what she could not express.

He smiled and patted her knee before pushing to his feet and moving to the fire, sitting himself on the floor between the two children and beginning to speak in a low voice with them.

"He's a good sort, Minnie," Cathy told her quietly. "I can sees it easy."

"He is," Minerva agreed, not quite managing to avoid her knowing smile. "Though he'd have given Ralph a run for his money, no doubt."

Cathy barked a surprised laugh at the mention of one of their more troublesome fellow street urchins. Ralph had always been the best of the pickpockets, even swiping things from the rest of them, and enjoyed nothing more than pranking them all when he could. He'd been press-ganged at fourteen, and no one had heard from him since, but the memory of him was always worth a laugh.

"How have you been, Cath?" Minerva asked her, turning serious. "Truly."

Cathy's eyes clouded and she looked away. "They raised the rents, and we're strugglin' to keep up. Agnes has had a cough for three months that won't shift, and the doctor won't come anymore, as I can't pay. Tommy's outgrown all his clothes and is already taller than Michael, so he can't wear his. And then…" She settled her hands on her stomach once more, her brow creasing.

"Again?" Minerva whispered, leaning forward and feeling a little teary. "How, Cath? Last time we talked—"

"Last time we talked," Cathy overrode in a surprisingly harsh tone, "I didn't have a sick little girl and a baby with bowed legs, let alone a son who needs an apprenticeship soon. What money I have goes to the roof over the heads of my babes and the food for their mouths. I can't make enough on laundry alone, so yes, I did what I had to do. Don't worry, I did not go back to Ethel's establishment. I did this on me own."

Minerva reached out and placed a hand on her friend's arm. "You know I don't judge you."

"I know," she replied, her voice breaking, "but I'm so ashamed. And it's so early to be this large, Minnie. I'm afeared it's twins, and what'll I do about that? Nine babies already—to have ten and eleven in the same breath, and no man about… What does the Almighty think of loose women who have no care for the lives they are giving their babies?"

"Cathy." Minerva gripped her arm hard, forcing her friend to look at her. "You have not abandoned a single one of your babies. You have been determined to keep each one and raise them in a home of love. You and I both know what sort of life they could be having, and you are keeping them from it."

"Barely." Cathy shook her head, tears falling from each eye. "Laura has already been propositioned once, Min. I dare not let her out anymore. I know how I first got this way, and she won't have to endure that, I'll make sure of it. But how long can I keep her safe? Or any of them safe?"

Minerva moved from her chair and folded her friend into her embrace, holding her close. "No one should have to endure what you have, Cath. Over and over again, your freedom has been taken from you. Yet you have fought your way through and survived in spite of it all. You are building a life for your children, and they adore you. They will not forget all that you sacrifice for them. And somehow, you will all rise above this. I promise."

Cathy gripped her shoulder, laughing a watery laugh. "You cannot promise that, Minnie. The only thing that rises in here is the bread. But thank you."

"As long as your children aren't raising glasses of Bert's ale before bed, I think you're on the right side of things." Minerva pulled back and patted her friend's arms with a cheeky grin.

"Well, I may use brandy to soothe the baby's gums when a tooth's comin' in," Cathy admitted, wrinkling her nose a little. "But who hasn't done that with a babe or three?"

Minerva giggled and shook her head. "Everyone and anyone, I am certain." She got to her feet and sighed. "Griff? Shall we let the Clarks go to bed?"

"I think we should," he replied, ruffling Michael's hair and shocking Minerva by getting a bright smile from the boy. "Miss Laura, I shall write to your mother if I can get an answer for you. Would that do?"

"Yes, sir, Griff," Laura said brightly. "It would do, all right."

He smiled at her and turned to face Minerva, hands on his hips. "Min?"

She swallowed and nodded. "Yes." She moved to hug Cathy again, this time quickly. "I should be in London for a bit. I'll try to come again."

"Don't put yourself out for us," Cathy said, as she always did. "We'd love to see you, but we know you are very busy." She pulled back and Minerva saw how fatigued the woman truly was. "Good luck with your hunt for him."

Him? Him who?

Belatedly, it occurred to Minerva that they had come here with a purpose, and Cathy had given her more than enough for a start.

"Yes," Minerva managed to respond, nodding rapidly. "Thank you."

Griff came to her side and offered Cathy a perfectly proportioned bow for her pride and her dignity, which was really more of a nod, but the lack of airs was perfection. "Miss Clark, it has been delightful to be in your home. I've had a chat with your two eldest and find them to be bright minds and good hearts, which is exceptional in any family. I may have put it into the head of Miss Laura that I may know of a situation where she might find education and training for any future of her choice without requiring any cost at all from you. But I shall not put any action forward if you do not wish me to. As I told your daughter, I can make no promises, but I may ask."

Cathy blinked at the suggestion and looked at Minerva, then back at Griff. "Are you having me on, Griffin?"

"Not even a little, ma'am," he answered adamantly.

She laughed a bit unsteadily. "Oh, please do ask. Laura is my second set of hands here, but I'd rather she have opportunity to improve herself, if she can. She'd not be taken away from me?"

"No, ma'am. She could return to you at any time you wish, based on the program schedule." Griff slipped his hands behind his back and smiled. "I will ask, and I will write when I know more. Will that do?"

Cathy nodded, swallowing hard, then came forward and kissed Griff's cheek. "Thank you, Griffin."

Minerva smiled as his cheeks turned pink. "I haven't done anything yet," he reminded her. "And it might not work."

"But you want to try," Cathy pointed out. "For my girl. That is worth all the hope I can muster. Thank you."

Minerva slipped her hand into Griff's behind his back and felt her heart warm when his fingers latched against hers. "Good night, then, Cathy."

They exited the house then and silently made their way down the London streets, Minerva leading the way again. Griff seemed content to walk beside her, their hands still entwined.

But Minerva needed to say something, now that she could. And before they got too close to their next location.

"You were thinking of the Rothchild Academy for Laura, weren't you?" she asked in a rough voice.

"Yes," he said simply. "I have no doubt you've thought of it before, too. I hope I didn't overstep."

Minerva shook her head, though he might not see the action that well in the dark of the night. "No, not at all. I have thought of it, but never considered actually mentioning it to Cathy. Or to Laura, for that matter. Perhaps I have been too close."

His fingers squeezed against hers for a moment. "It became very clear to me that both Laura and Michael are very bright, but their situation will never allow for them to be truly educated unless they are fortunate with their futures. Laura is a born storyteller. You should have heard her talk about her siblings. And Michael… I've never seen any lad of eleven so skilled with wood and knife. He ought to be a carpenter, if not something far more intricate. We can find a situation for him, I have no doubt. But Laura… Whether or not she becomes an operative for the Crown, you and I are uniquely placed to give her access to the Academy. And you could always keep an eye on her as a member of the school faculty."

The more fervently he spoke, the tighter Minerva's throat became, until finally she could only bleat some strange, guttural sound of emotion.

Griff stopped, his thumb brushing against her hand. "What is it?"

Minerva swiped at her tearing eyes, cursing herself in Russian.

"No, hey…" Griff tipped her chin up and gave her a searching look. "Minerva, what?"

"This is personal for me," she ground out, clenching her teeth hard against the truth of her life suddenly burning to get out. "Far more personal than…"

"I figured as much," Griff said simply, his smile turning gentle.

She blinked in surprise. "What?"

"This makes far more sense to me," he explained, his finger tracing beneath her chin softly. "You're not just some governess from Norfolk turned operative. You couldn't be. I'm not asking you to reveal life secrets but give me some credit. I've been to Downham several times, and I've never met anyone there who could pick locks like you. And my associations were far from polite."

The swallow Minerva needed refused to fully complete, and she cleared her throat, exhaling. "I was a Rothchild girl, Griff. In every sense of it. I was plucked up from this life. I was Laura, only I had no loving mother to protect me from… anything. To show me love and compassion. No one to offer me opportunity. It was only by sheer luck that anyone found me and thought I would be worth the scholarship."

Griff's hand gently came to the side of her face and smoothed away a tear. "And look what you have done. Look how your life has blossomed. How your mind has been cultivated. You are the prime example of how it should work and what could be possible. Don't you see how marvelous that is?"

Minerva shook her head, trying to look away, but he held her fast.

"Min," he whispered fiercely, leaning closer, "there is nothing to be ashamed of. Yours is a tale of success and victory. Of triumph. And no matter how you were plucked up and placed on that road, you are the one who made something of it."

"But why me and not Cathy?" Minerva asked with a hitch in her throat, her tears continuing. "Why not Annie or Jack or Ellie or Tess? There were so many of us, Griff. So many."

Griff pulled her against his chest and wrapped his arms around her, his mouth pressing into the cap upon her head. "We cannot save everyone, darling. You cannot torture yourself like this. We do what we can, and work to improve things for everyone. Why do you think Gent stays where he is instead of taking a promotion? Or Rogue? Or Trick? There are many of us who work down here, you know that. We do what we can. You were selected for a reason, and the lives you have saved and changed and bettered should be proof enough of that."

Minerva nodded against him, keeping her arms curled into her own body rather than wrapping them about him in return. She needed the comfort that only he could provide, the embrace she had longed for as a child on these very streets and had never found.

"Now," he said roughly, "I need to ask you something. Something personal and something difficult."

Again, Minerva nodded, turning her face against his chest.

She could hear the groan that came from the center of his chest and never quite reached his lips. "Were you ever... taken advantage of in the way that Cathy was? Were you ever reduced to the same situation before the Academy? Had you been...?" He trailed off, and she felt the pressure of his mouth increase at her cap.

Minerva closed her eyes and allowed her fingers to gently brush against his chest as he struggled for words.

"It would not change how I feel about you," he eventually went on. "My… my respect would not lessen, and I would not think any less of you. Or judge you. Or… anything else. I just…" He exhaled shakily and shook his head. "Please, for the love of God, Minerva, tell me the truth. I cannot bear not knowing."

She laid her palm flat against the pounding of his heart. "No," she whispered. "No, I was never in that situation. It is an advantage in these circles to be late in developing, as I was. I had only ever been propositioned in the weeks before I left for the Academy. But many of my friends… most of them, actually…" She opted not to finish, knowing he would understand after seeing Cathy's life and her children.

His shoulders sagged in relief, and his hold on her tightened briefly. "Thank you."

How long they stood there, Minerva wasn't certain. There was nothing romantic in the thing, only consolation and support, which somehow seemed a rarer, more precious thing.

Only when Griff's arms dropped from around her did she step away from the warmth of him, and she looked up into his eyes with a new vulnerability.

He looked back with an inscrutable expression. "I take it we are heading for Blaine's house?"

Minerva nodded, feeling her operative nature slip back into place. "Yes. Not to intrude, but to examine. And Ears should be meeting us somewhere around here."

"Good plan," he praised, turning to continue their walk and taking her hand again. "I hope she brings Rudder."

"You know him?" Minerva demanded, grinning at the idea that Griff had crossed paths with Ears's husband Teo already. The man had only been brought on as an asset in the spring, but he had been eager to get to work.

Griff chuckled. "Very briefly last month. I like him immensely. Can the Beddingsfords meet up with the Vickers? He is a baronet, isn't he?"

Somehow, their conversation turned rather chatty as they ambled down the dank streets of this quarter of London. As it was not unusual to see commonly dressed people in these sections in any given town, they were not a spectacle for anyone else to see, so they did not need to make efforts to sneak anywhere. They were investigating, but without the need to enter anyone's residence or place of business. That would come later, of course, but not tonight.

Had Minerva been paying an appropriate amount of attention to her surroundings, she might have noticed how much quieter it was getting, and that the area of Blaine's house was darker than it ought to have been, given the other buildings along the way. She might have seen something that would have enlightened her to danger she ought to have appreciated.

But only when their conversation was broken by a gunshot did she even think to properly look about her.

And only after Griff shoved her into an alley, hissing in pain, did she acknowledge the danger.

"Griff?" she whispered, gripping his jacket as he hissed through his teeth.

He shook his head. "I've been shot, love. Not badly. You lead, I'll follow."

She stared at him in shock, not quite comprehending. How could he have been shot? They would have noticed a gunman, wouldn't they? They were operatives, highly skilled and trained, and they would know if they were walking into danger.

Shot? How could he have been shot?

"Minerva," he grunted, pushing her firmly down the alley, still hissing between his teeth. "Guns. Shot. Danger. Go. Now, please."

Right. That she could do.

She turned around and started to move, glancing behind to make certain he was still there. When he was, she reached a hand back, needing to be certain he was actually staying with her.

His hand slid into hers neatly, and his fingers gripped hers. Hard.

She picked up her pace and began to run.

Chapter Twenty

Getting shot always stung, no matter how severe the wound.

Having alcohol, no matter how weak, placed against a gunshot wound always burned like hellfire.

Griff clenched his teeth against the pained groan from that telltale burn but forced himself not to lean away from it. "Damn, Suds," he gritted out. "What are you using back there?"

The old man wheezed a laugh behind him. "French brandy. A gift from Gent; you should be honored."

"Pour me a glass of it, and I'll toast you both." Griff made a face, exhaling in irritation. "It feels like a grazing. Is that true?"

"More or less," Suds confirmed, dousing his rag in more of the liquid. "Clipped you a bit. What happened?"

Griff would have shrugged had his right shoulder not been currently undergoing treatment for the aforementioned gunshot wound. Instead, he looked over at his partner, who had not said more than three words since they had arrived at the grizzled operative's home for his help with Griff's wound.

Minerva stood across the room, arms tightly folded, cap gone, her brow furrowed, and she stared at Griff with single-minded intensity. Except she did not react when his eyes met hers. She seemed to be looking through him rather than at him, if she was seeing him at all. It seemed almost more likely that her eyes were fixed on some absent location in his direction while her mind spun and whirled on thoughts and images that were far removed from their present location.

He hated seeing her look like that. He had begun to read her expressions for entertainment and had found he was correct more often than not. But this one… this nearly blank, distant, coldly vacant mask she wore was heartbreaking. The furrow in her brow spoke of concern, but beyond that, there could have been a hundred or so emotions wrapped up in the nothingness she expressed.

He had seen her vulnerability after visiting Cathy and the children, held her in an attempt to soothe the child within her who had seen and felt so much loneliness and hurt. Such feelings were not easily escaped, and he knew better than to believe that their moments of lightheartedness following the experience had solved anything.

In fact, by doing so, he had missed whatever danger had surrounded them, which had led to his getting shot. Clipped, really. A haphazard grazing of a bullet. It could have meant nothing. London was dangerous in certain parts, and it was entirely possible that they had simply been in the wrong place at the wrong time.

But Griff had lived too long and seen too much to believe in coincidences.

And he suspected Minerva had as well.

"All right there, Mirrors?" he called out gently.

She blinked and her eyes seemed to focus on him. "Fine," she murmured with a faint nod.

Ah. Absolutely not fine, then.

Good to know.

If Minerva was anything like him, she would be replaying every single aspect of their walk before the gunshot to find the bits and pieces they missed. She would be blaming herself for not being more observant. She would curse herself until she was able to atone, in her own way, for her mistake. No matter that they had both been there and ought to have mutually been able to note the danger; she would take the blame wholly upon herself.

Griff had not come to that point yet, mostly due to the pain and stinging of his wound and its treatment, but it would certainly be occupying his mind shortly and extensively.

Another set of footsteps sounded, and Griff tensed, looking towards the front of the house. But it was only another woman dressed as a man, followed by an actual man with darker skin and a scruff that Griff envied.

This man he knew.

"Rudder!" he cried in delight, holding out his right hand to shake as much as he was able with Suds working on the back of that shoulder. "Great to see you again."

Rudder, a Spaniard by birth, though half-English in truth, came over and gripped his hand, his smile holding a touch of irony. "You said we'd see each other soon, *amigo*. I did not think you meant it this way."

Griff barked a laugh. "I didn't mean in this way. Unintentional clipping, this one."

"Well, do let me know if you intentionally get clipped anytime soon," Rudder grunted with a wink. "I'd like to see what that looks like."

Minerva marched over to the duo. "What did you find, Ears?" she demanded of the woman.

Ah, the inestimable Ears. If Griff was correct, she had been doing operative-like work for years purely to make money as a journalist and had done rather well for herself in telling the stories of the underworld of London. It had been only by chance that she had stumbled upon Faction sympathizers in her work, and thus had begun her introduction into the world of covert operations.

Poor thing. Though, if he were to be fully honest, Griff would admit that the woman could probably handle herself better than most of the men who were brought in at first, purely based on her own development of the habit of sneaking around London dressed as she was. That was certainly some gumption, and he would give her full credit for it.

"There's nothing happening at the house at present," Ears told Minerva, putting a hand on her arm. "Not a meeting, not a gathering, nothing. There is a watchman holed up across the street in the dead end, and when we got there, he was passed out with drink. So it may very well be that you played into his drunken imaginings, and he was careless."

Minerva frowned rather darkly at that. "Careless? He was simply firing at wandering people? That won't go over well with the neighbors."

Ears scoffed to herself. "Most people don't wander near the

place, in case you haven't noticed. Even without the ties to the Faction, Blaine is a heartless creature. The tales of those in his debt would make even your blood run cold, Mirrors. After what happened in the spring, it is no wonder that he takes more care."

"And no one was curious about the firing of a gun in the middle of the night?" Griff asked, breaking into the conversation.

Ears glanced at him, raising a brow. "Nobody asks questions about anything there. One gunshot does not frighten anyone unless they are the target."

Griff raised the glass beside him, containing some of the brandy Suds was using on his shoulder. "Consider me warned." He downed it, then winced as Suds pressed against the cut with fresh burning.

"Have you told Gent?" Minerva asked them, not looking at Griff. "He'll need to warn his band."

Rudder cleared his throat. "We had a message sent. I have no doubt he'll take care of things on his end."

"We ought to make sure it gets to the Shopkeepers," Griff pointed out, shifting uncomfortably as Suds began to bandage him up. "Gent isn't the only one who has contacts in the underbelly of London. We can get any number of eyes on this place."

Minerva nodded, but still would not look at him. That was interesting, but not in a way he liked.

Still, Minerva was the sort of person to let him know exactly what she was doing and what her thoughts were on the situation.

She just would not do so in front of anyone else.

"I can post one of my assets there for now," Ears offered with a shrug that was perfectly suited to her present ensemble, but certainly would not have done for the lady she was in reality. "They are used to remembering details with exactness for my articles. They won't think twice about it."

Griff grinned at her. "And will you plant a story in the papers to throw them off our scent?"

Ears flashed a quick smile in response. "I am certain I can come up with something, if necessary. It would mean putting my present story on hold…"

Rudder laughed and slipped an arm around his wife's waist. "I don't think that one will be going anywhere, *cariño*. It will take quite some time for that one to fully develop."

"True," Ears mused, leaning into him while pulling a playfully thoughtful face. "There is still quite a bit of investigation to do, and then there is the twist…"

"Care to share?" Griff asked, sitting forward as much as he could. "I'd love a hint."

"There is no time for that now," Minerva interjected with surprising sharpness. "We cannot look for Mist's mark where he was last seen because of a bloody watchman with a rifle. That leaves us with no avenue to explore there unless we take him out."

"Well, that would leave quite a mess," Griff told her, only half teasing. "They tend to complain about that."

Her glare was quick and potent, but at least she had looked at him, however briefly.

"We'll circle back," Rudder suggested easily, his dark eyes darting between the two of them as though he could sense the tension Griff was feeling. "Examine the areas around the house and see if there are any other traps set for the innocent bystander."

"Or the less innocent," Griff suggested with a raised brow.

Rudder nodded in acknowledgement, his mouth quirking.

"It would only be a cursory look," Ears agreed, keeping her attention on Minerva. "We won't be in danger."

"Neither were we," Minerva murmured, her folded arms somehow tightening further against her body. "But do what you need to do."

Griff looked at his partner in some concern, unsure why she was acting this way and what would make her so on edge. They were operatives—sudden danger was part of the task. She was used to that sort of thing, had been through far worse situations and come through without any lasting issues.

Yet here she was, short and terse, distracted and distant, cold and retreating. In an evening full of high emotion, the shift to almost no emotion was unnerving.

Ears and Rudder left to survey the area around Blaine's house again, and then they would undoubtedly go home after making their reports and completing their portion of the unexpected assignment.

The moment they left, Minerva began to pace about the room,

pausing only a little by the fire each pass, as though the reminder of the warmth was needed each time. She said nothing, her arms still practically clenched against her body, and she seemed determined to not look at anyone, though there were now only three people in the room.

It was almost hypnotic to watch her walk, though his concern and curiosity was continuing to grow with every passing moment.

"Arm up," Suds gently commanded from behind him. "Just a little."

Griff complied and held perfectly still as Suds rolled a length of linen beneath his arm and around his torso, then over his shoulder to cross over the bandage.

"There, that should hold." He patted Griff's good shoulder, exhaling swiftly. "It shouldn't bleed much longer, truly. It'll burn like hell as it heals and scabs over, but I didn't need to stitch anything. You should be able to move your arm decently, but don't go doing anything stupid."

"Unfortunately, I can't promise that," Griff admitted with a resigned sigh, glancing over at the old man, moving his arm and shoulder to test any restrictions. "I do stupid things without thinking."

Suds wheezed his usual laugh and shook his head, moving towards the front of his house, the only part that faced the street and would give no hint to what went on within. "Then try thinking a little more, my friend. For all our sakes." He pointedly shifted his eyes towards Minerva, then back to Griff, raising a sharp brow before leaving the room entirely.

Alone at last, Griff exhaled and took a quick drink of brandy. "Well, that was a bit of a mess."

"Is that what you call it?" Minerva retorted, her tone clipped.

He narrowed his eyes as she continued to pace. "Yes… What else should it be called when an unexpected accident takes place during a mission?"

"It should be called 'pay more attention' or 'dangers of distraction' or something like that," she muttered, a strange hitch escaping through her words.

Griff's brows slowly rose as he heard it, and he decided he

needed to tread carefully, tease things out a little to get at their root. "Those sound like dreadful novel titles."

Minerva ran a hand over her face, a completely uncharacteristic move for her. "My entire life could be a dreadful novel."

"I'd read it," he offered, as though it would help.

She did not respond to that, and her pacing seemed to grow less steady in its path.

Griff watched for a moment more before saying, "Minerva, surely you've had missions with minor setbacks before. It happens, and it happens frequently. You heard what Ears and Rudder said. A drunk with a firearm. After what Ears uncovered earlier this year, it is no wonder Blaine is suspicious and wants protection for himself."

"You have an answer for everything, don't you?" she snapped, whirling to face him. "You've already determined why we missed the situation for what it was, written it off as an accident based on the preliminary information, and consoled yourself with whatever the easiest answer is so you don't have to look at the problem in the same way anymore. Does that make you feel better? Will you be able to sleep tonight, with your wound still burning—" Her voice broke and she looked down, swallowing hard.

"Is that what this is about?" Griff asked her, his voice dropping to nearly a whisper as he looked at the almost trembling figure of the strongest woman he had ever met.

Her eyes squeezed shut, and she looked to her right, a faint sniffle escaping.

A wave of tenderness washed over Griff, his entire body seeming to sink into the table upon which he sat.

"Please tell me you aren't feeling guilt for this," he pleaded, his hands gripping the table edge to keep himself from reaching for her. "This is no one's fault."

"I know that," she whispered, swiping at her cheek. "I know that no one is to blame, and we could not have expected it. But the fact remains that you got shot, and I was there, and I couldn't do a bloody thing about it. It was the most afraid I have been in years." She exhaled, and the sound was choked with tears. "And I hate being afraid."

Griff blinked at her admission. "A man holds a gun in your face, and you don't bat an eyelash, but I get winged, and you go to pieces?"

She sniffed harshly. "Yes!"

"Good heavens, woman," he muttered before he could stop himself, running a hand through his hair as he tried to decipher the revelation before him.

"Don't do that!" Minerva cried, almost curling into herself as she glared at him. "Don't pretend that this shouldn't be agony for me!"

Agony? For him to be shot, even though it was minor and easily healed from?

Griff shook his head, the tender feeling curling in his stomach again. "Why should it be?"

Minerva swallowed, shaking her head as well. "If you don't know, then you're an even greater idiot than you pretend to be."

He knew the several complicated reasons why it would bother him if she got shot, but he couldn't pretend to understand her side of things.

And he needed to understand.

"Tell me," he urged softly.

She stiffened at the request, then seemed to set her jaw. "How did you feel when you thought I was going to die?"

Griff inhaled sharply, the memory of seeing the gun against her head something that still turned him cold from the inside out. He still woke up in the night in a cold sweat because of it, and he knew full well that he would never forget that feeling.

And that was what she had felt?

Minerva nodded as he felt an echo of that anguish across his face. "Exactly."

"Exactly what?" he managed to force out, trying to play off anything she thought she saw, anything he was presently feeling. Anything at all. It was too much, too complicated, too real.

Minerva shook her head and marched across the room to him, gripping his head in her hands and crashing her lips down upon his. There was nothing tender in it, only desperation and need.

And fear. A whole world of fear.

Griff gripped her sides as she pulled back, wondering what she had done with the air from his lungs.

"I can't lose you," Minerva hissed harshly as she touched her brow to his, her tears returning with a vengeance. "I can't."

The pain in her voice echoed everything he was feeling, and he pulled her flush against him, burying his face into her shoulder, gripping the pinned masses of her hair with tight, trembling fingers. He couldn't say a word, seemed to be choking on the very attempt to form them, and only the feeling of the trembling figure in his arms seemed to ground him to the earth at all. He breathed her in, ignoring the burning in his shoulder as he held her tightly, wishing he could pull her inside of himself to keep her safe.

To keep this feeling between them safe.

To never feel this same fear over anyone else ever again.

"I hate this," Minerva hissed, her arms wrapped tightly around his neck. "I absolutely hate this."

"I know," Griff told her, his voice hoarse. "You know that I know."

He felt her nod against him, felt her mighty exhale, felt her body relax in his hold, and felt himself finally relax as well.

Minerva pulled back and looked at Griff, her gray-blue eyes searching his, her tears finally gone. "Are you well? Truly?"

Griff nodded, putting a hand to her cheek and smoothing the surface with his thumb. "Truly. Suds cleaning it was worse than actually receiving it. You heard him. No stitches, no extensive damage. I barely feel it, now that it's bound."

Minerva nodded, inhaling shakily. "I'll try to remember that. You're unharmed. I am unharmed. And it does not appear as though the attack was intended against our persons."

"Correct," Griff replied as he slid his hand to her neck, letting his thumb rub against the tender skin there. "They'll look into it from every angle, and if there is anything that ought to concern us, we'll be notified before we can sing 'God Save the King.'"

That made her smile, and it seemed a victory of historic proportions to see it.

"There, now," he mused, touching the corner of her smile with his thumb. "That's what I needed to see."

Faint color rushed into her cheeks, and she took his hand in hers, lacing their fingers. "Can we do something just for ourselves tonight? No social gatherings for information, no sneaking about the streets, just… something you and I can enjoy."

It was the sweetest request he had ever heard, and the grin on his face was as helpless as it was giddy. "Yes," he told her with more firmness than he'd ever said anything. "Yes, anything. Just us. What would you like?"

Minerva's smile turned almost girlish, and he was heady with the effect of it. This rosy-cheeked, breathless, practically giggling creature before him would have upended his entire world with one look had he met her ten years ago. He'd have given up his budding career as an operative and run away with her to Gretna Green in a heartbeat. He would have taken up residence at Worsley Park in truth rather than in appearances only, and they would have a passel of children now, as many as she could bear.

He would never have been able to leave her alone, poor thing.

He suddenly ached for that imagined future with a depth that stole his breath and crippled his limbs. Even now, he would take it.

Except he could not exactly retire his position at present, and nor, he suspected, could Minerva.

And she would have something to say now about his attentions, especially those leading to children.

And she would be far more difficult to sweep off her feet at this point compared to who she might have been ten years before this.

And…

There were a host of differences, he would admit freely, but in that moment, Griff truly believed they could all be overcome in the face of his rather profound love for her.

Love.

Well. There it was.

As clear as day, as uncomplicated as sunshine. He loved her. The deadly operative, the prickly spinster, the clever teacher, the deeply vulnerable woman with more defenses than any fortress—he loved each of them and all of them, wrapped up in the loveliness that was Minerva.

And he would give her anything and everything she asked for if it would bring her the smallest ray of happiness.

"Could we…" Minerva began before hesitating, biting her lip and driving Griff mad in doing so. "Could we go to the theater? We have not done so yet, and I almost never get to attend."

Theater was on the very top of Griff's list of things he found nearly unbearable, and he had done his utmost to avoid the thing as regularly as he could.

But suddenly, it was the most thrilling idea anyone had ever had, and he wanted nothing more than to attend.

"Of course we can," he told the stunning woman before him, leaning forward to give her a soft, sweet kiss. "Let us tell Suds we're going home. Then we will both get some sleep, write up our reports, do our due diligence and all that, and then tonight, we will go to the theater. I want you to wear whichever of Tilda's dresses you hate the least, have your maid arrange your hair in the way you like it, and we will see whichever opera or play you choose." He kissed the back of the hand he held and grinned at her. "Lord and Lady Beddingsford may be attending the theater according to everyone else, but I am going to the theater with you, and I want you to go to the theater with me."

"Yes," Minerva replied, giving him an adorably firm nod. "Yes. It will just be us. You may wish to reserve a box. So that it remains just us."

A slow grin crossed Griff's lips, and he could only hope it was the sort to make the lady's toes curl. "A private box for the Beddingsfords. Yes, my lady."

"No," Minerva corrected softly. "A private box for us."

Chapter Twenty-One

"You are certain this is the best one? Absolutely certain?"

"Yes, Minerva. Having seen you in each, I can say with absolute certainty, as your maid and your colleague, this one is the best of the bunch."

Minerva grunted in satisfaction at Anna's answer. "Excellent. Why?"

Anna met her eyes in the looking glass. "Why? Why what?"

"Why is it the best?" Minerva asked, splaying her fingers out for emphasis. "I need to know. I am unconscionably nervous, and I need logic to settle me."

If Anna was confused further by the request, or suspected anything by it, she gave no indication. She resumed her work on Minerva's hair, curling and folding the dark tresses in a far more gentle, elegant fashion than Lady Beddingsford would typically have worn it.

"The blue is a magnificent shade that complements your eyes well," she explained in her thick Irish accent, her tone remaining rather matter of fact. "You know your eyes have the ability to change shade based on what you wear, and they really shine out as a striking blue in this. Your complexion is subtle enough to work well with the bold color, and the simplicity of the accessories helps to accentuate your natural beauties."

Minerva found herself nodding at each and every point, not in agreement, but as a mark of reassurance.

It was the most intimidated she had ever been in her entire life, dressing for a night at the theater with Griff. It felt stupid to be like this, but she was. She had no confidence that the woman she was when she was not on assignment was enough to entertain or please a man like him, and the desire to please him was suddenly paramount.

She had never respected herself less than at this moment.

And yet…

There was something perfectly natural in this stupidity. She didn't understand how, but it was there. The notion that this was a profoundly human experience, one endured by innumerable souls over the ages and somehow conquered. That she was simply another passenger along this strange, vulnerable ride that she didn't quite like.

She hated it, in fact. But she knew no other course than to move forward in the face of the blatant discomfort of her entire being. The inner discomfort made the outer discomfort more important, oddly enough. And worth the effort. There was a strange yearning within her for all of this, the whole occasion, the madness she felt and was engaging in—and the entire focus and being of that yearning was Griff.

God help her.

"And you're sure about the pearls?" Minerva asked Anna, clearing her throat against the admission she'd just made to herself.

"Yes," Anna replied without giving the question any consideration, beginning to set her hair with pearl pins. "Anything more would make you uncomfortable."

"Everything feels uncomfortable at the moment," Minerva muttered, placing a freezing-cold hand against her throat. "My own skin, in fact."

"That happens," came the same sort of reply from her maid.

Minerva glanced heavenward, wishing for some reminder that she was still herself, no matter how unremarkable her current state was for anyone else in the world. It was foreign to her, and discomfort was never more unpleasant than when it was foreign.

"Damn."

Minerva blinked at her reflection, then looked towards the door.

Griff stood there, mostly ready for the evening, though his jacket was missing, and his cravat was loose about his neck. And he did not so much stand as lean against the doorjamb, and there was something about the comfort in his stance, in his appearance, in his manner that took Minerva out of their present positions and relationships and sent her reeling hard into the world of imagination.

Some easy, unexceptional evening of two people who lived their lives together, without artifice or ceremony, without walls or secrets, and found simple pleasures in entangling their lives with the other.

Was that what love was?

She almost gagged at the word.

Love? Whoever had said anything about love? This wasn't that. Couldn't be that. Love was for ordinary people in extraordinary circumstances, for those with few calls upon their time and their life, for those who could not see the world for what it truly was. Love was for those who were naïve enough to believe in something intangible that was only ever handled by unreliable mortals.

It was not for her. It never would be.

But what, then, was this instinct to smile in his presence? What was the tightening of her chest and the flushing of her cheeks? What was the tugging sensation behind her navel that made her want to flock to his side like some perfectly trained puppy? Why did she feel so exposed simply by existing, and somehow not mind nearly as much as she should?

Madness. It wasn't love, it was madness.

As she took in the figure of him and felt the deep, almost feral satisfaction in taking pleasure at the sight of him, her mind fumbled over the madness, and her lips burned with the other word instead.

Love.

She cleared her throat, hoping to clear such things from her voice. "What? Have I missed something?"

"No, but I feel as though I have," he replied, his eyes slowly traveling the length of her.

Minerva quickly looked at herself in the mirror to save herself from sighing. "I could have told you that. You've missed so very many things over the course of your life; that much has been painfully obvious from the beginning."

He chuckled, the sound deep and rumbling, somehow reaching the soles of her feet first.

One's toes should not curl at the sound of someone else's laughter. It was too unnerving.

"How much more time do you need for your masterpiece there, Anna?" Griff called.

Anna placed another pearl pin and stepped back with a nod. "Done now."

"Aye, so you are," Griff replied in an Irish accent to match her own. "Loveliness itself, and a credit to your fine handiwork, so it is."

Minerva snorted softly. "Is his accent as offensive as I think it is?"

"Worse," Anna quipped, smiling. "But I know he can do a worthy one. He spent over a year in Ireland on a mission without anyone knowing the difference."

"Did you really?" Minerva asked, turning to face Griff as he started into the room.

He shrugged his broad shoulders with his practiced nonchalance. "It wasn't long ago, and it was one of my very favorite missions. Ireland is special, no question about it."

Anna's smile was as proud as it was delighted. "True enough, sir. True enough."

Griff nudged his head towards the door, and Anna went, glancing over her shoulder at Minerva with a quick wink that she wasn't sure she cared for at all.

What in the world could she be winking for?

Minerva moved away from the mirror and realized, with some confusion, that Anna had not done up the back of her dress before leaving. She had only finished her hair and then done as Griff had indicated and left.

There was no possibility that Griff could have seen that from his vantage point, but Anna would have known full well it needed doing up.

Was that what the wink was for?

There would be words later with the maid, no question.

Of course, between the petticoats, chemise, and stays, there wasn't much to see there, and Griff had seen her in less. But there wasn't anything more comfortable about this than there had been on their previous occasions. In fact, this... this was much worse.

This was no mission, and he wasn't changing his clothing.

Just her.

"Is everything ready?" Minerva asked, pretending to examine the elegant designs along her hem. "For the theater, I mean. I can see that your cravat isn't done, so you are not quite ready."

"No, Tobin is hunting for the perfect cravat pin," Griff told her, jerking his thumb in the direction of his rooms. "I don't know what must be so perfect; I didn't give him a theme."

Minerva shook her head in amusement. "Poor Tobin. Tilda must have frightened him with her strictness, and without a theme, he is doubting everything."

Griff sat on the edge of Minerva's bed, grinning. "He will need to find some semblance of instinct if he is going to continue working as a valet for his cover. Not every mission will have a dresser-in-chief such as Tilda." He paused for a yawn, covering his mouth with the back of a hand. "But yes, everything else is ready. I've secured the box, the carriage will be here to get us to the theater in plenty of time to take our ease before the opera begins, and the box has a perfect view of the stage."

"Thank you," Minerva said softly, excitement over the prospect slowly take over her nerves. "I am… well, I may say that I am truly looking forward to it."

"I know you are," Griff replied, his smile crinkling his eyes in a way that tickled three of her ribs. "I can tell."

Something about the way he said it made her stomach drop to the furthest extent possible within her, and she had to bite her lip in response. Slowly, pointedly, and with a bit of a wild thrill hitting her heart, she turned her back to him. "Will you do me up, please? Anna seems to have forgotten."

She waited there, one hand still at her throat, the other pressing against the neck of her gown. It was a modest neckline, would create a smooth line directly to the edges of her shoulders, though she would have a faint hint of decolletage due to her stays, but only what was fashionable, not enough to be scandalous or daring. She need not feel more exposed than necessary.

It seemed as though a cool breeze crossed the gaping back of her gown, eliciting gooseflesh to raise along her entire back and shoulders, though only a small glimpse of her back would even be visible above the layers back there. What in the world was taking Griff so long?

Then his fingers were there, doing up the buttons in a slow, almost methodical process. Had she not felt the very faint pulling of fabric together, she might not have known he was there at all. She could barely feel the heat of his presence, had no hint of fingers brushing her stays or chemise in the natural motion of fastening buttons, could not even feel the breath of him as he worked. It was the strangest lack of sensation she had ever known, and the more buttons that were completed, the more she cursed herself for building up whatever expectations that left this moment so completely bereft for her.

Why in the world should the innocent doing up of her buttons be an experience at all?

Idiot woman. She fancied herself in love with a man, and suddenly thought every second of her existence ought to reach untold heights of something or other. No wonder Griff had been grazed by a bullet the night before—she was distracted by her own stupidity.

The sooner this mission was completed, the better. She had sanity to regain.

"How is your shoulder?" she asked, amazed that she could sound composed and careless in the asking when it had so tormented her before.

"Fine," he replied tersely, his attention on his task. "Barely feel it. Lot of fuss for a scratch, don't worry about it."

Minerva swallowed in lieu of nodding, looking up at the ceiling and suddenly wishing that he would leave her room and leave her alone. If she continued to make a fool of herself, even if she was the only one who knew she was doing it, she would be in for a night of despair, shame, and this twisted, gnawing feeling that made her want to hide in her bedcovers for hours on end.

Did that emotion have a name? Or did it just have a description that every woman would comprehend?

"There," Griff said, moving back to the bed, but not sitting. "All done."

Why did he sound relieved by that?

Minerva's cheeks suddenly felt hot, and she moved to the toilette to fetch the pearl ear bobs that Anna had set out. "Thank you. It is very convenient to have a partner who doesn't care about such things."

"I didn't say that," Griff broke in at once, his pitch a little odder than normal. "Though it would be better if you didn't ask me to do it again, for both of our sakes."

Minerva turned, working at the ear bob on her left ear. "What? I thought you said you could handle this. You told me you could."

Was she seeing things, or were his cheeks a trifle colored, just as hers felt?

He nodded tersely, his arms folded. "In a pinch, yes. On assignment, when I'm focused, yes. When I don't feel… well, that was then. This isn't the same thing."

Minerva stilled, her fingers midway to reaching for the other ear bob. "Isn't it?"

"No," Griff insisted, his head moving from side to side in pointed, slow motions. "Right now, I would much rather stay here with you looking just as you were than complete any mission, assignment, or duty. And the fact that I managed to help you just now without kissing you in a way that would probably have me knocked unconscious should earn me a damned medal."

She was suddenly hot all over and cold at the same time. Her eyes were dry, her fingers no longer existed, and there was nothing at all tying her to the ground.

And him… dash it, she could barely breathe for the look in his dark eyes. It was something powerful and consuming, something that wrapped her up and set her free all at once, something that set her aflame and made her soar.

Why were they doing this? Why were they dancing circles around this fire between them, refusing to name it and explore it and share it with each other? Why was she letting herself hurt with it rather than losing herself in him and forgetting thought and sense and even feeling?

If this was love, and she thought it might be, why weren't they falling headfirst into it?

Or was that precisely what they were doing, and she simply didn't know it?

"Griff? Griff! I've found the pin!"

Minerva couldn't tell if she breathed first or Griff did, but someone breathed, and then he was moving for the door without a word.

She couldn't let him leave like that, not without a response from her.

"Which gloves should I wear, Griff?" she called, more out of desperation than anything else.

He paused a step, then half turned, giving her a crooked grin. "Surprise me, love. It would suit me best if you went without gloves, but I suppose we must be polite, mustn't we?"

Minerva's throat went dry, and she had never felt more delighted by such a thing. "I suppose we must. More's the pity."

She could hear his groan from where she stood, and grinned when he turned and started down the corridor away from her without another word.

Knowing he found her attractive and appealing, considering she found him the same, was a heady thing indeed, and playing with that knowledge was the most fun she'd had in ages. And if she could keep that in mind, she might be more comfortable with the evening after all.

Not many minutes later, they were loaded into the carriage and on their way, Griff having bestowed the most heated examination upon Minerva as she descended, though his words had been few. The carriage ride would be short, thank heavens, as she wasn't certain an extended time in a confined space without an audience of eyes to keep in mind would be wise.

Griff seemed to be thinking along the same lines, his eyes trained firmly out of the window and not upon Minerva at all.

But she knew better than to be wounded by that. She had a keen sense of observation, and all that she had observed in him prior to getting to this point would be enough to content her for ages.

Ages and ages.

And yet… would it truly have been too much to hope for a little bit more?

Her cheeks heated in the dark of the carriage as they rode, and she looked down at her gloves. Long white gloves, not that it mattered. They were called opera gloves, so she had supposed they would be the most appropriate choice for the evening. There was something almost too pristine about them, too perfect, too pure. But they matched her pearls and kept her polite and respectable in appearance and ensured that Lady Beddingsford's tradition of elegance would remain intact.

It was a silly thing, focusing on her gloves and thinking so much about them. She could not recall the first time she had been forced to wear gloves, but they were still the most foreign garment of clothing to her. Still felt too fine for her. Still seemed pointless and extravagant. Still rubbed against her fingers in a way she didn't like.

Would she always be that London street urchin at heart? Or could she ever truly be Lady Beddingsford and the like?

Griff was the brother of a duke. Nearly a sort of royalty among London society. She was a street urchin who still found gloves strange after all this time. No matter how perfect they might feel in their operative world, they could not be less so in the real one.

What did it matter how she felt if that was the truth?

What did love matter then?

"We're here," Griff announced unnecessarily as the carriage pulled to a stop before the King's Theatre. He craned his neck, the beautiful pearl cravat pin remaining perfectly fixed in place as he did so. "Ready?"

He exited the carriage before she answered.

"Of course," she murmured as she reached for his hand and allowed him to help her down. "What are we seeing tonight?"

"If I read the advertisement correctly," he mused, holding his arm out for her to take, "we are seeing *Aureliano in Palmira* by Rossini."

Minerva frowned a little as they walked towards the entrance. "I've never heard of it."

"Neither have I, so we are in for a surprise," he returned. He covered the hand she'd set in his arm and squeezed her fingers gently. "It doesn't matter anyway. I am pleased just to be here with you. And you already know how beautiful you look."

"Do I?" Minerva managed a slight smile, nodding at someone she recognized from some occasion or other. "I don't recall having heard anything of the sort."

His hold tightened on her fingers. "No? I am quite certain I made my feelings clear on the subject."

She looked up at him in playful surprise. "Was that what your squawking was? I thought you had finally found some language you speak that I do not. I had no notion of what you were saying."

Griff released a sigh and patted her hand before releasing it. "My dear woman, when you hear the language known as man's incoherency in response to your appearance, it is the purest and most natural expression of approval and appreciation that exists."

"Well," Minerva said with a pretend huff, "why not simply say, 'I approve and appreciate,' in plain English and save a lady the doubt?"

"Minerva…"

"What?" She grinned up at him, knowing somehow that he would enjoy seeing a wide smile on her face, as she rarely did so under usual circumstances.

Sure enough, his eyes darkened, and he pulled her a little closer as they moved into the theater. "I approve," he murmured, his mouth almost directly at her ear. "And I appreciate. Very much."

A dozen shivers raced down her spine and up again, sending sparks throughout her entire frame. Heat pulled her in twelve directions, and the back of her neck seemed to be on fire. Yet somehow, her feet continued to move at the same sedate pace they had maintained previously, as though her world hadn't just been flipped on its head and spun like a top.

It was all she could do to avoid leaning into him as they walked. Nothing would have felt more pleasurable at that moment, she was certain, but even the Beddingsfords had some sense of decorum.

And while they were not at the theater for the Beddingsfords, they had to appear for the other people present as the Beddingsfords.

It was an oddly complicated relationship for the first time since they'd begun.

Thankfully, no one was particularly interested in speaking with the Beddingsfords at the moment, so they were able to go almost directly to their box, which, just as Griff had said, provided a perfect view of the stage. There would be nothing to distract from the beauty of the music, the costumes, the story, the entire experience of the opera itself.

Apart from the maddeningly attractive and charming man presently situating himself in the chair to her right.

Minerva exhaled slowly, wishing she had brought her fan with her.

"Bless the King's Theatre," Griff said with a sigh as he sat. "Such a smooth and splendid path to our box, we weren't even stopped by anyone. And there is no room here for anyone else, so there will be no interlopers. Just us."

Just us.

Heavens.

Minerva tried to swallow but could not quite manage it. She put a hand to her throat, trying once more.

"Are you all right?" Griff asked, his voice mildly concerned but holding a laugh in its tone.

If he only knew.

"Yes," Minerva managed, failing again at the swallow. "I simply cannot decide if the pearls were the right choice this evening. There are some blue gems that would have done beautifully, and Anna could have put flowers and ribbons in my hair to match—"

Griff took her hand from her throat and laid his palm against hers, matching finger to finger, though his hand was a great deal larger than hers. "Minerva. Why are you worried about that? I've told you how beautiful you look. You chose the gown you wanted, the hair you wanted, everything. You've never been so anxious about your appearance, even when trussed up like Tilda's dreams come true. Is this how you wanted to look and feel tonight?"

Minerva looked down at her hand, placed so securely against his, and felt her breath come more easily as he slowly laced their fingers. "I think so. I have always preferred simple elegance, and I don't feel as though I am on display or playing a caricature as I do with our usual ensembles."

"Then what?"

"This is the most like me I have been," she whispered, her fingers shifting against his. "And that is almost more uncomfortable."

Griff brought their hands up, and her eyes followed, locking on his. "It shouldn't be," he murmured, kissing the back of her hand.

"You, just as you are, happen to be my preferred company. And while I may not be the arbiter of taste, admittedly, I cannot see any other sentient, logical, philosophical, or artistic view from anyone else differing on the subject."

Tears, of all things, began to burn in her eyes, and she lowered them to focus on his cravat. "No one has ever said that before. I don't know what to say or what to think."

"See, that is a problem for me." He forced an almost harsh exhale and shook his head. "The incompetence of other people where you are concerned has left me in a position of not being believed and possibly being accused of insincerity. What would it take for you to believe me?"

"I believe you," Minerva admitted with a small laugh. "I didn't say that."

Griff's low laugh tickled something in the back of her throat, and suddenly, she could swallow.

Miraculous.

"It just doesn't feel real," she went on. She bit her lip, shaking her head. "To me. You are real, obviously. And I believe you. But…"

"Minerva, love. Look at me."

She did so, almost embarrassed to be saying so much.

Griff's smile was gentle, tender, and perfect. "Stop thinking so much. Stop analyzing everything. Just stop. Breathe it in, and let it be. Let it exist. Can you do that?"

If his thumb continued to rub against her hand like that, and his smile in her direction continued to be so sweet, she could let almost anything exist.

She nodded, wanting to cry again for whatever reason. Thankfully, the overture for the opera started, and their attention was forced to the stage, though Minerva struggled to recognize anything she saw, as her attention was wholly focused on what was happening with her right hand.

The actors and the music were stirring, and their ability to captivate the audience was unmistakable. It was not the first time that Minerva had been to the opera, but it was the first time she had been to the opera for her own pleasure, and the experience transcended any other she could recall. Whether she could credit that wholly to

Griff or only partially, she didn't know, but she would safely admit that he had a great deal to do with it.

Or perhaps it was more to do with her feelings for him.

Her feelings from him.

All of it and then some. But it all revolved around Griff, of that she was certain.

She heard him suddenly hiss a dark Hindustani curse and glanced over in surprise. "What in the world was that for?" she whispered.

He was not looking at her, nor the stage, but across the theater to another box that was almost pointedly empty.

"What?" she whispered again.

"Chorlton," he grunted. "And Pryce and friends. All of whom just left their box one by one. The intermission isn't for another few songs."

Truth be told, Minerva had long lost track of the progress of the opera and had simply been enjoying her time in it. But the return to reality, and the jarring appearance of their assignments when they were supposed to be away from all of that…

Well, it was disheartening, to say the least.

But true to form, her instincts kicked in, and the alertness she had trained for sprang to life. "Then it seems a good time to go and find them, don't you think?"

Griff looked at her, smiling tightly, regret tingeing the edges of it. "It would appear that it is. But is it terrible that I don't want to?"

Minerva managed a smile in return, despite wanting to scream her irritation at the interruption of their lovely evening. "Not terrible, though it does not matter, does it?"

"No," he admitted softly, rising to his feet. "No, it does not."

Chapter Twenty-Two

"The Key is safe and guarded, and he will remain so until further notice."

"And your assignment to destroy his records?"

"Complete."

"And the Hand?"

"Wants us to continue our plans. The Key is not necessary for them."

Griff frowned as he listened to the conversation within the retiring room just beyond them. It had not been overly difficult to find the group once he and Minerva had begun looking. There were only so many places a decent number of people could go during an opera and not raise comment. And he was fairly certain none of them would have left the theater, given the delicacy of maintaining reputation and avoiding speculation when in Society gatherings.

But a retiring room, when they clearly had men and women within, was an interesting choice.

Fortunately for Griff and Minerva, they had not completely closed the door, and there was space enough for both of them to listen. Even with the sounds of the opera continuing about them, the words of the speakers were clear enough for their well-trained ears.

Mostly.

"Have you collected enough support for the arrival?" a deep voice asked.

"We believe so. Our plant has a certain charm about him, and he has encouraged many to host more. Between his work and our roots, we are prepared for twenty, if not more."

"Excellent, nicely done."

"Unfortunately, Herschel wouldn't fall for the story, and with his wife behind bars, he is more suspicious than ever."

"We can forget about him, then. Lady Lavinia was useful to us, but he never was. It does not matter. The Hand will be pleased to have so many new recruits in the ranks. And to be able to free up the Key to return to work shortly."

Griff didn't like the sound of any of this. Hand and Key were clearly code names for certain individuals, and the mentions of arrivals and recruits was unnerving, to say the least. They hadn't noted any indication from their assignments that three of their marks were preparing for anything in particular. Recruiting possible sympathizers, certainly, but when were the Faction supporters not doing so?

He glanced at Minerva across the doorway from him, listening intently. She met his eyes, shaking her head very slightly. She didn't like this either, that much was obvious.

What in the world had they stumbled upon?

"Martin is Key?" she mouthed, twisting her fingers to indicate a key unlocking.

Griff's brows rose. That was a genius speculation, and was more than likely correct, the more he thought about it. He nodded once, agreeing with that assertion.

He held up his hand and pointed to it with a finger, mouthing the word as a question.

Unfortunately, Minerva shrugged a little, indicating she had no answers there.

"When will the arrival take place?" asked a feminine voice that was certainly not Miss Pryce. This one sounded almost elderly, which was startling to Griff. How could an elderly British woman be of any use to the Faction?

"Monday at midnight. It is all above board. We've even got a charity providing resources to the 'poor, helpless refugees,' and no one can claim anything else. It's perfectly orchestrated."

"Of course it is. Anything by the Hand always is."

The room seemed to chuckle together at that, and Griff wanted to groan at hearing it. A group of operatives, agents, conspirators, or sympathizers were going to make their way to British shores on

Monday, and there wasn't a damn thing they could do about it. Refugees could not be turned away, and if that was what they were claiming, there wasn't much hope of stopping them.

Why were they coming? What was about to happen that required so many people of their persuasion to be on British shores?

This was different than Ears uncovering mass assassination attempts to achieve a particular goal, though Griff was certain the shipment of apparent refugees coming in would also bring in unreported goods that wouldn't be so above board.

Perhaps that was it…

A twofold delivery? One to provide personnel that would raise no questions, and goods that accompanied them that no one would consider asking questions about. But how would they intervene there? How could they do anything if all of the paperwork they were submitting to authorities would look accurate?

The fallout from the foiled plot was creating new ploys, Griff realized slowly. The bill to impose certain sanctions on shipping had been halted, which meant the play for control over gaugers and water channels had failed. They were trying other ways to get what they wanted, but it would likely still involve the same players.

Roots and plants…

This was a full-scale infiltration with longstanding supporters as well as new ones and stopping it might not be the most important detail.

Identification would be.

Griff nodded to himself as he thought through that notion. The identification of those coming in and the identification of those who were housing them. Of course, they would also need to know what goods were coming in and where they would be stored, but that was simple enough, all things considered. They had any number of contacts at the docks who could monitor that much alone.

But where were they going to find enough of their own people to track the individuals involved?

"How will we know where to go?" Chorlton asked. "There are any number of docks and wharfs."

"St. Saviour's, of course," came the grizzled response. "As our cause is so righteous. Go to your box number. Clear enough?"

Again, dark laughter resounded from the group, and Griff shook his head. What he wouldn't give for a company of soldiers to march within the room and arrest all of them for conspiring with foreign powers or some such, just to shut them all up. But as per usual, he was bound by his duty to report everything he saw and heard to the powers higher than he so a strategic plan could be implemented that would not disrupt the lives of British citizens and would serve the greater good.

And that was what he would do.

"Well," someone said with a sigh, "that is all we can do for now. *J'ai vecu.*"

The phrase of support and loyalty was uttered by them all, and Griff looked at Minerva quickly, recognizing that the statement was that of a close to the meeting.

They needed to move. Now.

He jerked his head to his side, and she came, somehow without any sound from her skirts. He took her arm and hurried them around the corner of the alcove the retiring room was situated in, then pressed her back to the wall, looming over her.

"Sorry," he hissed, leaning in at once.

He caught her brief nod before pressing his lips to hers, and genius woman that she was, her fingers dug into his hair, pulling him further against her. One of her stockinged feet latched around the back of his knee, locking him to her rather effectively, and if his heart hadn't already been pounding from anticipation of being found out, it would have begun doing so then.

It was a strange thing, kissing Minerva without actually kissing Minerva. Their mouths were fused together, it was true, but there was nothing in it but the positioning. His arm was wrapped around her waist, the other hand bracing them both against the wall, and for all appearances, they were in a passionate and thorough embrace.

In truth, they were only standing there, wrapped in each other, connected in a show of intimacy. The breathless panting was not from their passion, but their adrenaline, though it added a convincing sound to the thing.

Footsteps came near, and Griff shut his eyes, forcing his mouth to move against Minerva's just enough.

She whimpered, whether in truth or in acting, he couldn't tell, but bloody hell, did it sound real.

His fingers gripped against her back in response, and her fingers slid against his scalp, creating the need in him to growl some sort of approval. But he made himself tamp it down, keep it constrained, reminding himself that this was not real. It was not real.

Was it?

Faint murmurs and snickers, if not a gasp or two, met Griff's ears, but he did not stop, knowing it was not worth the risk. He deepened his kiss for show, Minerva sighing loudly, and the footsteps shuffled away, the exact number of them impossible to count with the deadening nature of the carpets.

When applause for the present song of the opera sounded, Griff broke the kiss, allowing his mouth to move towards Minerva's cheek as he glanced to his left, knowing she would do the same to her right, if she had sense remaining. He was struggling to find his own, but he was not so far gone as to forget how they found themselves here.

"Gone?" he whispered against her ear, pausing there.

"Yes," she replied in a low, almost guttural tone.

His right knee buckled very briefly.

Griff exhaled and pressed his brow against the wall next to Minerva's head. She took the cue and released her hold on his hair, letting her wrists dangle at his shoulders, leaning into him.

Now they could breathe. Now they could relax.

Now they could…

"Good thinking," Minerva whispered, one hand patting his neck.

He laughed once. "Want to know where I got the idea?"

She scoffed and her hand moved to bat the back of his head. "I know exactly where it came from, thank you very much. Turnabout is fair play, no?"

"Something like that." He straightened slightly, shaking his head. "There is so much to report from that. How did our assignments wind up so complicated?"

"Why shouldn't they?" Minerva asked, sobering as she leaned her head back against the wall. "Everything else has."

Griff gave her a bemused look. "Everything?"

She nodded, her eyes finding his.

Somehow, against reason, he found himself leaning in. "Everything?" he asked again, dropping his voice.

"Hasn't it?" she whispered, a strange wavering sound hitting her voice.

He paused there, a hairsbreadth from kissing her again. She was arching towards him, but not leaning in. And that waver did not sound like desire. It sounded more like…

Fear. Trepidation. Hesitation.

But not reluctance.

Griff searched her eyes, so close it seemed as though he could see into her very soul. If only he could truly see so far, he might find more answers than Minerva would give him voluntarily. He loved her, that much he knew easily and clearly. She liked him, he could safely say, and did not object to his attentions. She had been almost eager for them of late, if he flattered himself, and she was anything but indifferent to him.

He could see a future for them. A creative, glorious future that would keep both of them sufficiently occupied and entertained in so very many aspects.

And yet she was not closing this distance between them. The invitation was there, his willingness plain, and she was waiting rather than moving.

Submitting, not selecting.

That was not how this should be.

But perhaps she was overwhelmed with what they had heard, and like him, her mind was going in a hundred directions and committing each aspect of the conversation to memory.

Perhaps it was simply bad timing. Perhaps she was tired. Perhaps the slow running of her finger along the juncture of his neck and shoulder was a sign of anxiety rather than encouragement.

Perhaps he was wrong. About everything.

Lord, don't let him be completely wrong.

"We should get back to our box," he murmured, his eyes darting to her lips with the strongest pang of longing he had ever felt for her.

"Yes," he watched them say, feeling the breath of them on his own lips.

But she did not move.

How did that feel like victory and defeat all in one?

Helpless, Griff closed the distance between them to kiss her softly, and Minerva kissed him back, the faintest pressure now against his neck.

She nuzzled against him, a hand moving to his jaw as she sighed with what seemed to be the weight of the world.

"What is it, love?" Griff all but begged, dusting his lips across her brow. "Tell me, please."

He felt her shake her head. "I can't," she breathed. "Not yet."

Not yet.

Had there ever been a phrase of more hope and more dread?

But he would trust in her and in what he knew she was capable of, so he nodded and, regretfully, stepped back, holding his arm out to her.

Her throat worked on a swallow, and she took it, silently allowing him to walk her back to the box. "During intermission," she murmured as he sat beside her, "will you see what box number they are in? You could be confused looking for a drink for me."

"Good thought," he replied with a nod. He took her hand, surprised at how cold it felt within her gloves. "A dutiful husband would undoubtedly go out in search of a drink for his lady."

"Suppose so," was all she said.

Griff glanced at her, finding no hint of a smile on her face, no inkling of joy in her features, and no indication that she was even aware of her present surroundings.

What a change this was from the warm, almost giggling figure she had been when they'd arrived. Yet they had been together every moment, experienced all of the same things, heard each of the details from their marks. He had not been offensive, had not seen her hurt, had not known anything that ought to have caused such a shift in her, and the not knowing was disconcerting.

But he would let her tell him when she was ready. Minerva never failed him with her words and opinions, and this would be no different.

The intermission came, and true to his word, Griff left his seat to identify the box that Chorlton and Pryce had been in, under the guise of finding a drink or refreshment for his wife. It took most of the length of the intermission, given the number of people who streamed out of their boxes to socialize, and the amount of jostling he endured just for a simple errand seemed wholly unnecessary.

But he was able to complete the task and return, with drink in hand, before the second act began, which was the only thing he could have wished for.

He handed the drink to Minerva and whispered, "Seven," before taking his seat.

She nodded, took one sip, and set the drink down on the floor beside her.

And said nothing.

Not one word.

The music struck up again, indicating the resuming of the opera, and Griff reached for Minerva's dangling fingers, knowing their hands would be out of sight of anyone else. He didn't care; that was the point. Griff wanted to hold Minerva's hand, and it had nothing to do with the Beddingsfords.

He held them for the space of two heartbeats, and then Minerva slowly pulled her hand away.

He glanced at her curiously, but her focus was on the stage, her hands securely in her lap.

Years of being a covert operative had taught him to suspect danger and trouble where it was not necessarily evident, and those trainings were putting him on the alert now. Something was troubling Minerva, and whatever it was, she did not want Griff to be involved.

Or to know.

She shifted slightly in her seat, then settled once more, this time leaning away from him, her expression unchanged.

Now he was irritated as well as curious.

From a kiss in the corridor to distance in the box, and only a handful of words to fill the time and space between.

That was not enough time or context for anyone to have offended another person, even when they were as classically irritating as Griff had the ability to be.

But clearly he had done something. Why else would she shy away from him now after all they had shared and been through? After all they had said, and all they had not said, she suddenly did not want him near.

He needed to give her the benefit of the doubt, he eventually decided. They could sit here and enjoy the opera and say nothing, pretend each other were not here, and then discuss the music or costumes or actors with great animation on the drive home. It could be a lovely distraction from the plot they had heard about and allow them both to be reminded of life outside of missions and spies and infiltrations.

Perhaps she simply did not wish to be touched when she was in this state. He knew several individuals like that, and he could respect such preferences. It seemed an odd time for such a proclivity to appear when they had been living together in such close quarters for so long, and had trained together beyond that, but he had heard of stranger things.

It would be fine. He would respect her space and her present silence and allow her to resume conversation and warmth at her leisure.

Provided her leisure was not sometime next week.

Because he loved her, damn it, and he wanted to hold her hand for no other reason than because it allowed him to be connected to her.

Was that too much to ask?

He'd have to tell her one of these days, or she would never fully comprehend his continuing to reach for her. Perhaps it was an annoyance when she wasn't aware of the strength and depth of his feelings, or in which avenues they moved.

He was going to drive himself mad with so much conjecture and no facts to support any of them.

There was nothing to do but wait, and so wait he would.

By the time the opera ended and the two of them had been loaded into their carriage, she still hadn't said a word to him. Nor did she speak on the carriage ride to their house. Nor did she speak as they arrived home, removed their cloaks, and were finally left alone in the entry hall.

She simply stood there and said nothing.

Griff was positively fuming as he stared at her now, watching her pull her gloves from her fingers and arms. He had been imagining doing that himself all night, given their earlier teasing about gloves and the like.

It wasn't that he resented being deprived of that. It was that something had caused Minerva to completely wall herself up against him over the course of the evening, and he had no bloody clue what it was.

Growling in irritation, he shucked his own gloves off and set his hands on his hips. "All right, what is it? What have I done now?"

Minerva jerked to look at him, her brow creasing. "I beg your pardon?"

"She speaks!" Griff cried, gesturing dramatically. "A miracle from on high if ever I saw one!"

"What the bloody hell are you on about?" she demanded, matching his pose, though he doubted it was intentional on her part.

"You!" Griff ran his hands through his hair, laughing that she was apparently clueless as to what had driven him mad all evening. "What started off as a lovely, promising evening that I have been looking forward to more than I let on, turned into some horrific exercise in torture through silence that has me questioning absolutely everything I thought I knew."

Her utterly dumbfounded expression and lack of response enraged him, and he whirled away, throwing his hands into the air. "Unbelievable. Still! Still doing it. What have I done, Minerva? I've gone over the entire night backwards and forwards, and I've got nothing to apologize for. So whatever sins you're laying against me are purely imagined."

"You are the most self-centered, impossible, deranged man I have ever met in my entire life," Minerva snapped. "I opt to say little, and you make the entire thing about you? Turn around and explain yourself, you bleeding idiot."

"Gladly!" He made a show of turning back around, bearing a taunting smile. "We interrupt our evening, which had been going beautifully, to see to our mission. We uncover a plot. We keep our covers with a kiss, which I apologized for ahead of time, I'll remind you, and which you were an active participant in, I must say. Thoroughly."

Her cheeks flamed a brilliant pink, and it was an oddly satisfying response.

"And then," he went on, taking two steps towards her. "Then! You completely disappeared into yourself. No explanation. No obvious reason. No words to me the rest of the night. Your partner."

"Why do I have to speak?" Minerva finally said, flinging a hand out. "I don't see the need to fill the air with sound every three seconds, unlike some people. I was watching the opera, which is why we were there."

Griff shook his head frantically in disbelief. "I can watch an opera any time I want! I wanted to be there with you, and you might as well have been there by yourself! I didn't expect a running commentary throughout the show, but for God's sake, woman, you could have said something."

"Like what?" she thundered, her tone taking on an icy edge he hadn't expected. "Like how I didn't know what to think about kissing you in the corridor for show because I wanted to do so in earnest? Like how it suddenly became an idea to run away with you rather than complete our assignment? Like how I still blame myself for you getting shot because we weren't paying enough attention? Because we were spending time with each other rather than doing our job and investigating, and that's how we missed an armed man guarding the place? How almost everything we have done together has been a disaster because we were, in fact, together? I am not an imbecile, I realize there is some degree of attraction here, and I wish to heaven, hell, and back again that there weren't!"

Revelation upon revelation lashed upon his cheek, a strange cacophony of pleasure and pain as she thrilled and devastated him in turn the more she spoke. No admission of feelings should sound with such anger, if not disgust, and to hear what he had enjoyed so much be described with such fury…

He was not about to take that lying down, or standing there, as it were.

He could match that fury, and God help him, he was about to.

"There wasn't another option but to do this together, remember?" Griff yelled, tugging at his cravat before it could strangle him in his rage. "We both tried to get away from that early on, and they said no!"

"I was there, I recall!" Minerva made a harsh growling sound between clenched teeth. "But you! You would not keep things professional between us! You had to tease and charm and toy, you had to make all of this a game rather than focusing on what we were supposed to do. And I will take my share of the blame here—I wasn't prepared for that. I should have kept my defenses up and forced us onto the right course."

"The right course?" Griff repeated. "Right? What the hell was wrong with what we did?"

Minerva put her face in her hands, the sounds of her seething eking through her fingers. "How could I have let myself get so distracted by you? How could I be so stupid? The biggest plot I have ever uncovered in the course of my career, and I am standing here in the foyer fighting with you. This is so bloody pointless!"

Griff released a harsh, almost forced laugh at that. "Well, I can agree with that!"

Her hands dropped, and she glared at him, belatedly causing him to wonder if she had a weapon on her person with which she might now kill him. "You make me a worse operative, Mist. You make me sloppy, emotional, unobservant, and weak, and that is unforgivable."

"I think you just complimented me on how I make you feel," Griff sneered, wishing his own words wouldn't make his stomach twist into knots. "How's that polite, professional distance working for you now, Mirrors? Take a look at yourself, why don't you?"

"Oh please, enthrall me," Minerva dared, folding her arms. "Astonish me with your keen powers of observation, oh mighty spy, and catalogue my faults."

"We don't have time for that list," Griff informed her smugly, "so I will confine myself to the relevant ones."

She snarled, and he would swear he could see her hackles raising like an alley cat.

"You are narrow-minded," he began, indicating the first flaw with a taunting finger. "Impossibly so. Cannot see past the end of your own nose. You have minimal imagination at best; everything has to go exactly as you've envisioned. Heaven forbid anything goes wrong; you cannot adapt to actually save your life. You fight like a woman in a tantrum, you waltz like your body is a ramrod, you have all the warmth of an ice block in January, and you make it utterly impossible to be an equal partner because you refuse to trust anyone but yourself. No wonder you've always worked alone. It's the only way you know how to live."

Minerva's mouth hung open, and she seemed to be trembling with fury, if the quivering of her ringlets was any indication.

It did not feel any better to have said what he did, Griff would admit. But there was an odd freedom in airing his resentment. Was that so wrong?

"Oh, and you have the boniest fingers I have ever held," he added, for some unknown reason. "Better you wear the gloves than not, if you wish to appear a fine lady."

"These fingers," Minerva muttered in the darkest voice any woman had ever used in the history of life itself, "are about to find their way into your eye sockets. And yes, I do know the proper way to go about it, thank you. Don't worry about holding them anymore. You won't have to."

Griff bowed slightly. "Yes, you made that abundantly clear this evening. Pulling away from me and leaning so far to the side, it's a wonder you didn't topple out of your seat. What excuses Lord Beddingsford would have had to make then."

"Devil take Lord Beddingsford," Minerva spat, "and may the devil spend eternity annoyed by him. Perhaps Lady Beddingsford simply preferred not to be touched at that moment."

"Her ladyship seemed keen enough moments before," Griff replied without concern.

"And a lady once willing must always be so, is that it?"

That was a trap, and Griff knew it well. He swallowed back a retort and shook his head. "That is not what I meant."

"Ah, forgive me for not understanding your true meaning, my lord," Minerva said with a derisive curtsy. "You always speak with such clarity, it must be my simple woman's mind unable to properly comprehend. If you'll excuse me, I have reports to write. And so do you." She turned on her heel and strode further into the house, muttering in dark German phrases he would have to be strung up to ever utter.

He shook his head to himself, looking down at the floor. She was right; he did have reports to write. And the sooner he did, the sooner this mission could be concluded, and he could get on with his life.

There was no satisfaction in that thought.

None at all.

"Well done, Griff, old boy," he mumbled as he moved to the study. "Bloody well done."

Chapter Twenty-Three

There was a strange loneliness in a house of silence. Minerva had never felt anything like it before, but she could not deny that it was true.

Three days of not seeing or speaking with Griff, and they were in the same house. She had checked to make sure he had not moved his things elsewhere, and thus far, he was still there.

He was still there.

She had only intended to avoid him for the first day. Her anger had been the most significant feeling she had ever known in her life, so consuming and all-encompassing. But when that had finally begun to fade, she had only felt hurt. Hurt for what she had said to him, hurt for what he had said to her. Yet… nothing she had said was a lie. None of it. She was an honest person, when she was herself, and she could not truthfully take back anything that she had said.

She could only take back the emotion with which she had said it. Griff was self-centered, but who wasn't? He was so much more than that. He was impossible, anyone would admit that. He did make her emotional, distracted, weak… He did make her a worse operative when they were together because all she wanted was him.

None of those things were truly drawbacks to him. They were simply part of his nature, and God help her, she loved him in spite of those things.

She loved him in spite of everything.

But she couldn't find him to tell him so. He was still living in the house, according to servants, but she had not seen him when she had time to seek him out. Between preparations for the upcoming mission and her reporting in on the progress of her own assignments, she was in and out of the house herself.

A counterplot to track the arrival of the agents and goods was underway, involving all of the departments and operatives from all areas of the service. There were too many unknowns, and the dangers were incalculable due to those unknowns.

Normally, Minerva would have been thrilled to take part in such a mission. Would love the risks and dangers, the ability to immediately provide useful information to the Shopkeepers, the mass cooperation of operatives she would never have had the opportunity to work with otherwise. And she was excited for the opportunity, she couldn't deny that.

But it was a tainted opportunity.

She wanted to talk to Griff. She wanted to sit on the floor of the drawing room and discuss the matter with him. She wanted to talk through the implications and the possibilities, wanted to pretend that they could control the outcomes for the sake of speculation, wanted to hear his thoughts on the topic and how he would manage the operation if he were the one in charge. She wanted to tell him how irritated she was at having to repeat herself multiple times for multiple committees of people with regards to their present assignment. Wanted to laugh about her materials report to Tilda. Wanted to tell him that she had actually provided an idea to Tilda and might be working with the woman on designing more functional costumes for the female agents.

He would never believe that.

She wanted to hold his hand.

That broke her heart. She had pulled away from him at the theater, but not for the reasons he thought.

She had been afraid. Afraid of what happened to her under the influence of his touch. Afraid of losing herself if she gave more to him. Afraid that she would never be the operative she once was if she let herself slide on that slope. Afraid…

Afraid to love him. Afraid to let him love her, if he wanted.

Just afraid.

And that fear had caused her to retreat, and caused her to lash out, and it was only in the silence of the house and her thoughts and her reverie that she had been able to put a name to the thing.

And then, of all things, to realize the truth.

She wanted him anyway.

But she had probably pushed him too far, said too much, angered him to a degree from which there was no return. Why else would he be impossible to find?

He would be involved in the mission tonight, of that she had no doubt. But would she be able to speak with him before they went to their assigned positions? Knowing how she would worry about him, if she let herself, knowing how tormented she currently felt, she needed to at least give good wishes. Touch his hand. Apologize for…

For…

Anything, really. How she had yelled. How she had retreated. How she had only given him half-truths during her tirade against him.

There wouldn't be time for how she felt, but at least she could make it clear how she did not feel.

Would that be enough?

"Mirrors? Time to go."

Minerva jumped, startled by the sudden appearance and address from Anna. "What?"

Anna raised a brow. "Time to go? Milliner has us all meeting together before we move to the assembly point."

"Right." Minerva blinked, staring down at the poor excuses for notes she had been writing out in her parlor. With no one in the house to address with her thoughts, and only needing to fill time before the mission, she had decided to set herself the task of polite responses to invitations.

But none of that would matter, would it?

The Beddingsfords might disappear from London after tonight, and never return. What a scandal that would be, but she would not be around to see it. She would have to return to the Convent and prepare for teaching, as the fall term was well under way.

Life as she had known it would return. But she would not be the same person she had known in that life.

How was she going to reconcile the two?

"Mirrors."

"Sorry!" Minerva pushed up from her chair and smiled for Anna, brushing at her gown. "Lost in my thoughts."

"You don't say," Anna murmured, handing over a hat and half cloak.

They would be proceeding out of the house as simply Lady Beddingsford and her maid leaving for an evening's entertainment and making their way to the designated meeting place for Convent agents in London.

Almack's.

It was a delightful advantage for the ladies to have Lady Cowper as an ally, as she was the clear grand dame of the Almack's patronesses and had been an agent herself at one time. She had repeatedly insisted that she was always available to help any of her fellow agents in need, but they tried to not require her services, simply due to her natural prominence.

But access to a highly exclusive location to meet together? That they could do.

And if Lady Cowper were ever asked about such things, as she was required to be there for their meetings, all she had to do was speak of one of the dozens of charities for which she was patroness, and all questions were removed.

The rooms were not brightly lit at the moment, but they were certainly alight enough to indicate activity. There was no way around that—a large group of women could not meet together without some difficulty. And if Minerva's instincts were correct, they would all be receiving costumes there and leaving in a very different manner.

Chairs had been set up in the ballroom, most of which were already full, but Minerva and Anna made their way to an open two and sat.

Milliner stood at the front of the room, already dressed in a clever costume of a hack driver. She nodded at Minerva as she entered, and then at the three women following.

"I think we are enough here to begin," she started. "Thank you to Lady Cowper, as always, for providing us the meeting space. Would you remind us of the story, should we be asked?"

Lady Cowper rose from the first seat of the room and faced them all. "Ladies, this is a meeting of the Irish Children's Hunger Committee. It will split opinion if expressed, so be prepared and remain ambivalent."

Milliner nodded at that. "We are not taking a stance on Catholic children or Protestant ones, so avoid that, if you can. And if questioned, tell them we haven't figured out the best way to help either side. Which is true, after all."

There was light, uneasy laughter from the group at that, and Minerva found herself nodding. The situation in Ireland was more complicated than anyone would have liked and, even in jest, had to be taken seriously.

Someday, perhaps she would be assigned to Ireland. She'd like that.

Griff had been there. Would he wish to join her?

She shook her head at the errant thought, forcing herself to return to the meeting at hand.

"Right, then," Milliner went on, "most of you know enough of the evening's task. There is a shipment of agents or sympathizers of the Faction coming on land, and they will also be transporting unreported goods. Our mission, along with the other operatives joining us, will not be to stop the operation, but to monitor it. We need to know where every passenger goes and where every item off-loaded ends up."

Heads nodded around the room, and Milliner swept her dark gaze around at them all.

"Weaver is leading the operation," she told them, "and he will determine assignments. This is one of the more unknown engagements we have had in recent days, so if there is anyone who wishes to back out, now is your chance."

Not a hair moved.

Milliner's smile was slight, but undeniably proud. "Excellent. Tilda has furnished us with a variety of options for the evening, so unless you have brought your own ensembles, please come find what suits you and get changed. We will leave for the assembly point in twenty minutes." She nodded once and stepped away, moving to speak with Lady Cowper privately.

Minerva looked at Anna with a tight smile. "Did you bring anything for us? I wasn't thinking and—"

"Yes," Anna interrupted, her smile far more easy. "I am well aware. I brought a few things."

The next few minutes were spent changing, with Lady Cowper and her staff taking on the task of returning belongings to each home. Minerva slipped into her breeches and boots, Anna adjusting the settings of her stays to form her figure into something less feminine. Then she had a coarse linen shirt, neck kerchief, and padded jacket.

Her hair had already been pinned up, but now she was fastened in a wig of shaggy black hair that made her look like a young man in need of a trim when she placed a cap atop the mass. It was a good disguise, if she did say so herself, and she had never been more grateful for the squarish set of her jaw than at moments like this. Whoever would have thought that a feature so unflattering for a woman would be so very useful for her instead?

A quick whistle rent the air, and the murmur of conversation silenced.

"Set?" called Milliner's barely disguised voice. "Servant passages. Follow Ivy."

Minerva's brows rose. Ivy was in the group this evening? That as an impressive feat. Ivy was one of the best agents to come out of the Convent, and her missions were usually of the utmost discretion and importance, due to the standing of her husband in Parliament. Last she had heard, Ivy had been part of the contingent helping Trace with a little problem involving his lady love up near Liverpool last year.

Interesting that this particular mission should take place while she was in London and draw her attention.

The women all trickled out of the ballroom as ordered, winding through the relatively narrow servant passages of Almack's, eventually leading them all out to the darkened streets behind the building. They would take none of the main roads towards the docks, keeping to the darker, quieter streets where no one would be looking. And they would split up naturally and wind their way there so as to avoid appearing as a mob marching through London. All of this was beyond habit, ingrained in them as much as their answers to the basic questions of capture.

Minerva, Anna, and another operative split off almost at once, looking for all intents and purposes like a trio of lads heading in for evening shifts, though they would probably raise some brows as to the actual workload they would be capable of. Still, not all dock laborers were required to lift massive amounts. Some were runners, recorders, lodging owners, market vendors, or chandlers.

And Minerva knew well that sometimes there were street urchins looking to make a few coins for simple errands.

They would blend in perfectly.

The abandoned warehouse in Upper Shadewell was before them, and they filed in through various doors, each guarded by a burly man at varying positions, each far more alert than an average passerby would think. But Minerva nodded with a faint grunt at each, and she wondered if she might know one in particular from somewhere, though there was not time to trace back through her memories for his face or nature.

He rather reminded her of Hal's protector turned house servant, a cantankerous rascal named Tad.

Weaver leaned against a wall on the far side of the warehouse, so far removed from his usual finery it was delightful, and he seemed perfectly content to watch operatives trickle in. Minerva took a good look around, seeing men and women she had known for years, had worked with previously, or whose faces she knew from previous interdepartmental exchanges. But as yet, there was no Griff.

Where was he?

A group of five men came into the space from the back door, and her attention went there in a moment, hoping against hope.

Sure enough, as though she had conjured him herself, there was Griff, accompanied by Draper and three others she did not know. If he saw her, he gave no indication, but she continued to stare at him without shame.

He could have been one of the heavy-lifting dockworkers. His athletic frame had never been so evident, the workmen's clothing suiting him somehow more perfectly than his finery, which she would never have anticipated. His hat was tipped ever so slightly back, allowing the minimal light in the space to give her full view of his face. He hadn't shaved in days, which added to his look, and gave him the rugged, dangerous, rough appearance one might wish for the occasion, but it also took her back to the young man she had pulled from the docks all those years ago. His stubble hadn't been so thick or dark then, but the shadow of it had been there.

Would someone have to pull him from the docks again tonight? Would someone need to pull her?

She couldn't bear the thought of it, and her chest grew tight with the fear.

Griff folded his arms as he listened to Weaver, now addressing them all, and Minerva's eyes fell to his wrist. Wrapped tightly there was the talisman, seeming no more out of place there than anything else about Griff. It was a part of him, and the sight of it did more to settle her than almost anything else could have. That talisman had gotten him through every mission and occasion before this, and she had to believe it would do so now. It was nothing more than her father's old button, slid through a long leather strap she had purloined from their home as a child, but over the years it had become a shield for this man.

Was that her father looking out for her from the other side?

She could only hope he would use his influence again tonight, if that was the case.

She looked into Griff's face again, and this time, saw him looking at her.

Breath seemed to fill her lungs rather than escape them, and the tightness in her chest eased. Something about the steadiness of him, of his look, the certainty of his bearing, was enough to ground her and give her confidence.

How could she tell him what she needed to across this space, with no time to say anything?

She swallowed and forced her lips to smile a little, though they did not need much prodding to do so.

The floor of her stomach caught fire when he returned her smile with a crooked one of his own. Small, slight, but certainly there and certainly Griff.

It ought to have been enough.

But it wasn't.

"Ears, Rudder, Mirrors, passengers," Weaver called out, drawing Minerva's attention to the meeting.

Minerva looked around for Ears and Rudder, nodding at both when she saw them. Without knowing the true number of passengers coming ashore, they could not be certain how many of them would truly be tracking anyone, or where it would take them. They could only hope to track all of them and to note the location of the goods, if assigned to do so.

It was the most unpredictable sort of mission they could ask for, which were not Minerva's favorites.

But they were Griff's.

"Gent, Mist, Beacon, passengers." Gent knew the city well, that was a good choice. And Beacon was the best sharpshooter the Convent had; she could take care of them both as well as herself.

They would be safe as a team. Good.

"Trick, Trace, Rogue, goods."

Minerva blinked at that. Trick was involved? The man had been so deep undercover, he hadn't surfaced for five years. They were bringing him in for this? But he was the best source in the London underbelly, so he would have a good sense of things. And Trace and Rogue knew the docks like the back of their hands. There was no accident in pairing them together.

The rest of the assignments went out smoothly, and then suddenly, Weaver was silent.

All eyes were on him.

"There is no telling what protections they have in place for this," he finally said. "Not enough time to prepare. We have some assets around to watch out for you, but we cannot possibly cover all of London with them. Keep your eyes open. Keep an eye on each other. Do not be seen. We may not get another chance like this if we disrupt them at all. Split up if you have to, leave someone if you must. There are no promises tonight, people. None." He looked around, then nodded once. "Get moving."

The group started to disperse, but Minerva could not go yet. Would not.

She turned and started towards Griff, her eyes fixed far ahead of him so no one would know. He was starting towards her as well, frowning slightly at her odd focus, she could see, but not saying a word. He slowed as she reached him and was starting to pass, but Minerva hooked her little finger against his—hard.

Clever man that he was, he turned at once to follow her, keeping their small fingers interlocked, his free hand taking hers and hiding them between them as they moved through the mass of other operatives.

Minerva walked them towards a tall series of crates and boxes, creating a sort of anteroom in the warehouse, and once sheltered, turned to face Griff, setting her back against the rough wood of the crates.

His mouth was on hers at once, and she arched into him, her fingers still behind her back, gripping against his with the same hunger her lips ached with. He was relentless against her, and she was just as voracious, giving as much as she was taking, pleading as much as she was declaring, and reveling as much as she was driving. It was a battle and a dance, a sparring session full of laughter and meaning, grazing fingers and teasing looks, a frenzy of feeling and a moment of madness.

Glorious, delicious madness.

Griff hummed into her mouth, releasing one of her hands to lean further into her, bracing himself on the crates behind her. Minerva used that newly freed hand to grip his shirt, keeping him close and pulling herself closer. Her right leg moved, wrapping around his and settling behind his knee, just as it had done at the theater the other night, locking him to her until she deemed necessary to relent.

That time might never come.

"Gads, my lady," Griff murmured against her lips, nipping just enough to tighten her hold on him. "Still you unman me."

Minerva laughed softly and fused their mouths together for another searing kiss, wishing there was time to curl herself fully into him. "That is my secret power, my lord."

"Is it?" He smiled against her, his lips dusting her cheek. "How delightful."

She sighed and moved her hand to his jaw. "Griff… I…"

He placed a finger against her lips, gently silencing her, his eyes steady on hers. "Are you about to apologize for what you said to me?"

Minerva cocked her head, curious about his tone, and smiled a little. "No…? I wasn't. My tone, perhaps, but the words…"

He chuckled and slid his hand behind her ear, careful not to disrupt her wig. "Good. I know you meant that. I meant what I said, too, but not how I said it. Because there's more, isn't there?"

She could not have said it better herself, not under these circumstances. "Yes," she whispered. "Yes, there is more."

He kissed her again, very softly, and touched his brow to hers. "But there's no time now."

"No. There isn't," she murmured, her voice hitching slightly.

He winced at that hitch. "Minerva, I wish…"

"I know." She took his hand and kissed the talisman at his wrist before cradling her own face with his palm, looking up at him as fiercely as she dared. "Please be careful," she whispered, the three words meaning something else entirely.

Griff's lips twitched, and somehow, she knew he understood. He kissed her once. "You be careful," he said with clear emphasis, his words taking on the same meaning.

She nodded, holding his hand against her for just a moment more. Then she arched up and brushed her lips across his, felt his take hers the same, and in a perfectly choreographed movement, they moved away from each other in opposite directions, heading for their assigned groups.

It was time.

Chapter Twenty-Four

$\mathscr{I}$t had been, without a doubt, the longest night of Griff's life.

The fact that it had only just ended at three in the afternoon might have had something to do with it.

But he, Gent, and Beacon had managed to track a passenger from the ship who had gone to a house from which there had been comings and goings all night and into the morning. Beacon had watched the back of the house, and her reports had been essential in ensuring that they did not miss a departure from the bustling location. With so much activity, Gent had been forced to involve his army of children to track each person that had left the house—on the chance the passenger had been one of the party to depart the residence—but one of the adult operatives had gone with them each time. Finally, they had accumulated all of the addresses, and each would now have a watch on it until their passenger would make themselves known at one of them.

Or the host presented them in public somehow.

How exactly this information was going to be acted upon had been less clear to them during Weaver's meeting, but Griff was certain some plan had been put in place by the Shopkeepers.

Or would be shortly.

It had been a surprisingly orderly mission, all things considered. The groups assigned to track passengers had lain in wait along the disembarkation route, signaling to each other when they would pick up a mark. The crew unloading the ship had made plenty of noise to give them cover, even if the passengers, and their escorts, had been mostly silent. Griff could not speak for any other set, but his team had not encountered any weapons throughout the ordeal. He had not heard any gunshots, scuffles, or sounds of struggle at all, so he could only hope that meant there had been no disruptions, let alone losses, among their ranks.

And as for the goods unloaded…

Well, he had no idea what they had been or where they had gone, but he was very curious to read through whatever after-action report the operatives were given in the coming days.

Not at the moment, of course. Presently, he was damn tired and wanted nothing more than to drop into bed and sleep until dawn.

But he had been the idiot to offer up submitting the report for his team, as the other two operatives had families and the like to return to, so he would have to get that done before he could rest at all.

And if Minerva was back…

His heart seemed to careen to the right, slamming into the ribs there somehow.

Minerva.

He had no words for the relief that had swept through him upon feeling that small finger of hers latch on to his and tug him rather pointedly to follow her. He had felt more settled about matters between them when he'd caught her watching him and seen her smile, but the firmness of her grip on him had told him everything he had needed to know. That they'd managed to find a moment for themselves at all, let alone one where they could share such an extraordinary series of kisses in each other's hold, had been remarkable. But to hear the meaning behind her words, 'Please be careful,' and to offer up the same to her had been liberating.

She loved him. It was as good as expressed, if not better than, and whatever explanation they would offer each other for their fight would pale in comparison to that. He loved her, and she loved him, and they matched each other in every way. In passion, in energy, in complication, in livelihood, in stubbornness…

Griff chuckled to himself, a trifle breathlessly, as he considered that particular point. There would likely be more fights in their future, which meant more such reconciliations, and any children they had would almost certainly be hellions in some way or another.

He'd never thought all that much about children, but it was suddenly a perfectly genius idea, if Minerva was their mother.

Knowing what sort of child he had been, he hoped, for her sake, they had very few boys.

He walked around to the back of their Grosvenor Street house, as though he were one of the footmen returning from holiday or some such, and slipped into the kitchen.

"All right there, sir?" the cook asked without looking up from his chopping.

"Perfectly, thank you," Griff replied, taking his cap off. "How's the mistress?"

At this, the cook paused, looking over at him in confusion. "D'you know, I'm not sure. I've not been asked to provide breakfast or luncheon, and no one has requested tea. She might not even be at home."

Something cold began to take the journey from Griff's throat to the pit of his stomach, as though he had swallowed a portion of ice. He did his level best to nod in response before heading out of the kitchen and trying to hasten his steps without looking frantic or desperate.

Why would Minerva not be at home? It would be unusual for anyone to be out as long as his team had been, unless all of the houses had been bustling. And just because he had not heard sounds of danger did not mean there had not been any in actuality. Especially once they were all spread out with the distribution of passengers. Houses could have been more protected than the docks, for all they knew. Just as Weaver had said, there were no promises with that mission, and none of them would know if harm had come to associates until all reports were in.

He rounded the stairs to the first floor and started looking for the housekeeper, whatever her name was. Or Pick, if he was around. One of them would certainly know if Minerva was back, and if they were not available...

"Mist, welcome home."

Griff's boots skidded on the floor as he came to a sudden stop, looking this way and that for whoever had called for him.

Anna, bless her, was coming down the stairs, back in her maid's uniform and clean as a whistle, unlike any of them the night before.

"Anna," he panted, hurrying to her. "Is she back? Is she well? Is she here?"

"Yes to all," Anna assured him in a firm voice before he could ramble further. "She's in the morning room. I've told her it isn't morning, but that's where she wanted to be."

His heart did not seem to hear her as it continued to thunder and pound with the same sort of panic. His mind, however, had heard and comprehended, and told his head to nod a few times.

"Good," his mouth said, his heart not paying attention to that either. "And, erm… how—how was your time?"

"Well enough," Anna said with a shrug, her smile telling Griff she knew he was only being polite. "Brick and Pen and I tailed a man to St. James. I can tell you more later, but I think you've something better to do, aye?" She nudged her head towards the morning room as she moved past him.

"You need a raise, Anna," Griff told her as he started in the direction she'd indicated.

"You don't pay my wages, but thank you!"

He grinned quickly at the quip, then sobered at once as he neared his preferred destination.

She was well, he reminded himself. She was well. And he was well. And they loved each other.

He thought. He thought they loved each other. Wasn't that what she was saying? That was what he was saying, but what if he had misinterpreted what she had meant by what she had said? What if she was only telling her partner to be careful, wasn't telling Griff that she loved him, and he was…

He wasn't going to get anywhere thinking himself into madness out here in the corridor. He needed to go into the room and face the woman of his dreams and discover if all of this was in his head or if it just might be possible that his dreams could become his reality.

What could possibly be worrisome in that?

Griff exhaled silently, his heart still pounding as though he were fleeing for his life, and moved into the room.

Minerva sat on the floor facing the fire, still in her costume from the night before, though her wig and cap were gone, and her hair was almost completely loose and streaming around her shoulders. She did not seem to hear him come in, and Griff took a moment to fully appreciate the sight of her, well and whole and thoughtfully gazing into a weak and sputtering fire.

Approve and appreciate, he'd once said.

Yes, he approved of her, and hell yes, he appreciated her, and he'd do so for the rest of his life.

His throat tightened, and he approached slowly, his steps creaking the floorboards beneath him.

Minerva glanced over towards the sound, and he stopped, smiling hesitantly at her.

He watched her reaction dawn, every shift of her emotions, every change of each and every feature, and the rise of color that appeared in her cheeks as she took in the sight of him.

"Thank God it's you," she finally whispered, swiping at her cheeks, which he'd previously thought were dry. She pushed to her feet and smiled tremulously, a pair of tears tracking down her face.

Griff closed the distance between them without haste, wrapping his arms around her with a heavy sigh.

Her arms reached around him in return, her face burying against his chest. For a long moment, they only stood there, holding each other and not moving the slightest inch. Simply breathing while being held was enough.

It would always be enough.

Griff slowly began running his fingers through her hair, pressing his lips against her scalp. "I like having your hair down."

"I almost never wear it like this," she murmured, shifting her face to lay a cheek against him. "Too much of a hassle to maintain."

"What if I brush through it for you?" he asked as he toyed with a few curling locks. "Would that help?"

"I could be convinced," she admitted, a slight giggle hitting her voice.

He laughed himself, kissing her head. "Cook says he hasn't done breakfast or luncheon. You should have at least had him make you eggs at some point. How long have you been here?"

"Hours." Minerva pulled back, looking up at him, tears gone, though her eyes were a trifle puffy. "I couldn't think of eating until I knew anything about how you'd fared."

Griff brushed his thumb across her cheek. "Darling love. I am fine, nothing extraordinary to report. You?"

"Same." She leaned into his hand, managing a soft smile. "I love you."

Were there ever more beautiful words uttered in creation?

Griff placed his other hand along her face, cupping it so she could clearly see his eyes, his lips, and feel his touch. "I love you," he told her, his fingertips applying just the faintest amount of pressure with his earnestness.

Minerva sighed a half laugh, her fingers wandering to his sides and drumming once there. "Just to be clear, right? I said it without saying it earlier…"

"So did I," Griff admitted, laughing in earnest. "Glad we've established that." His hands slipped to her shoulders, and he exhaled. "I didn't mean to lash out at you after the theater. I was afraid that you were actually pulling away from me when you were physically pulling away from me."

"And I was afraid that I couldn't be who I was if I loved you as I did," Minerva admitted, her nose wrinkling with a grimace. "That somehow I would be diminished if I gave myself up to it." She swallowed, gripping the sides of his jacket as she rose up to arch into him. "And now I don't care if I am. I am worse without you than I could ever be with you."

Griff kissed her, tenderness and adoration filling him, knowing he could never possibly earn a portion of the love of such a woman. "I am nothing without you," he insisted against her lips. "I've known that from almost the first moment I met you."

"Are you always going to try and outdo me?" Minerva whispered with a playful tilt to her head, lowering herself back down.

"Probably," he admitted without shame. "I am monstrously competitive." He kissed her again before she could retort further, then decided to play the ace up his sleeve. Something he had been waiting weeks to share, and finally could.

He pulled back and began to work at the leather strap bound around his wrist, keeping his eyes on Minerva, wondering how she would respond. Her eyes flicked between his fingers and his eyes, confusion brewing there. When the strap and charm were free of him, he took one of her hands and dropped the length of it into her open palm.

Minerva's fingers curled into the leather, and she traced the surface of the button with her other hand. "What's this for?"

"I'm giving it to you," he said, closing her hand around the whole of it.

Immediately, she shook her head, her eyes darting down to her closed fingers. "No, Griff, this is yours. It means so much to you."

He covered her hand with his. "You misunderstand me. I am giving it *back* to you."

Minerva looked up at him, her gray-blue eyes wide and startled.

Griff smiled, cupping her cheek. "Hello again, Hatch."

Thankfully, Minerva did not try to deny it, though her throat worked twice for a swallow, and her tongue darted out to wet her lips before she could speak. "How long have you known?"

"Since before I told you the story," he confessed with a small laugh. "I suspected, especially when I spent enough time looking in your eyes, and then I knew for certain when I did tell you. You didn't gasp in the right places. You didn't gasp at all. I should have told you then, but I couldn't let go yet. Now I can. I can put this, and myself, safely in your care."

Her beautiful eyes welled with tears. "Griff…"

He leaned forward and gently kissed her. "Thank you, my love. For your bravery. For your stubbornness. For saving me. Then and now."

Minerva put a hand to his face, bringing her brow to his. "Oh, Griff."

"Marry me, Minerva," he murmured. "Marry me in earnest. Marry me and take me by surprise for the rest of my life, especially if you're going to do it like the first day of our mission."

Minerva's hand moved to the back of his head, smacking him lightly. "Griff!" She laughed and latched her hand behind his neck, bringing their noses to touch. "We'd scandalize all of Society and become quite infamous."

"Naturally. Passionate love must always draw attention, and I'd welcome it, especially if it means we don't have to be in London anymore." He sighed and smiled at her. "So what about it? Will you be my true Lady Beddingsford?"

"I would love nothing more," she told him in that low, husky tone of hers he so adored. "But Griff… I come from nothing. I'm a nobody. You're the brother of a duke."

Griff tsked, shaking his head. "Darling Mirrors, if you are good enough to risk your life and limb for king and country, you are certainly good enough to marry the younger brother of any member of the peerage, especially if the owner of that peerage is also married to a woman risking life and limb for king and country. And if you ever claim yourself beneath your station again, I'm taking you to Weaver so you can explain to him why you don't believe his scholarship program truly makes any difference in the world. Though what we are going to tell Laura Clark when she gets her admission letter, I could not say. You will have to let her down gently, my love. And after all the promises I made…"

Minerva beamed at him and slid her fingers into the hair at the base of his neck. "You are a bleeding idiot, Mist. But at least I can claim you as my idiot."

"Dash it, my lady," he murmured, grinning as devilishly as he dared, pulling her close. "Was there ever any doubt of that?"

Epilogue

"$\mathcal{I}$ still don't understand why you aren't making a bigger fuss about this."

Griff sighed impatiently at the annoyed statement from his sister and looked at his brother, lifting a superior brow.

Hawk ignored them both, as he had been doing all day.

Minerva laughed as she looked between the two brothers, then looked at Clara, who also seemed rather bemused by them.

"Damned nuisance," Griff muttered, shaking his head beside her.

"I am not," Adrianna insisted from across the table, glaring fiercely at him. "I am your sister!"

"As I said…" Griff lifted his glass and sipped slowly while his sister sputtered in indignation.

Hawk exhaled loudly from the head of the table. "So delightful to have the whole family together, isn't it?"

"It's Griffin's wedding," Adrianna pointed out unnecessarily. "A day you thought would never come. Where else would we be?"

Minerva choked back a laugh, hiding her mouth in her linen napkin as Griff gave his brother another look, this one far more intrigued.

"You thought I would never marry?" Griff asked him. "With all of my charm and attractive features?"

Hawk looked at Minerva morosely. "You won't ask for an annulment, will you? I know he's a trial, but I really cannot take him back, not like this."

Minerva took Griff's hand, lacing their fingers. "No, Your

Grace, I am afraid he has rather charmed me, in spite of his many flaws, and I am quite irreparable."

"My condolences," Hawk offered, toasting her with his wine. "Very good of you not to object, as this is all clearly against your will."

"Clara, my dear sister," Griff announced loudly, turning to face the duchess at the other end of the table. "You are looking very well, indeed. Glowing with imminent motherhood. Are you as well as you appear, or will you give all women unjust assumptions about this interesting condition?"

Clara chortled, sitting back in her chair, her hands going to her stomach. "Oh heavens, Griff. Don't."

"Please, don't," Adrianna begged, her eyes widening as she speared a piece of potato on her plate. "That is the last thing I need at this meal."

"I beg your pardon?" Hawk asked, turning his attention to his sister, this time raising his own superior brow.

Adrianna Russell, however, was not cowed by either of her brothers, and Minerva knew that well. Had known it from the first day she had met the girl. And marrying into the family that morning had only solidified that knowledge.

Especially when she could see the girl match either brother with her own superior expressions, as she was now.

"What?" Adrianna retorted, tossing the dark tendrils of her coif over a shoulder. "You don't think I should find it even remotely odd that you have both married my former teachers? The woman who taught me art and French is carrying your child, George, and that isn't supposed to be something I am reminded of from time to time?"

Hawk winced at being called his given name and looked down the table at his wife, who was completely unruffled by the statement.

Adrianna looked at her as well. "I adore you, Clara. You know that. It is only a fact."

Clara shrugged easily. "I know, *cherie*. No harm done."

"And you," Adrianna said to Griff, as though the duchess had not responded at all, "have married the woman who taught me comportment, elocution, philosophy, and logic. What do you make of that?"

Griff made a face of consideration. "I've always wanted to marry an intelligent woman, and now I have." He took a bite of ham and gestured with his silverware that he wasn't particularly bothered by the fact.

Minerva bit her lip on a laugh, unsure how any of them were going to survive this meal. Or a lifetime of being a family.

Adrianna rolled her eyes and pushed back her chair. "My appetite is sated. I am going for a walk before the day turns, and I will join you all at supper." She strode from the room without another word or a look at any of them.

There was a long pause of silence, and then both brothers groaned in eerie unison.

"I am sorry, Minerva," Hawk said simply, his expression full of concern. "It's not personal. Well, it is, but it's about us, her brothers, not you. This is not a demonstration against the match, she's only headstrong."

Minerva waved off his concern. "I am well aware, Your Grace, having faced Adrianna's nature many, many times. She was very sweet to me this morning, so I know how she truly feels. You both bring out the willfulness in her, and that's better than anyone else doing so, is it not?"

Hawk sighed at that, shaking his head. "I suppose so."

Griff took Minerva's hand and kissed the back of it tenderly. "You are a good and generous soul," he murmured against her skin.

Minerva winked at him. "Not that good, I promise."

"Promise?" he repeated, a brow quirking. "Do tell, wife."

"Not now," she hissed as she rapped his thigh. "Good heavens."

"One can only hope," her incorrigible husband replied.

Minerva cleared her throat and looked at Clara. "Have you heard from Pippa?"

Clara nodded around a mouthful of luncheon. "I have. She sends her regards. I'll tell you about it when the gentlemen leave."

"And so the secrets begin," Griff sighed dramatically. "*Et tu, wife?*"

"You'll survive," Minerva replied dryly, patting his hand.

Hawk grinned, then looked back at his brother. "How are they going to handle the fallout from your assignment, Griff? Still on it?"

Griff shook his head soberly. "No, they've handed it off to Trick, given what we now know. He's best suited to further the work there. I'm helping the London League to secure their records and families, since there is no telling how much compromise there has been."

"They're relocating the families?" Clara put a hand to her heart, making a pained sound. "Those poor babies. And the wives! Ugh, I cannot imagine it."

"Nor I," Minerva echoed, shaking her head. She had been married all of three hours, and already, she could sympathize with being parted from one's spouse for an unknown amount of time.

"I've offered up Worsley for their use," Griff told them all, though Minerva was already well aware. "I think Rook's family is going to take me up on it."

Hawk pushed back his chair and gestured for him to follow. "Let's look at my estates. I think we can offer one, if not two."

"I thought you might," Griff laughed, rising himself and kissing Minerva's brow before following his brother out of the dining room.

Minerva waited until they were gone, then looked at Clara quickly. "I take it she said no?" At her friend's nod, she sighed. "She's really not going to let us tell them about Duchess?"

Clara shook her head. "She insisted they be kept in the dark. Duchess has all the necessary paperwork. It was simply not understood what it was for, and she did not elaborate on the subject at the time."

"How are we going to keep this a secret?" she hissed. "They're our husbands, Clara!"

"And her brothers," Clara replied. She rubbed her brow, sighing a little. "We'll have to hope they forgive us and blame her. Her first mission is after Christmas. That much I know."

Minerva sat back against her chair, shaking her head. "God help us all. She'll be amazing, of that I have no doubt. But I will not want to be there when our husbands find out."

"Ideally, they never will."

"Amen to that."

Coming Soon

Agents of the Convent
Book Four

"Fair is found, and found is fair..."

by

Rebecca Connolly

About the Author

Growing up, Rebecca Connolly wanted to be Elizabeth Bennett, Mary Poppins, or British royalty, so it came as a great shock when she discovered she was an American girl from the Midwest. She started making up stories when she was young, and thanks to a rampant imagination and a fairly consistent stream of hot chocolate, ice cream, and cookie dough, she's kept at it. She loves a good love story, and a good swoon, and tries to share that with her readers. She still lives in the Midwest, has two degrees in non-writing fields, and dreams of one day having a cottage of her own in her beloved British Isles.

Rebecca is a huge fan of period dramas and currently writes in the Regency era, though she refuses to rule any other time period out. You just never know where the imagination will take you, and she'll write whatever story comes to her whenever it's set! There is always a story to tell, and she wants to tell them all!

You can find out more at www.rebeccaconnolly.com.

www.ingramcontent.com/pod-product-compliance
Lightning Source LLC
Chambersburg PA
CBHW072026220726
48293CB00016B/453